CARTOON NETWORK

STEVEN UNIVERSE

CRYSTAL CLEAN

kaboom!

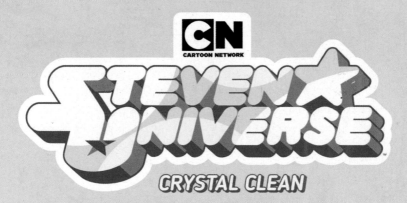

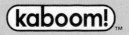

STEVEN UNIVERSE: CRYSTAL CLEAN, April 2020. Published by KaBOOM!, a division of Boom Entertainment, Inc. STEVEN UNIVERSE, CARTOON NETWORK, the logos, and all related characters and elements are trademarks of and © Cartoon Network. A WarnerMedia Company. All rights reserved. (S20) KaBOOM!™ and the KaBOOM! Logo are trademarks of Boom Entertainment, Inc., registered in various countries and categories. All characters, events, and/or institutions depicted herein are fictional. Any similarity between any of the names, characters, persons, events, and/or institutions in this publication to actual names, characters, and persons, whether living or dead, events and/or institutions is unintended and purely coincidental. KaBOOM! Does not read or accept unsolicited submissions of ideas, stories, or artwork.

For information regarding the CPSIA on this printed material, call (203) 595-3636 and provide reference #RICH - 883295.

BOOM! Studios, 5670 Wilshire Boulevard, Suite 400, Los Angeles, CA 90036-5679. Printed in USA. First Printing.

ISBN: 978-1-68415-507-1, eISBN: 978-1-64144-665-5

CARTOON NETWORK

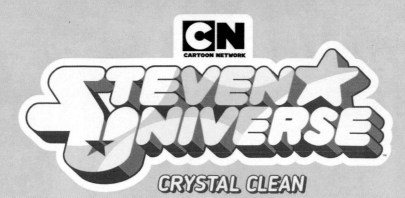

STEVEN UNIVERSE

CRYSTAL CLEAN

created by
REBECCA SUGAR

written by
TALYA PERPER

illustrated by
S.M. MARA

colored by
KIERAN QUIGLEY

lettered by
MIKE FIORENTINO

cover by
JAMIE LOUGHRAN

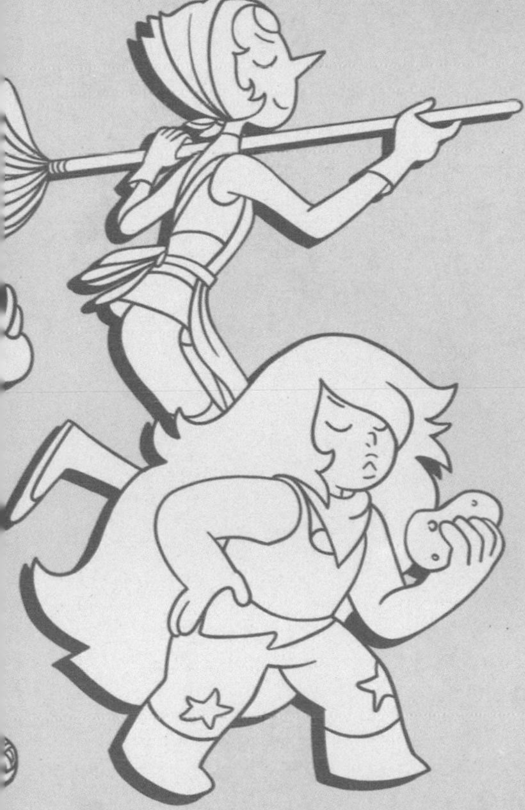

designer
MARIE KRUPINA

assistant editor
MICHAEL MOCCIO

editor
MATTHEW LEVINE

With Special Thanks to
Marisa Marionakis, Janet No, Austin Page, Conrad Montgomery,
Jackie Buscarino and the wonderful folks at Cartoon Network.

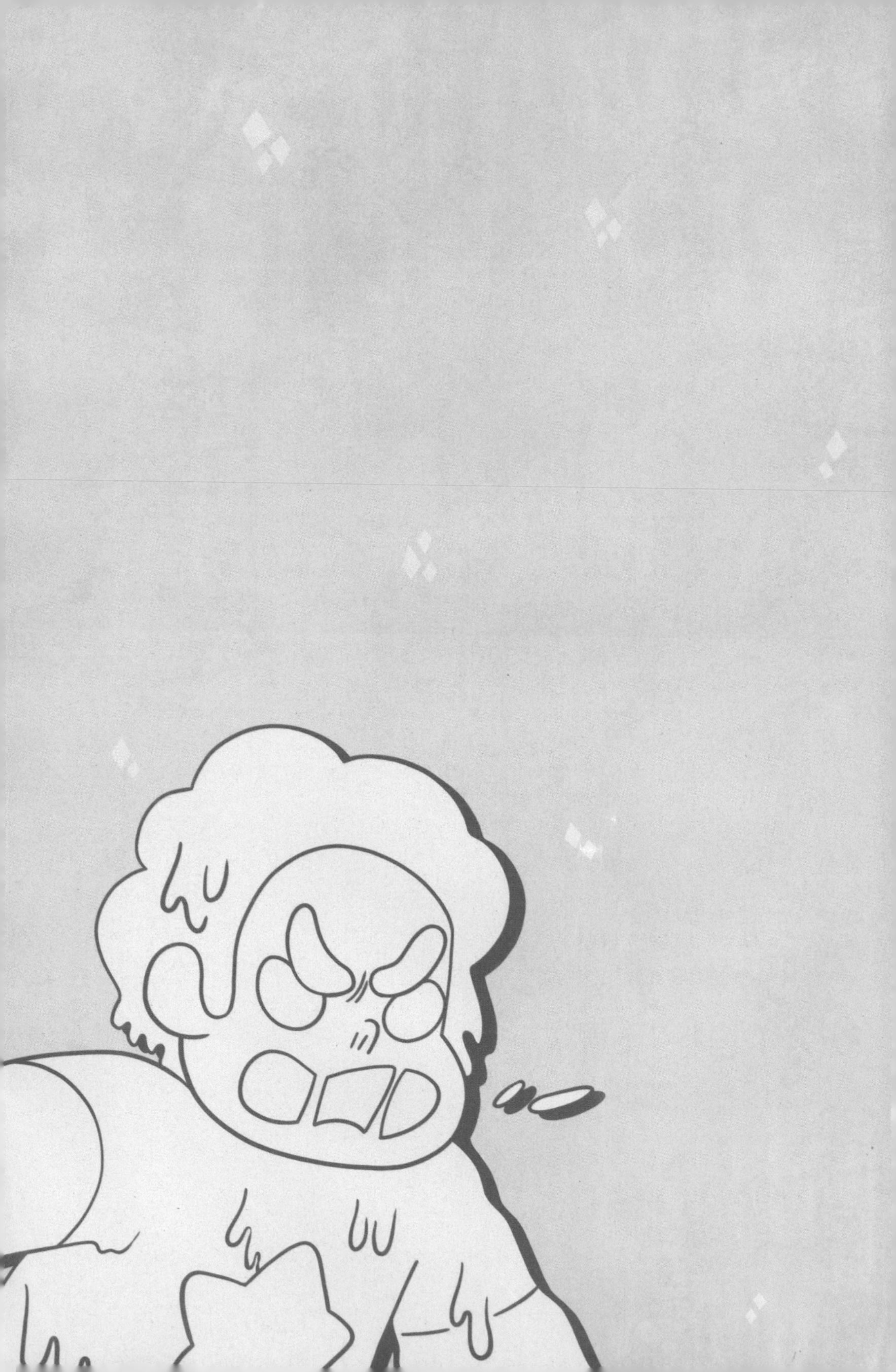

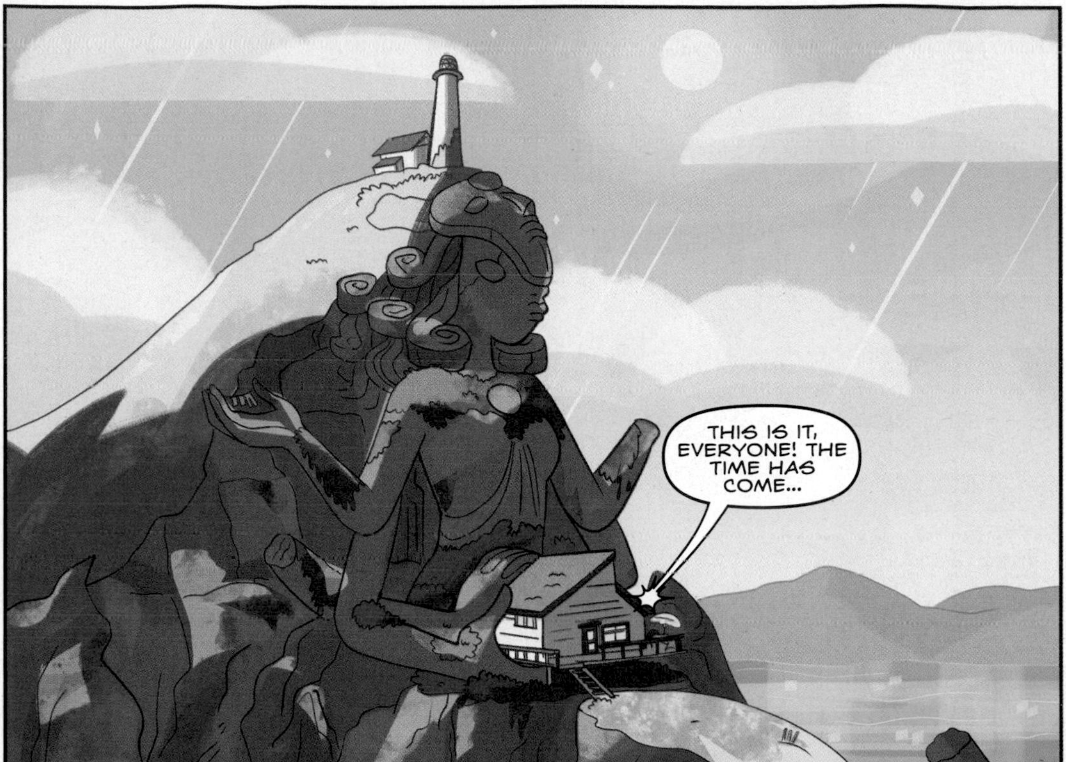
THIS IS IT, EVERYONE! THE TIME HAS COME...

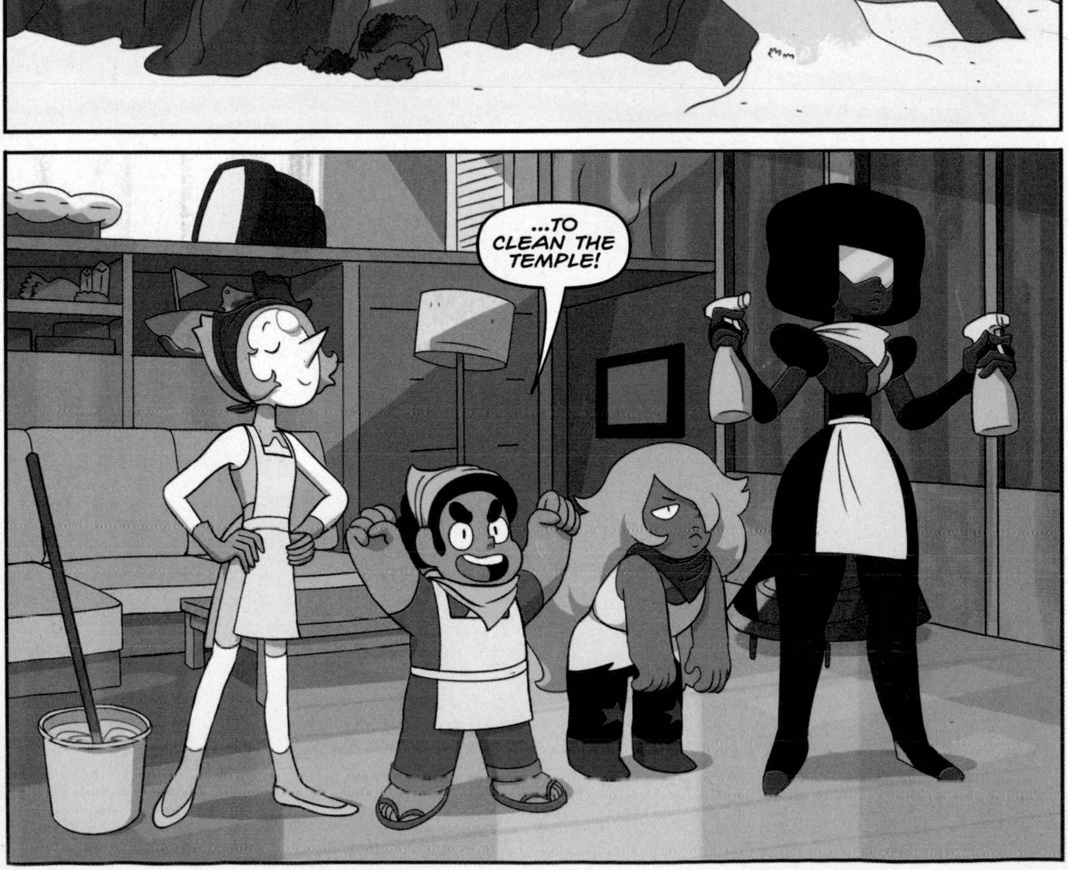
...TO CLEAN THE TEMPLE!

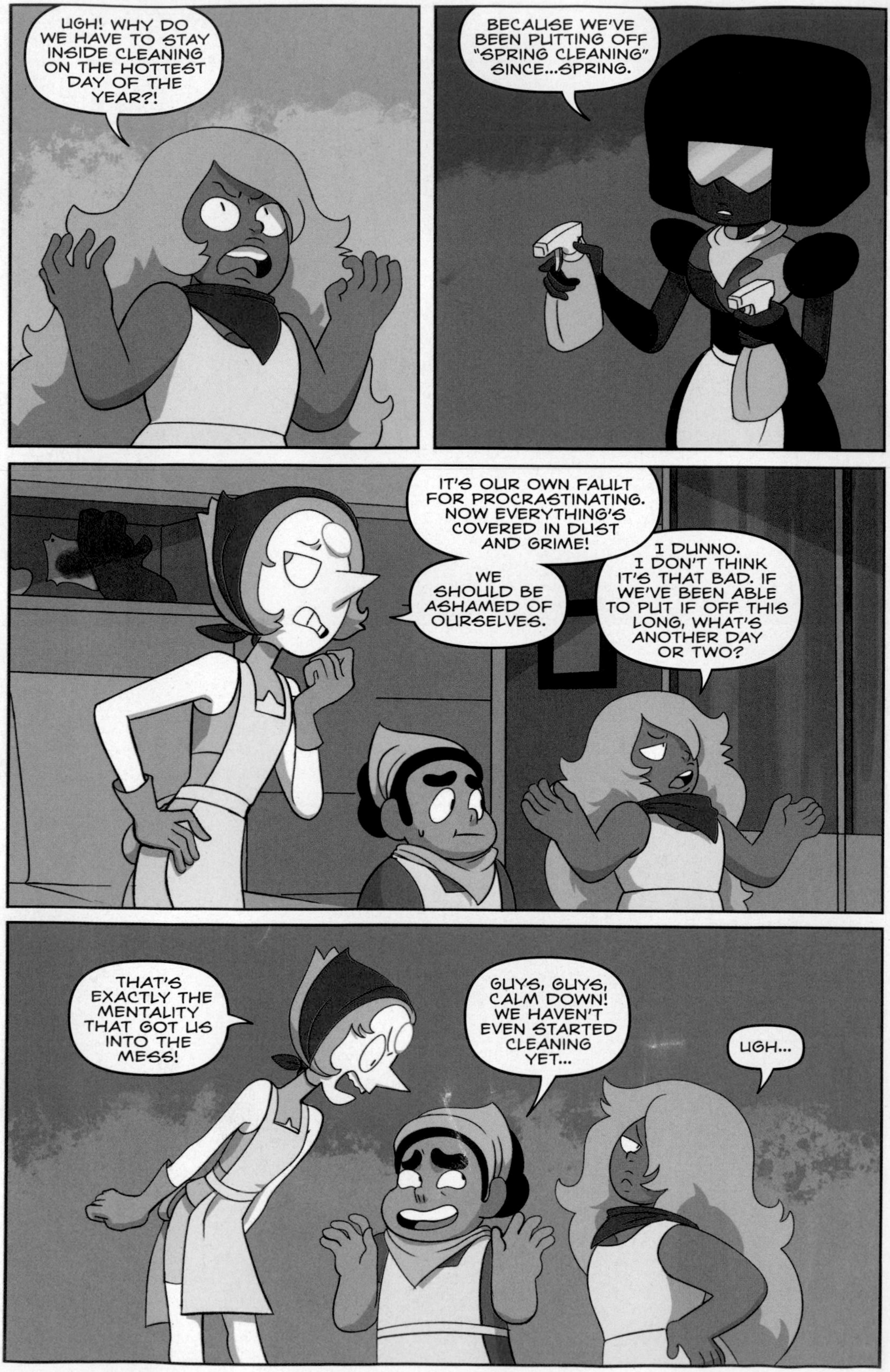
UGH! WHY DO WE HAVE TO STAY INSIDE CLEANING ON THE HOTTEST DAY OF THE YEAR?!
BECAUSE WE'VE BEEN PUTTING OFF "SPRING CLEANING" SINCE...SPRING.
IT'S OUR OWN FAULT FOR PROCRASTINATING. NOW EVERYTHING'S COVERED IN DUST AND GRIME!
WE SHOULD BE ASHAMED OF OURSELVES.
I DUNNO. I DON'T THINK IT'S THAT BAD. IF WE'VE BEEN ABLE TO PUT IF OFF THIS LONG, WHAT'S ANOTHER DAY OR TWO?
THAT'S EXACTLY THE MENTALITY THAT GOT US INTO THE MESS!
GUYS, GUYS, CALM DOWN! WE HAVEN'T EVEN STARTED CLEANING YET...
UGH...

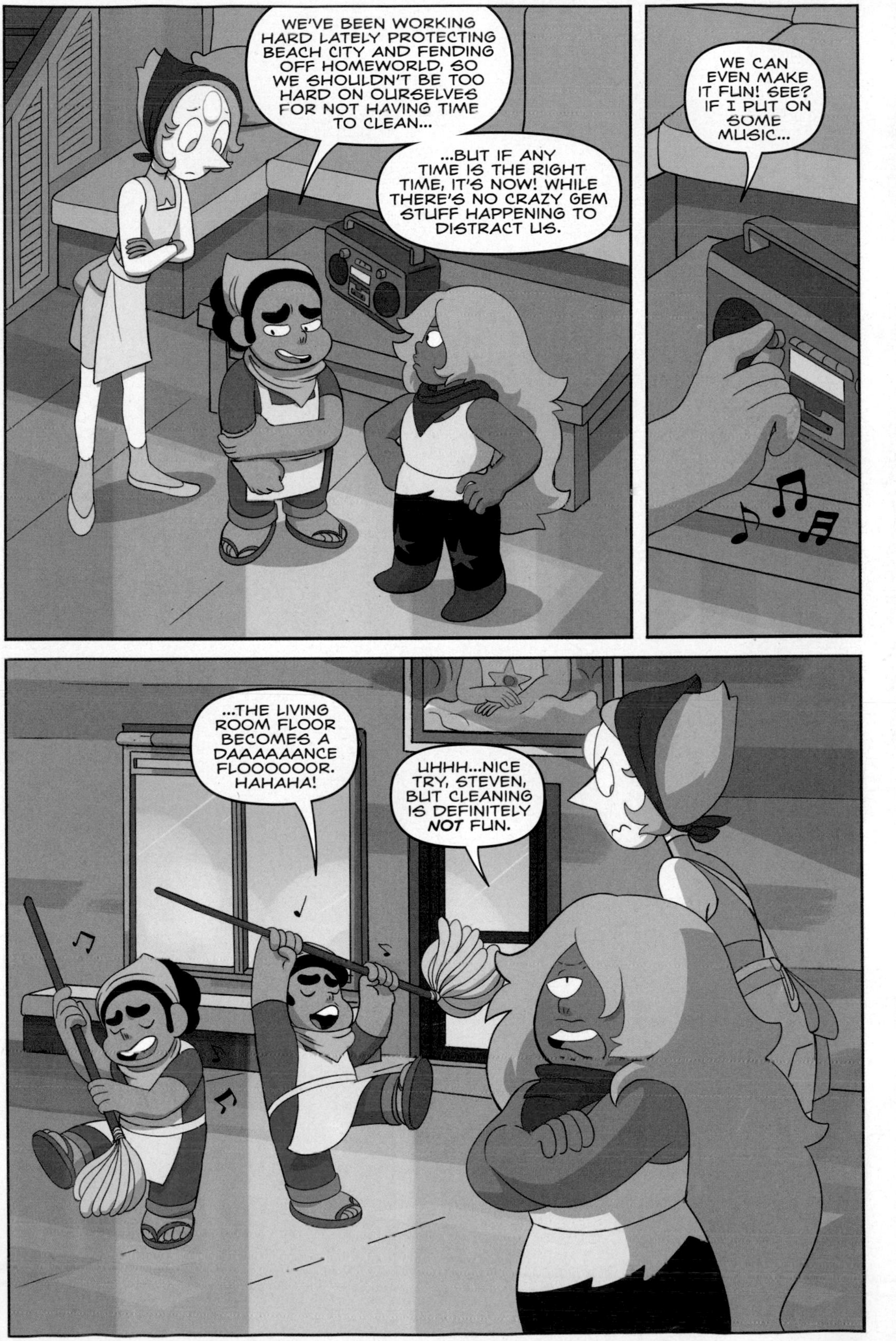
WE'VE BEEN WORKING HARD LATELY PROTECTING BEACH CITY AND FENDING OFF HOMEWORLD, SO WE SHOULDN'T BE TOO HARD ON OURSELVES FOR NOT HAVING TIME TO CLEAN...
...BUT IF ANY TIME IS THE RIGHT TIME, IT'S NOW! WHILE THERE'S NO CRAZY GEM STUFF HAPPENING TO DISTRACT US.
WE CAN EVEN MAKE IT FUN! SEE? IF I PUT ON SOME MUSIC...
...THE LIVING ROOM FLOOR BECOMES A DAAAAAANCE FLOOOOOOR. HAHAHA!
UHHH...NICE TRY, STEVEN, BUT CLEANING IS DEFINITELY *NOT* FUN.

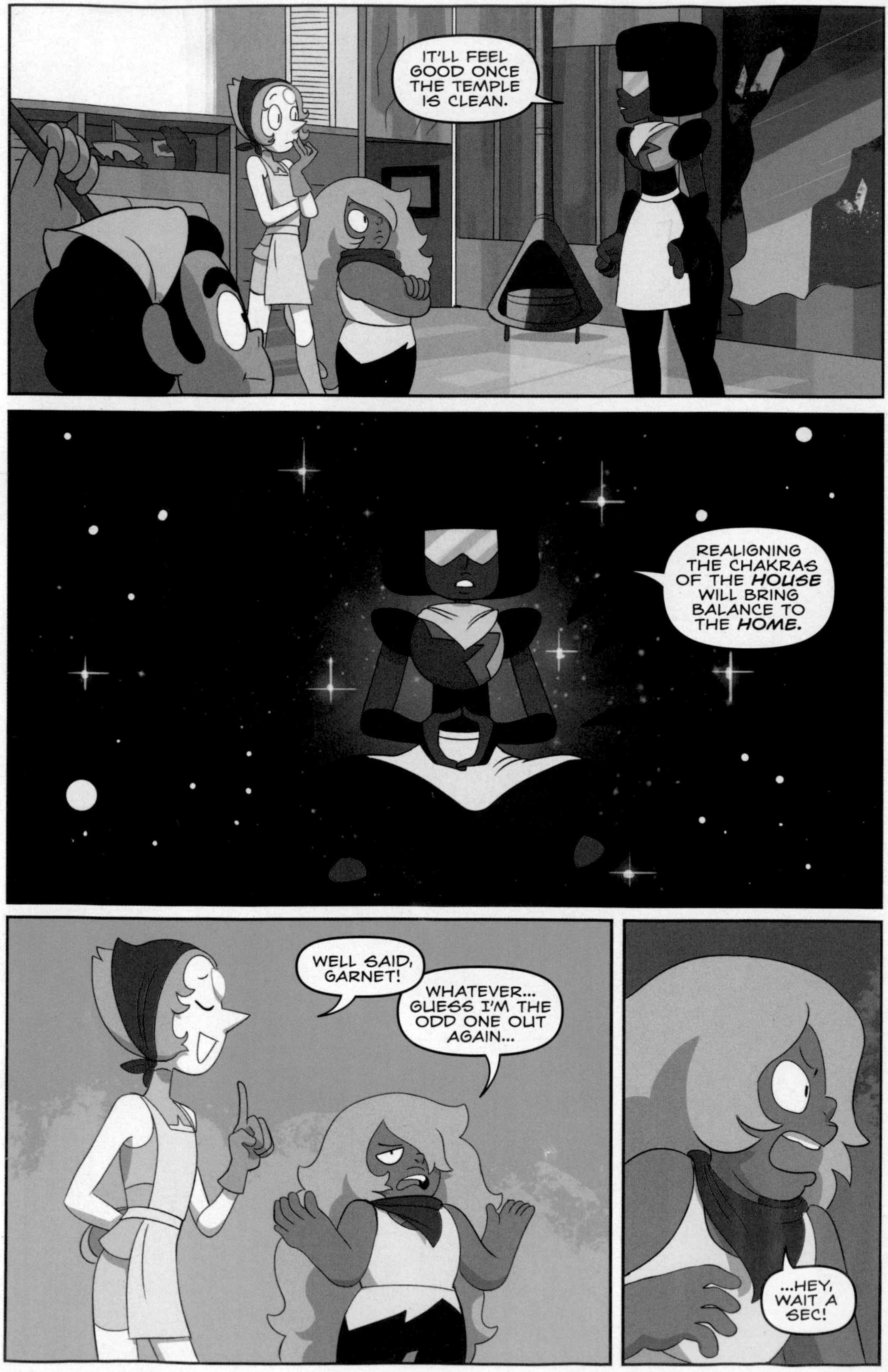
IT'LL FEEL GOOD ONCE THE TEMPLE IS CLEAN.
REALIGNING THE CHAKRAS OF THE *HOUSE* WILL BRING BALANCE TO THE *HOME.*
WELL SAID, GARNET!
WHATEVER... GUESS I'M THE ODD ONE OUT AGAIN...
...HEY, WAIT A SEC!

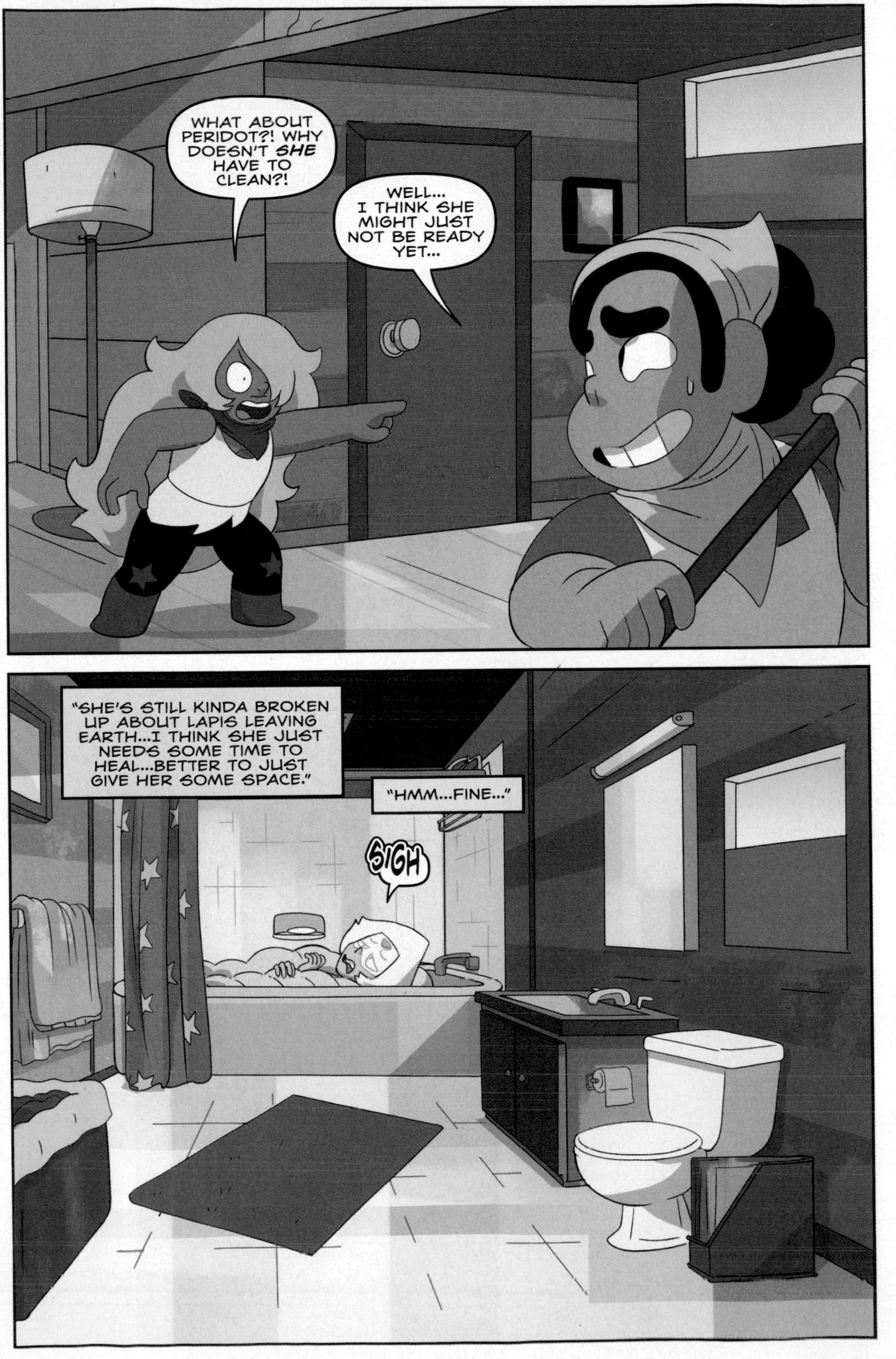
WHAT ABOUT PERIDOT?! WHY DOESN'T *SHE* HAVE TO CLEAN?!
WELL... I THINK SHE MIGHT JUST NOT BE READY YET...
"SHE'S STILL KINDA BROKEN UP ABOUT LAPIS LEAVING EARTH...I THINK SHE JUST NEEDS SOME TIME TO HEAL...BETTER TO JUST GIVE HER SOME SPACE."
"HMM...FINE..."
SIGH

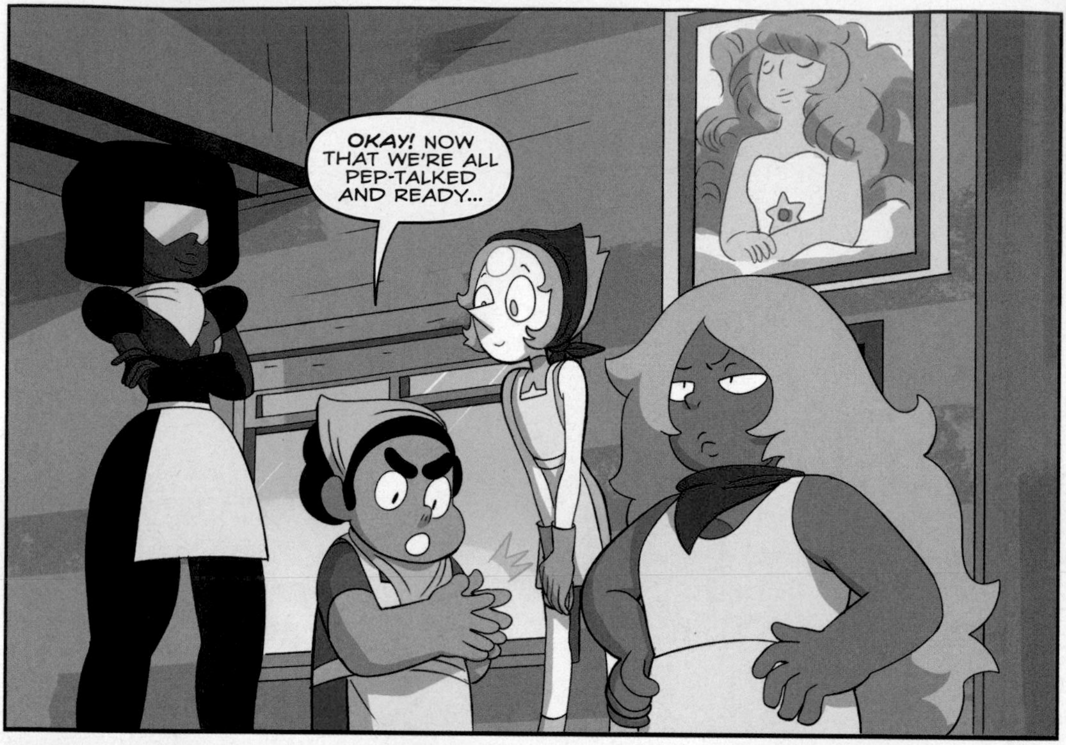
OKAY! NOW THAT WE'RE ALL PEP-TALKED AND READY...

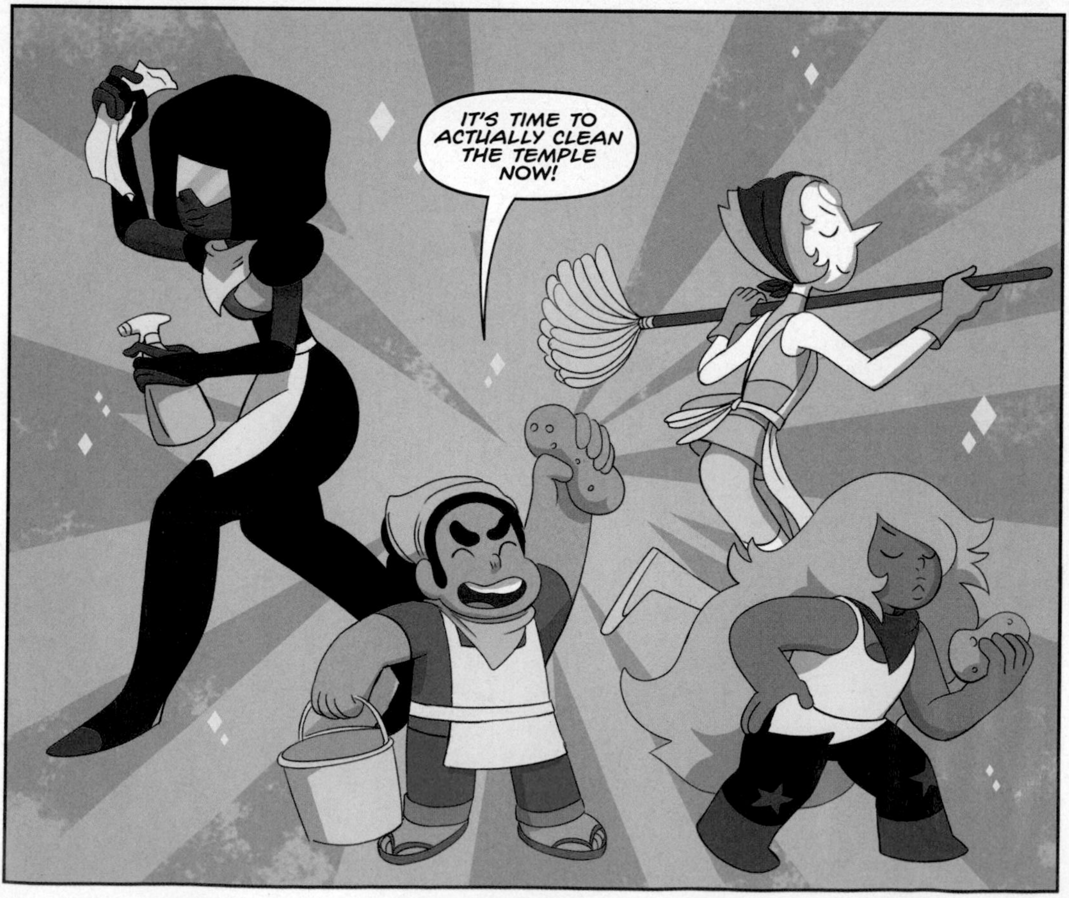
IT'S TIME TO ACTUALLY CLEAN THE TEMPLE NOW!

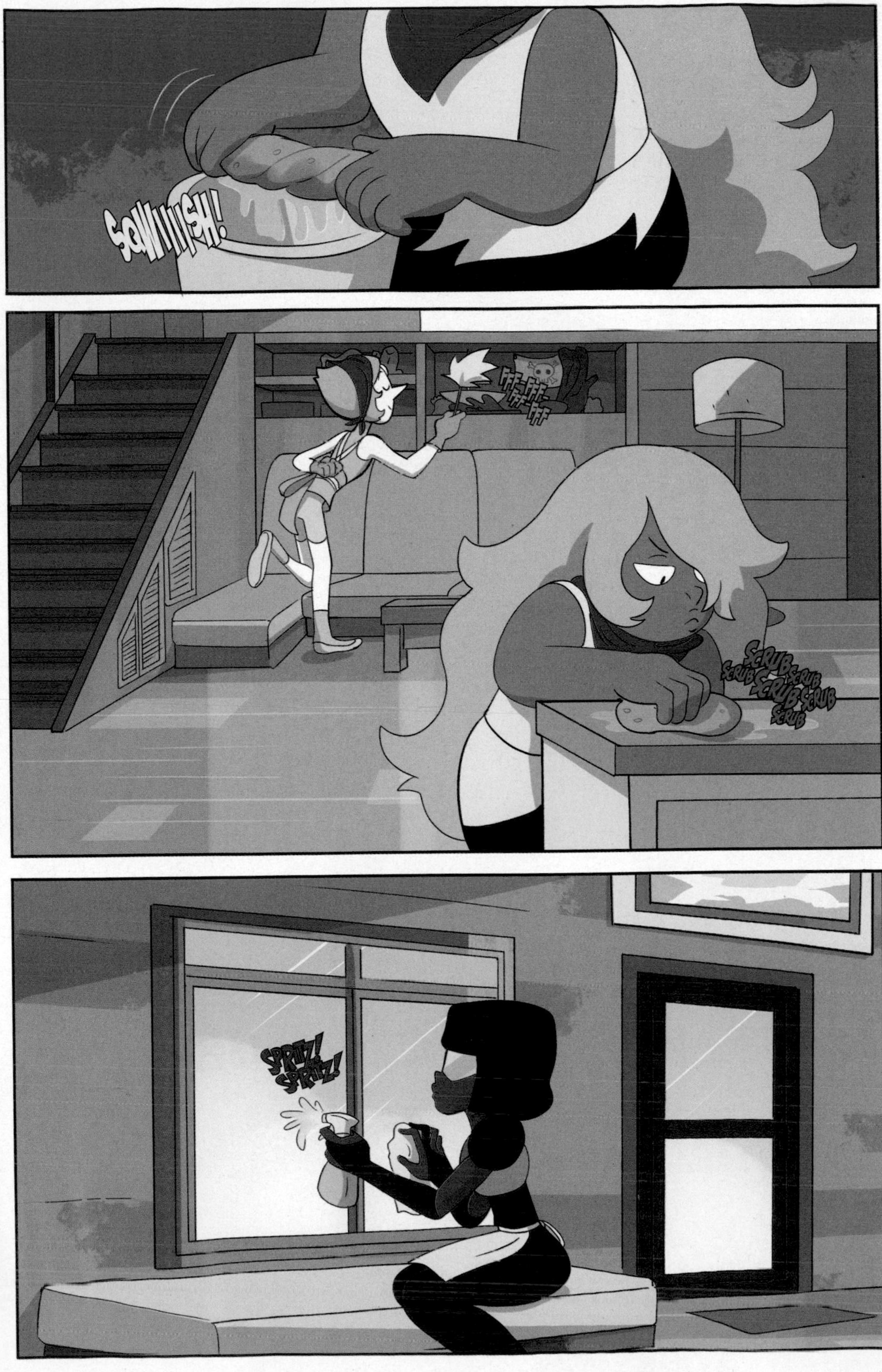
SQUIIIISH!
FFF-FFF-
FFF-FFF
SCRUB SCRUB SCRUB SCRUB SCRUB SCRUB
SPRITZ! SPRITZ!

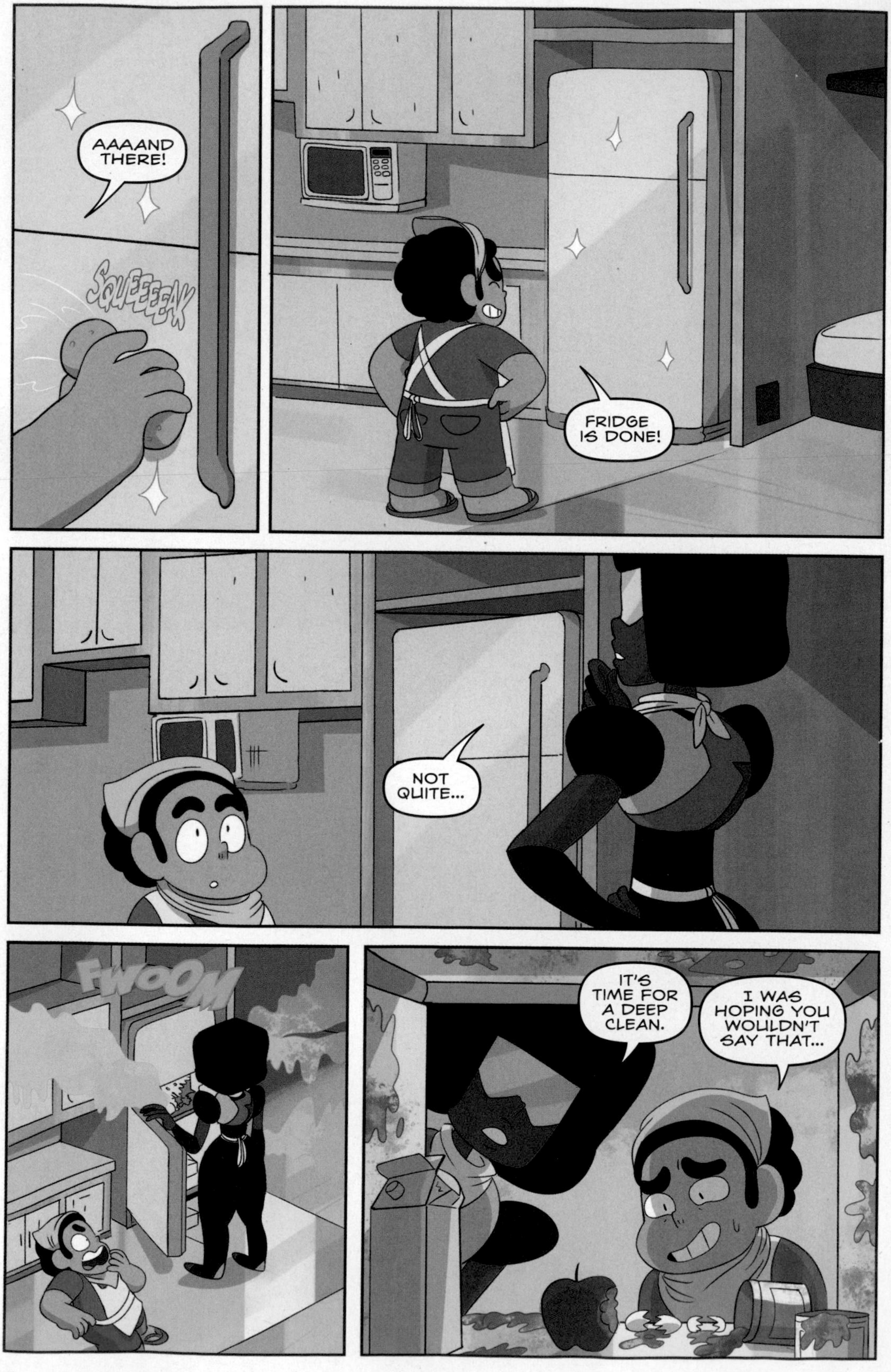
AAAAND THERE!
SQUEEEEAK
FRIDGE IS DONE!
NOT QUITE...
FWOOM
IT'S TIME FOR A DEEP CLEAN.
I WAS HOPING YOU WOULDN'T SAY THAT...

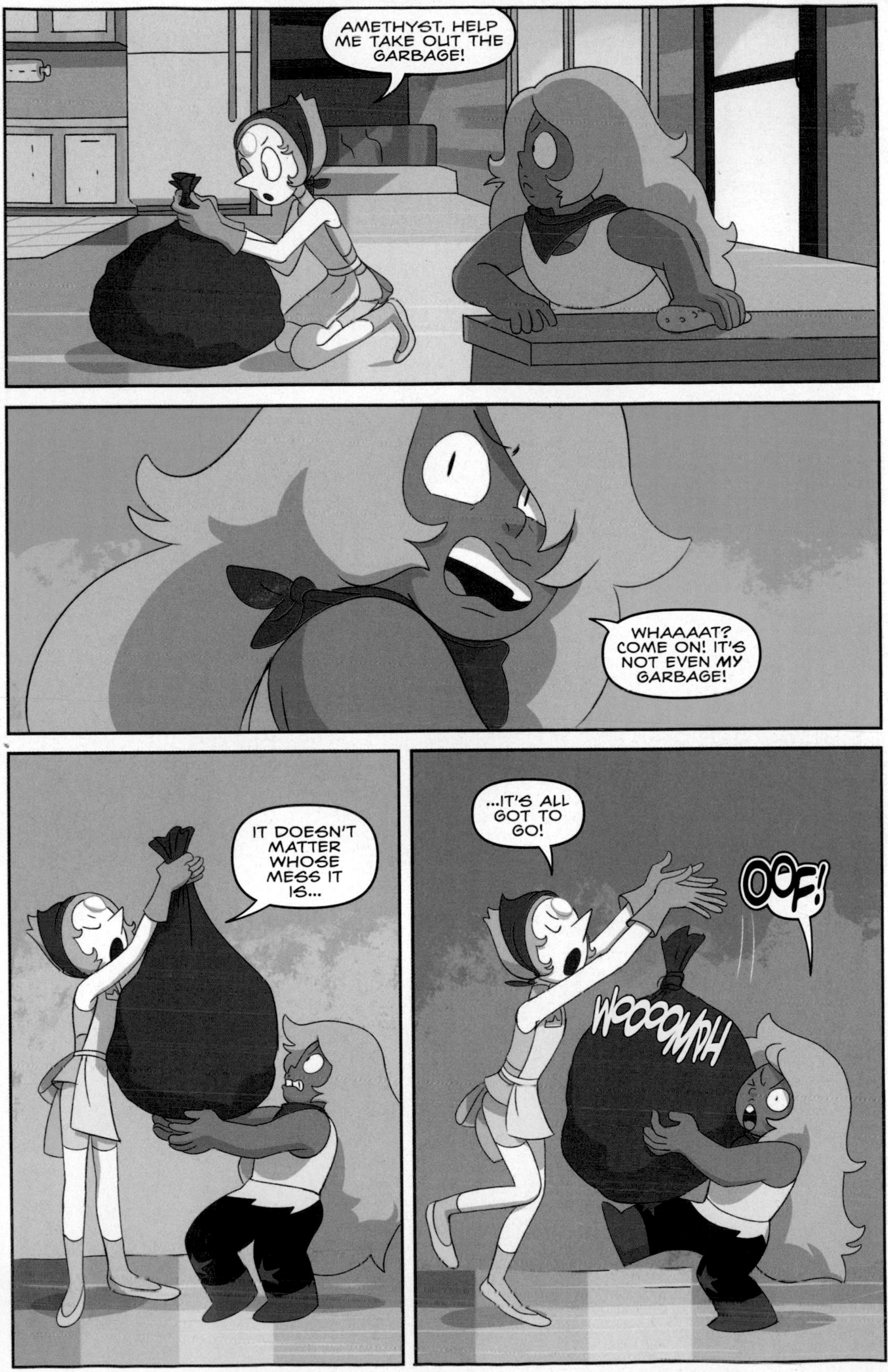
AMETHYST, HELP ME TAKE OUT THE GARBAGE!
WHAAAAT? COME ON! IT'S NOT EVEN MY GARBAGE!
IT DOESN'T MATTER WHOSE MESS IT IS...
...IT'S ALL GOT TO GO!
OOF!
WOOOOMPH

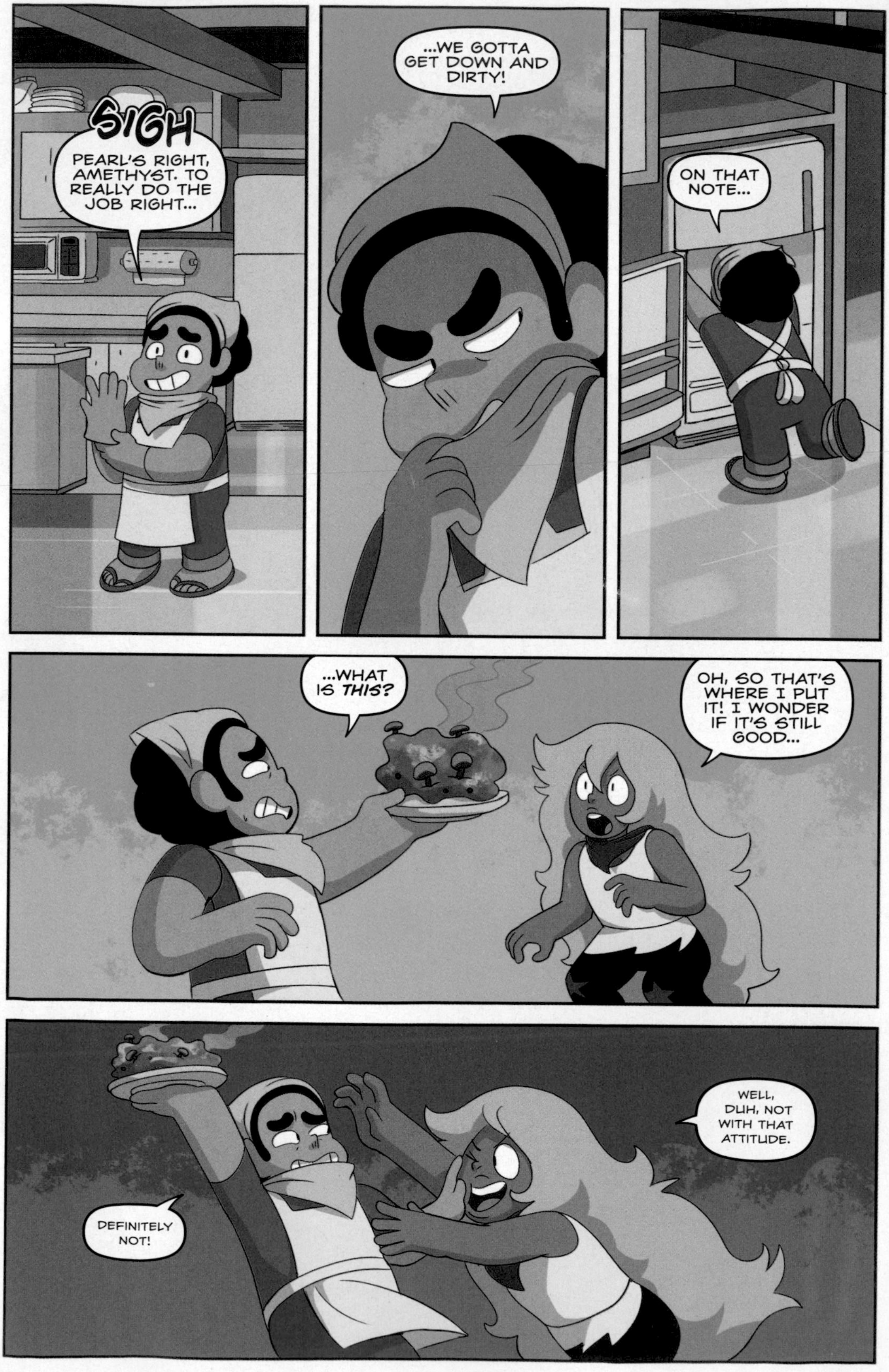
SIGH
PEARL'S RIGHT, AMETHYST. TO REALLY DO THE JOB RIGHT...
...WE GOTTA GET DOWN AND DIRTY!
ON THAT NOTE...
...WHAT IS *THIS*?
OH, SO THAT'S WHERE I PUT IT! I WONDER IF IT'S STILL GOOD...
WELL, DUH, NOT WITH THAT ATTITUDE.
DEFINITELY NOT!

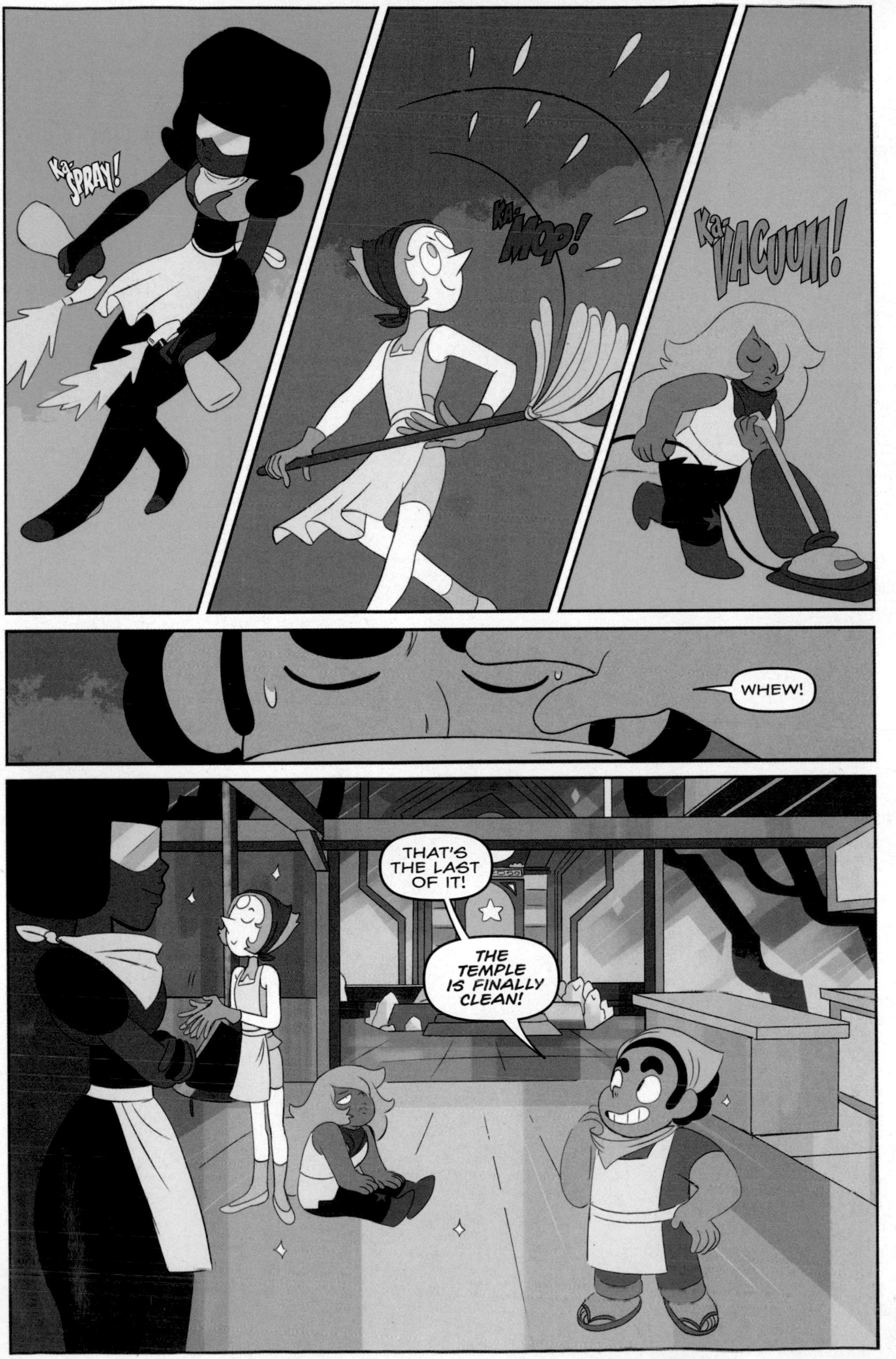
KA-SPRAY!
KA-MOP!
KA-VACUUM!
WHEW!
THAT'S THE LAST OF IT!
THE TEMPLE IS FINALLY CLEAN!

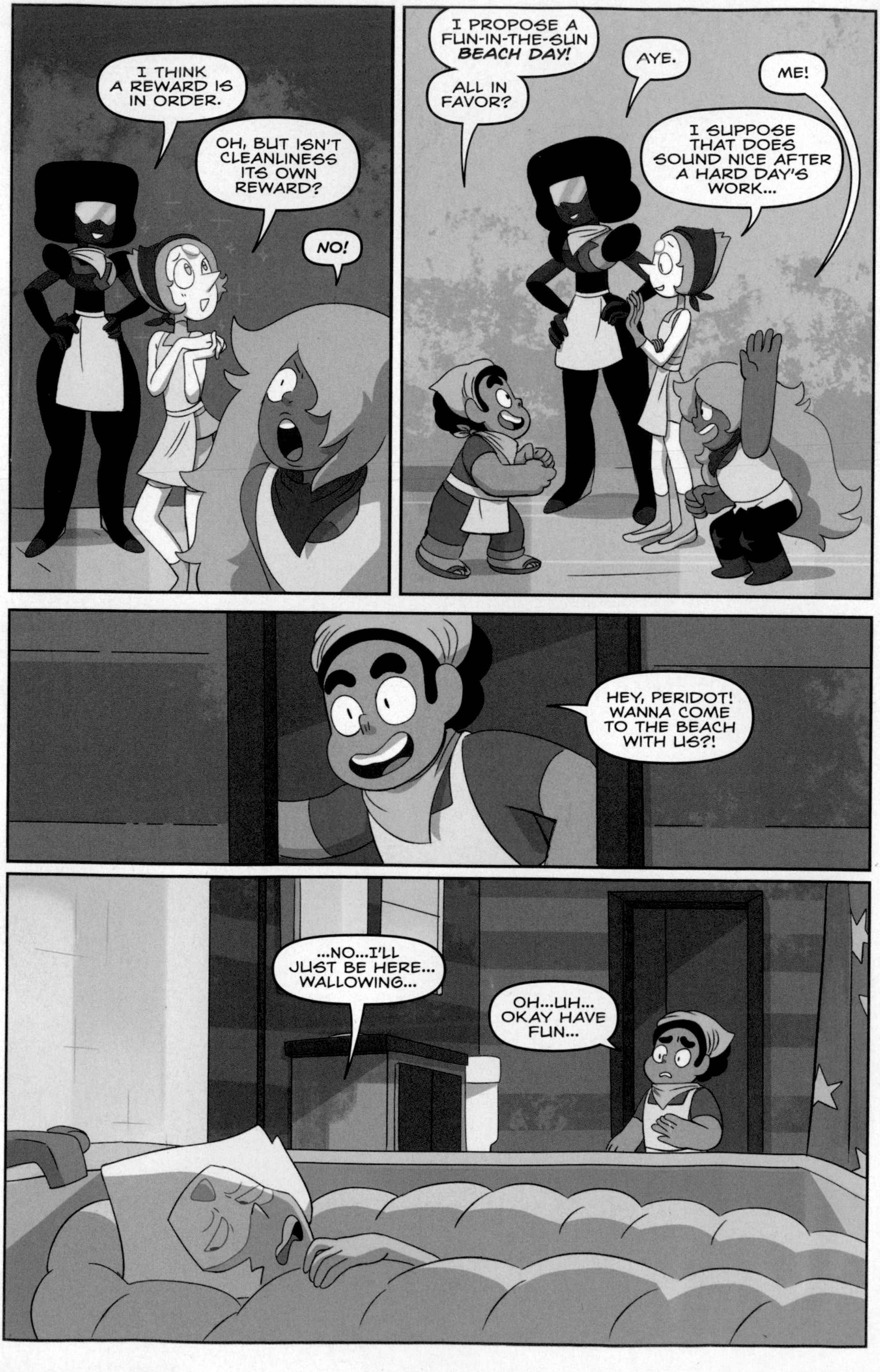
I THINK A REWARD IS IN ORDER.
OH, BUT ISN'T CLEANLINESS ITS OWN REWARD?
NO!
I PROPOSE A FUN-IN-THE-SUN BEACH DAY!
ALL IN FAVOR?
AYE.
ME!
I SUPPOSE THAT DOES SOUND NICE AFTER A HARD DAY'S WORK...
HEY, PERIDOT! WANNA COME TO THE BEACH WITH US?!
...NO...I'LL JUST BE HERE... WALLOWING...
OH...UH... OKAY HAVE FUN...

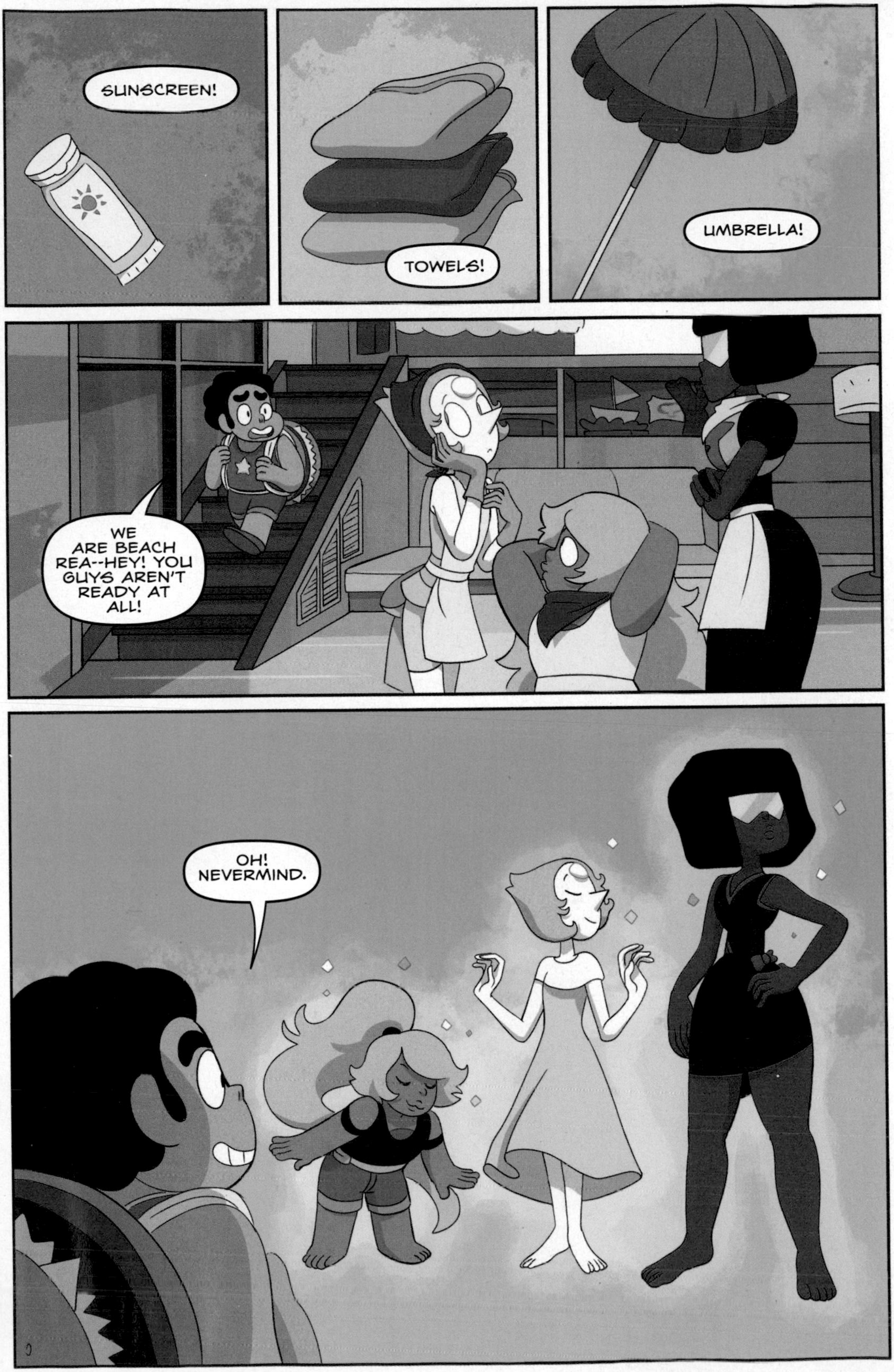
SUNSCREEN!
TOWELS!
UMBRELLA!
WE ARE BEACH REA--HEY! YOU GUYS AREN'T READY AT ALL!
OH! NEVERMIND.

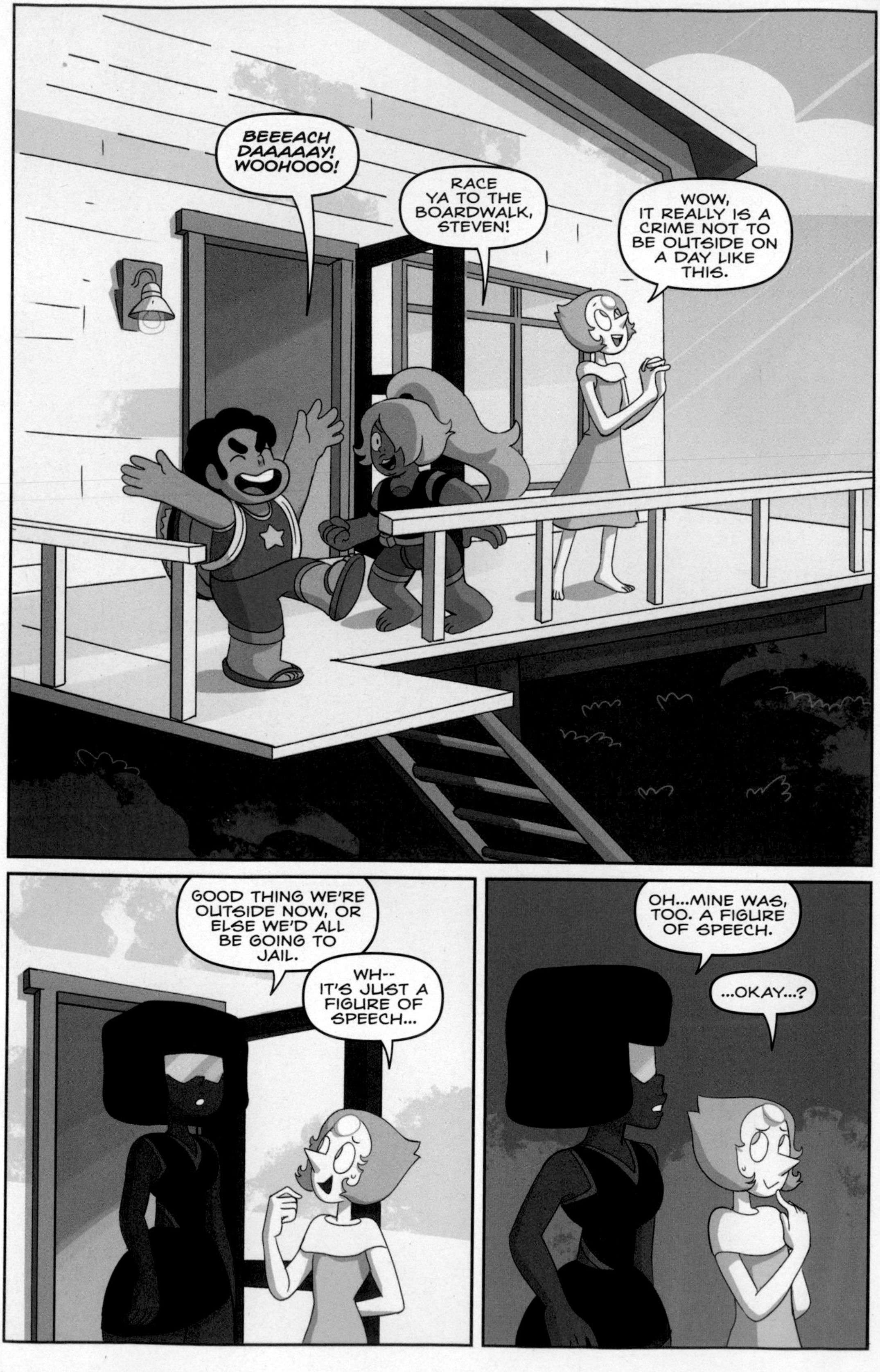
BEEEACH DAAAAAY! WOOHOOO!
RACE YA TO THE BOARDWALK, STEVEN!
WOW, IT REALLY IS A CRIME NOT TO BE OUTSIDE ON A DAY LIKE THIS.
GOOD THING WE'RE OUTSIDE NOW, OR ELSE WE'D ALL BE GOING TO JAIL.
WH-- IT'S JUST A FIGURE OF SPEECH...
OH...MINE WAS, TOO. A FIGURE OF SPEECH.
...OKAY...?

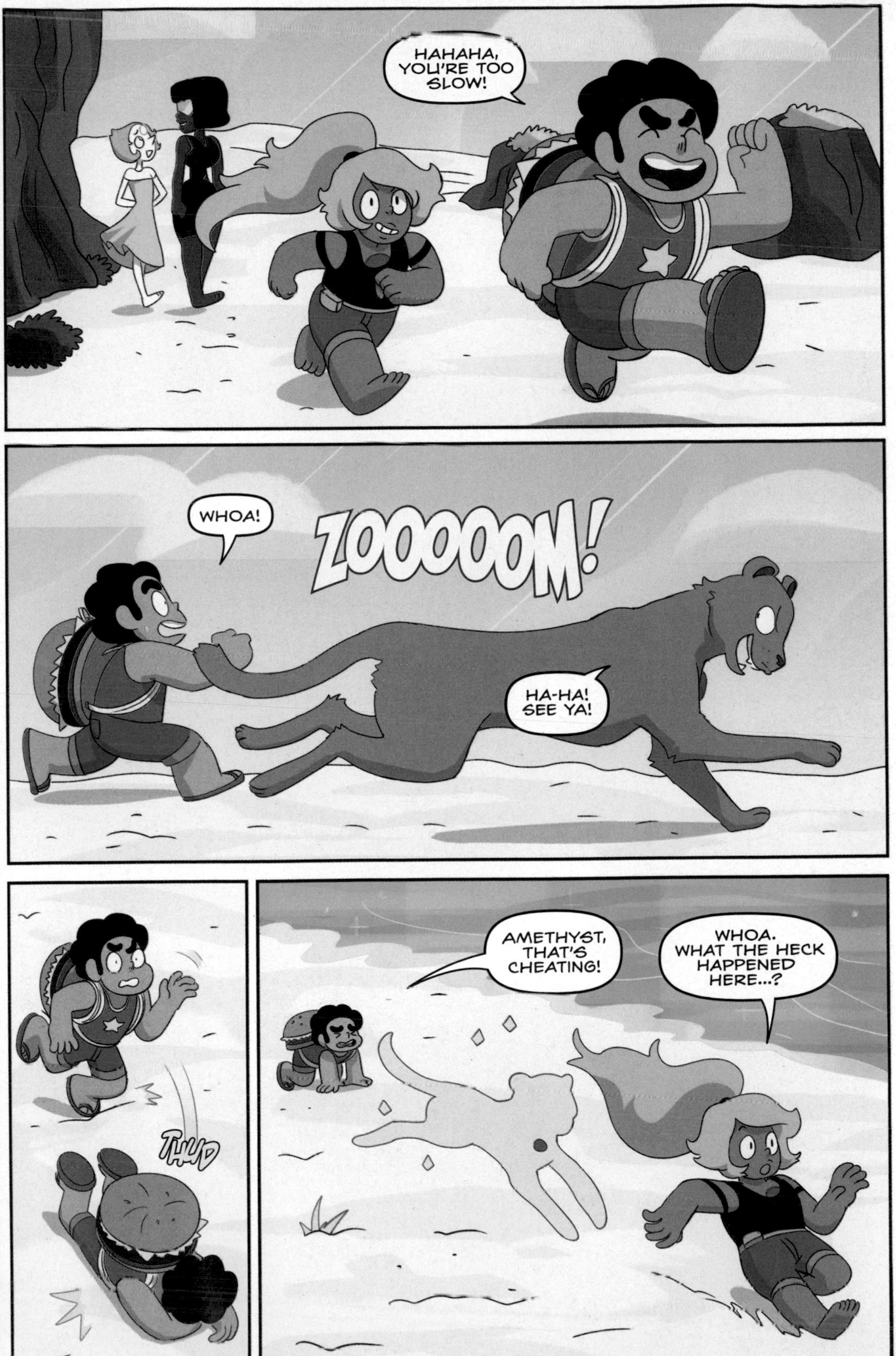
HAHAHA, YOU'RE TOO SLOW!
WHOA!
ZOOOOOM!
HA-HA! SEE YA!
THUD
AMETHYST, THAT'S CHEATING!
WHOA. WHAT THE HECK HAPPENED HERE...?

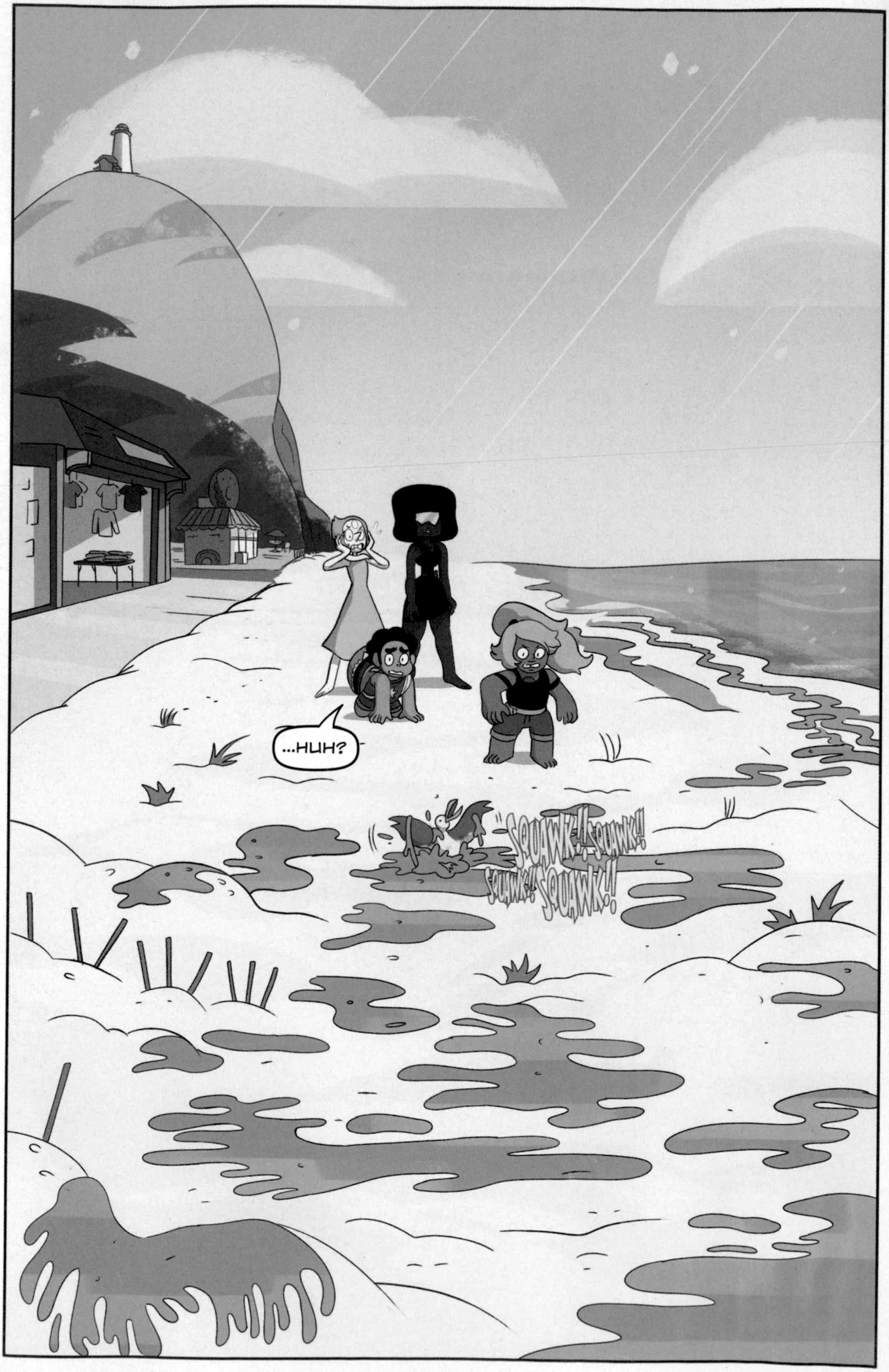
...HUH?
SQUAWK!! SQUAWK!!
SQUAWK!! SQUAWK!!

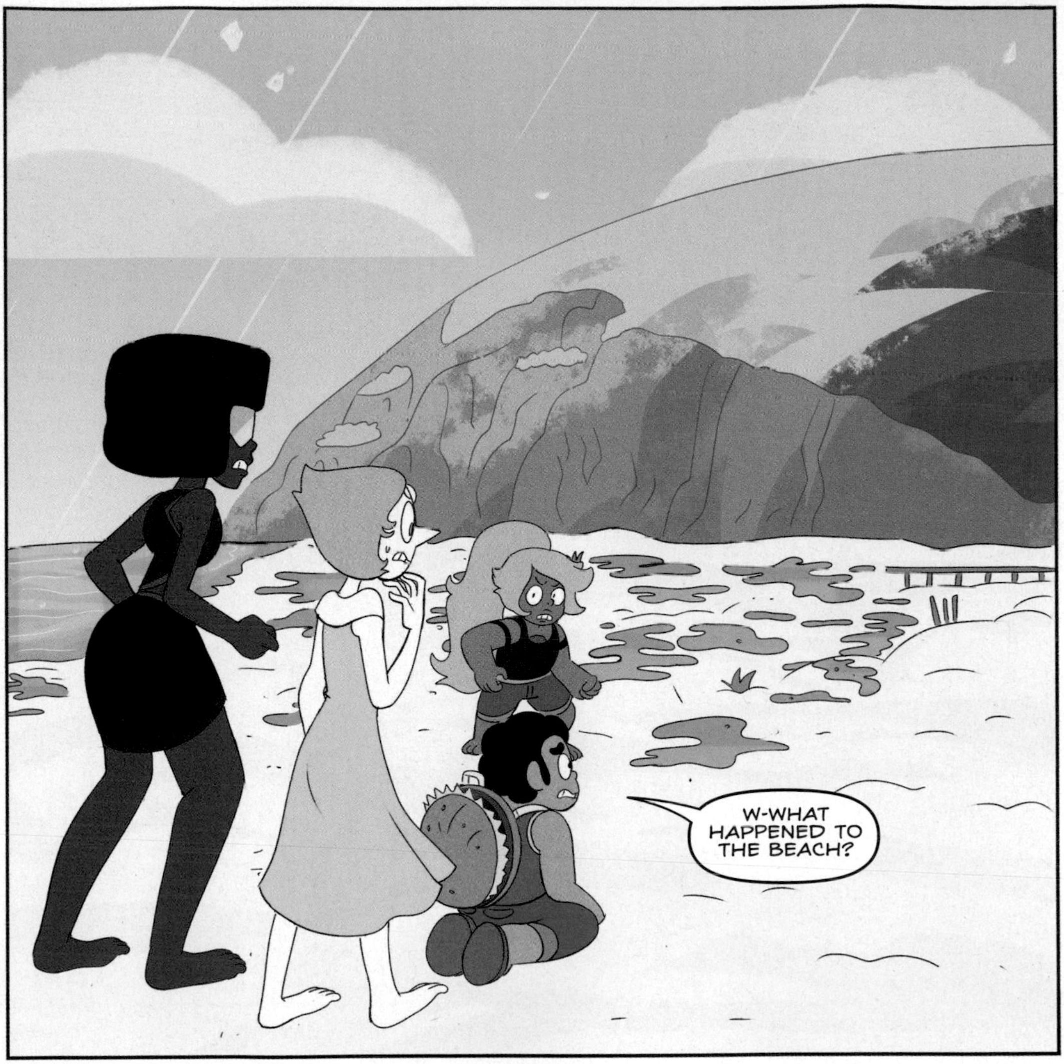
W-WHAT HAPPENED TO THE BEACH?

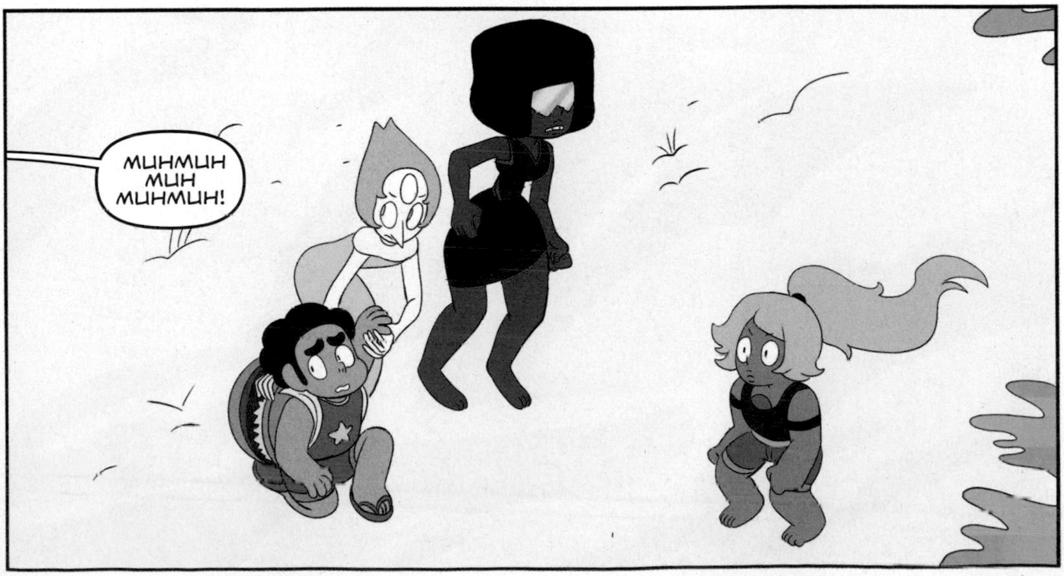
MUHMUH MUH MUHMUH!

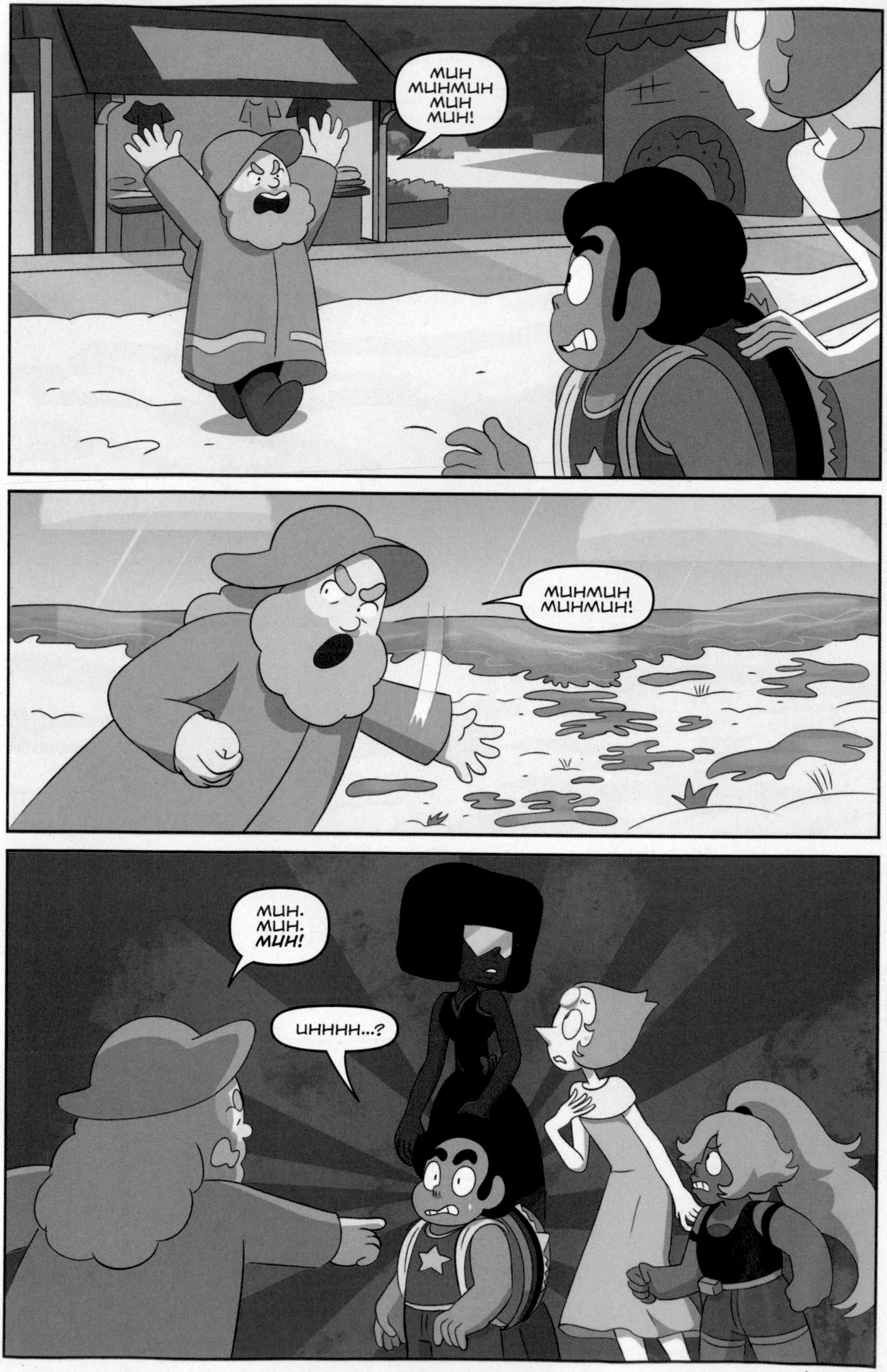
MUH MUHMUH MUH MUH!
MUHMUH MUHMUH!
MUH. MUH. MUH!
UHHHH...?

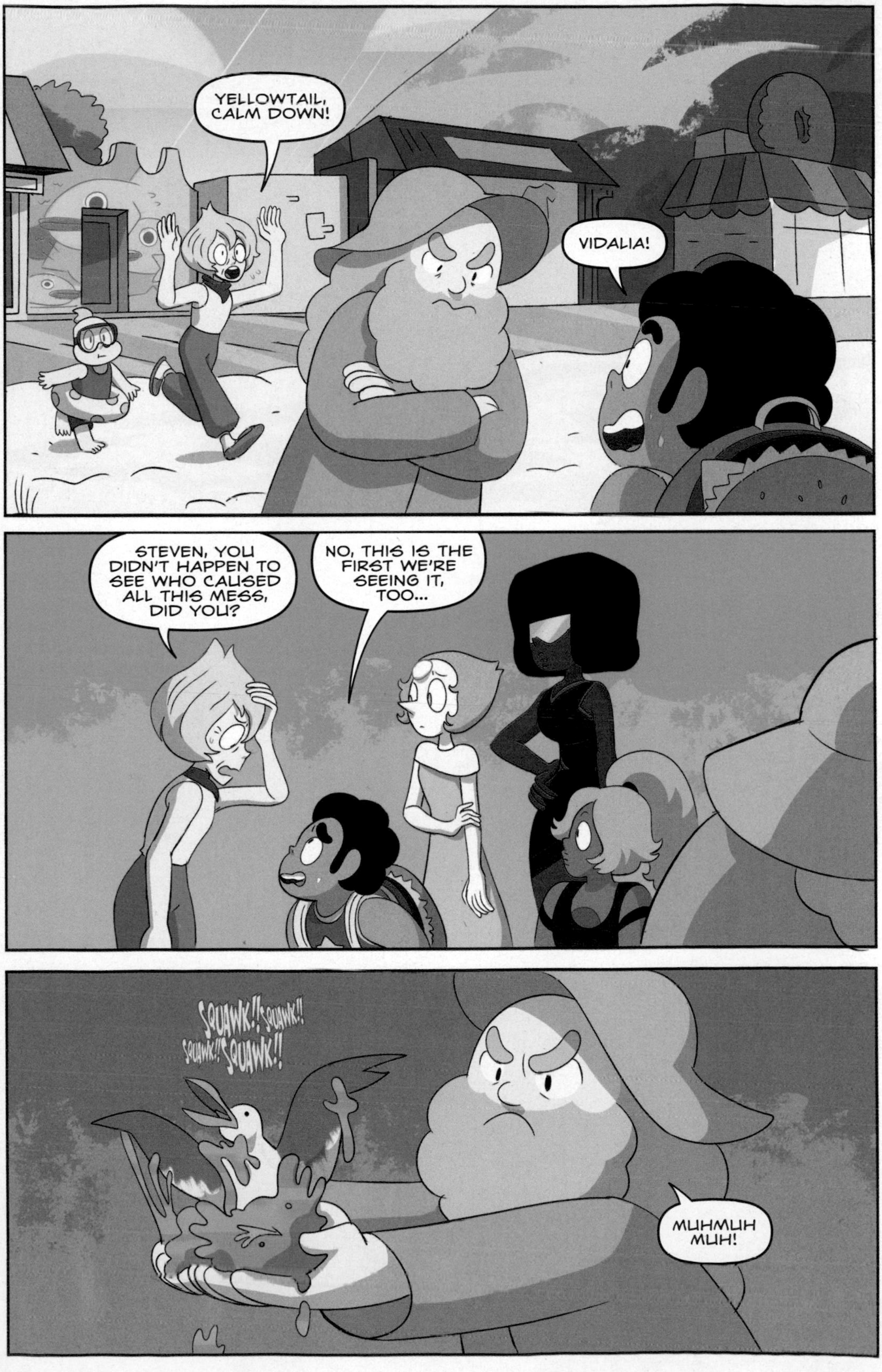
YELLOWTAIL, CALM DOWN!
VIDALIA!
STEVEN, YOU DIDN'T HAPPEN TO SEE WHO CAUSED ALL THIS MESS, DID YOU?
NO, THIS IS THE FIRST WE'RE SEEING IT, TOO...
SQUAWK!! SQUAWK!! SQUAWK!! SQUAWK!!
MUHMUH MUH!

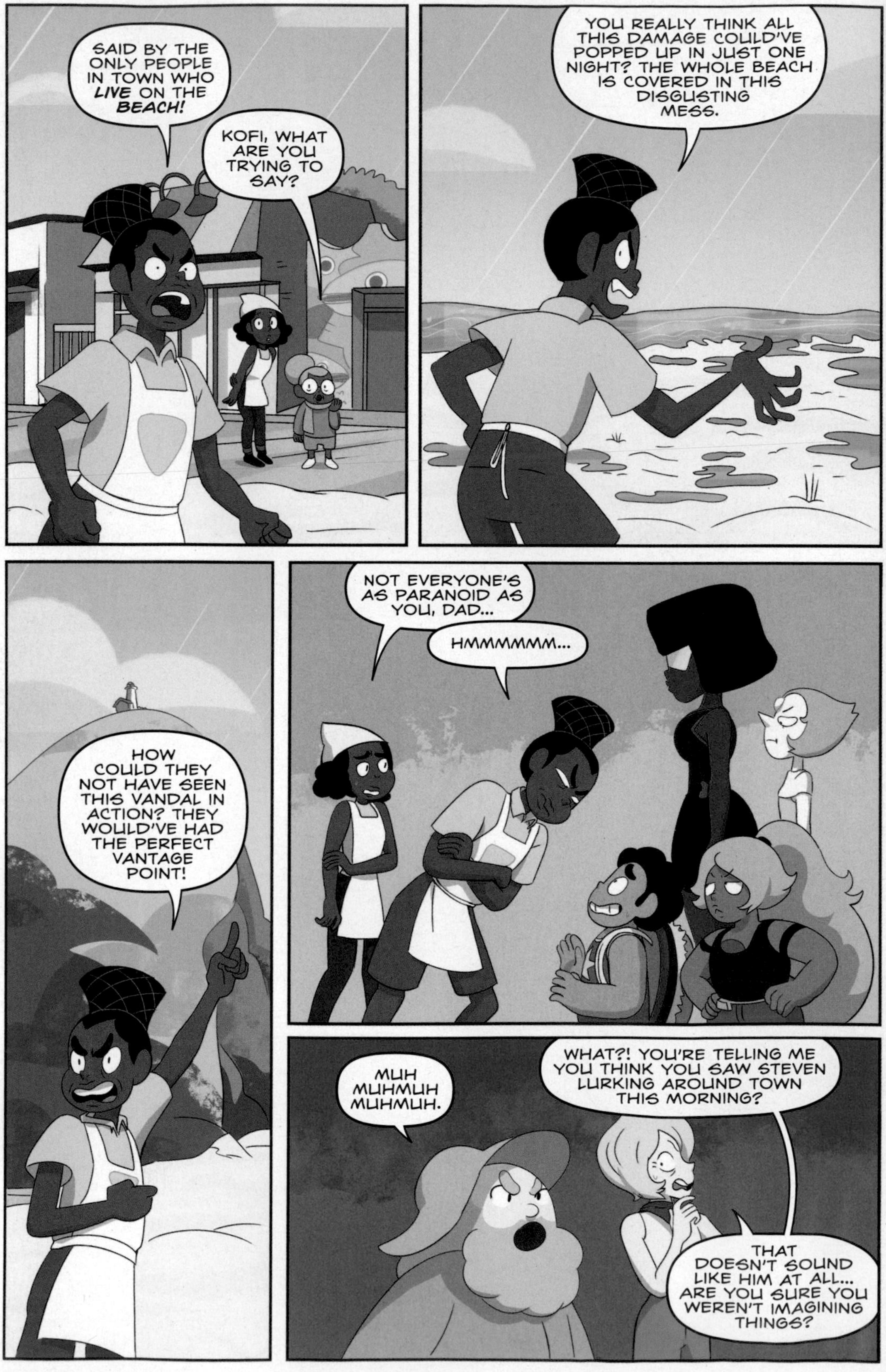
SAID BY THE ONLY PEOPLE IN TOWN WHO *LIVE* ON THE *BEACH!*
KOFI, WHAT ARE YOU TRYING TO SAY?
YOU REALLY THINK ALL THIS DAMAGE COULD'VE POPPED UP IN JUST ONE NIGHT? THE WHOLE BEACH IS COVERED IN THIS DISGUSTING MESS.
HOW COULD THEY NOT HAVE SEEN THIS VANDAL IN ACTION? THEY WOULD'VE HAD THE PERFECT VANTAGE POINT!
NOT EVERYONE'S AS PARANOID AS YOU, DAD...
HMMMMMM...
MUH MUHMUH MUHMUH.
WHAT?! YOU'RE TELLING ME YOU THINK YOU SAW STEVEN LURKING AROUND TOWN THIS MORNING?
THAT DOESN'T SOUND LIKE HIM AT ALL... ARE YOU SURE YOU WEREN'T IMAGINING THINGS?

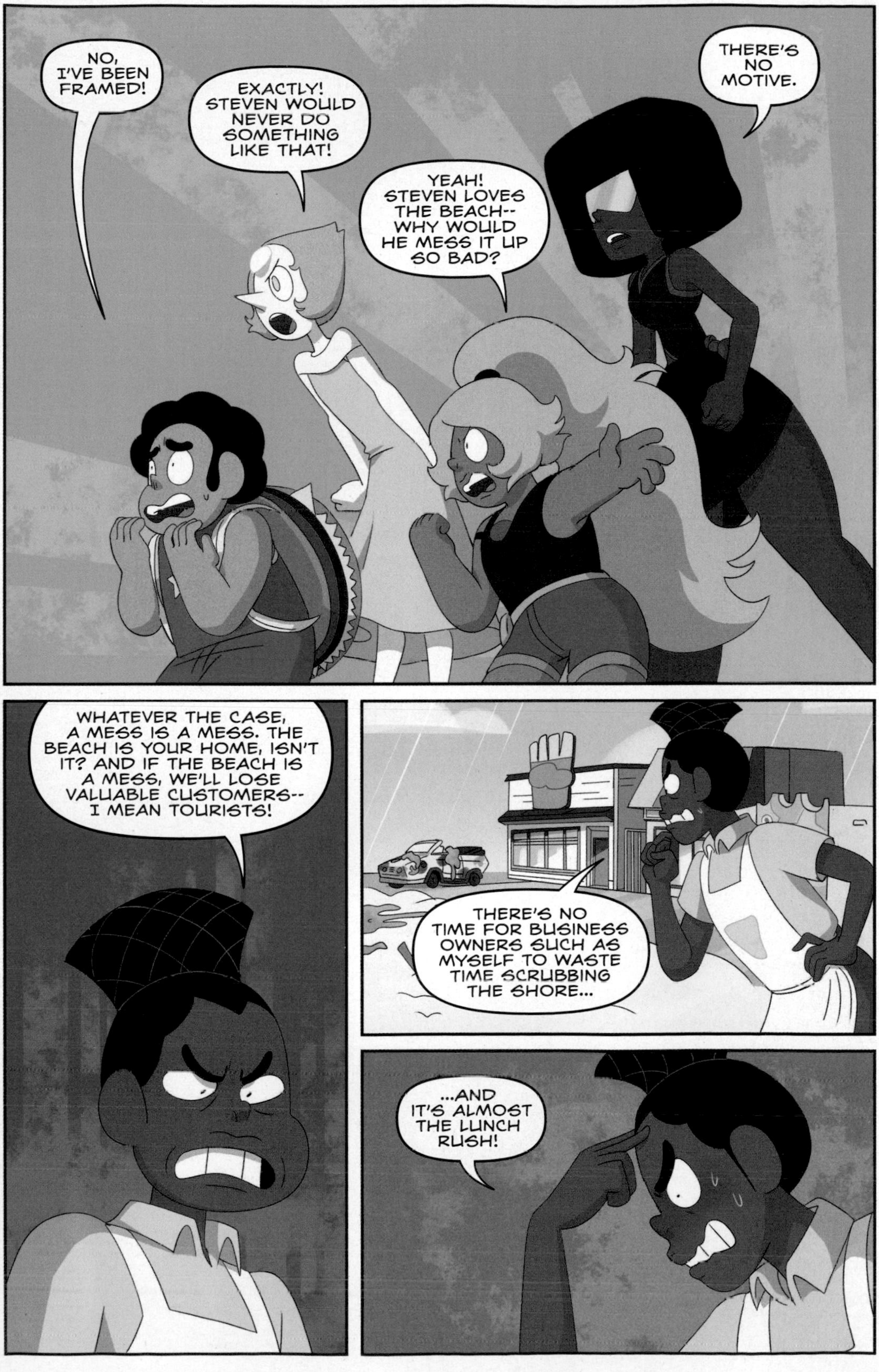
NO, I'VE BEEN FRAMED!
EXACTLY! STEVEN WOULD NEVER DO SOMETHING LIKE THAT!
YEAH! STEVEN LOVES THE BEACH-- WHY WOULD HE MESS IT UP SO BAD?
THERE'S NO MOTIVE.
WHATEVER THE CASE, A MESS IS A MESS. THE BEACH IS YOUR HOME, ISN'T IT? AND IF THE BEACH IS A MESS, WE'LL LOSE VALUABLE CUSTOMERS-- I MEAN TOURISTS!
THERE'S NO TIME FOR BUSINESS OWNERS SUCH AS MYSELF TO WASTE TIME SCRUBBING THE SHORE...
...AND IT'S ALMOST THE LUNCH RUSH!

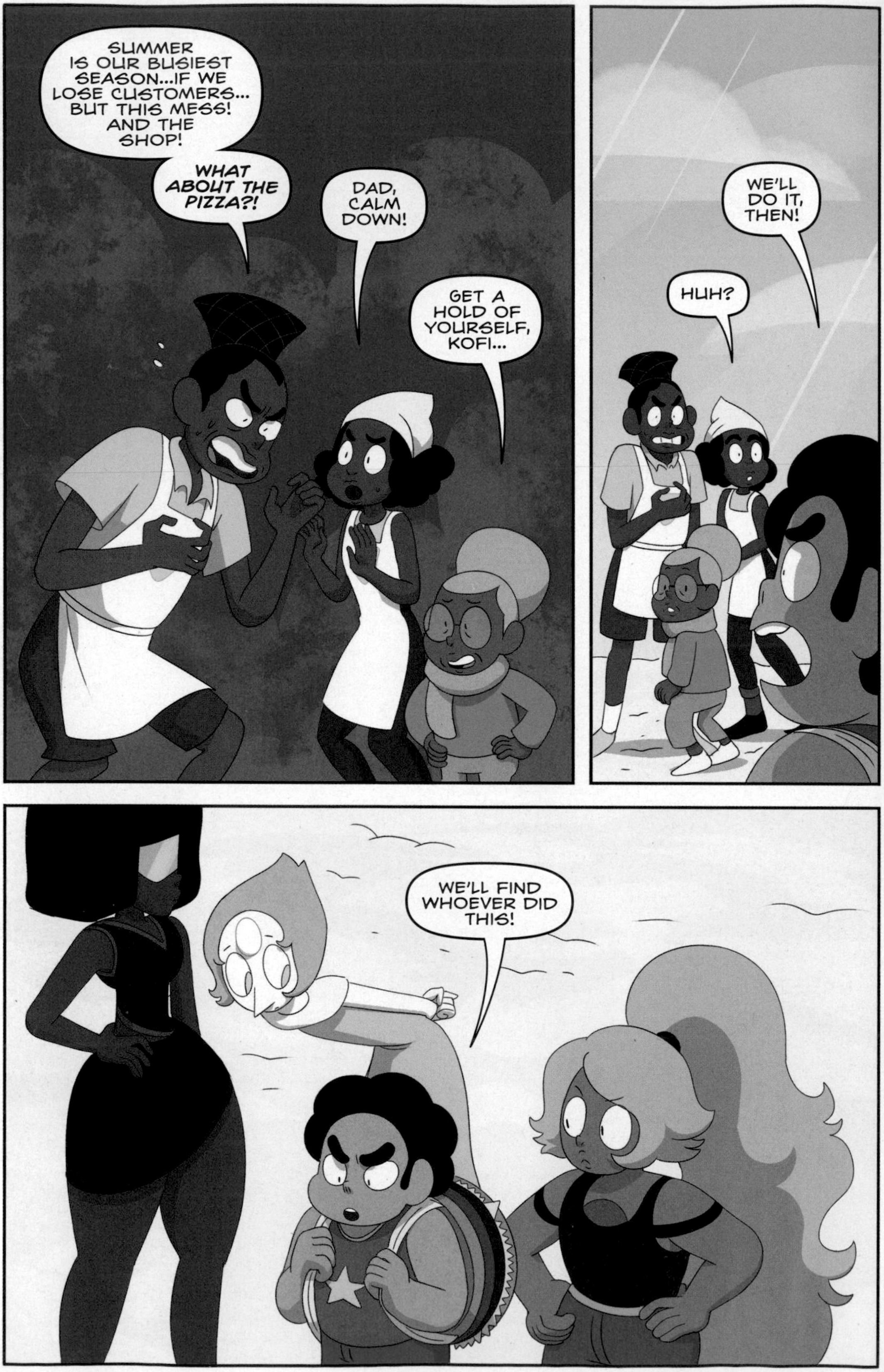
SUMMER IS OUR BUSIEST SEASON...IF WE LOSE CUSTOMERS... BUT THIS MESS! AND THE SHOP!
WHAT ABOUT THE PIZZA?!
DAD, CALM DOWN!
GET A HOLD OF YOURSELF, KOFI...
HUH?
WE'LL DO IT, THEN!
WE'LL FIND WHOEVER DID THIS!

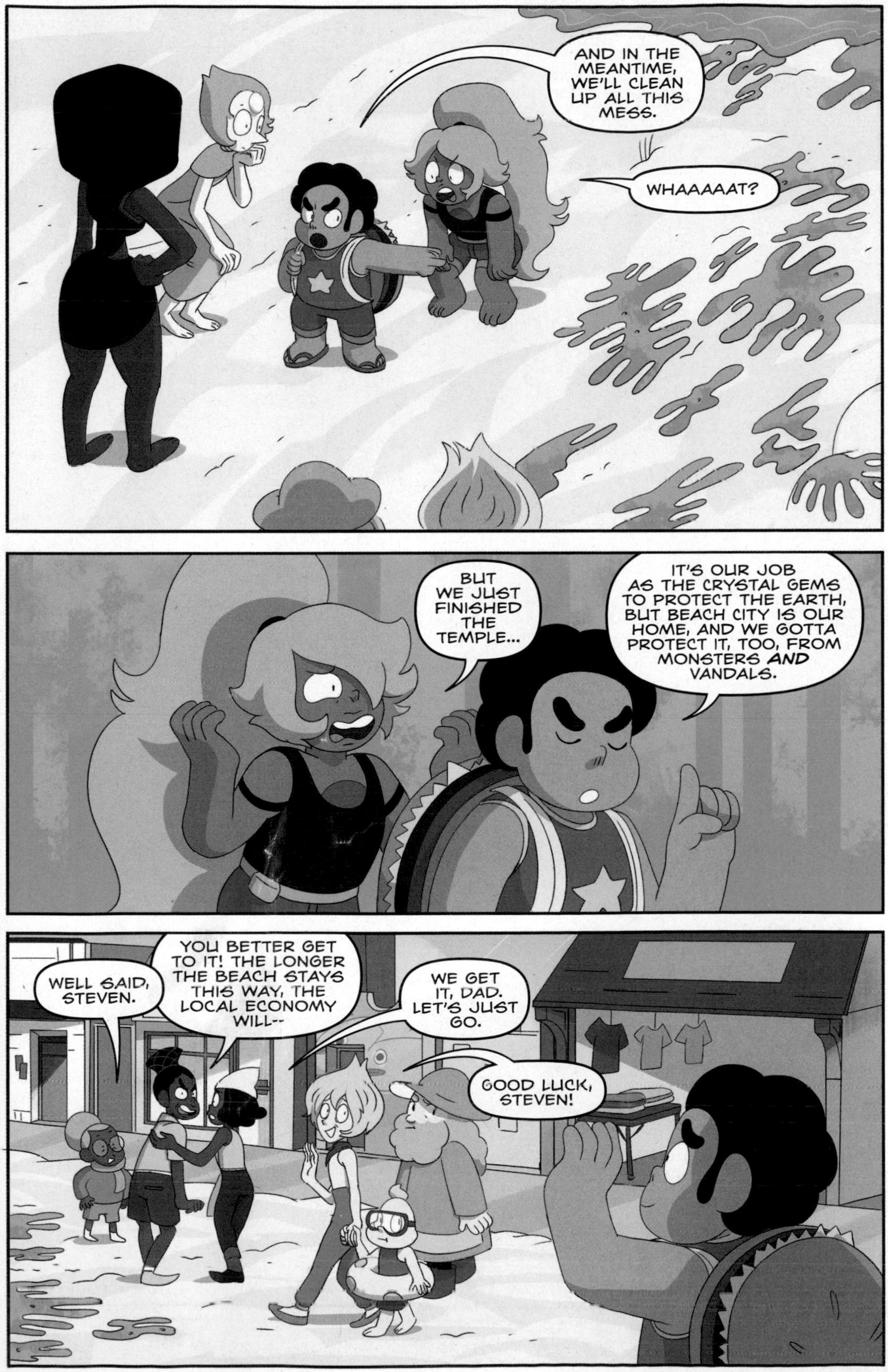
AND IN THE MEANTIME, WE'LL CLEAN UP ALL THIS MESS.
WHAAAAAT?
BUT WE JUST FINISHED THE TEMPLE...
IT'S OUR JOB AS THE CRYSTAL GEMS TO PROTECT THE EARTH, BUT BEACH CITY IS OUR HOME, AND WE GOTTA PROTECT IT, TOO, FROM MONSTERS AND VANDALS.
WELL SAID, STEVEN.
YOU BETTER GET TO IT! THE LONGER THE BEACH STAYS THIS WAY, THE LOCAL ECONOMY WILL--
WE GET IT, DAD. LET'S JUST GO.
GOOD LUCK, STEVEN!

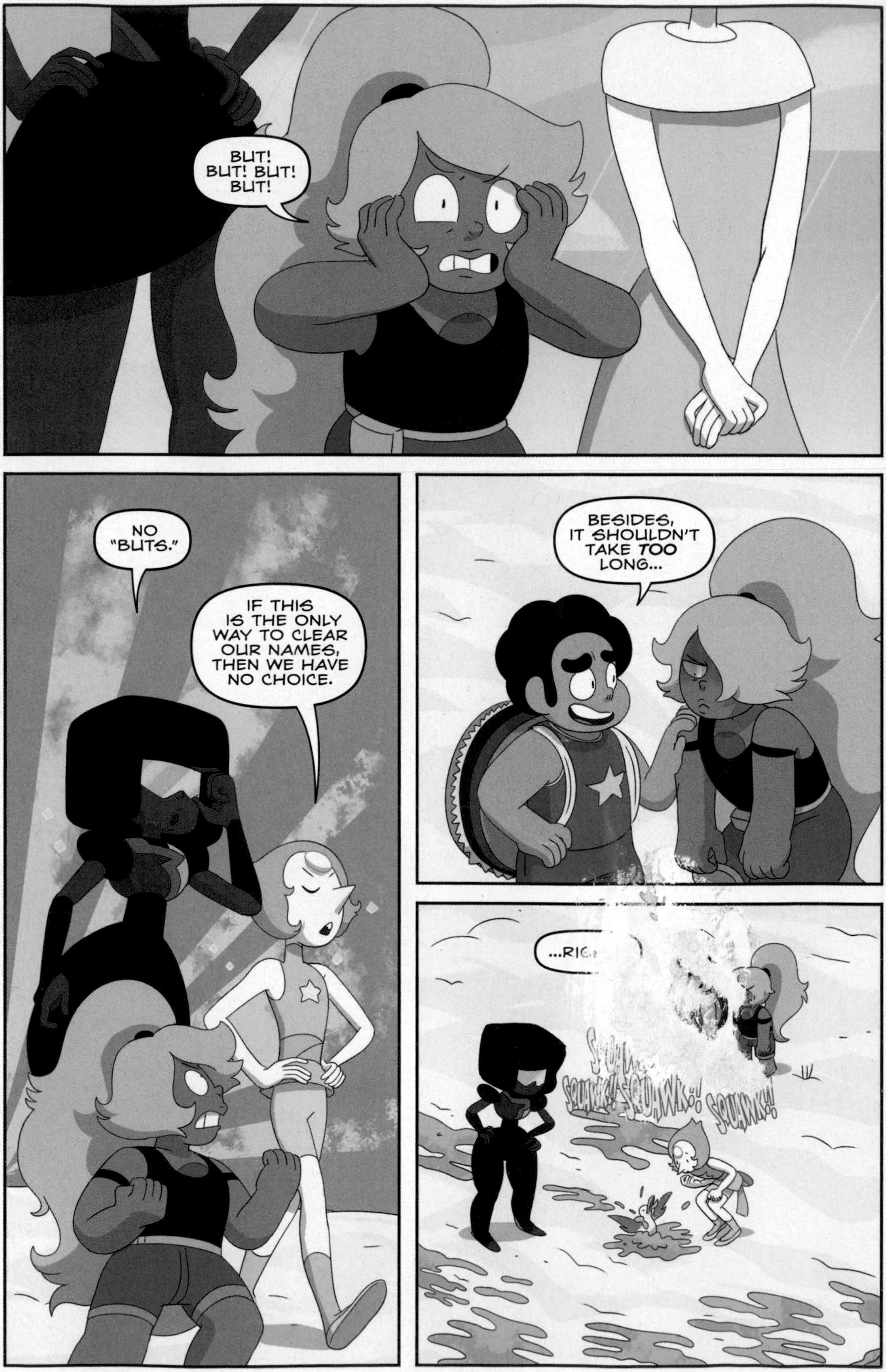
BUT! BUT! BUT! BUT!
NO "BUTS."
IF THIS IS THE ONLY WAY TO CLEAR OUR NAMES, THEN WE HAVE NO CHOICE.
BESIDES, IT SHOULDN'T TAKE *TOO* LONG...
...RIG
SQUAWK!! SQUAWK!! SQUAWK!! SQUAWK!!

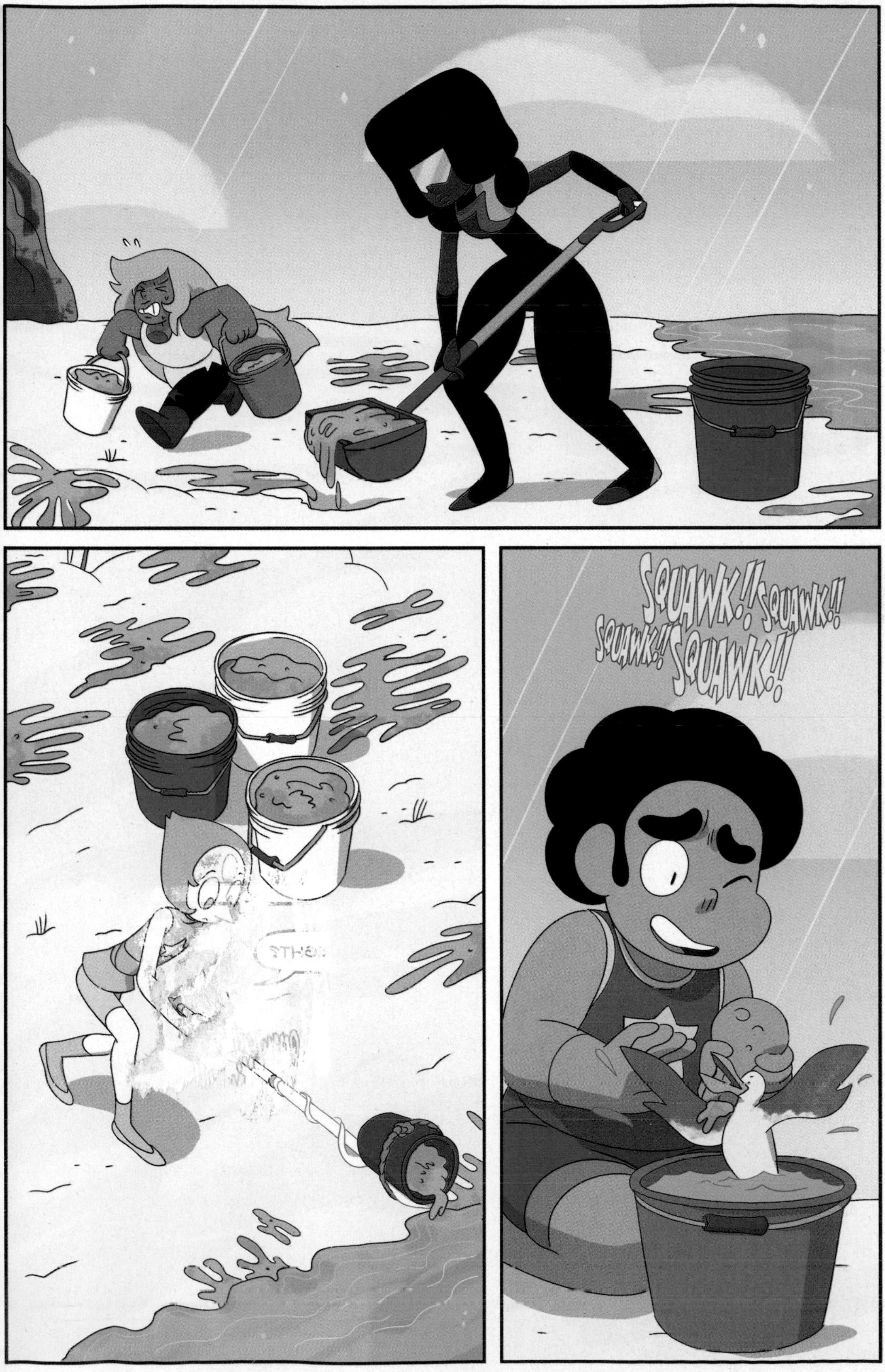
SQUAWK!!
SQUAWK!!
SQUAWK!!
SQUAWK!!

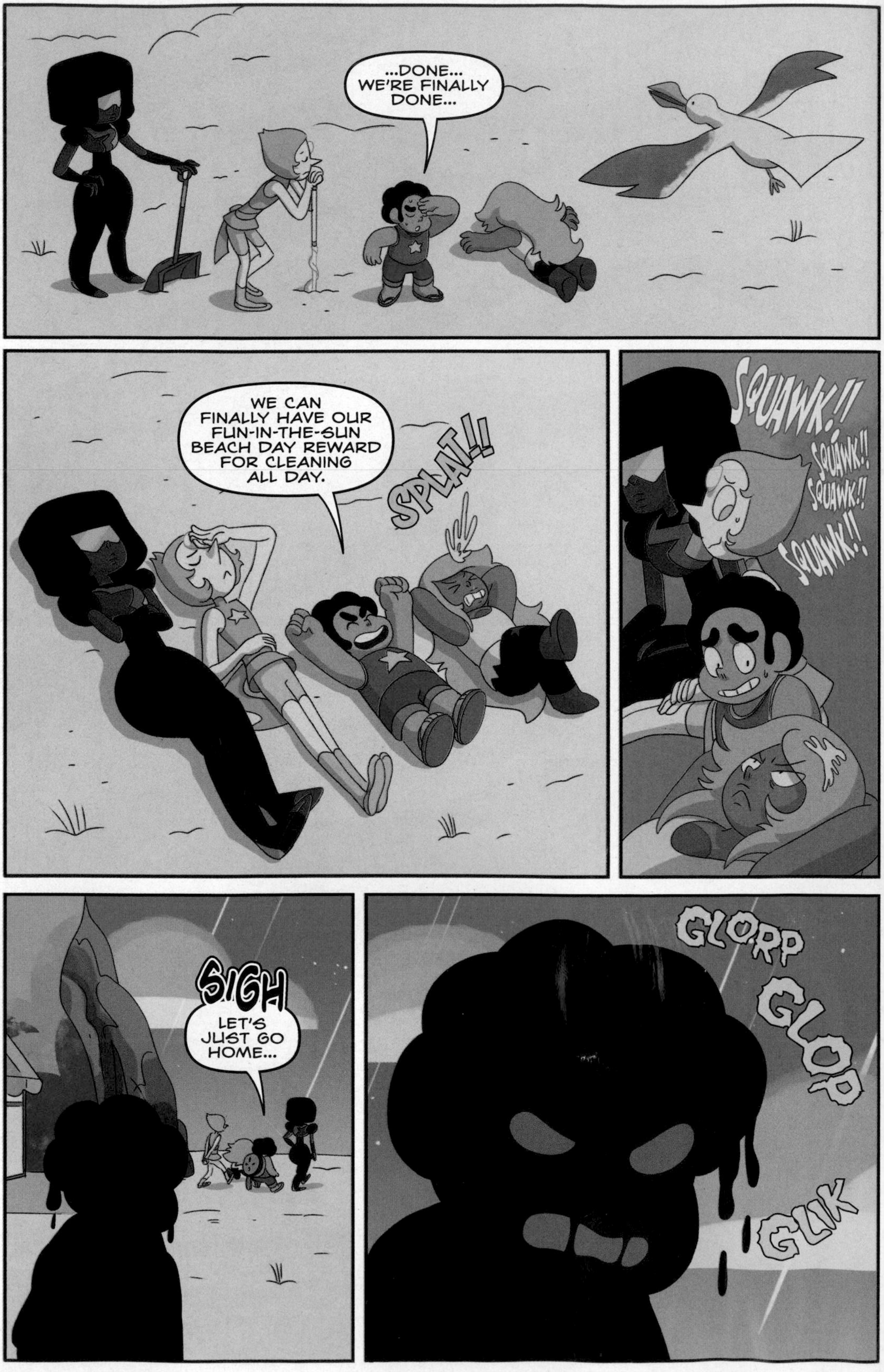
...DONE... WE'RE FINALLY DONE...
WE CAN FINALLY HAVE OUR FUN-IN-THE-SUN BEACH DAY REWARD FOR CLEANING ALL DAY.
SPLAT!!
SQUAWK!!
SQUAWK!!
SQUAWK!!
SQUAWK!!
SIGH
LET'S JUST GO HOME...
GLORP
GLOP
GLIK

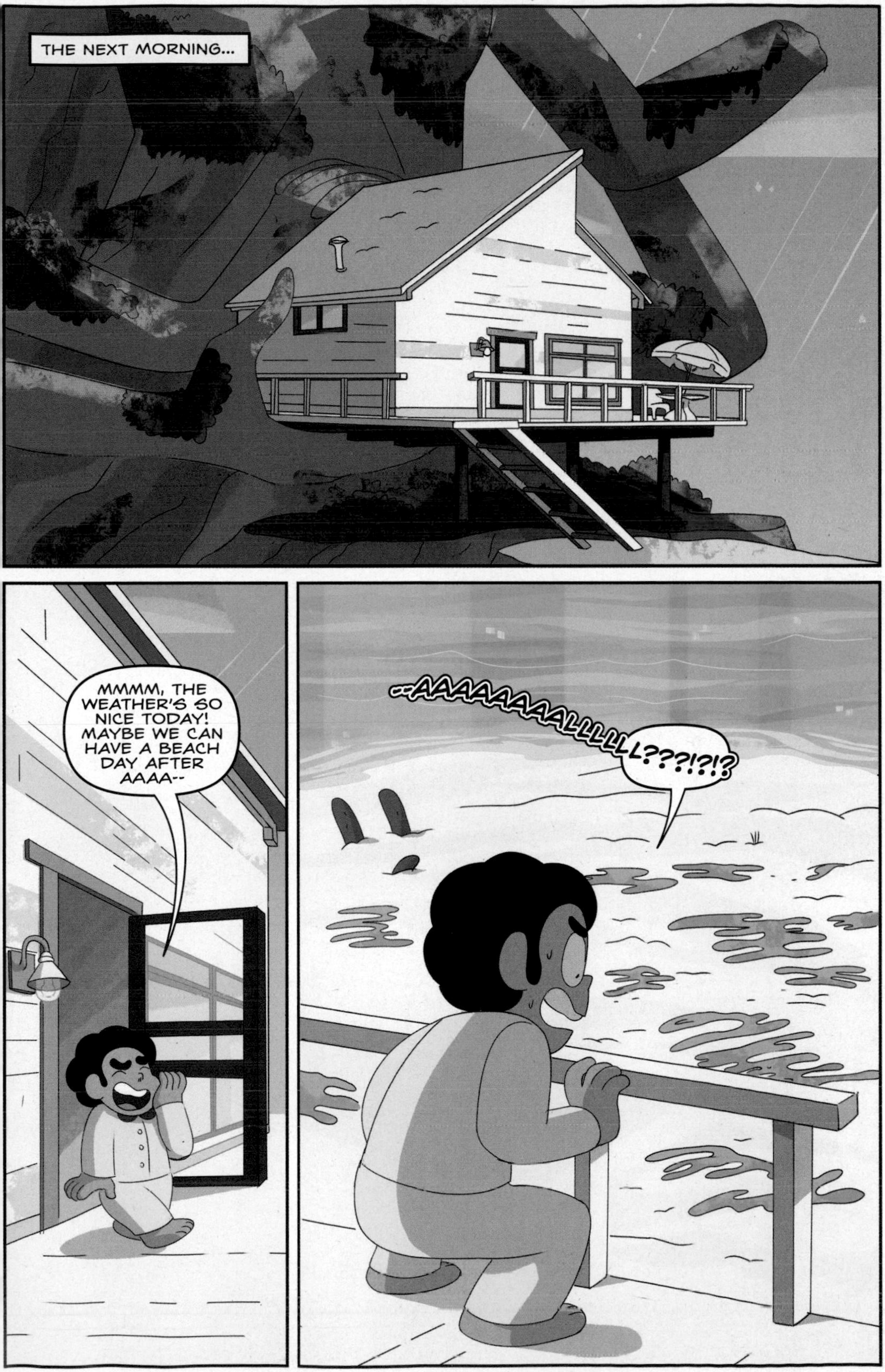
THE NEXT MORNING...
MMMM, THE WEATHER'S SO NICE TODAY! MAYBE WE CAN HAVE A BEACH DAY AFTER AAAA--
--AAAAAAAAALLLLLL???!?!?

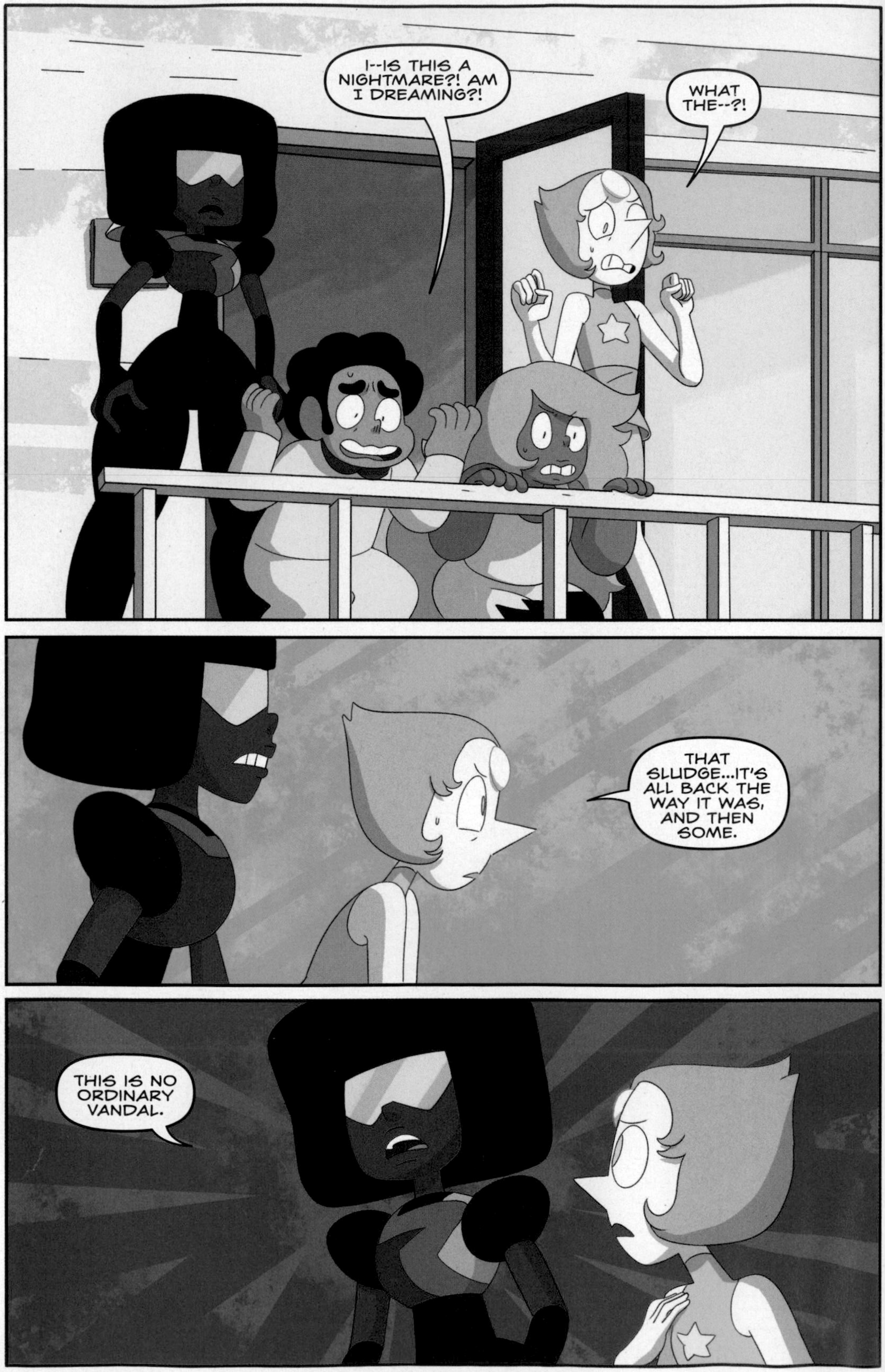
I--IS THIS A NIGHTMARE?! AM I DREAMING?!
WHAT THE--?!
THAT SLUDGE...IT'S ALL BACK THE WAY IT WAS, AND THEN SOME.
THIS IS NO ORDINARY VANDAL.

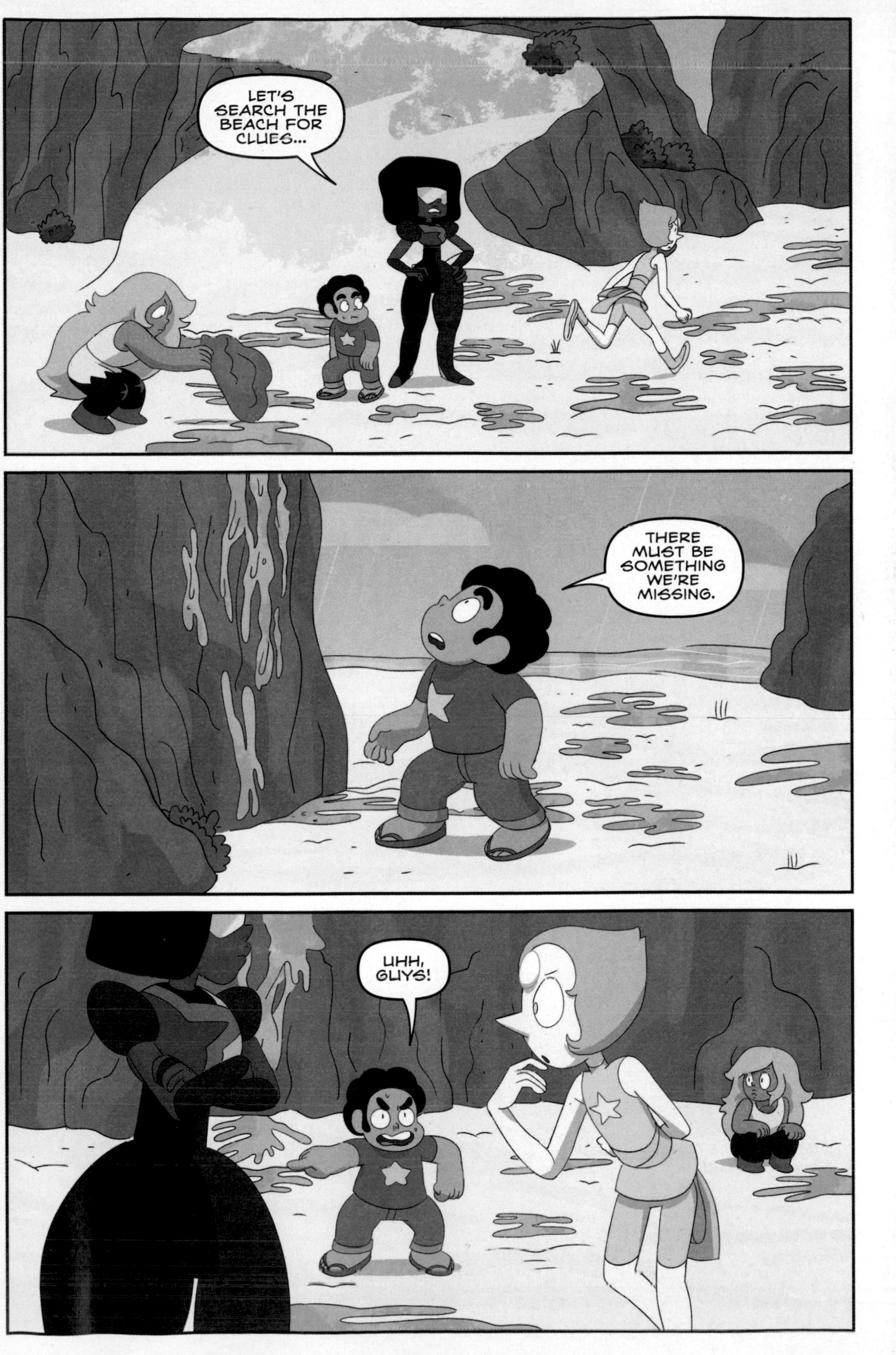
LET'S SEARCH THE BEACH FOR CLUES...
THERE MUST BE SOMETHING WE'RE MISSING.
UHH, GUYS!

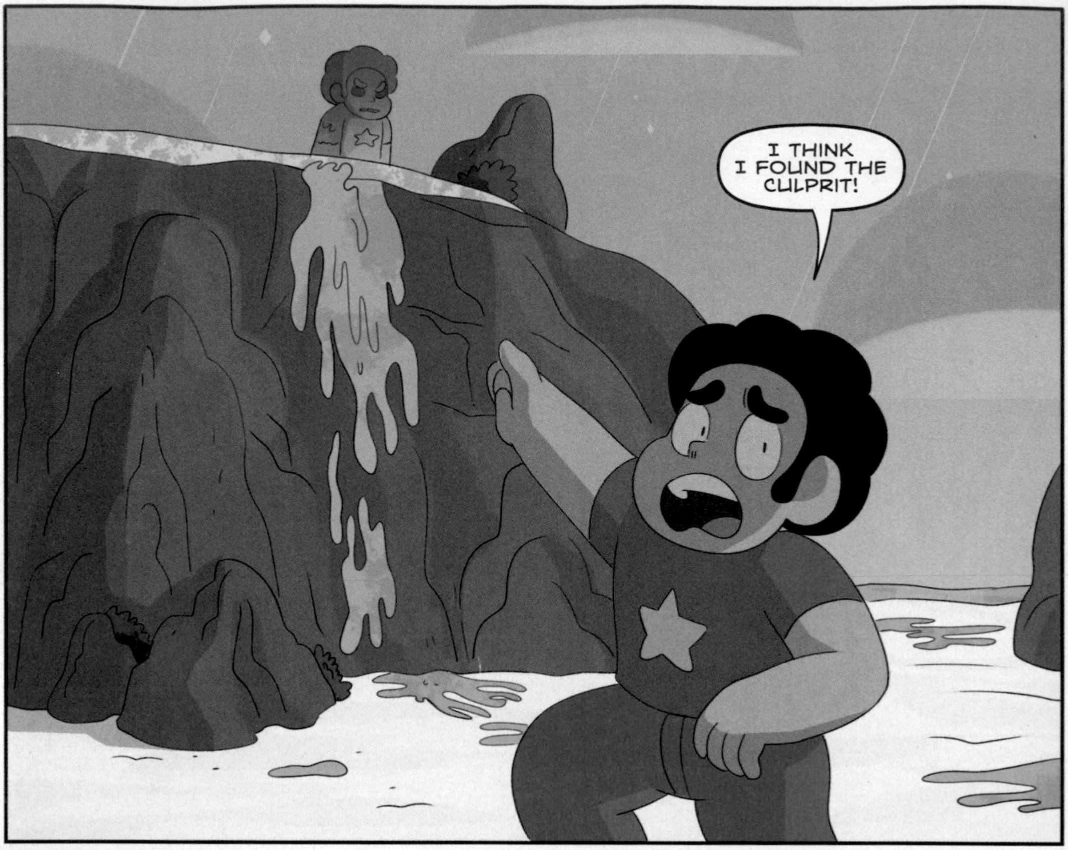
I THINK I FOUND THE CULPRIT!

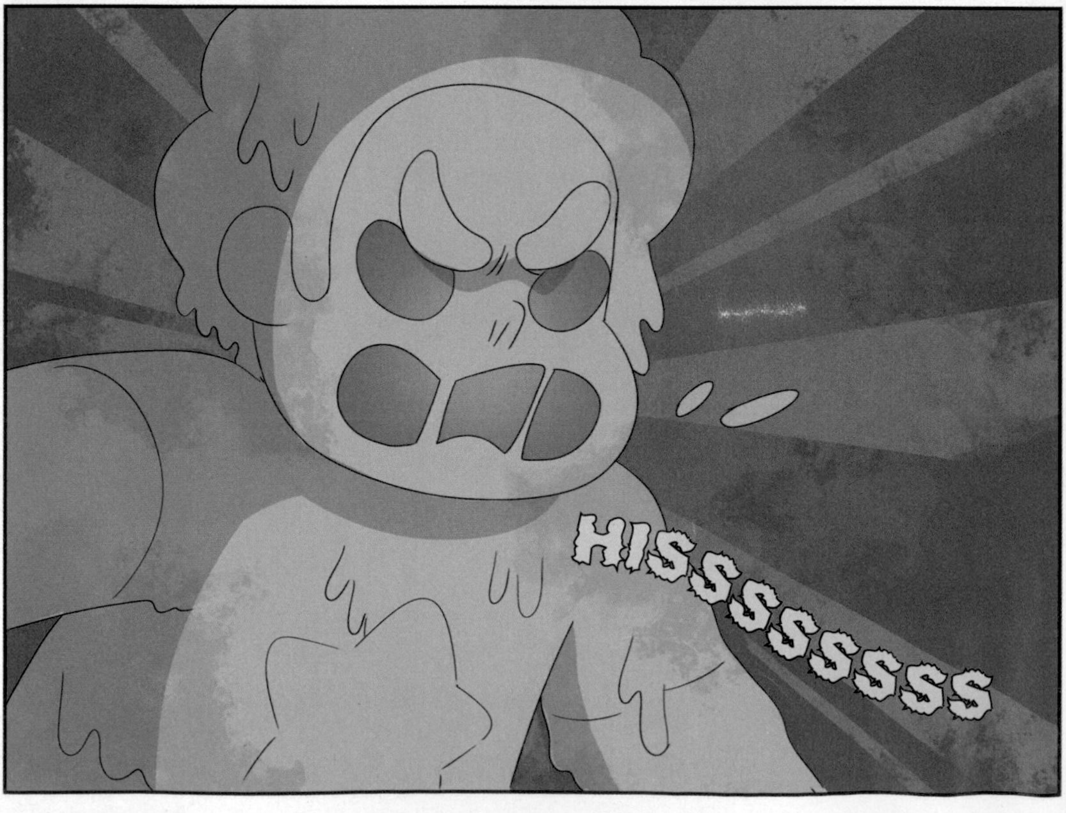
HISSSSSSSSSS

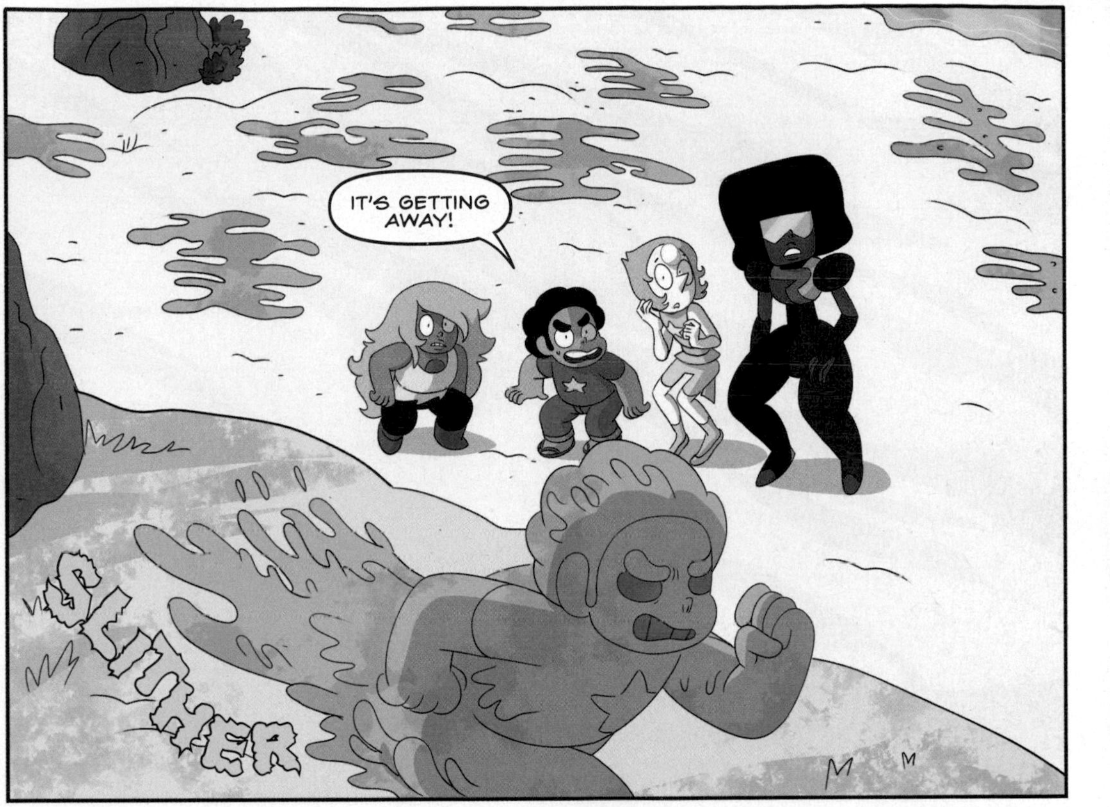
IT'S GETTING AWAY!
SLITHER
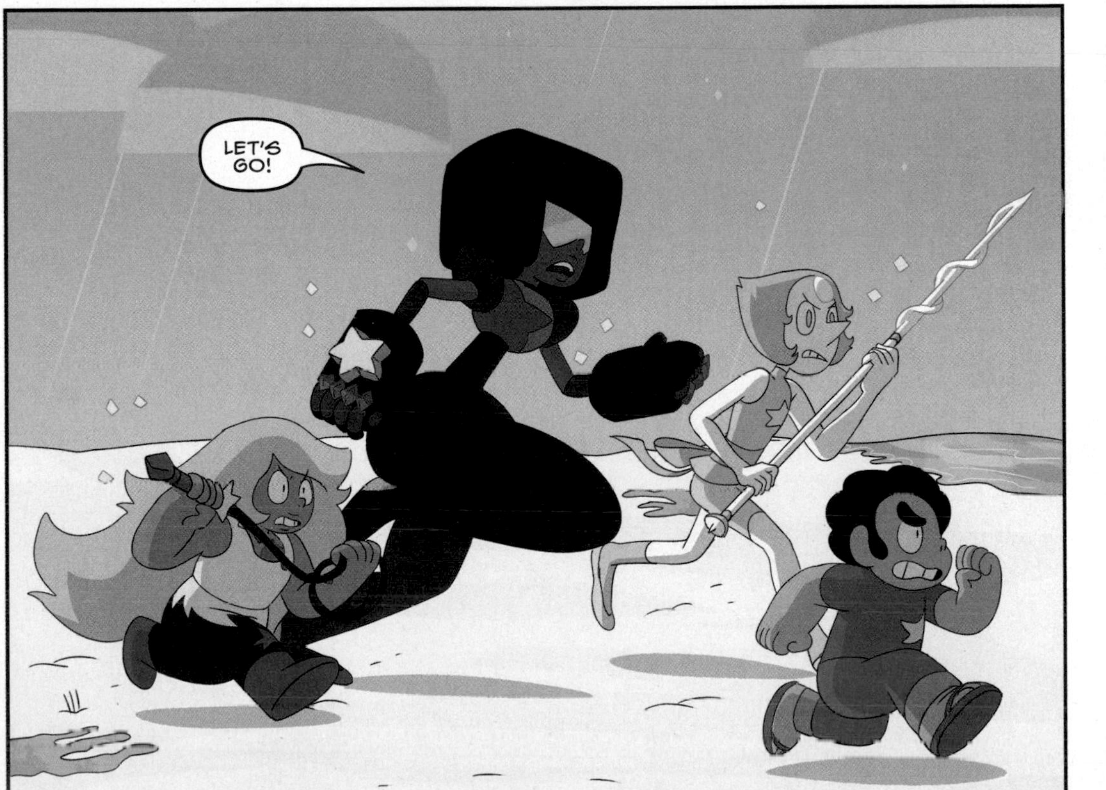
LET'S GO!

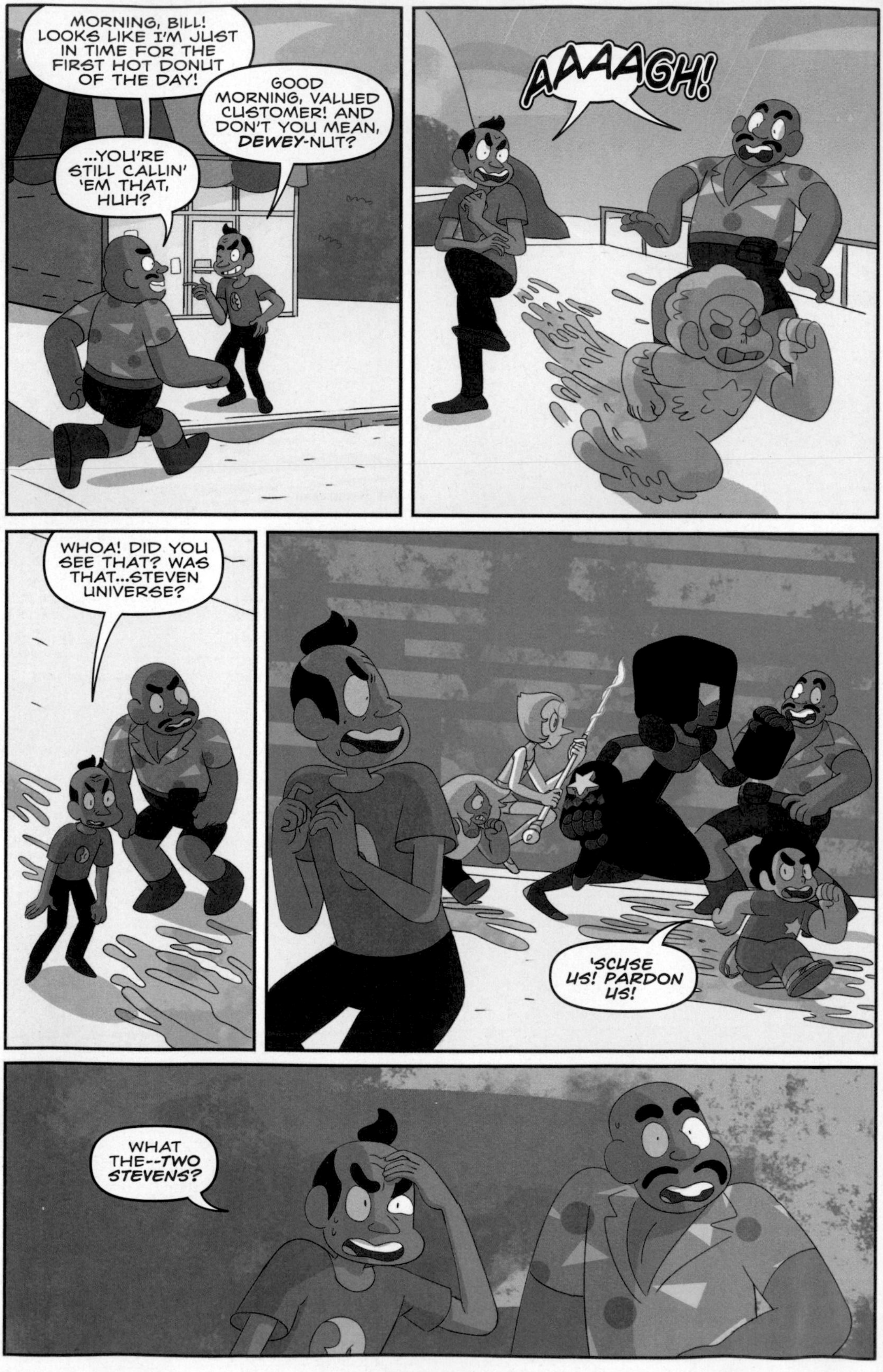
MORNING, BILL! LOOKS LIKE I'M JUST IN TIME FOR THE FIRST HOT DONUT OF THE DAY!
GOOD MORNING, VALUED CUSTOMER! AND DON'T YOU MEAN, DEWEY-NUT?
...YOU'RE STILL CALLIN' 'EM THAT, HUH?
AAAAGH!
WHOA! DID YOU SEE THAT? WAS THAT...STEVEN UNIVERSE?
'SCUSE US! PARDON US!
WHAT THE--TWO STEVENS?

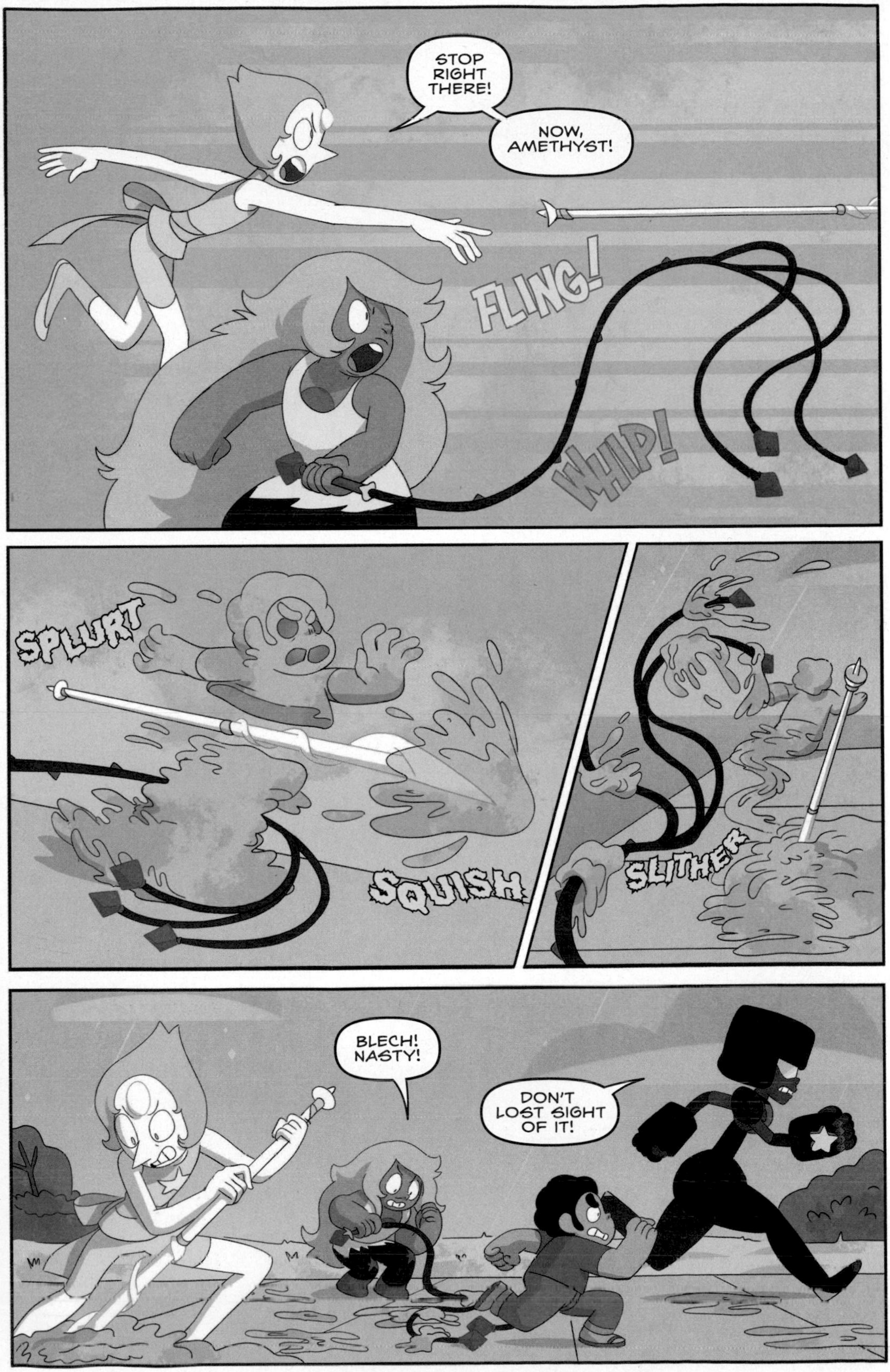
STOP RIGHT THERE!
NOW, AMETHYST!
FLING!
WHIP!
SPLURT
SQUISH
SLITHER
BLECH! NASTY!
DON'T LOST SIGHT OF IT!

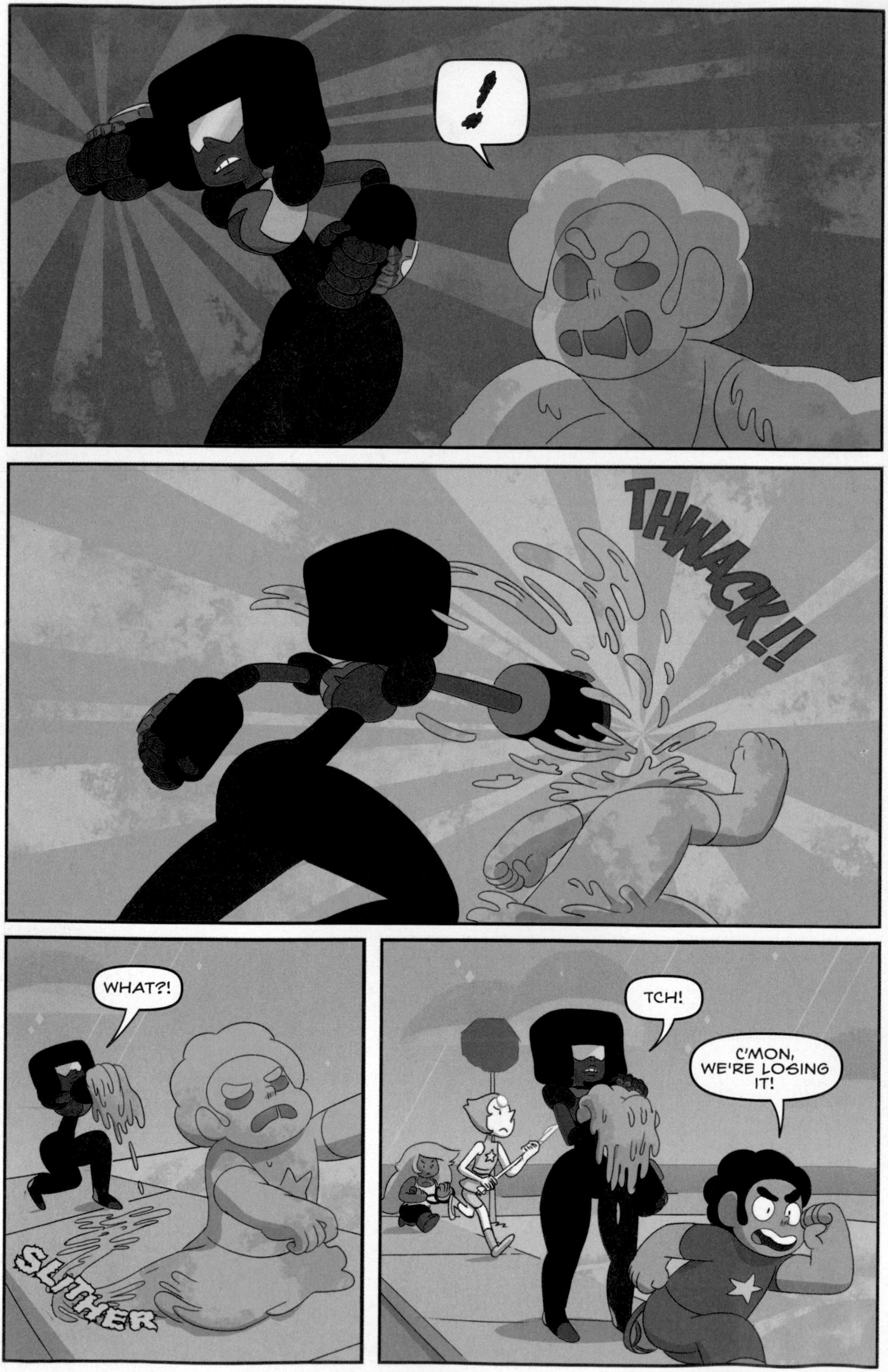
!
THWACK!!
WHAT?!
SLITHER
TCH!
C'MON, WE'RE LOSING IT!

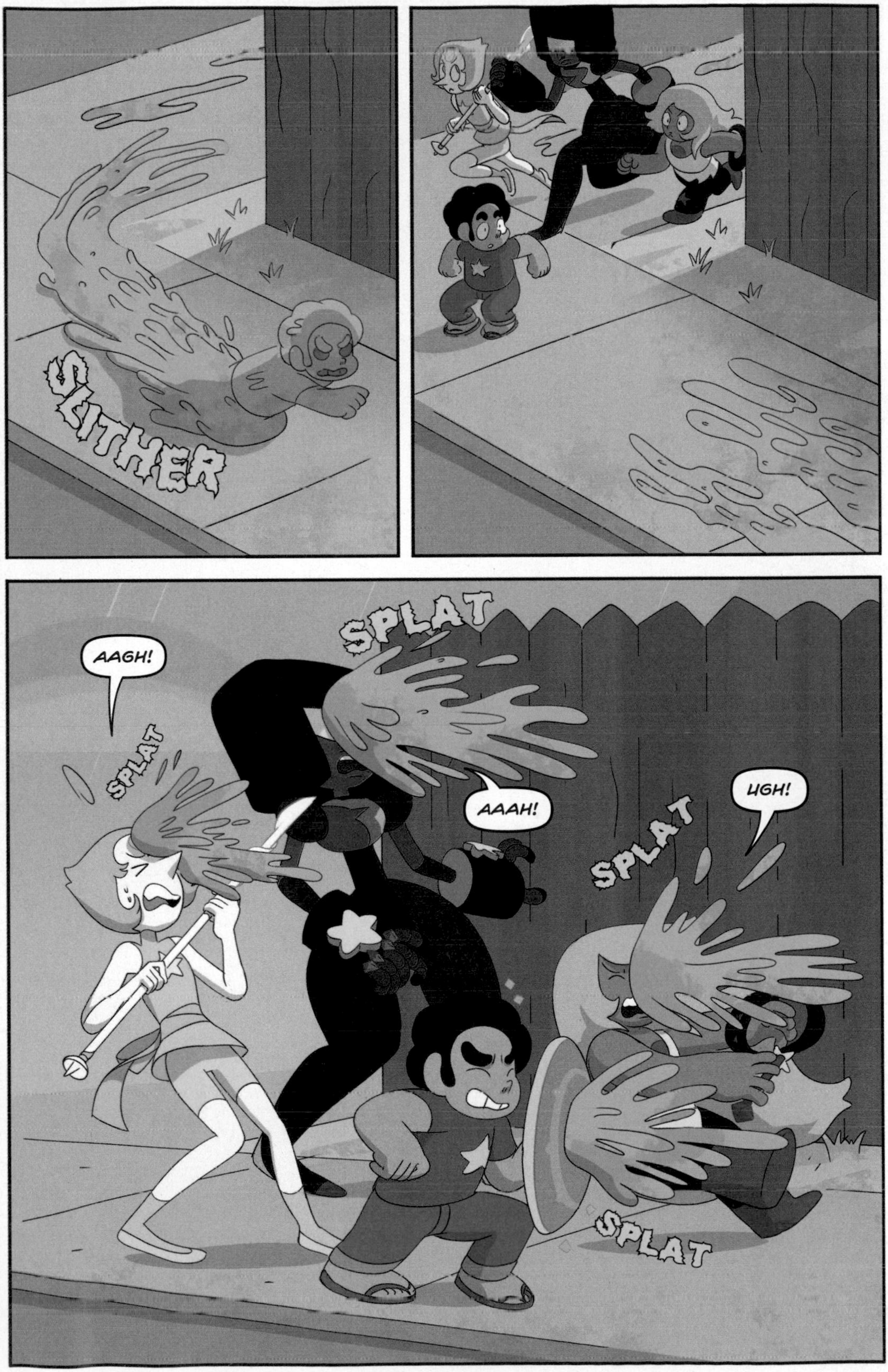
SLITHER
SPLAT
AAGH!
SPLAT
AAAH!
UGH!
SPLAT
SPLAT

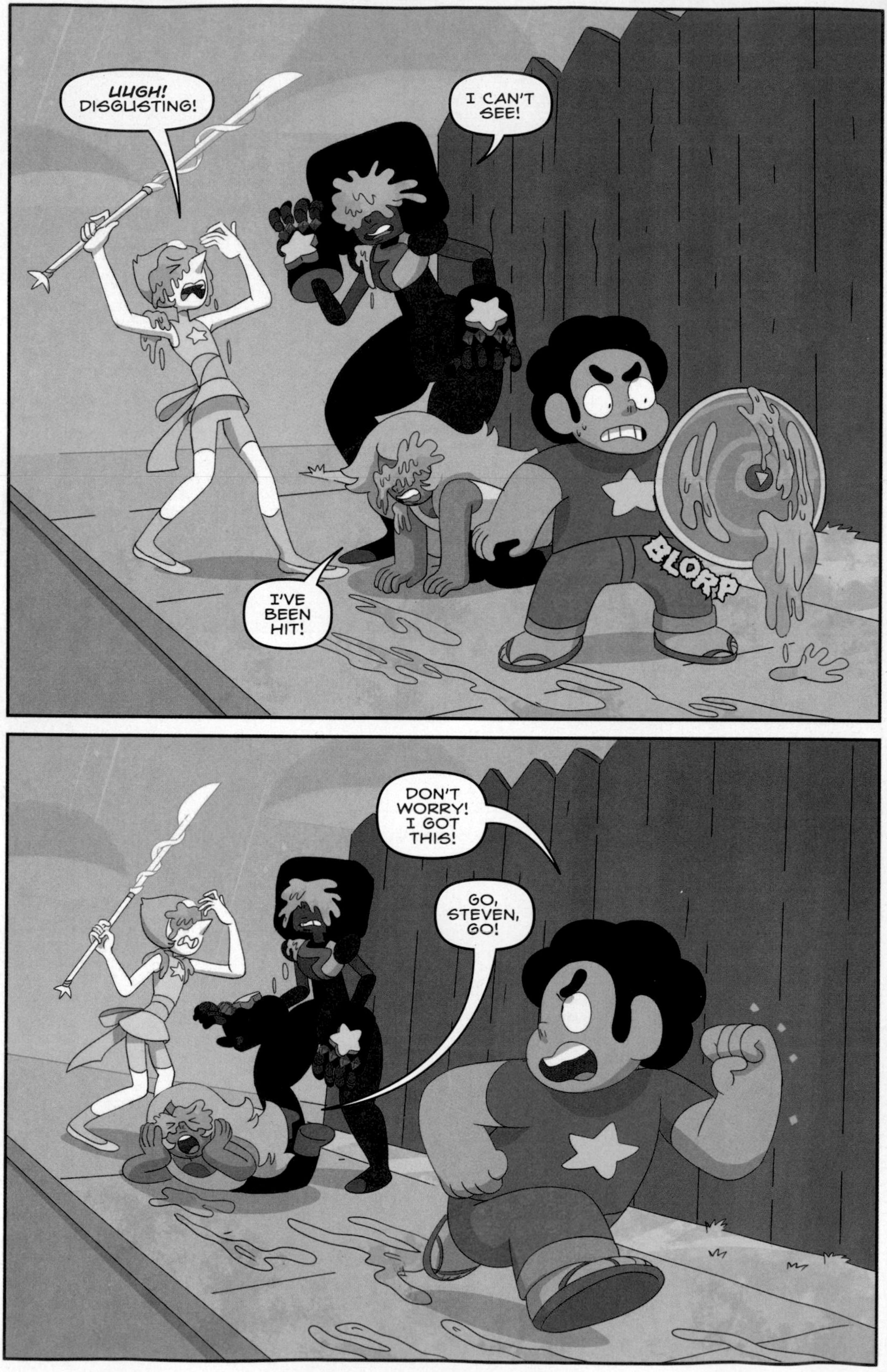
UUGH! DISGUSTING!
I CAN'T SEE!
I'VE BEEN HIT!
BLORP
DON'T WORRY! I GOT THIS!
GO, STEVEN, GO!

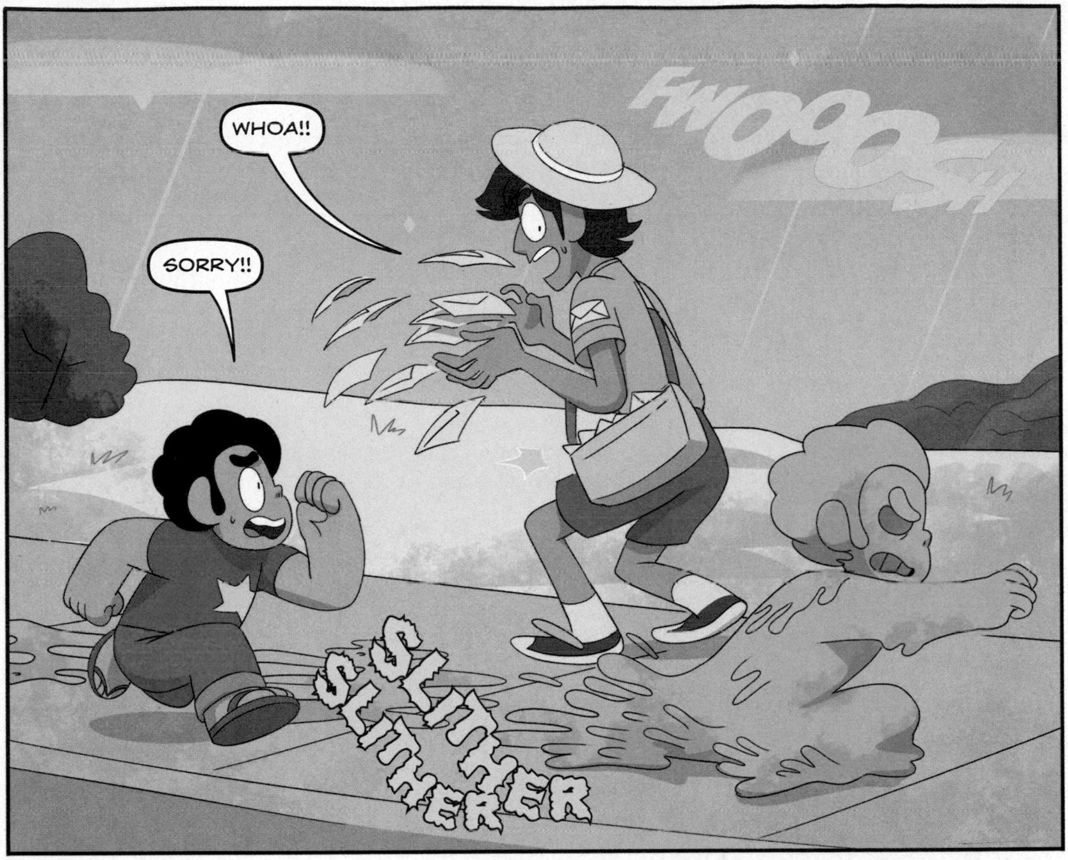
FWOOOSH
WHOA!!
SORRY!!
SLITHER
SLITHER

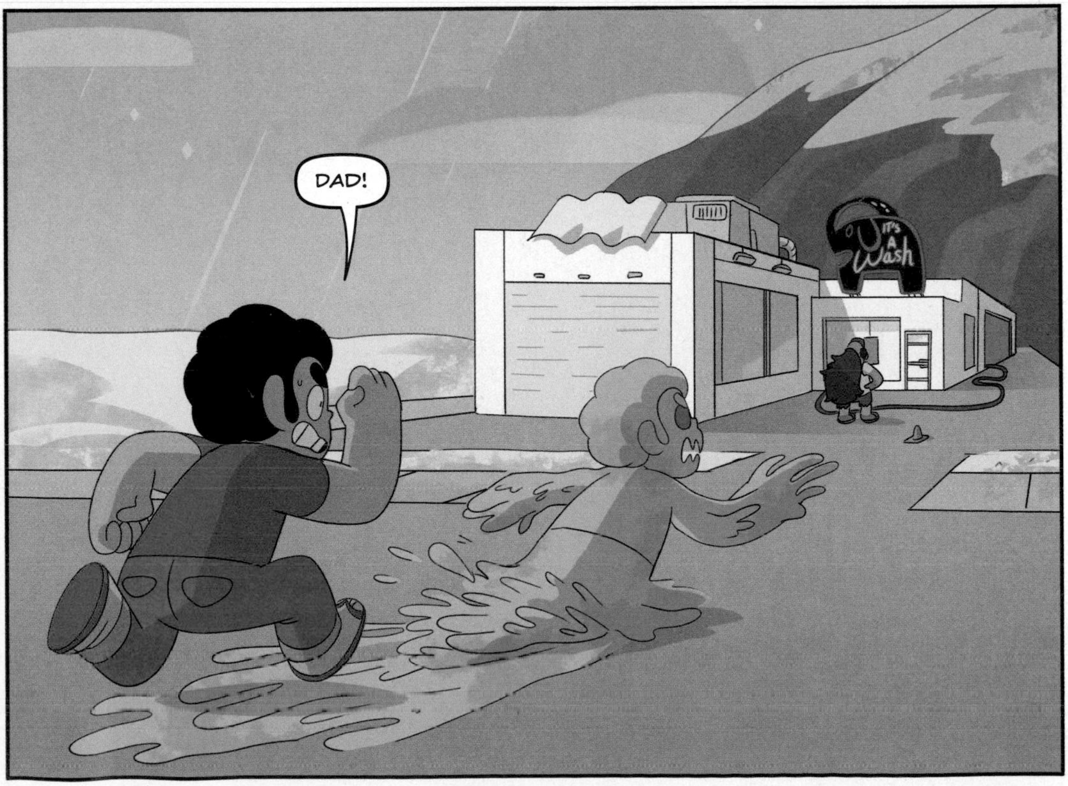
DAD!
IT'S A Wash

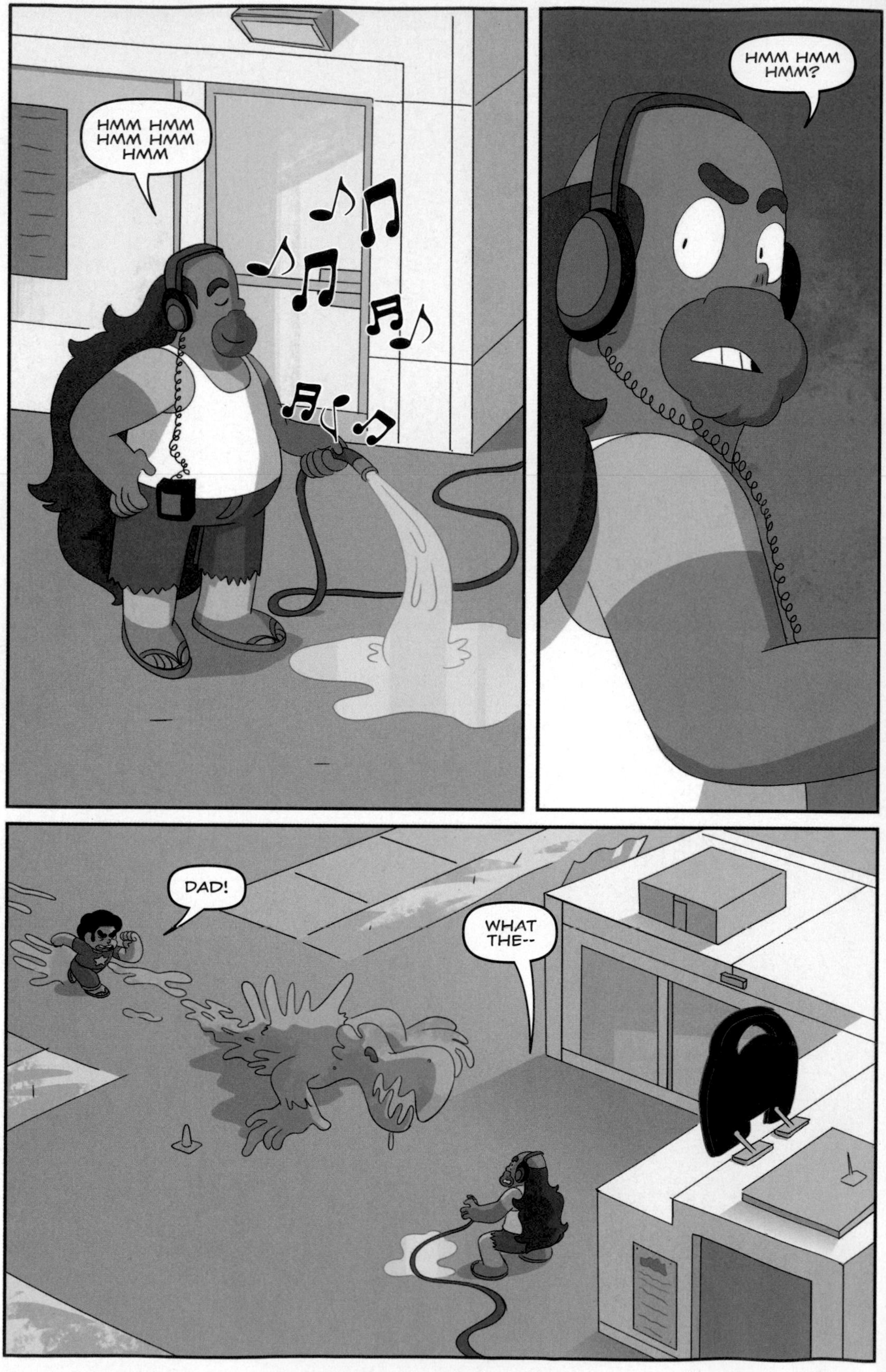
HMM HMM
HMM HMM
HMM
HMM HMM
HMM?
DAD!
WHAT
THE--

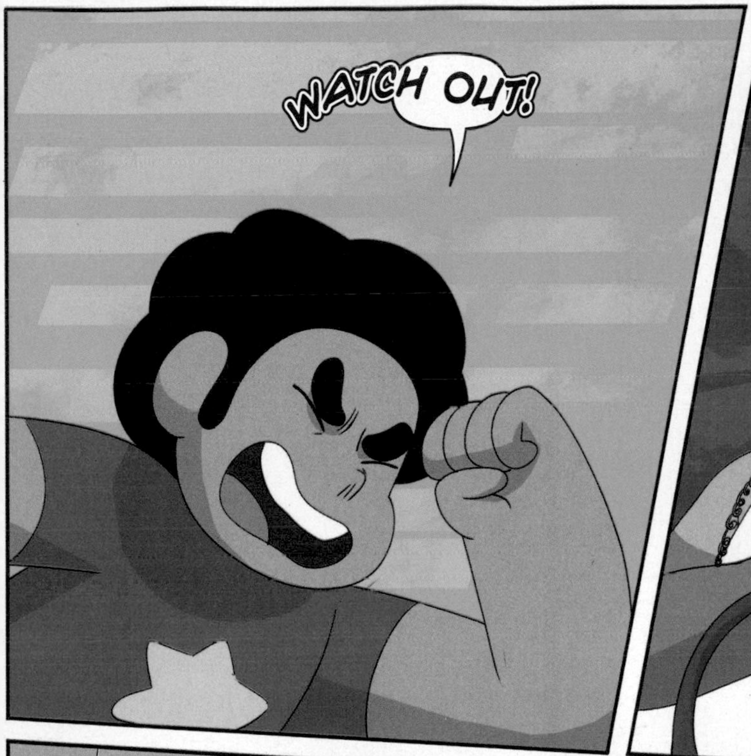
WATCH OUT!
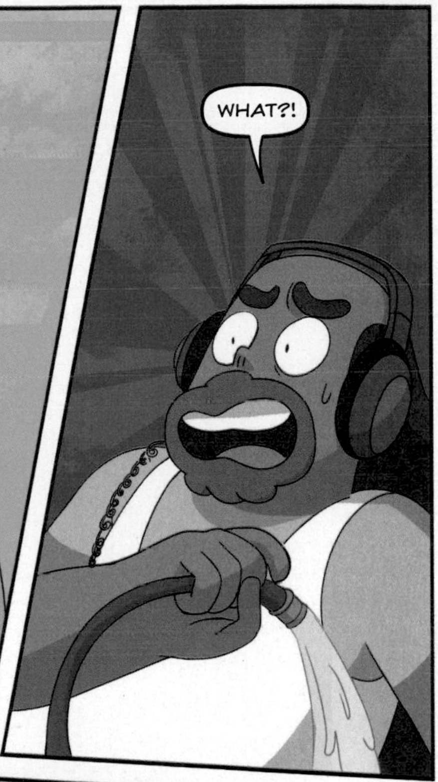
WHAT?!
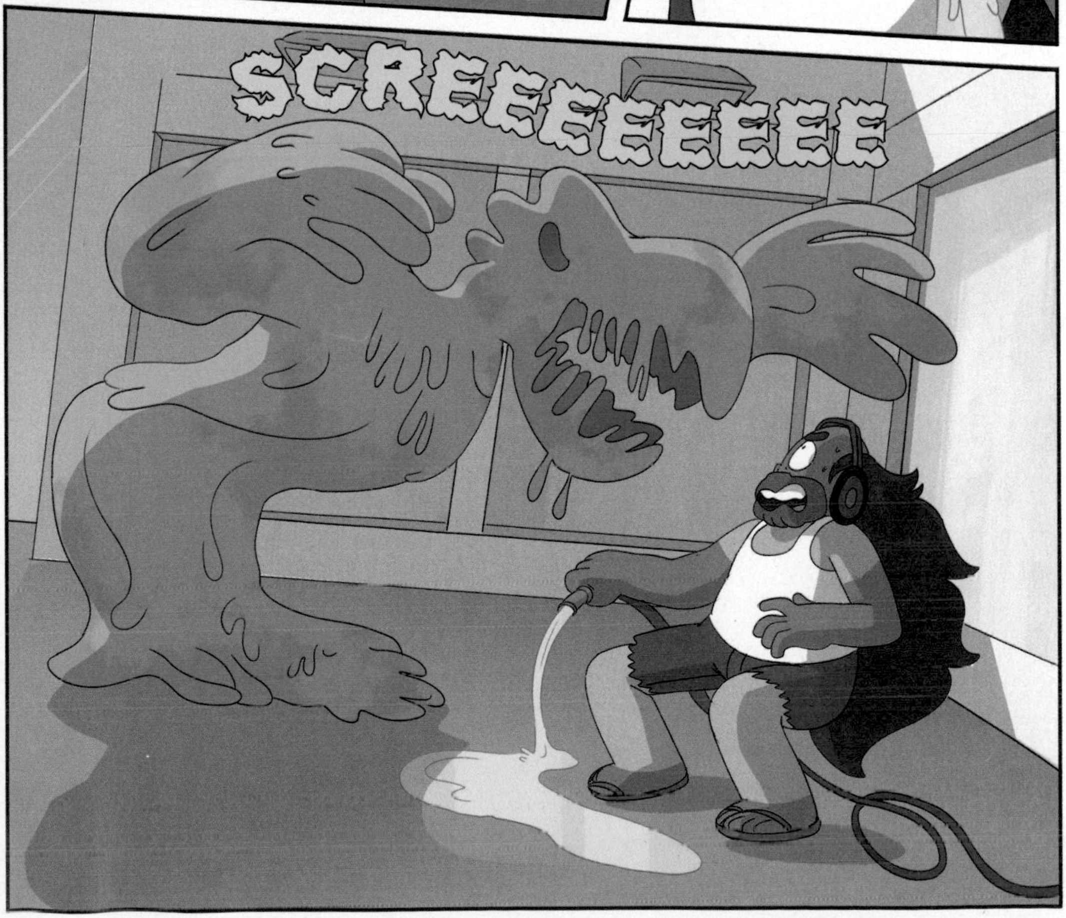
SCREEEEEEEEE

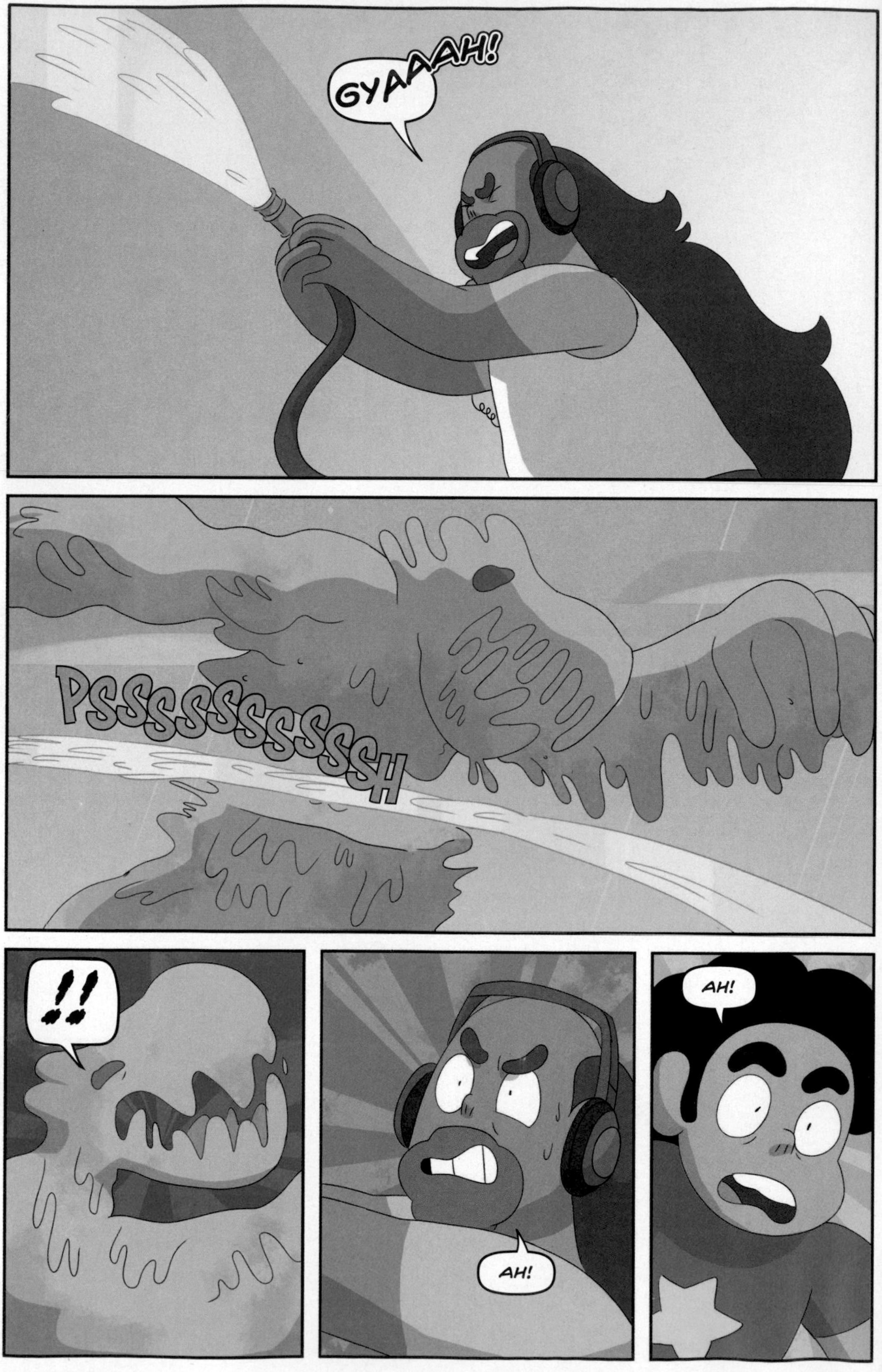
GYAAAH!
PSSSSSSSSSSH
!!
AH!
AH!

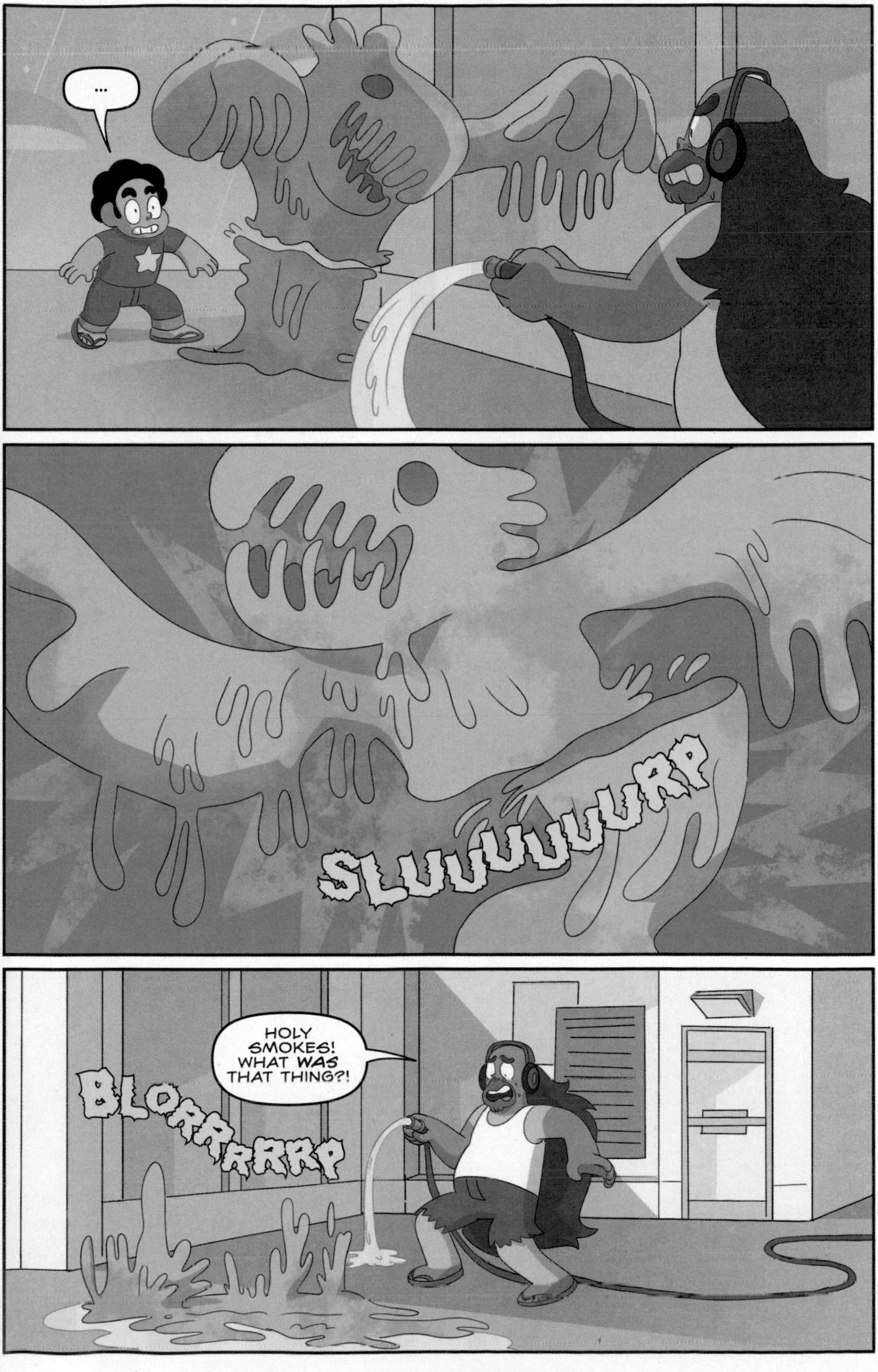
...
SLUUUUUURP
HOLY SMOKES! WHAT WAS THAT THING?!
BLORRRRRRP

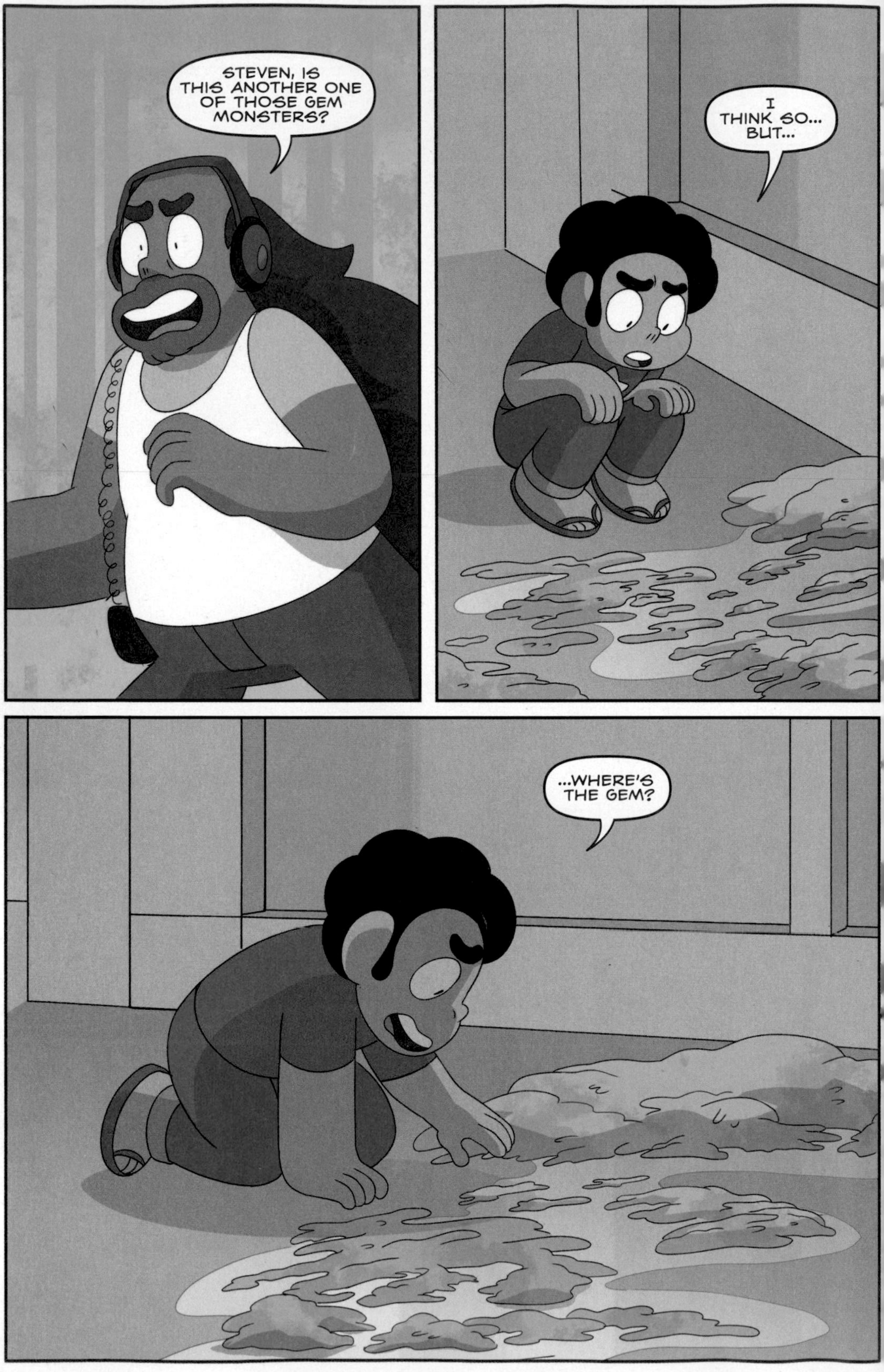
STEVEN, IS THIS ANOTHER ONE OF THOSE GEM MONSTERS?
I THINK SO... BUT...
...WHERE'S THE GEM?

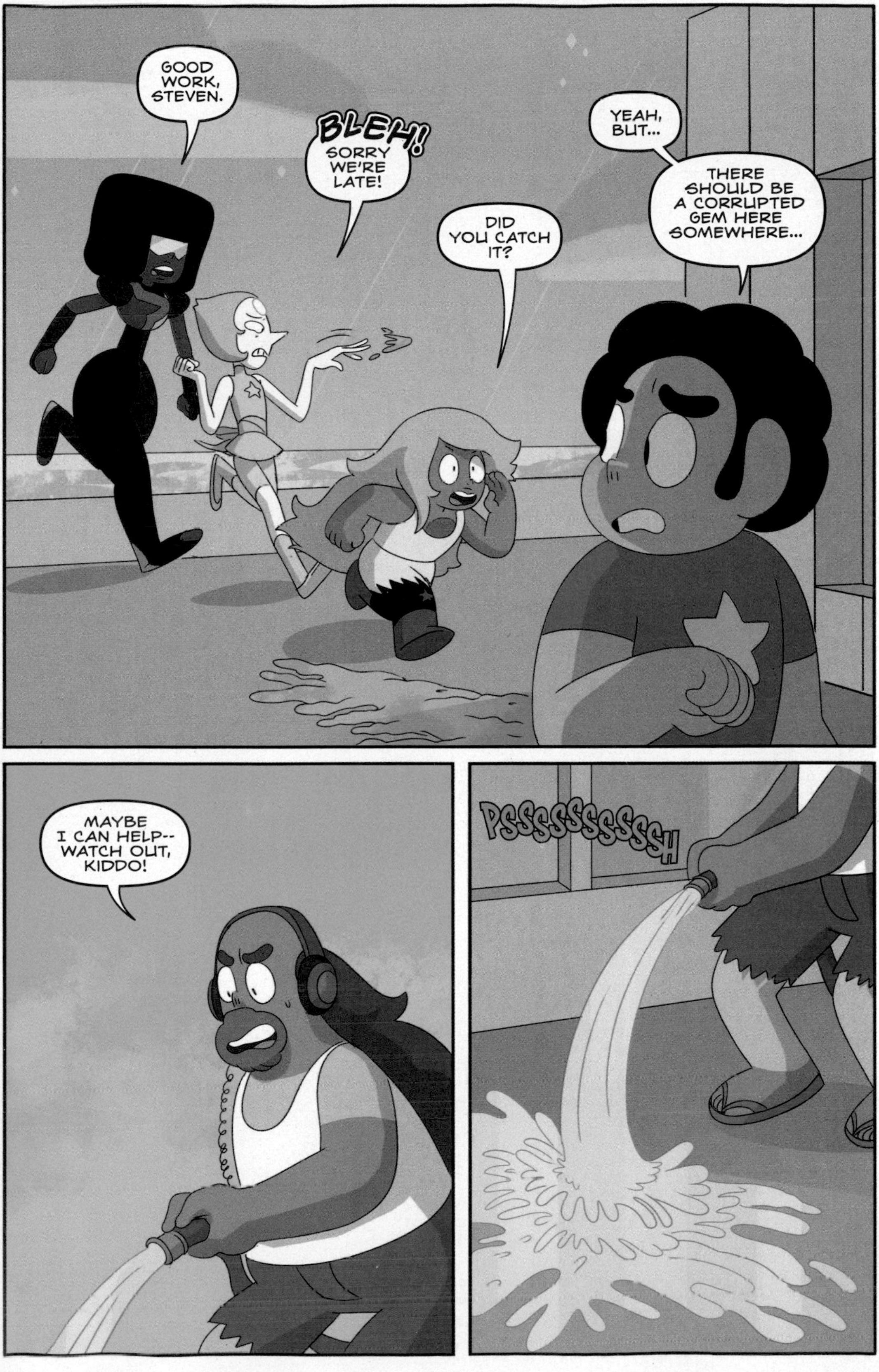
GOOD WORK, STEVEN.
BLEH!
SORRY WE'RE LATE!
DID YOU CATCH IT?
YEAH, BUT...
THERE SHOULD BE A CORRUPTED GEM HERE SOMEWHERE...
MAYBE I CAN HELP-- WATCH OUT, KIDDO!
PSSSSSSSSSSH

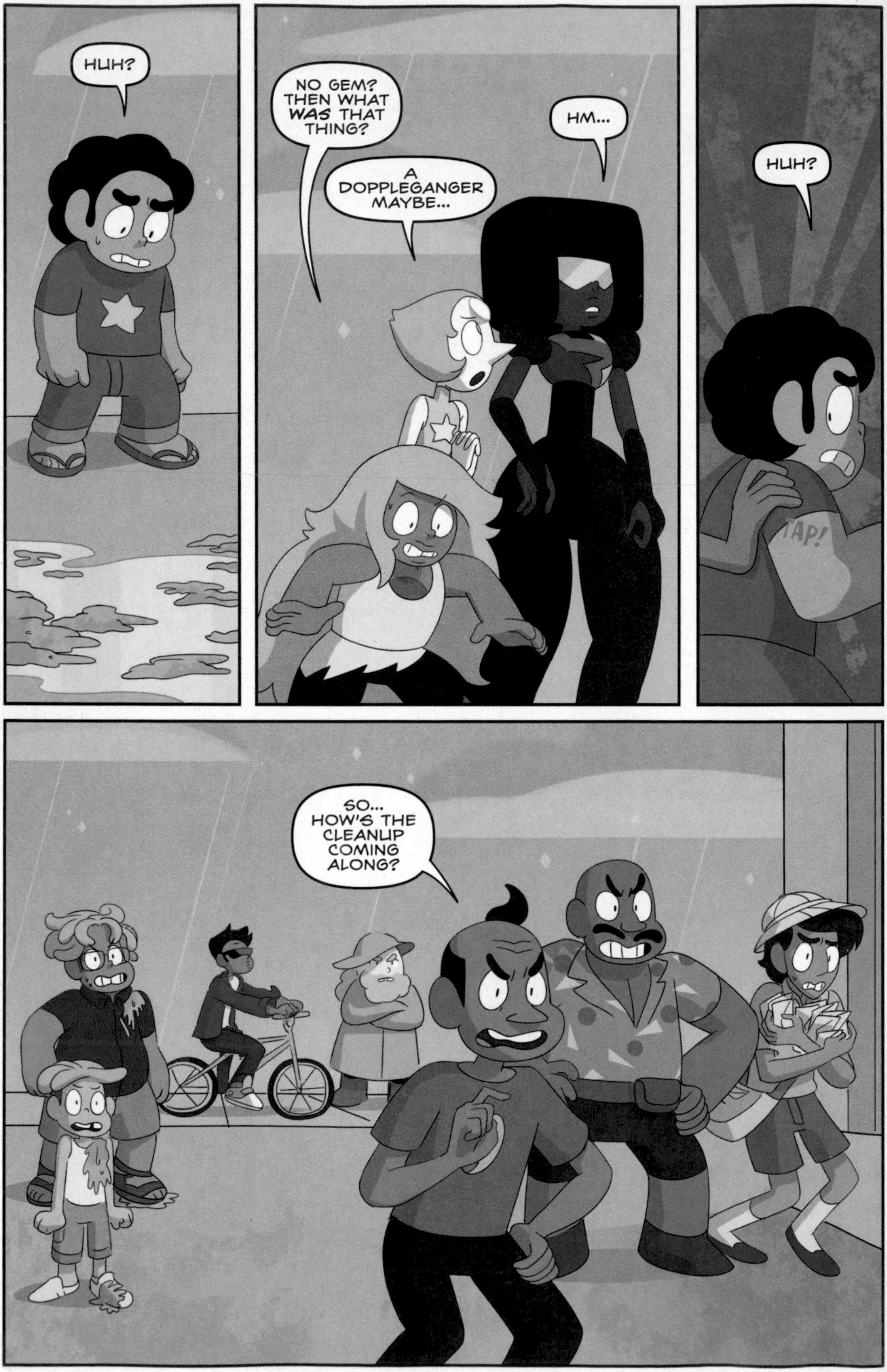
HUH?
NO GEM? THEN WHAT WAS THAT THING?
HM...
A DOPPLEGANGER MAYBE...
HUH?
TAP!
SO... HOW'S THE CLEANUP COMING ALONG?

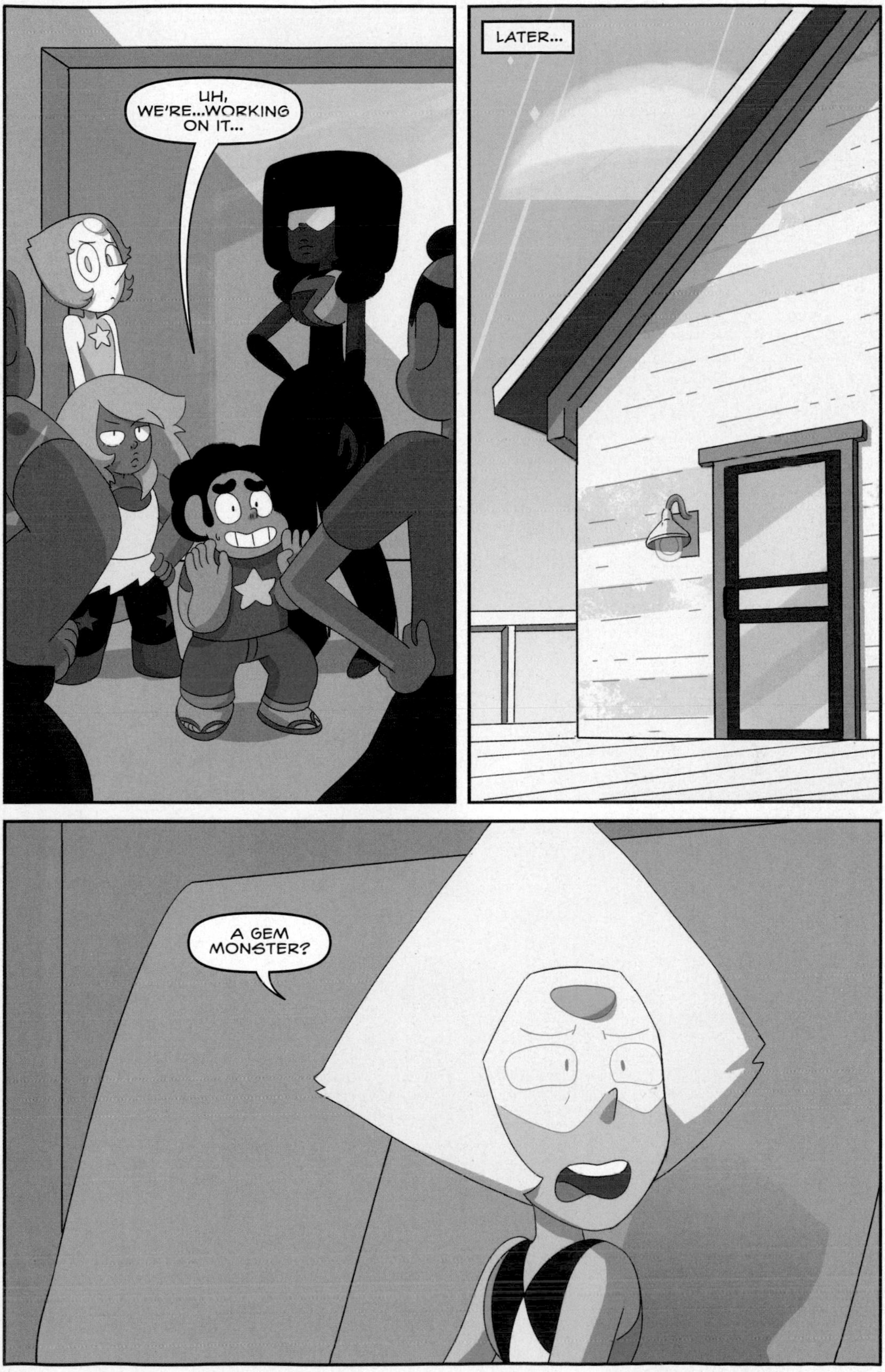
UH,
WE'RE...WORKING
ON IT...
LATER...
A GEM
MONSTER?

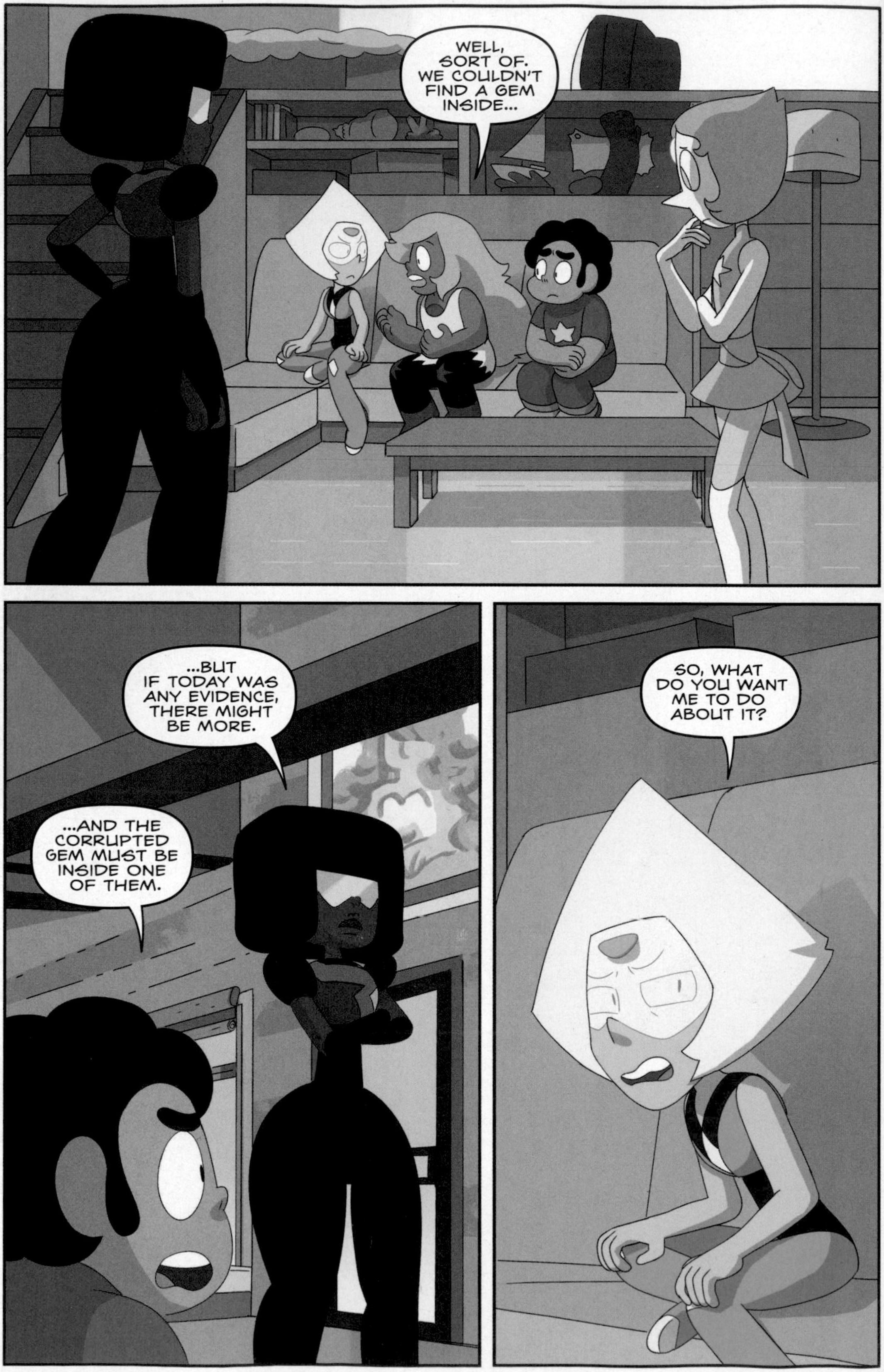
WELL, SORT OF. WE COULDN'T FIND A GEM INSIDE...
...BUT IF TODAY WAS ANY EVIDENCE, THERE MIGHT BE MORE.
...AND THE CORRUPTED GEM MUST BE INSIDE ONE OF THEM.
SO, WHAT DO YOU WANT ME TO DO ABOUT IT?

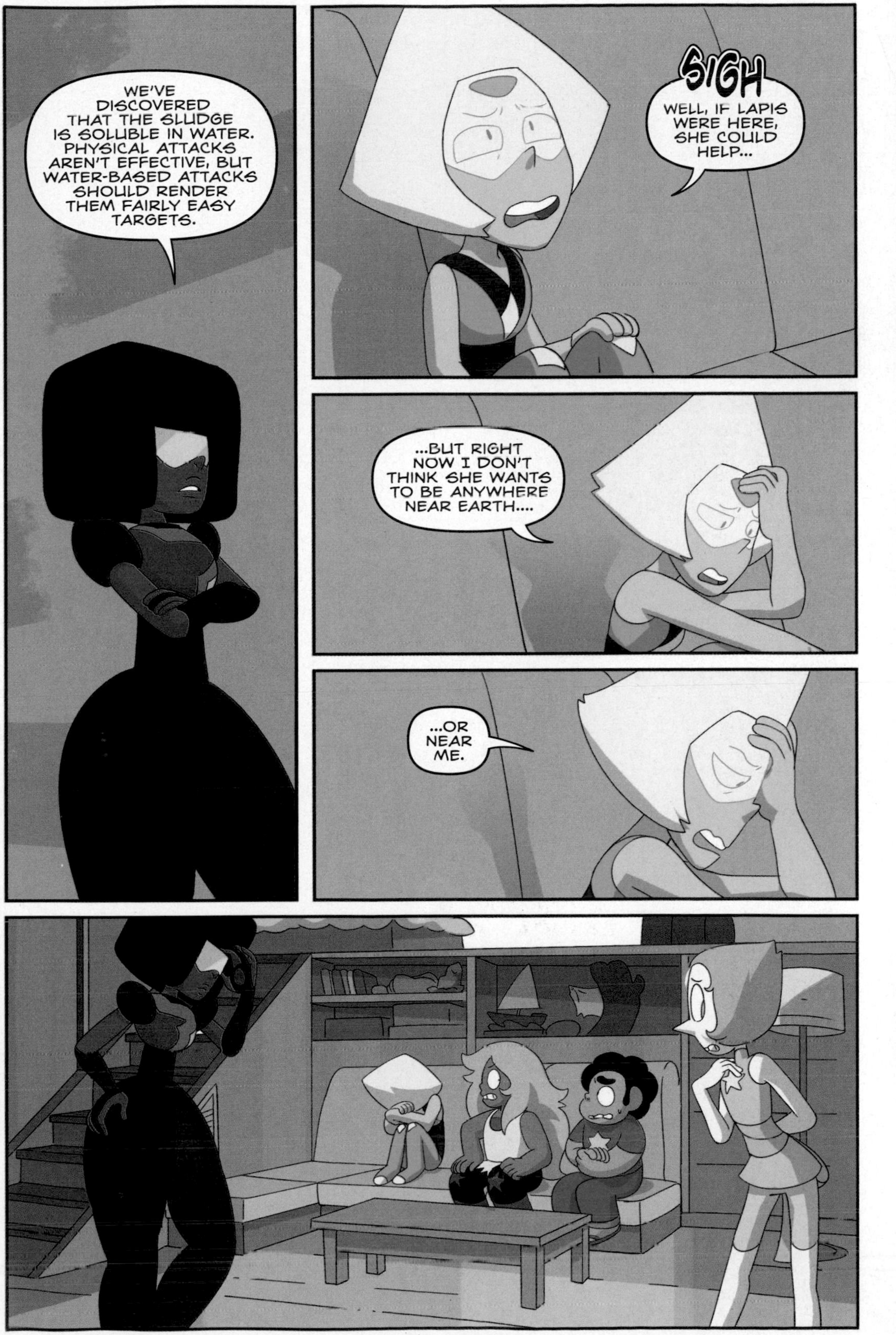
WE'VE DISCOVERED THAT THE SLUDGE IS SOLUBLE IN WATER. PHYSICAL ATTACKS AREN'T EFFECTIVE, BUT WATER-BASED ATTACKS SHOULD RENDER THEM FAIRLY EASY TARGETS.
SIGH
WELL, IF LAPIS WERE HERE, SHE COULD HELP...
...BUT RIGHT NOW I DON'T THINK SHE WANTS TO BE ANYWHERE NEAR EARTH....
...OR NEAR ME.

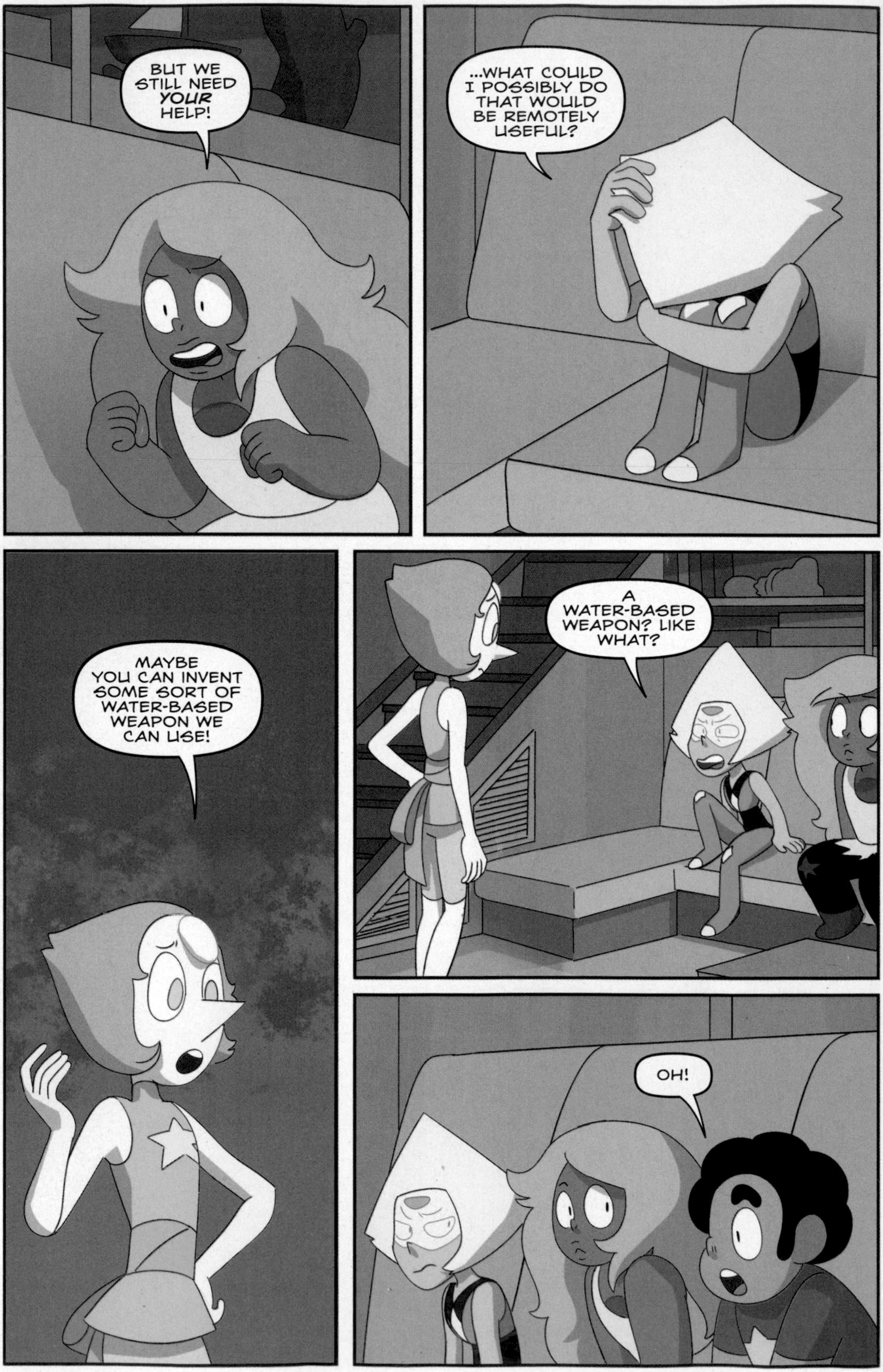
BUT WE STILL NEED *YOUR* HELP!
...WHAT COULD I POSSIBLY DO THAT WOULD BE REMOTELY USEFUL?
MAYBE YOU CAN INVENT SOME SORT OF WATER-BASED WEAPON WE CAN USE!
A WATER-BASED WEAPON? LIKE WHAT?
OH!

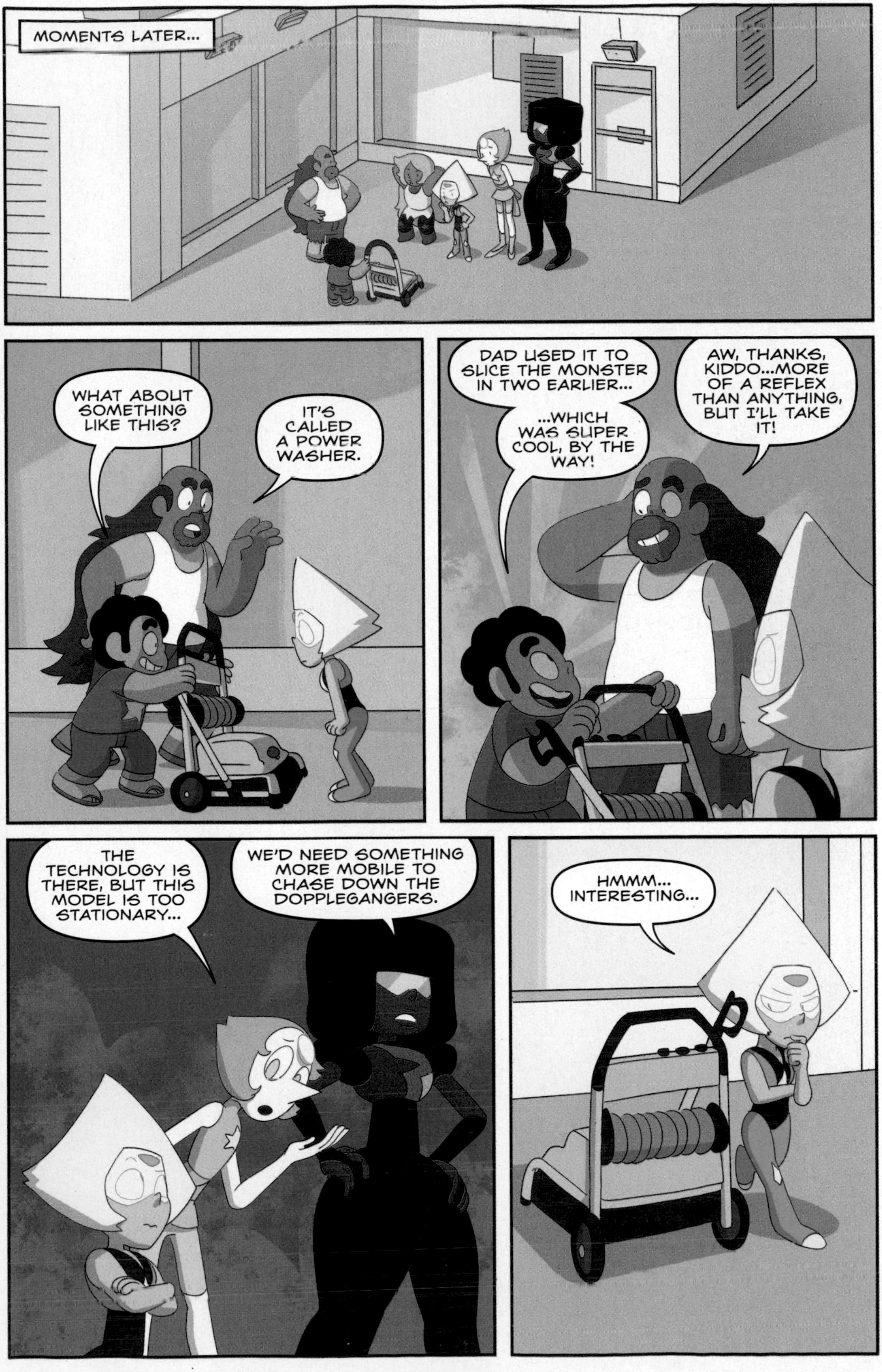
MOMENTS LATER...
WHAT ABOUT SOMETHING LIKE THIS?
IT'S CALLED A POWER WASHER.
DAD USED IT TO SLICE THE MONSTER IN TWO EARLIER...
...WHICH WAS SUPER COOL, BY THE WAY!
AW, THANKS, KIDDO...MORE OF A REFLEX THAN ANYTHING, BUT I'LL TAKE IT!
THE TECHNOLOGY IS THERE, BUT THIS MODEL IS TOO STATIONARY...
WE'D NEED SOMETHING MORE MOBILE TO CHASE DOWN THE DOPPLEGANGERS.
HMMM... INTERESTING...

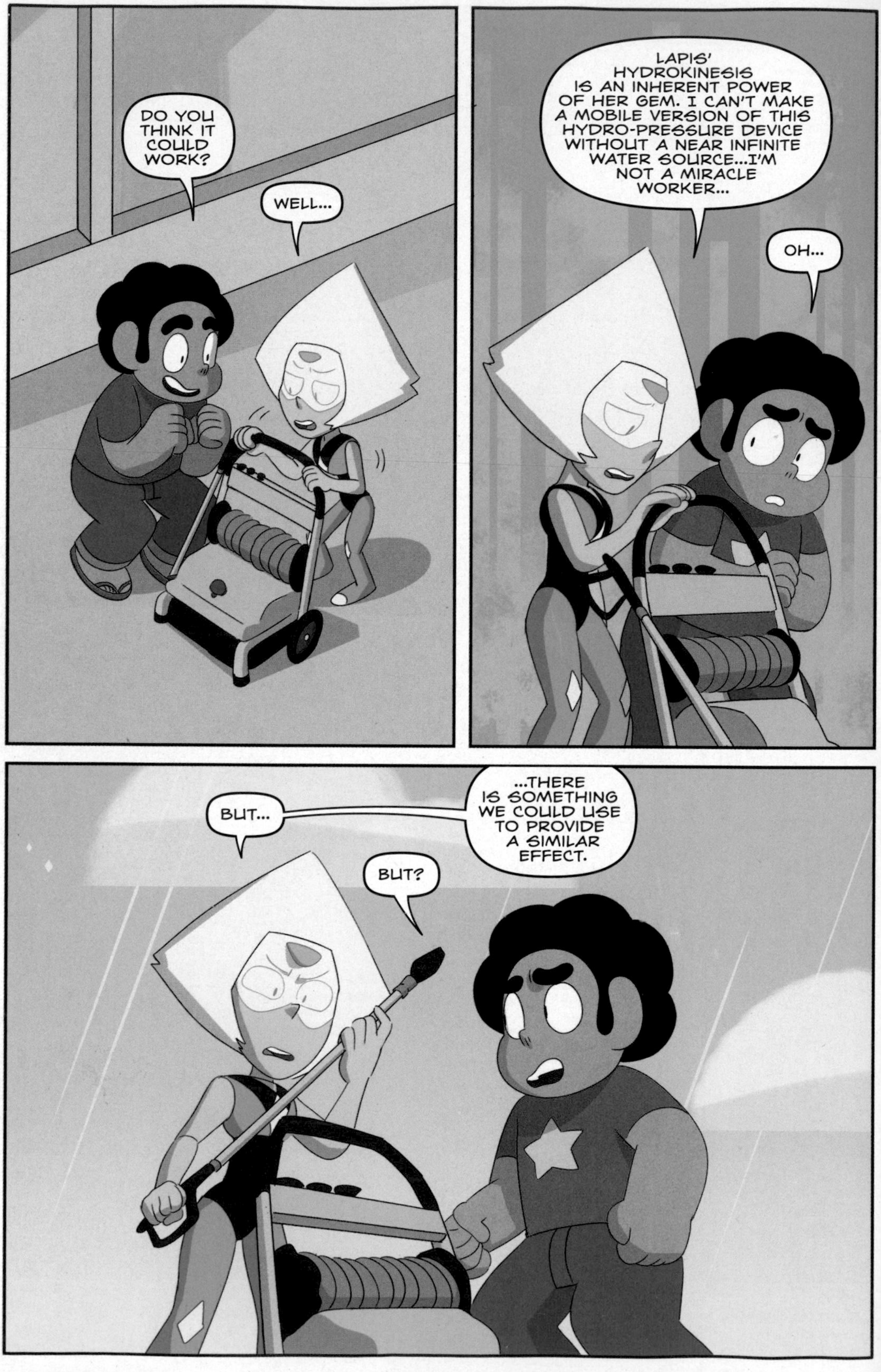
DO YOU THINK IT COULD WORK?
WELL...
LAPIS' HYDROKINESIS IS AN INHERENT POWER OF HER GEM. I CAN'T MAKE A MOBILE VERSION OF THIS HYDRO-PRESSURE DEVICE WITHOUT A NEAR INFINITE WATER SOURCE...I'M NOT A MIRACLE WORKER...
OH...
BUT...
...THERE IS SOMETHING WE COULD USE TO PROVIDE A SIMILAR EFFECT.
BUT?

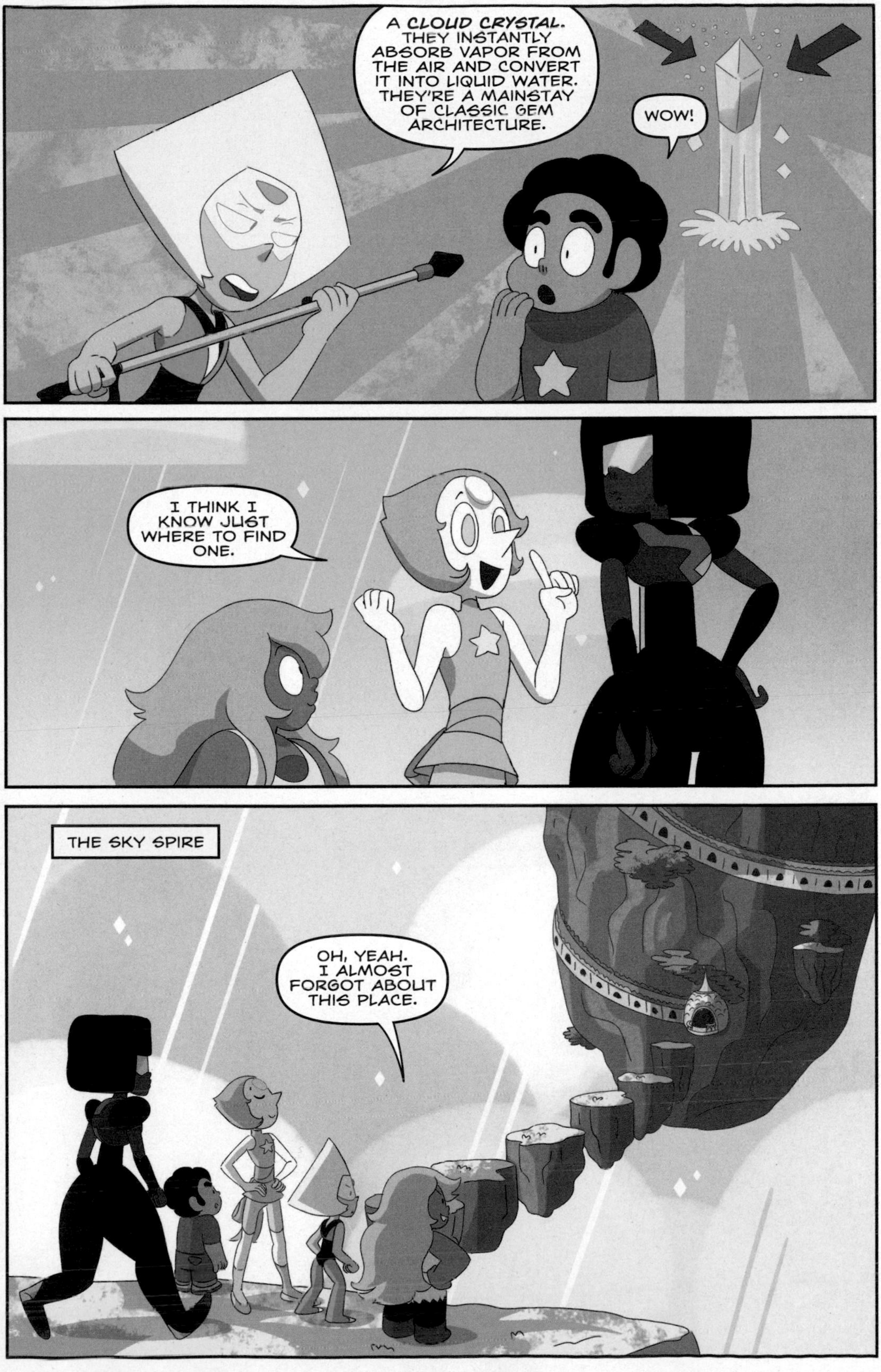

A CLOUD CRYSTAL. THEY INSTANTLY ABSORB VAPOR FROM THE AIR AND CONVERT IT INTO LIQUID WATER. THEY'RE A MAINSTAY OF CLASSIC GEM ARCHITECTURE.
WOW!
I THINK I KNOW JUST WHERE TO FIND ONE.
THE SKY SPIRE
OH, YEAH. I ALMOST FORGOT ABOUT THIS PLACE.

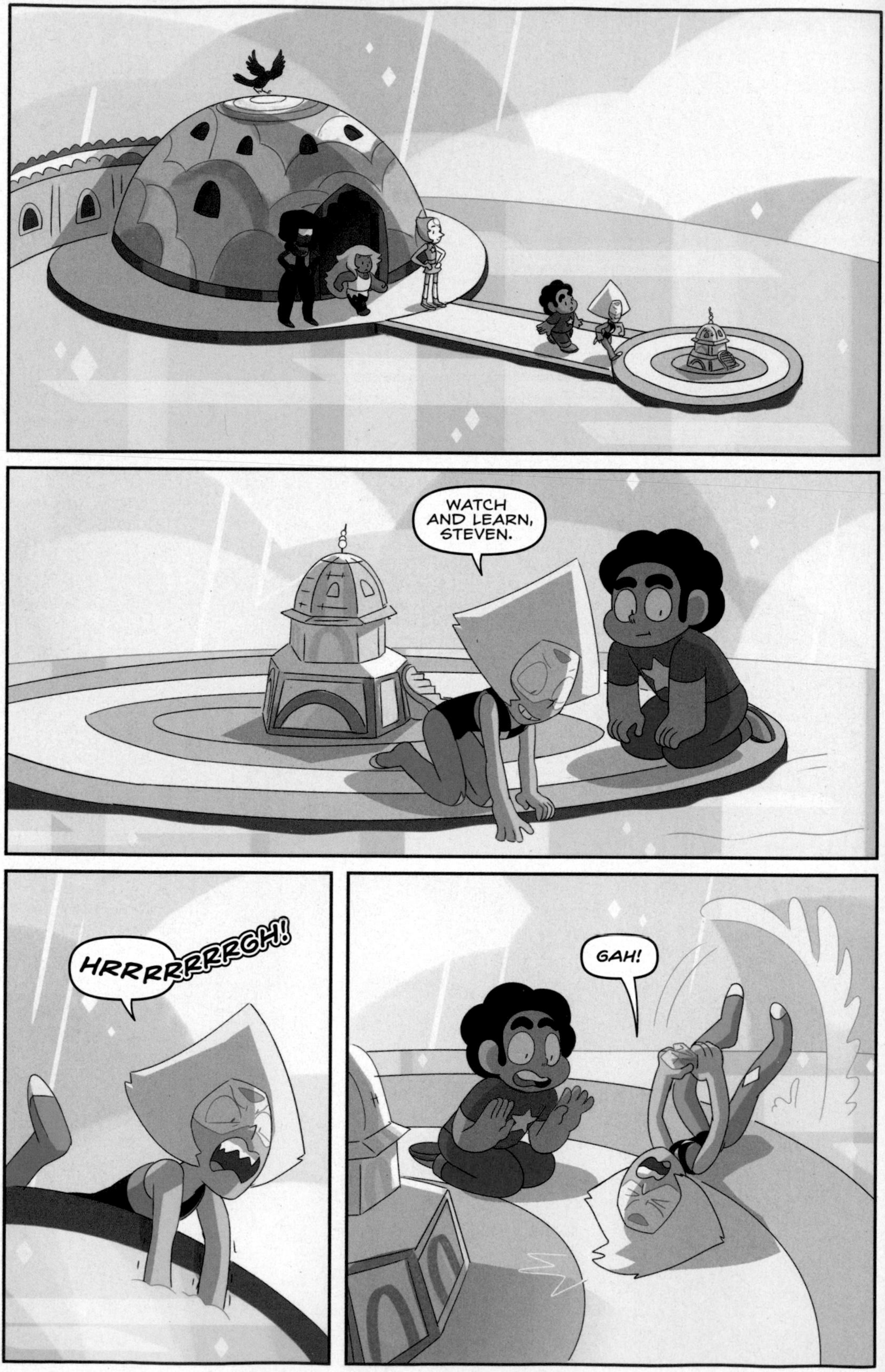
WATCH AND LEARN, STEVEN.
HRRRRRRRRGH!
GAH!

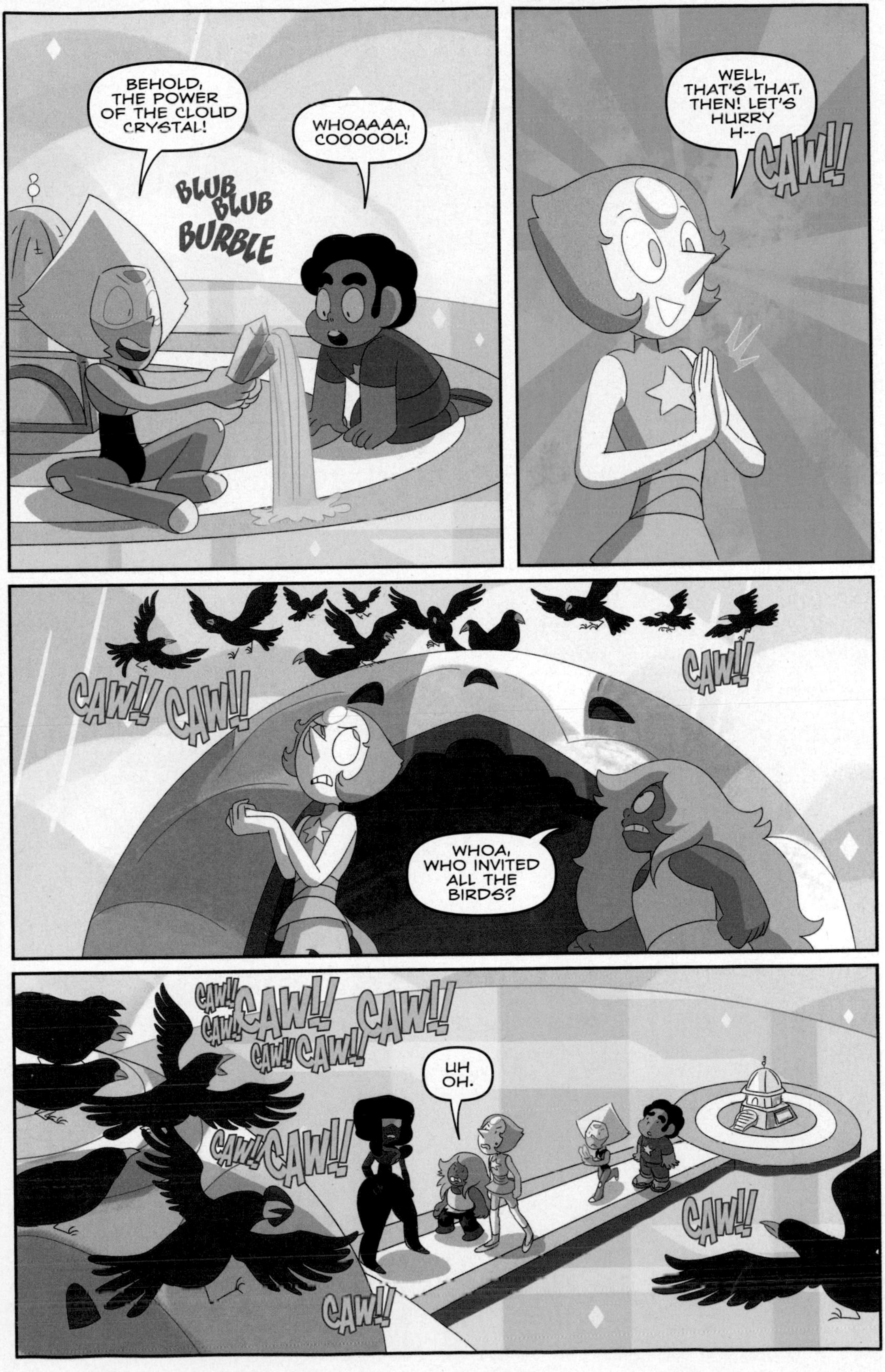
BEHOLD, THE POWER OF THE CLOUD CRYSTAL!
BLUB BLUB BURBLE
WHOAAAA, COOOOOL!
WELL, THAT'S THAT, THEN! LET'S HURRY H--
CAW!!
CAW!! CAW!!
CAW!!
WHOA, WHO INVITED ALL THE BIRDS?
CAW!! CAW!! CAW!! CAW!!
CAW!! CAW!!
UH OH.
CAW!! CAW!!
CAW!!
CAW!!

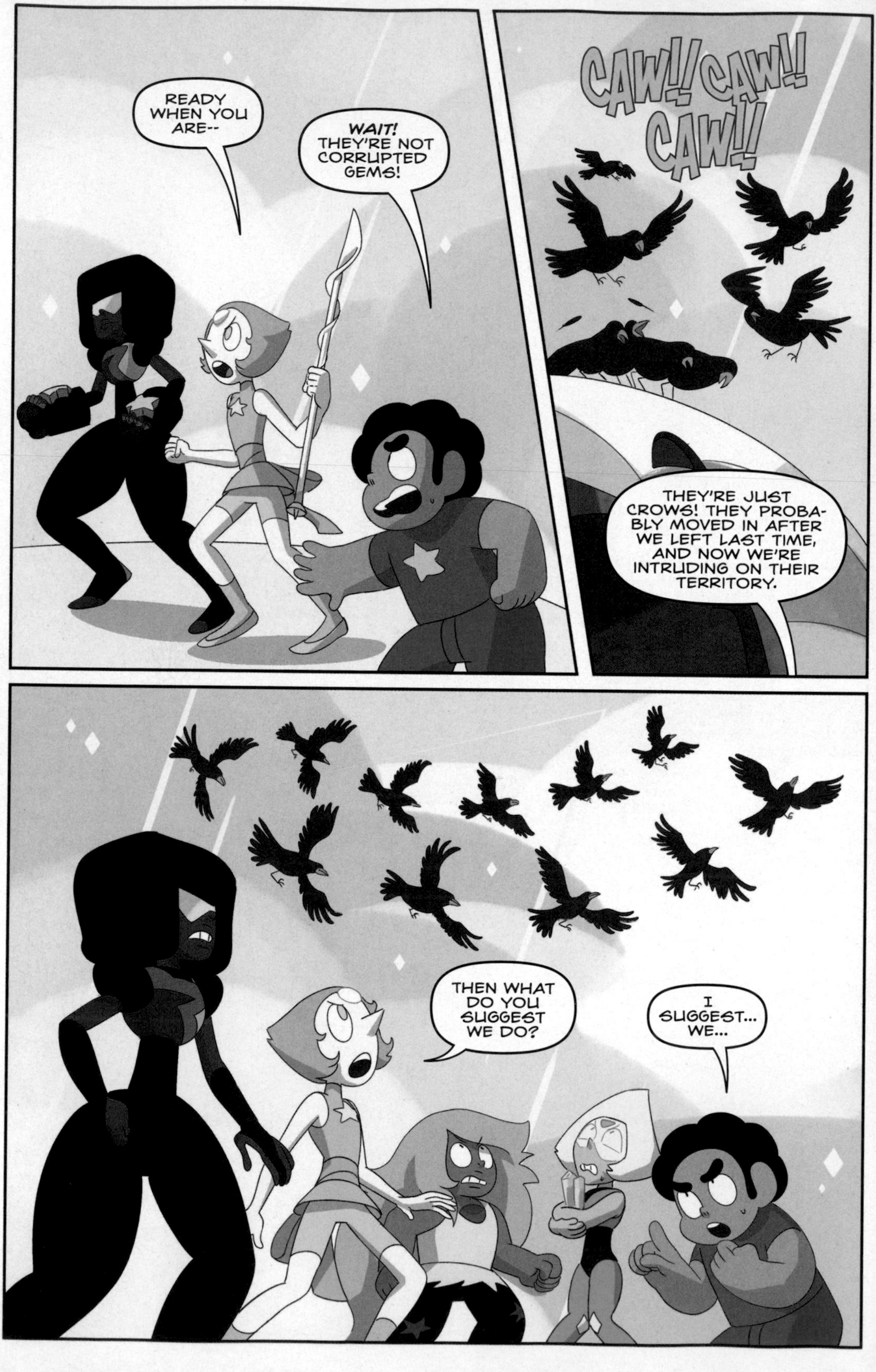
READY WHEN YOU ARE--
WAIT! THEY'RE NOT CORRUPTED GEMS!
CAW!! CAW!! CAW!!
THEY'RE JUST CROWS! THEY PROBABLY MOVED IN AFTER WE LEFT LAST TIME, AND NOW WE'RE INTRUDING ON THEIR TERRITORY.
THEN WHAT DO YOU SUGGEST WE DO?
I SUGGEST... WE...

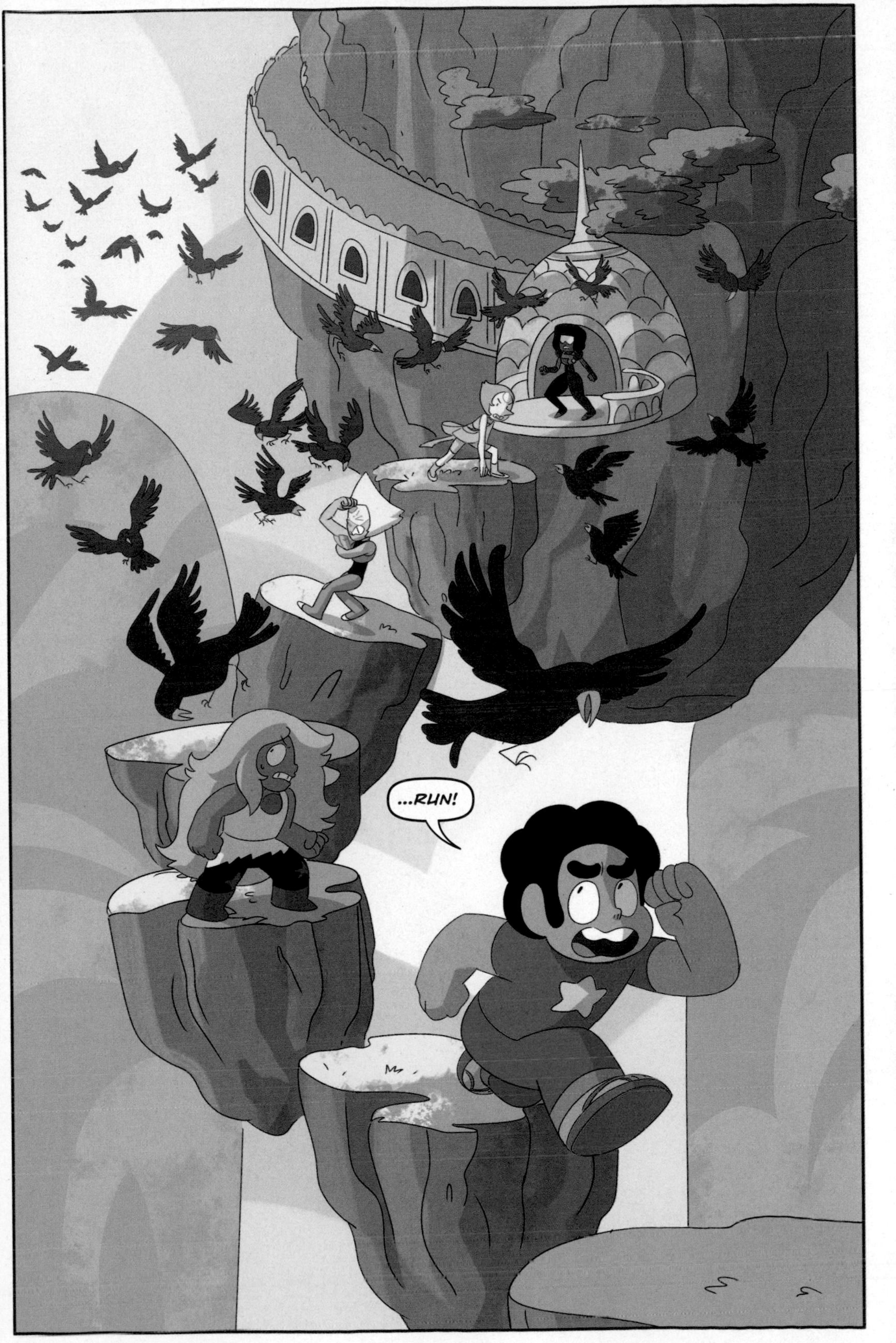
...RUN!

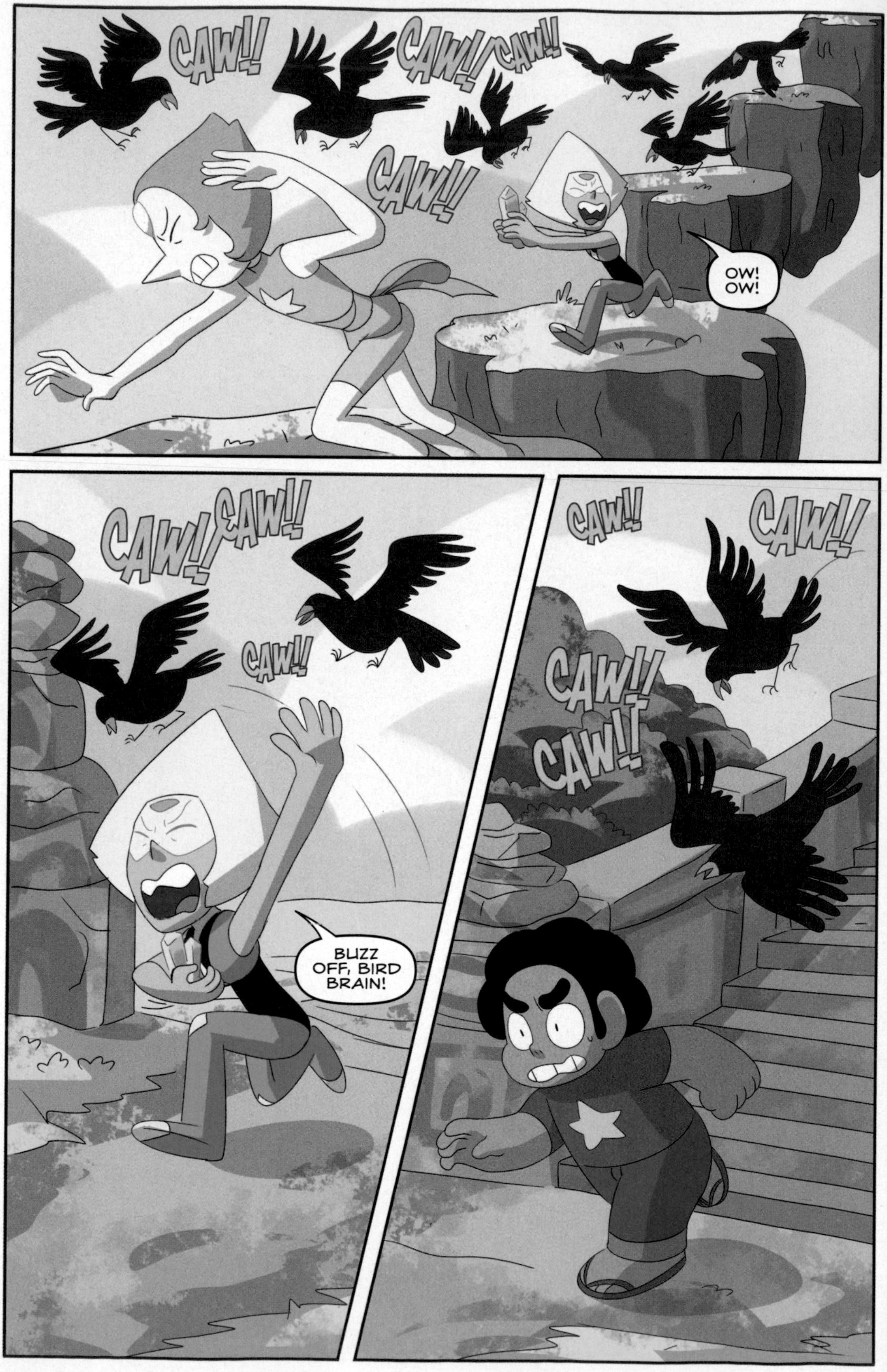
CAW!!
CAW!!
CAW!!
CAW!!
OW! OW!
CAW!!
CAW!!
CAW!!
BUZZ OFF, BIRD BRAIN!
CAW!!
CAW!!
CAW!!
CAW!!

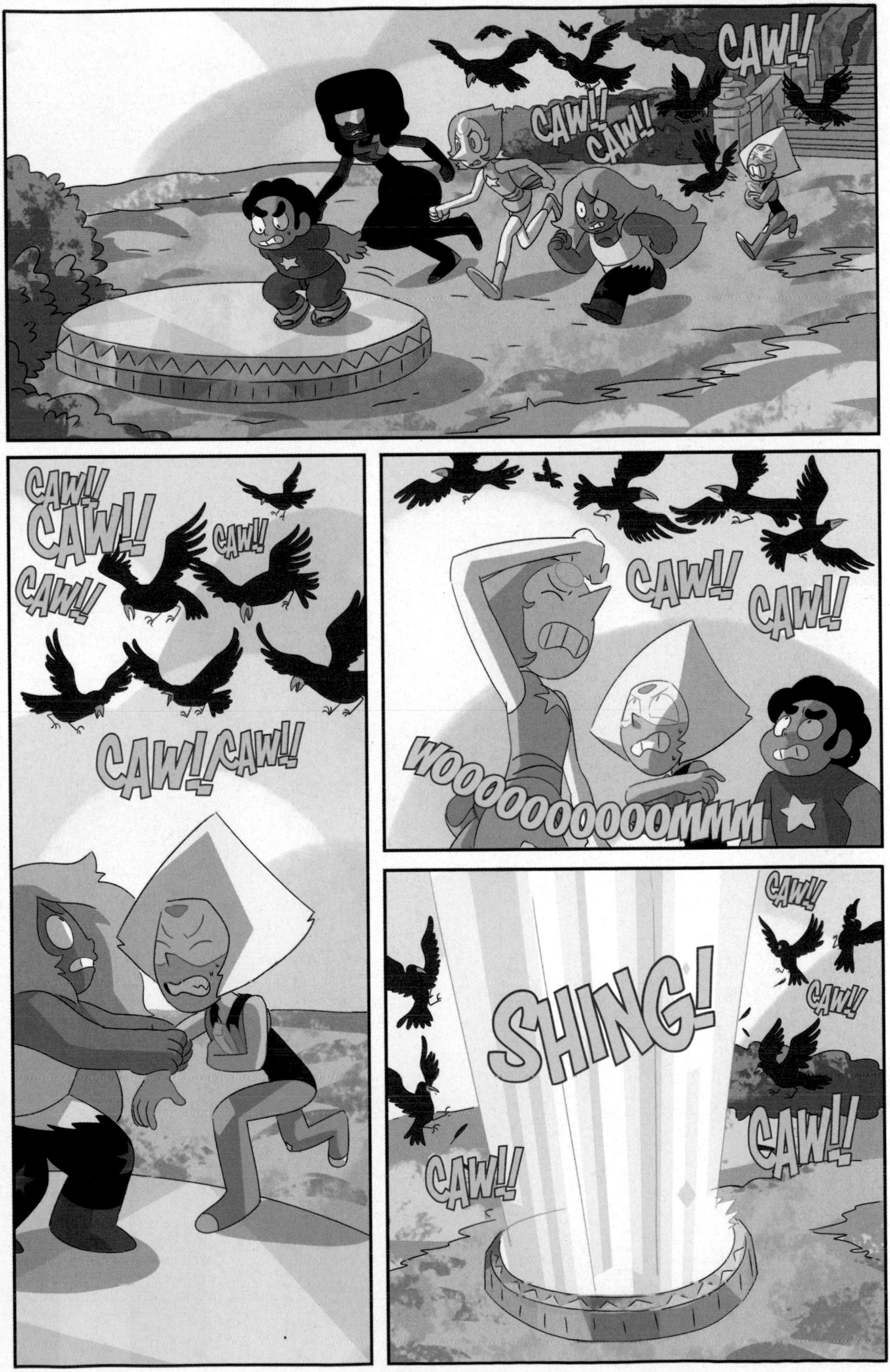
CAW!!
CAW!!
CAW!!
CAW!!
CAW!!
CAW!!
CAW!!
CAW!!
CAW!!
CAW!!
CAW!!
WOOOOOOOOOOOMMM
SHING!
CAW!!
CAW!!
CAW!!
CAW!!

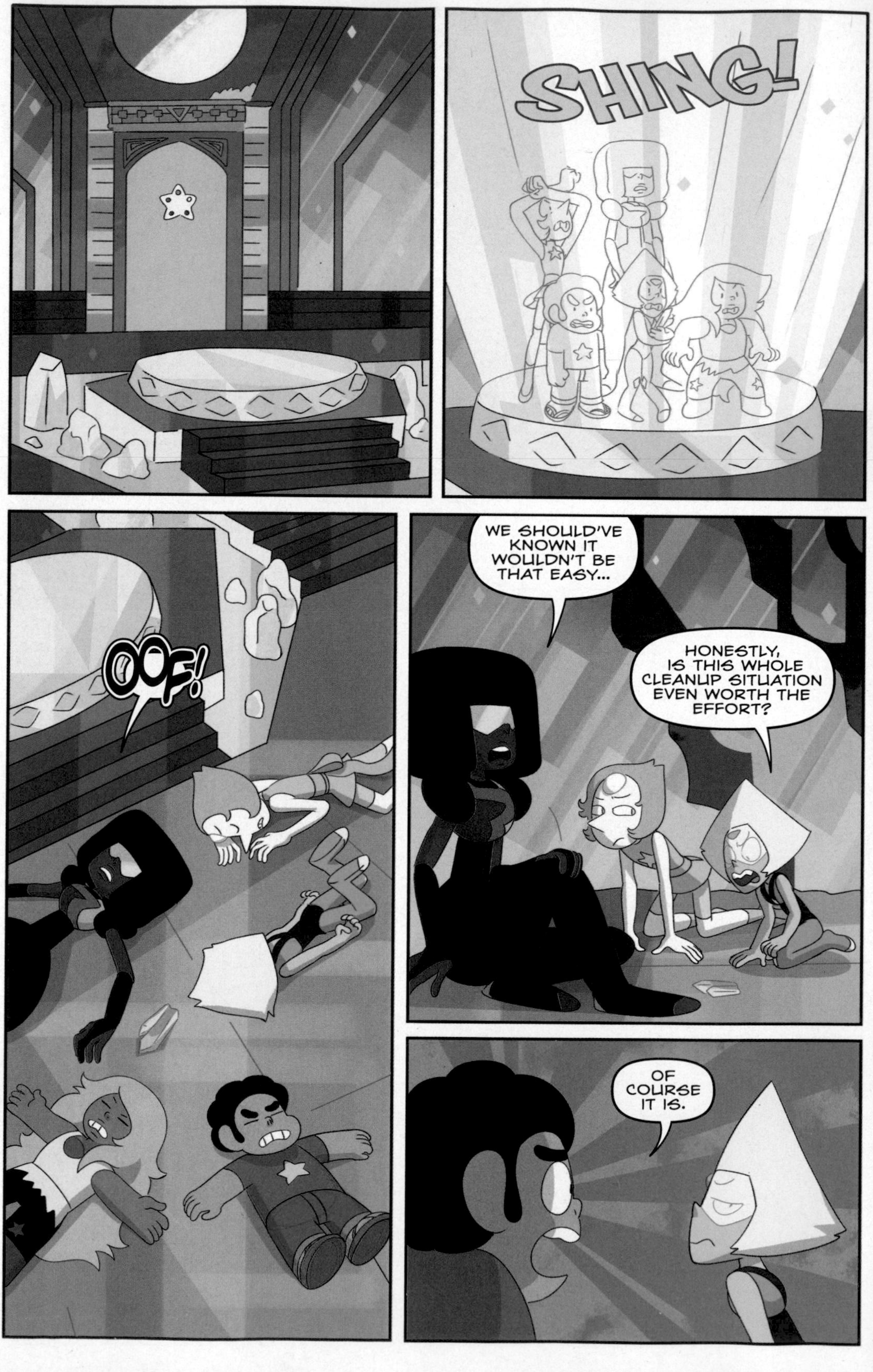
SHING!
OOF!
WE SHOULD'VE KNOWN IT WOULDN'T BE THAT EASY...
HONESTLY, IS THIS WHOLE CLEANUP SITUATION EVEN WORTH THE EFFORT?
OF COURSE IT IS.

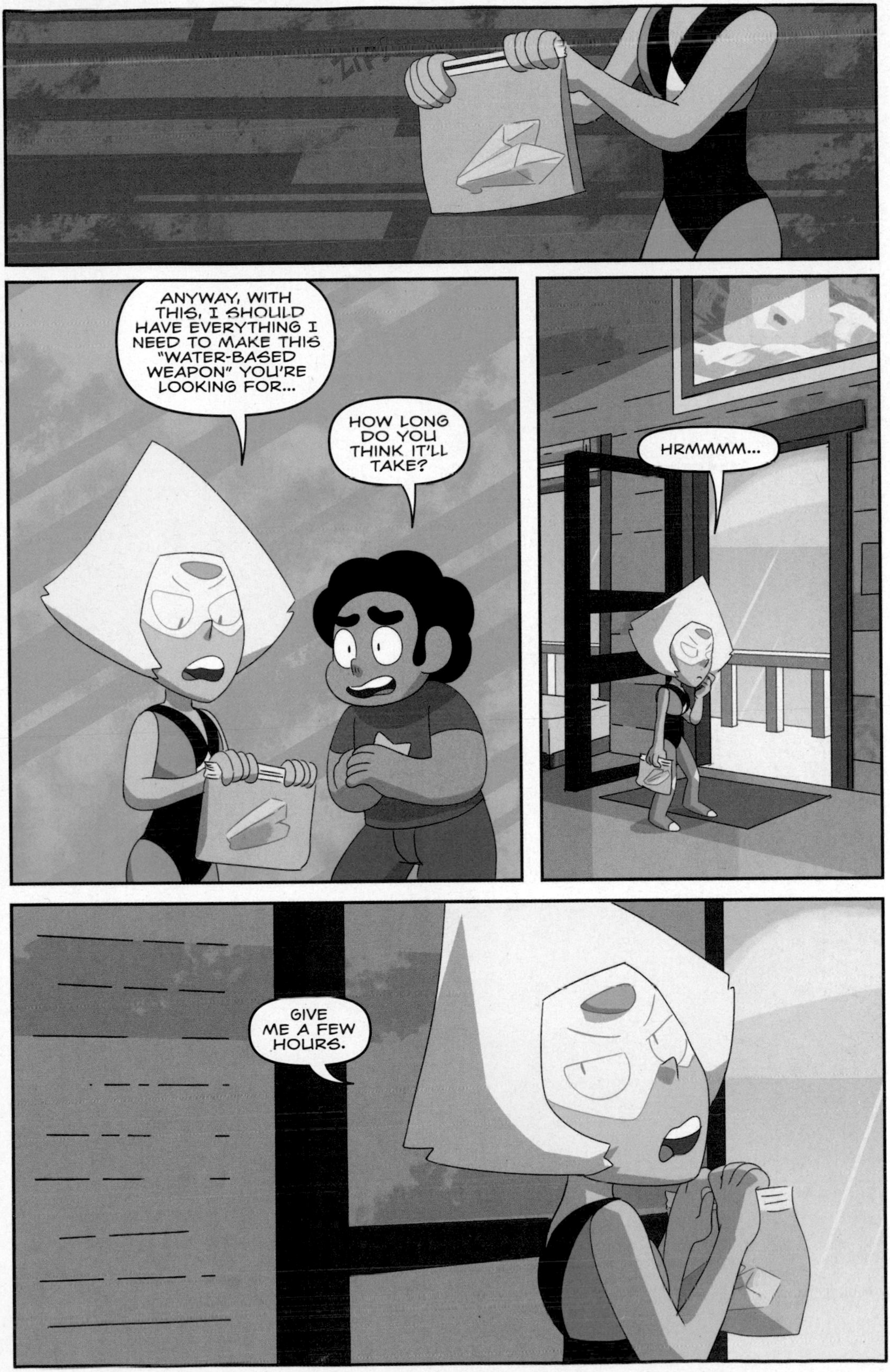
ZIP!
ANYWAY, WITH THIS, I SHOULD HAVE EVERYTHING I NEED TO MAKE THIS "WATER-BASED WEAPON" YOU'RE LOOKING FOR...
HOW LONG DO YOU THINK IT'LL TAKE?
HRMMMM...
GIVE ME A FEW HOURS.

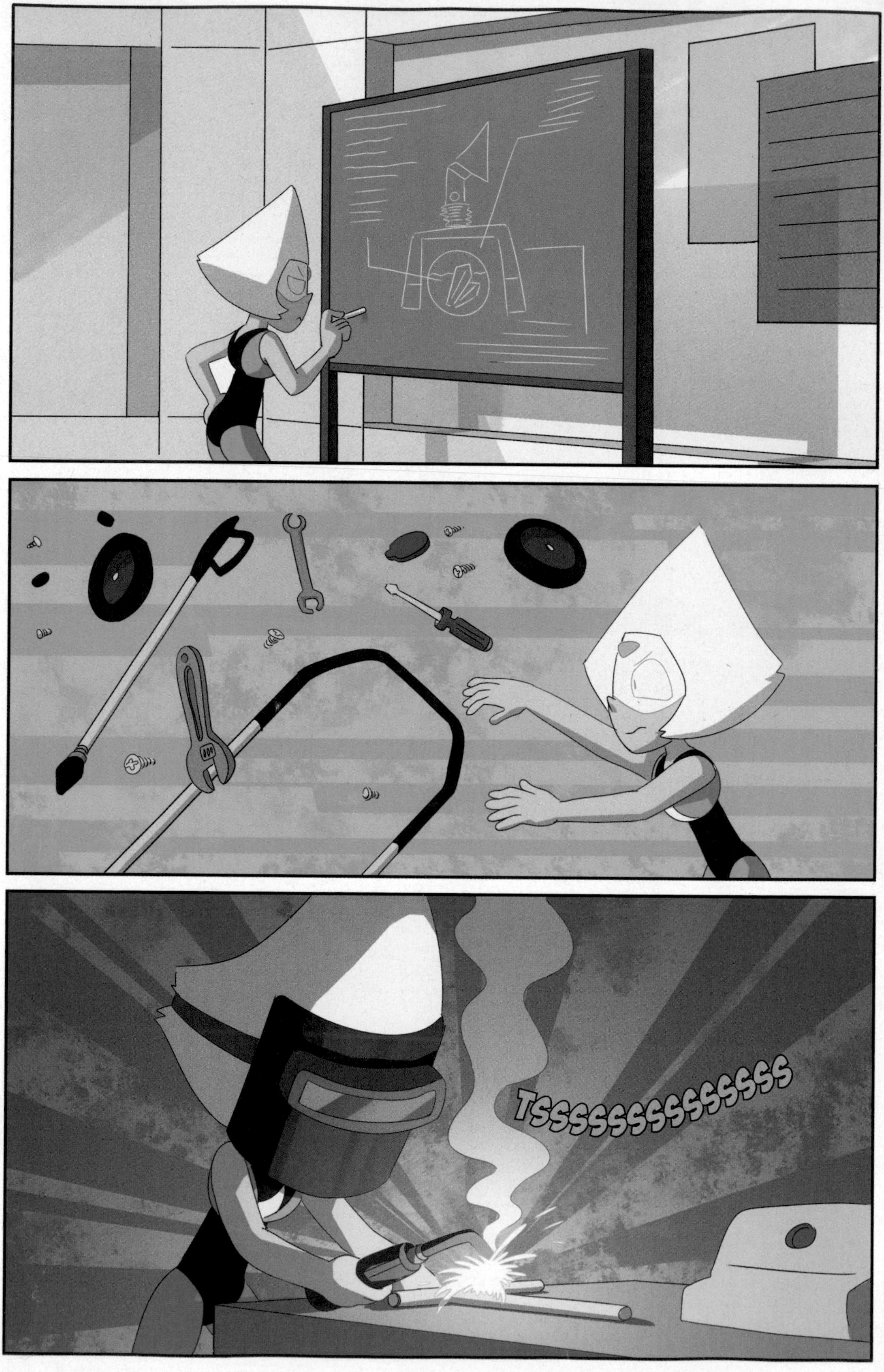
TSSSSSSSSSSSSSS

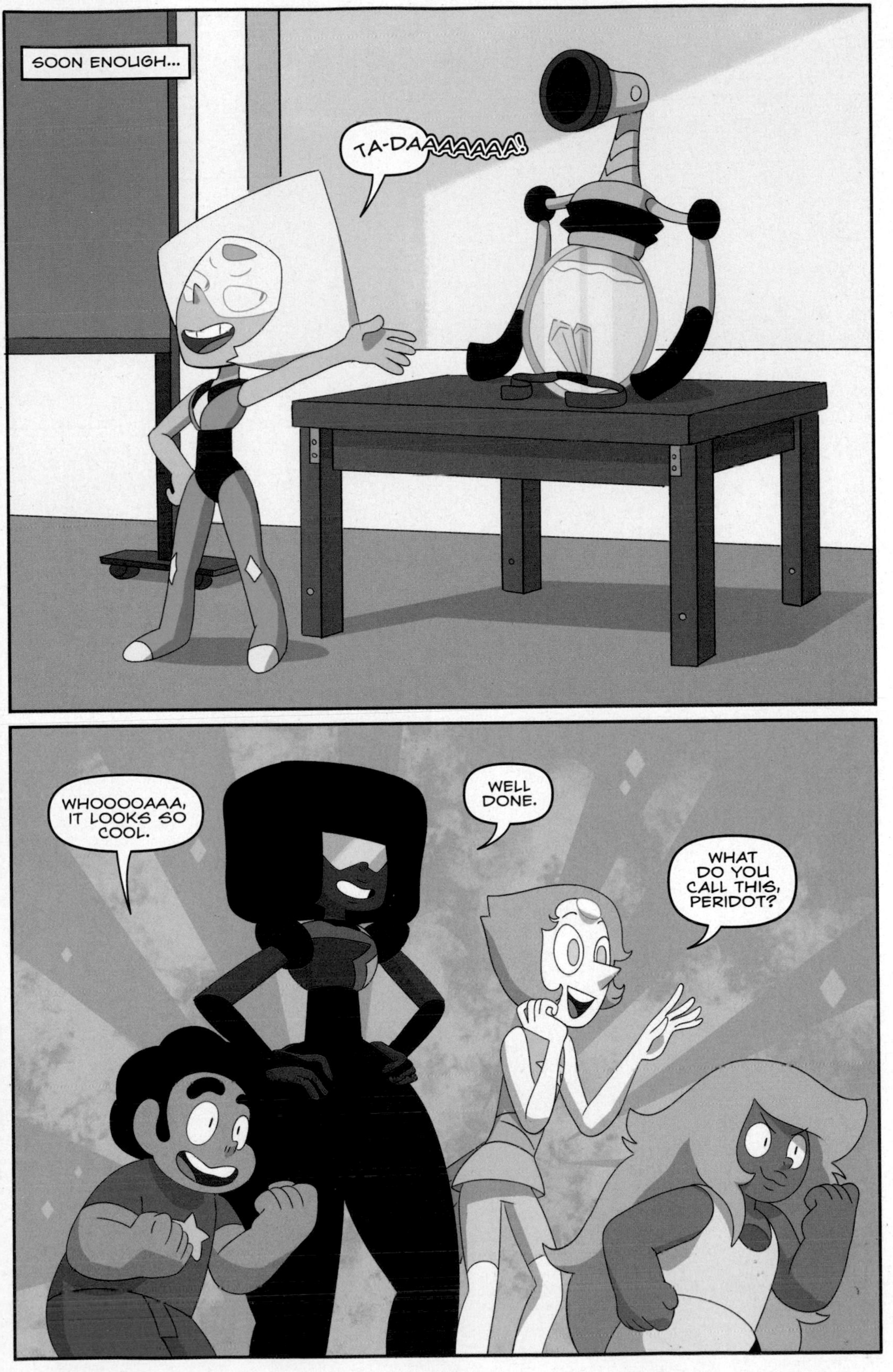
SOON ENOUGH...
TA-DAAAAAAAA!
WHOOOOAAA, IT LOOKS SO COOL.
WELL DONE.
WHAT DO YOU CALL THIS, PERIDOT?

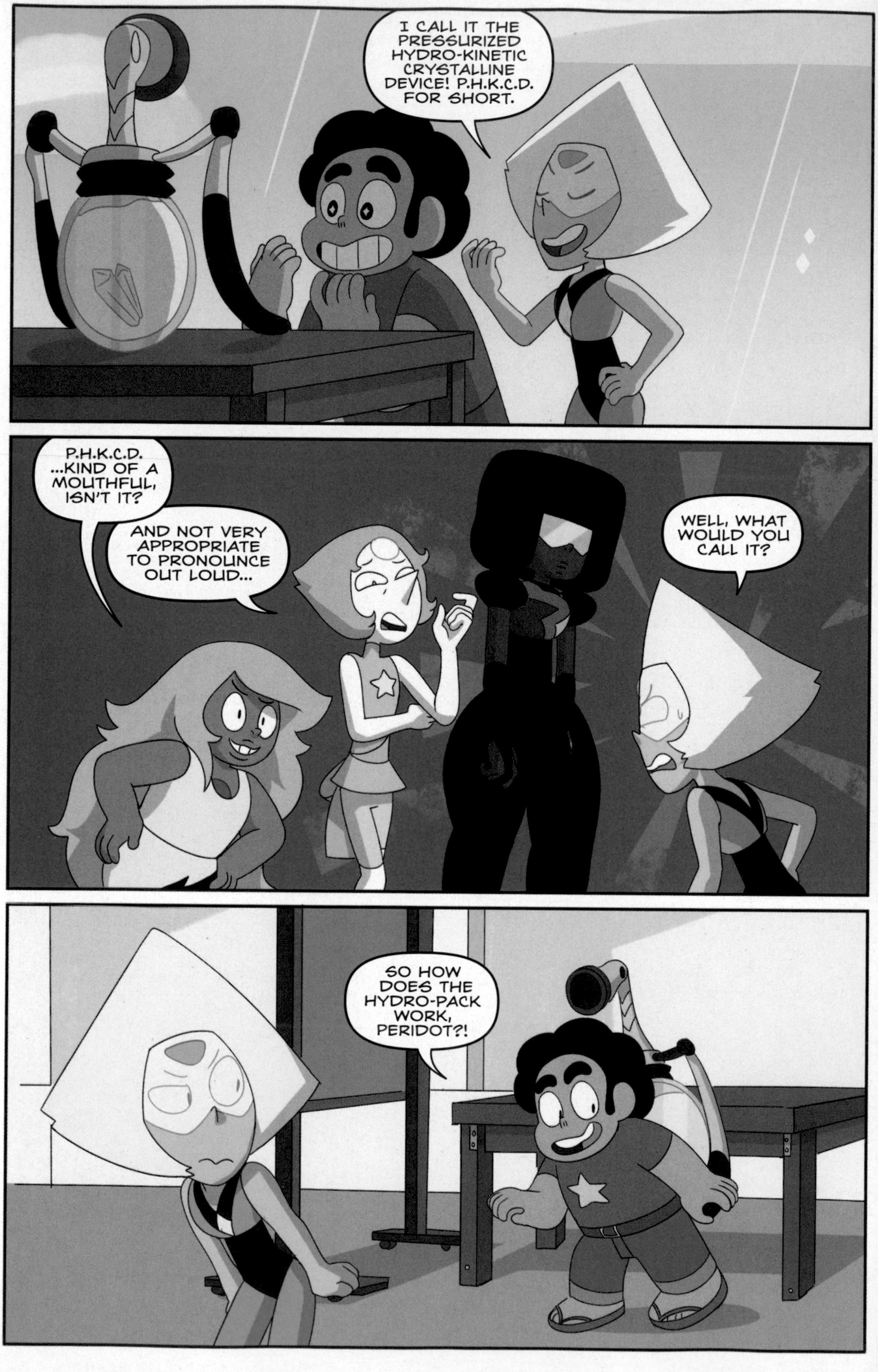
I CALL IT THE PRESSURIZED HYDRO-KINETIC CRYSTALLINE DEVICE! P.H.K.C.D. FOR SHORT.
P.H.K.C.D. ...KIND OF A MOUTHFUL, ISN'T IT?
AND NOT VERY APPROPRIATE TO PRONOUNCE OUT LOUD...
WELL, WHAT WOULD YOU CALL IT?
SO HOW DOES THE HYDRO-PACK WORK, PERIDOT?!

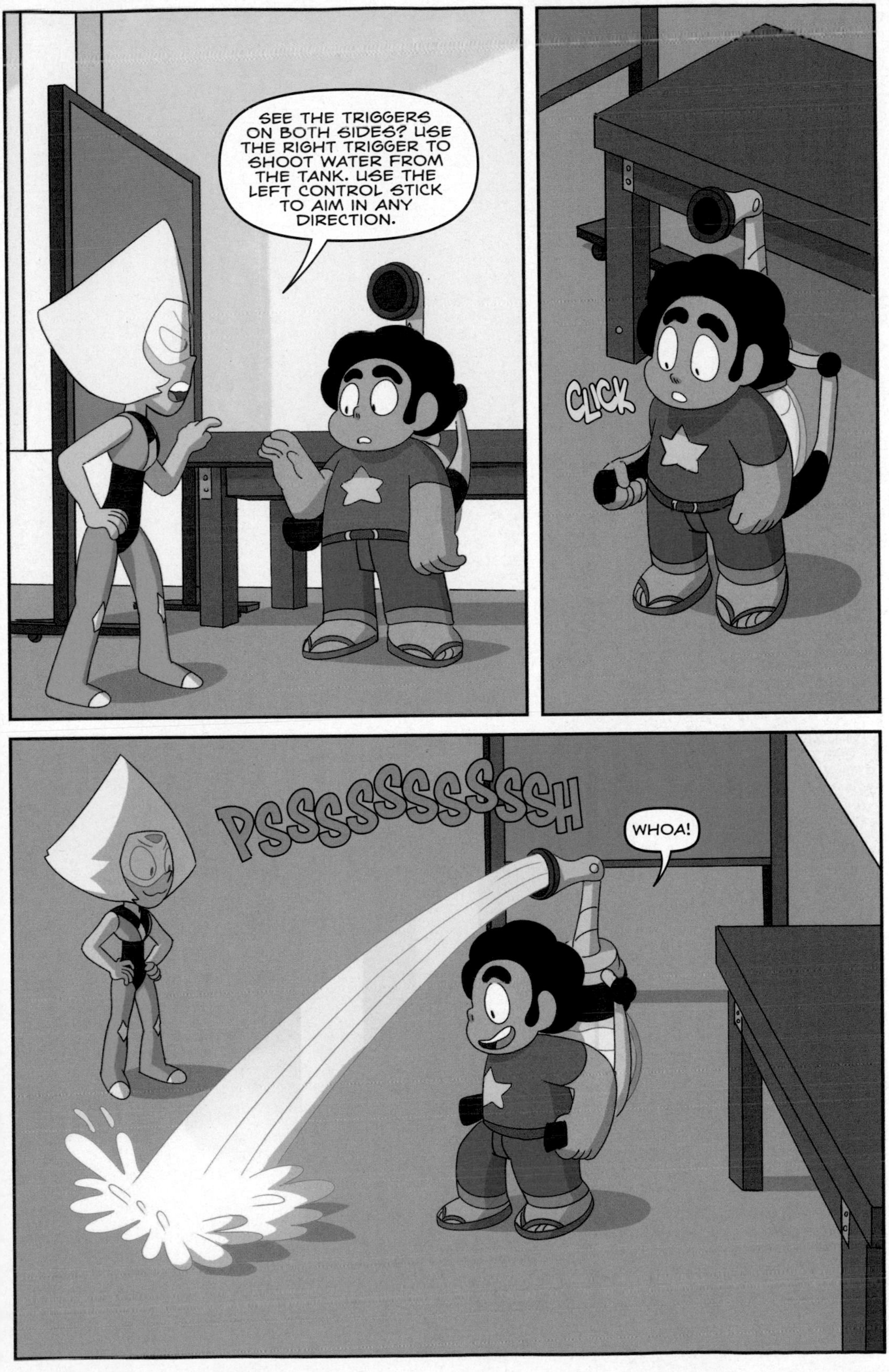
SEE THE TRIGGERS ON BOTH SIDES? USE THE RIGHT TRIGGER TO SHOOT WATER FROM THE TANK. USE THE LEFT CONTROL STICK TO AIM IN ANY DIRECTION.
CLICK
PSSSSSSSSSSSH
WHOA!

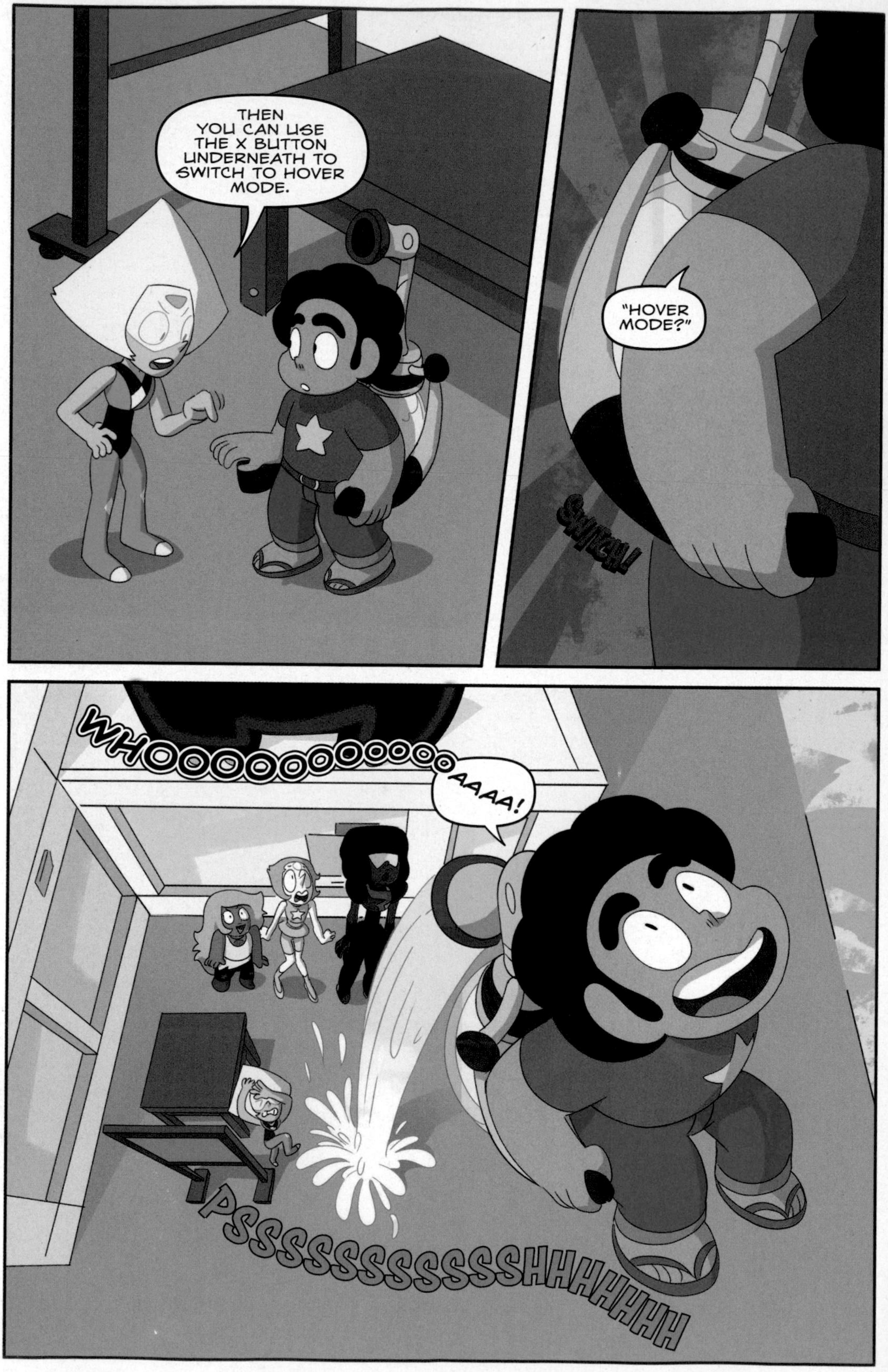
THEN YOU CAN USE THE X BUTTON UNDERNEATH TO SWITCH TO HOVER MODE.
"HOVER MODE?"
SWITCH!
WHOOOOOOOOOOOAAAA!
PSSSSSSSSSSSHHHHHHH

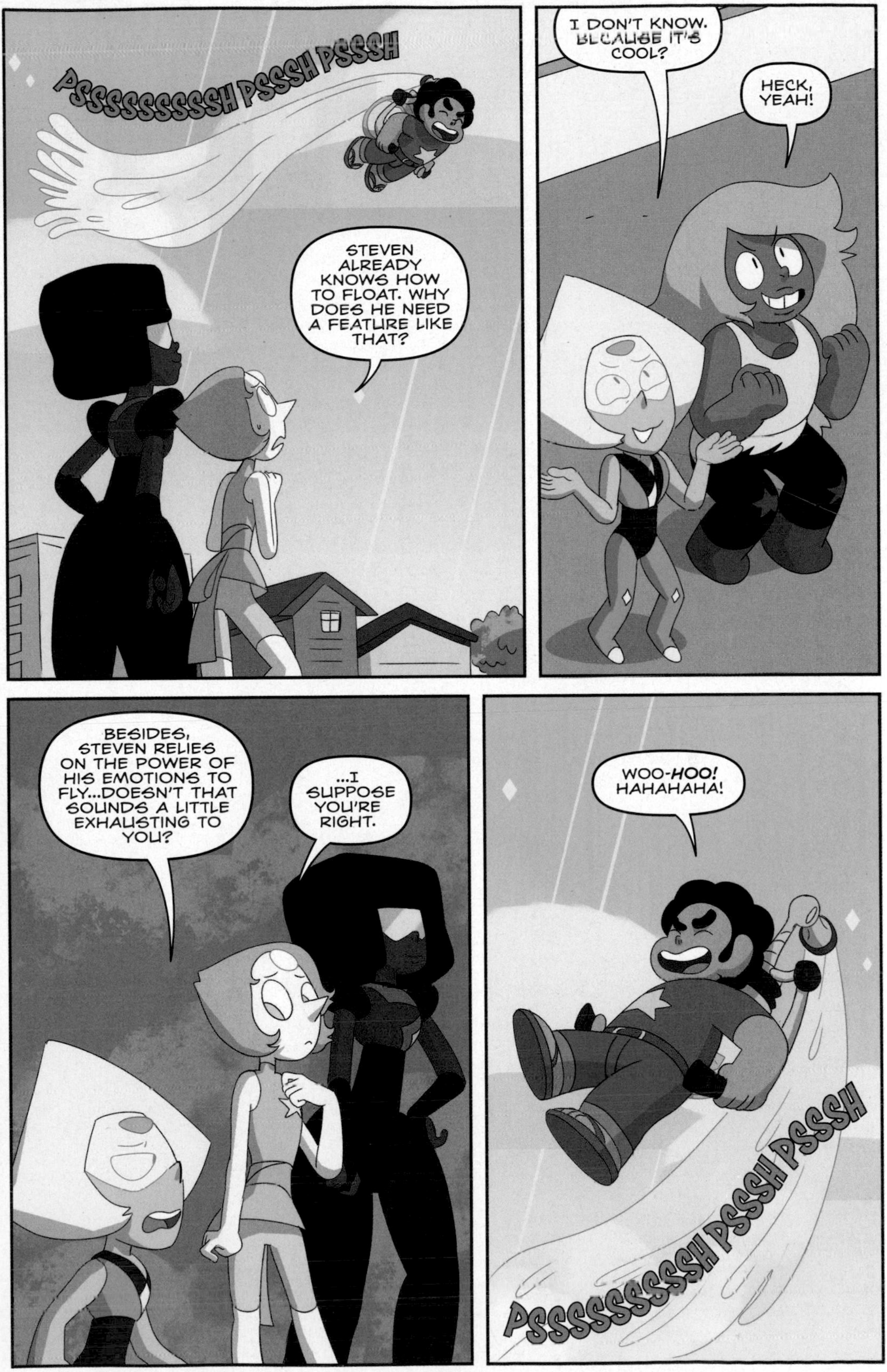
PSSSSSSSSSH PSSSH PSSSH
STEVEN ALREADY KNOWS HOW TO FLOAT. WHY DOES HE NEED A FEATURE LIKE THAT?
I DON'T KNOW. BECAUSE IT'S COOL?
HECK, YEAH!
BESIDES, STEVEN RELIES ON THE POWER OF HIS EMOTIONS TO FLY...DOESN'T THAT SOUNDS A LITTLE EXHAUSTING TO YOU?
...I SUPPOSE YOU'RE RIGHT.
WOO-*HOO!* HAHAHAHA!
PSSSSSSSSSH PSSSH PSSSH

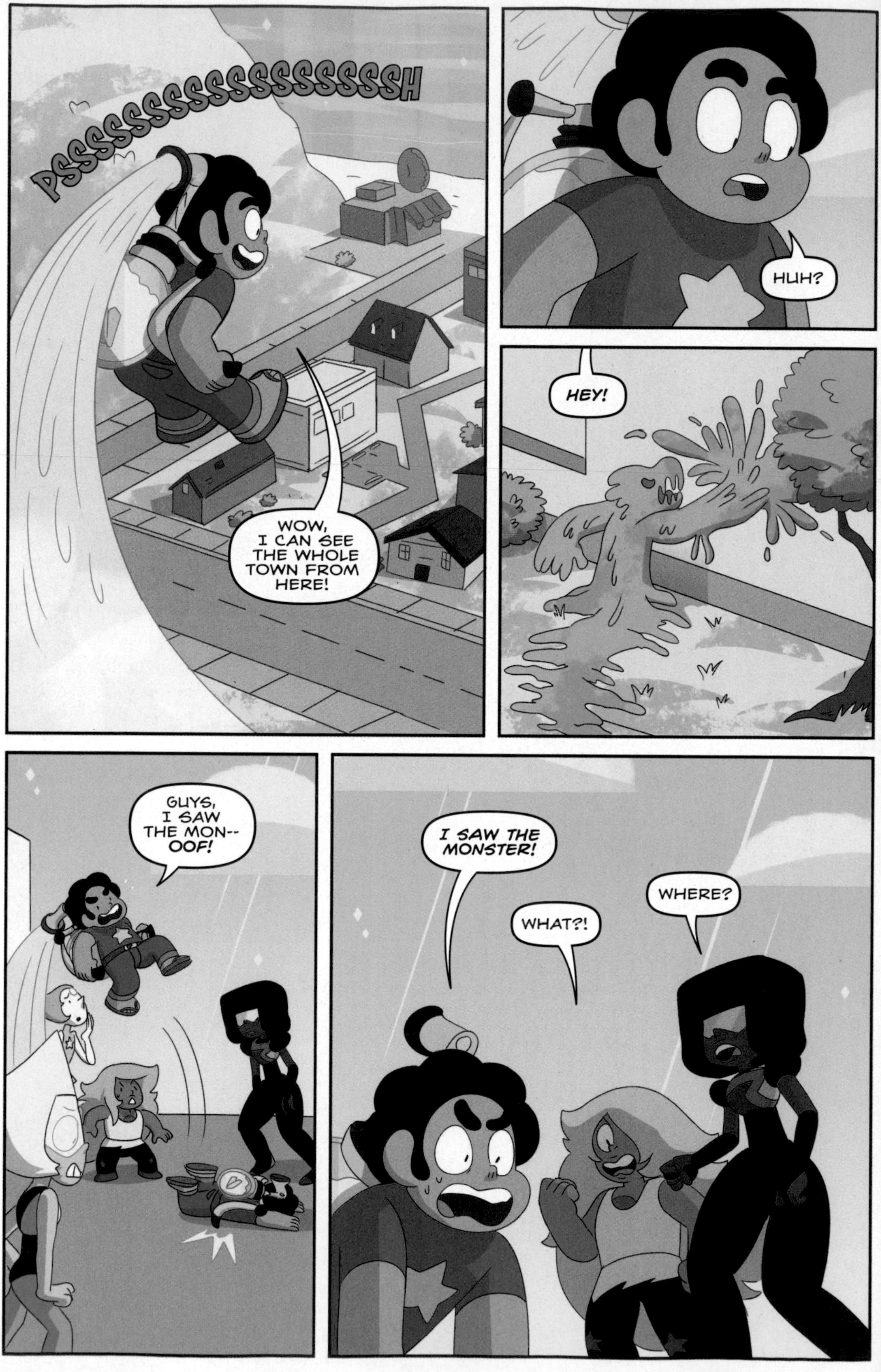
PSSSSSSSSSSSSSSSSSH
WOW, I CAN SEE THE WHOLE TOWN FROM HERE!
HUH?
HEY!
GUYS, I SAW THE MON-- OOF!
I SAW THE MONSTER!
WHAT?!
WHERE?

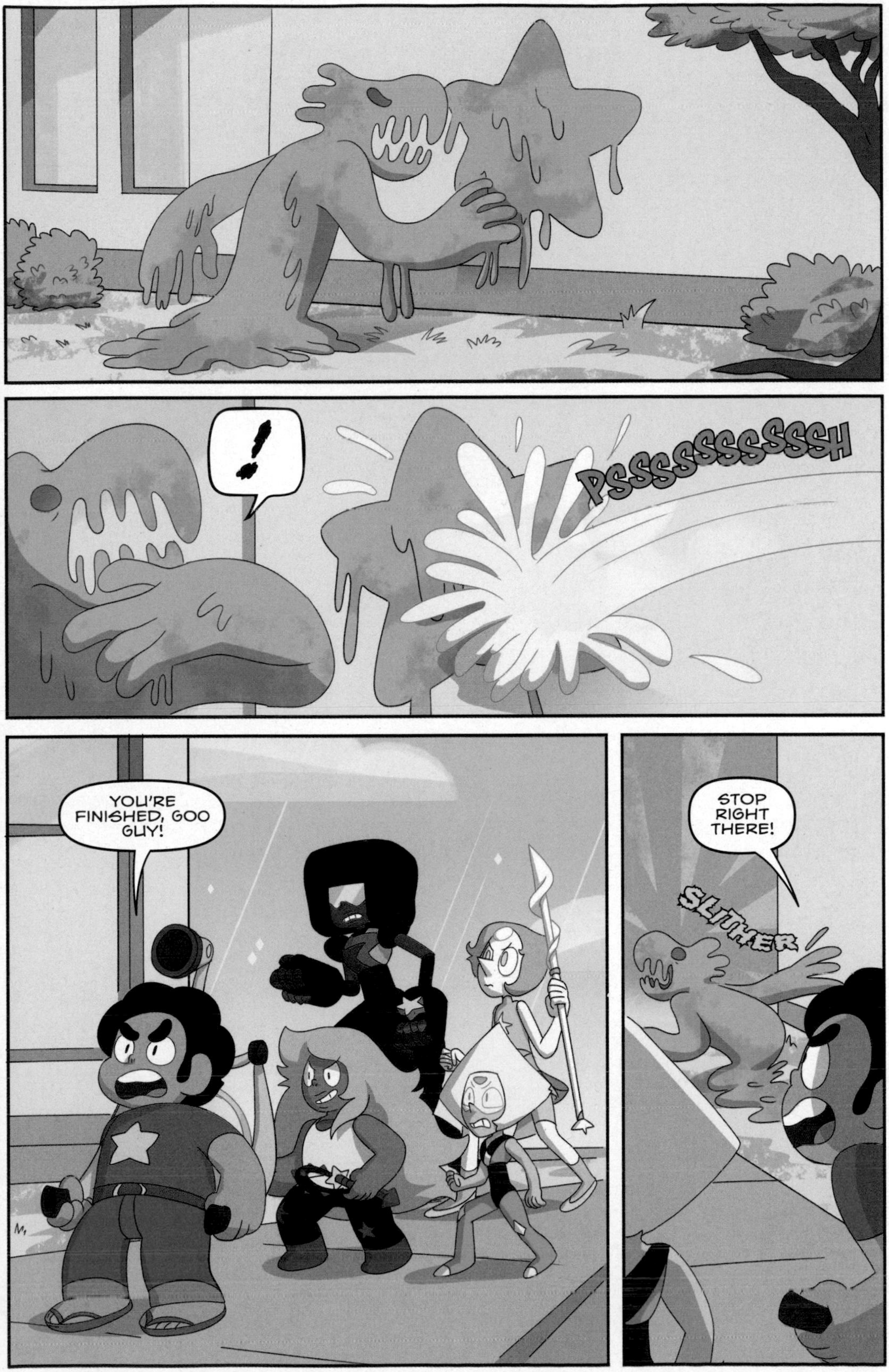
!
PSSSSSSSSSSH
YOU'RE FINISHED, GOO GUY!
STOP RIGHT THERE!
SLITHER

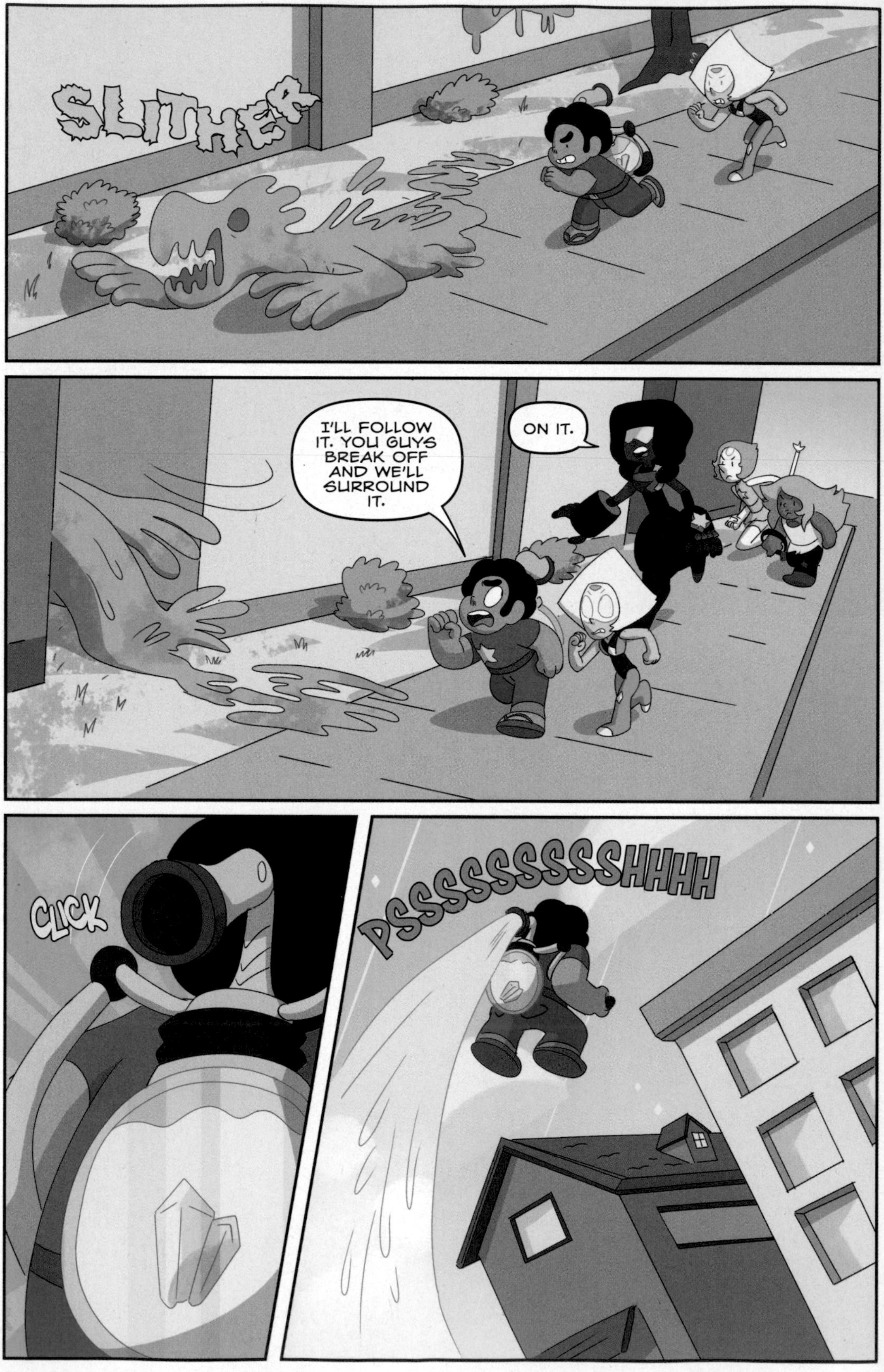
SLITHER
I'LL FOLLOW IT. YOU GUYS BREAK OFF AND WE'LL SURROUND IT.
ON IT.
CLICK
PSSSSSSSSSHHHH

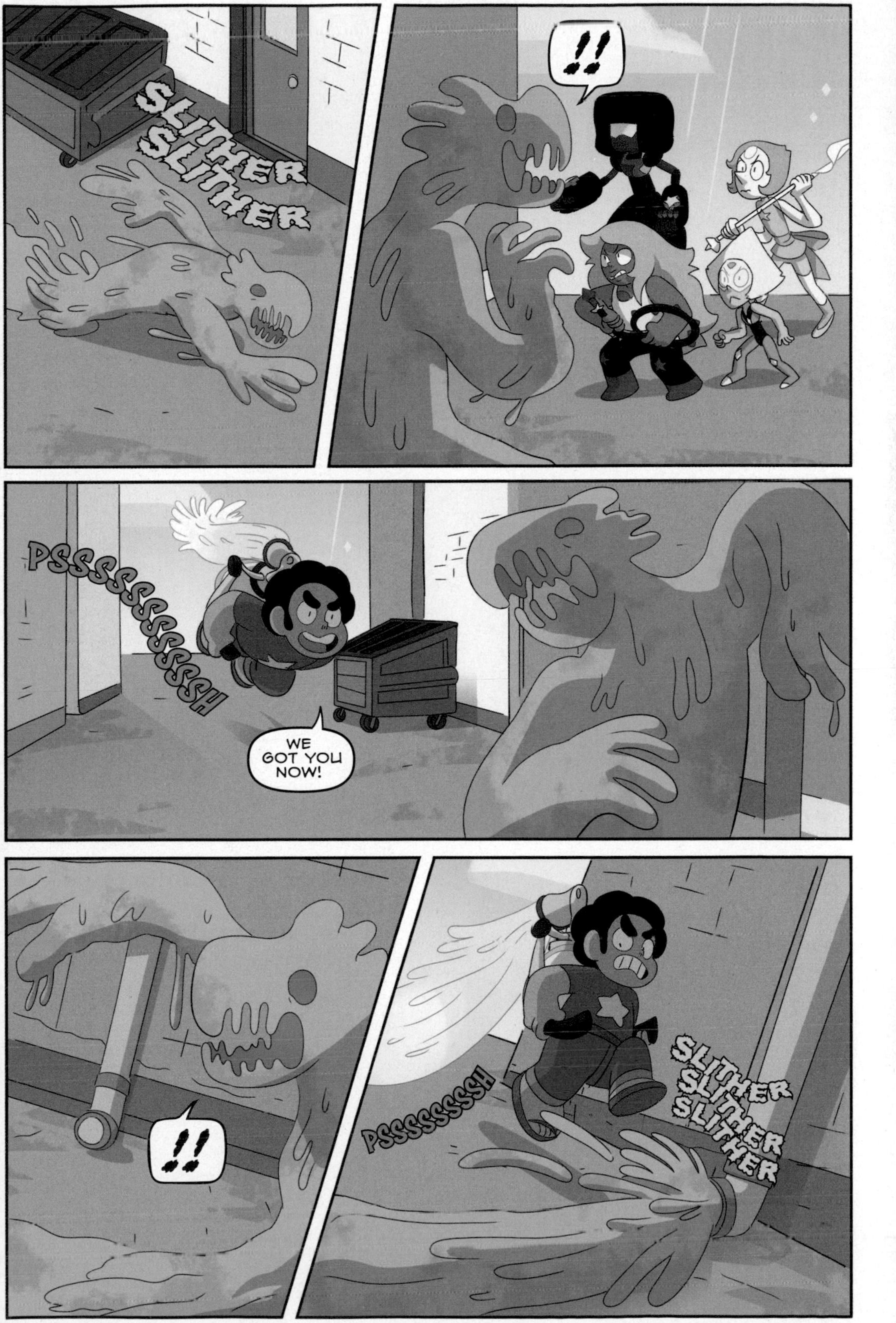
SLITHER SLITHER
!!
PSSSSSSSSSSSSH
WE GOT YOU NOW!
!!
PSSSSSSSSH
SLITHER SLITHER SLITHER

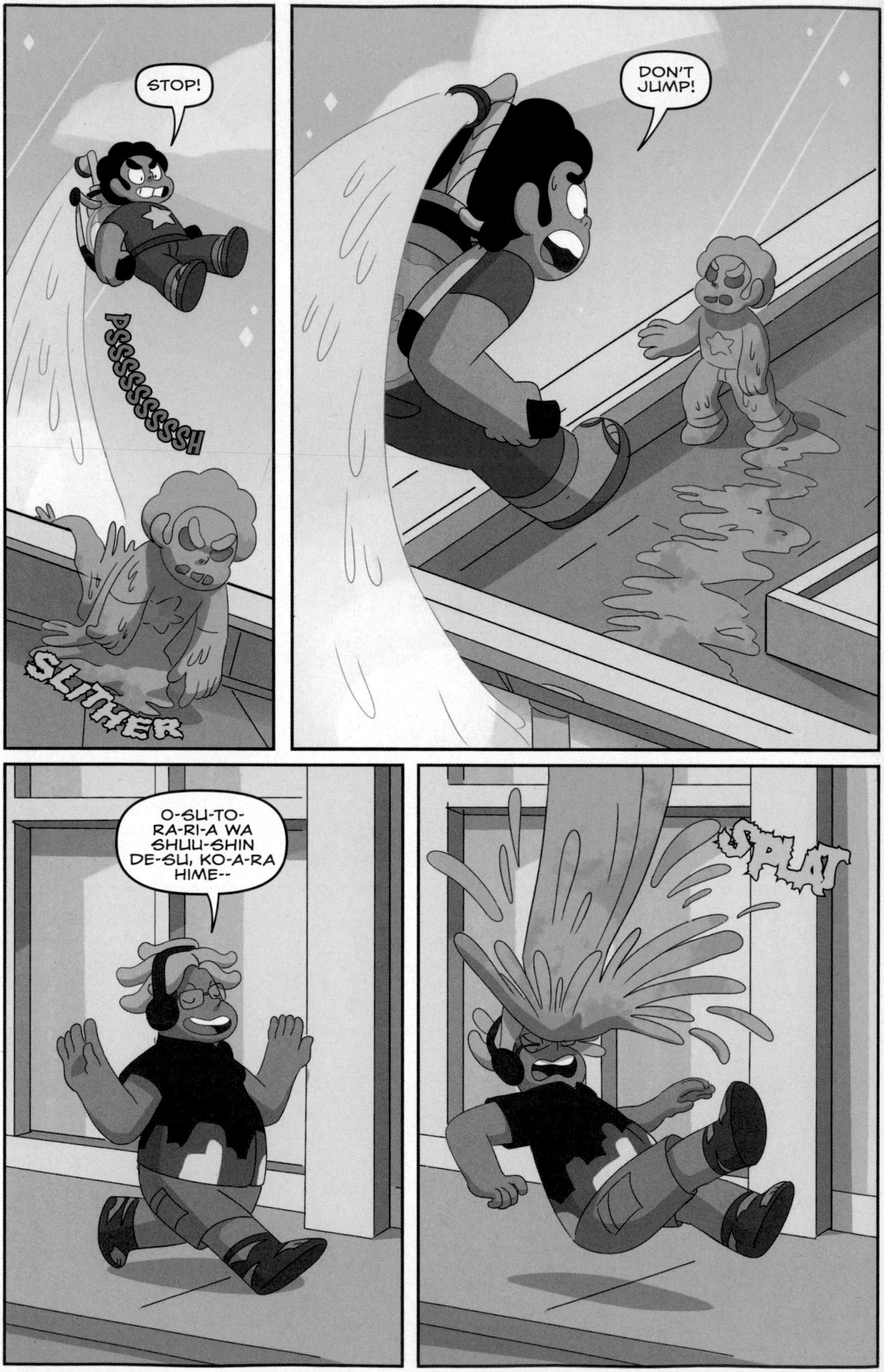
STOP!
PSSSSSSSSSH
SLITHER
DON'T JUMP!
O-SU-TO-RA-RI-A WA SHUU-SHIN DE-SU, KO-A-RA HIME--
SPLAT

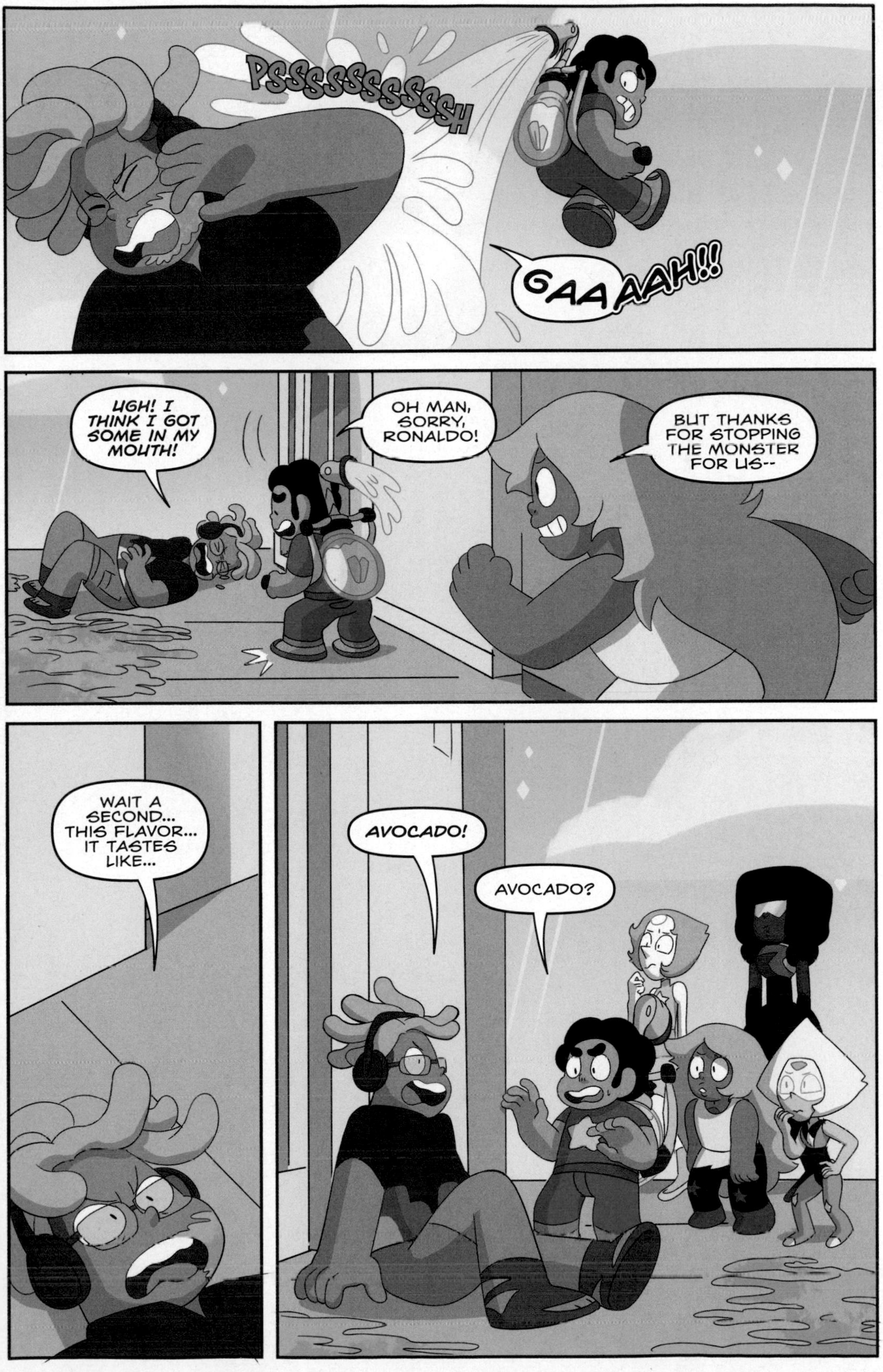
PSSSSSSSSSSSH
GAAAAH!!
UGH! I THINK I GOT SOME IN MY MOUTH!
OH MAN, SORRY, RONALDO!
BUT THANKS FOR STOPPING THE MONSTER FOR US--
WAIT A SECOND... THIS FLAVOR... IT TASTES LIKE...
AVOCADO!
AVOCADO?

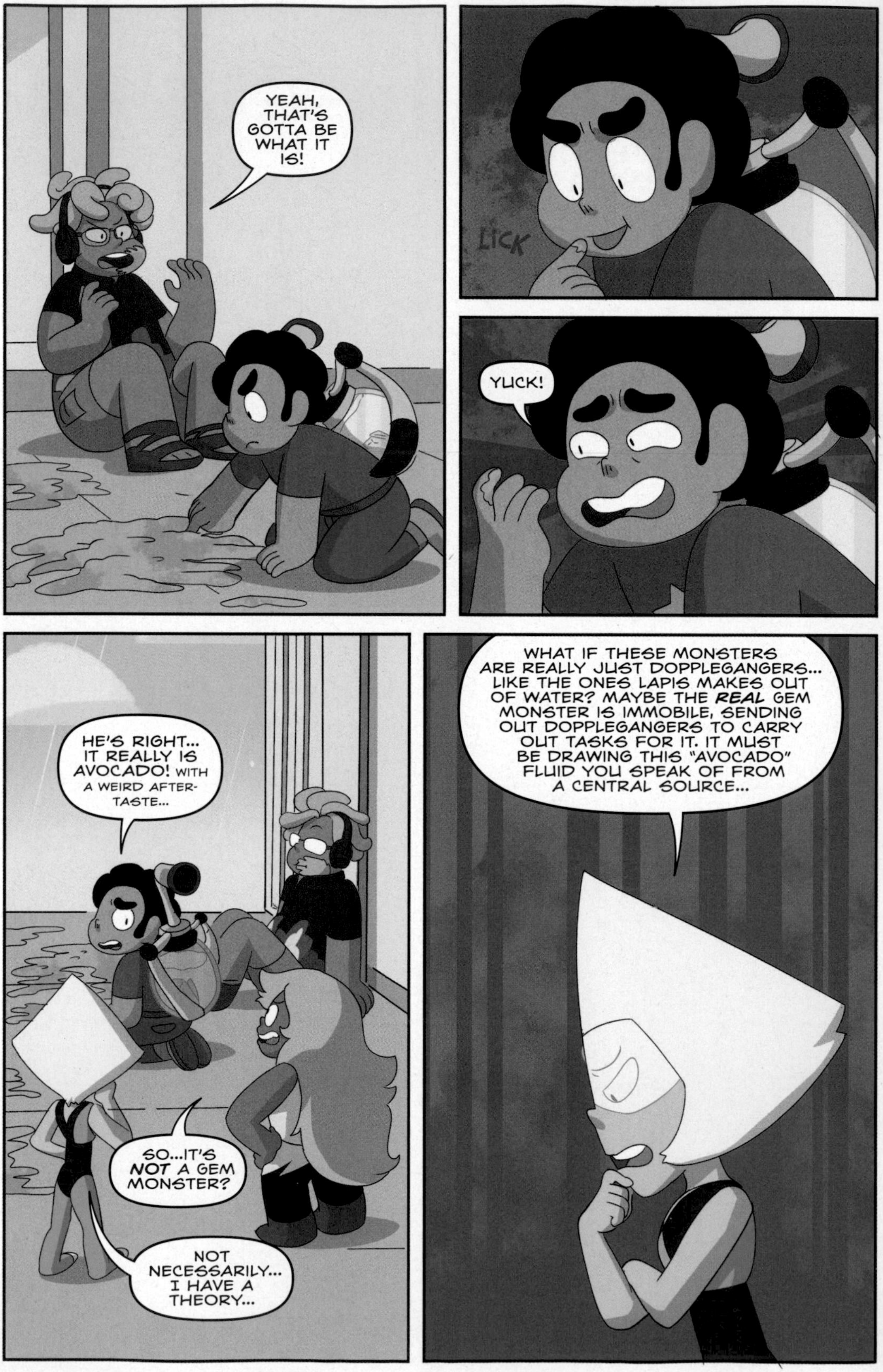
YEAH, THAT'S GOTTA BE WHAT IT IS!
LICK
YUCK!
HE'S RIGHT... IT REALLY IS AVOCADO! WITH A WEIRD AFTER-TASTE...
SO...IT'S NOT A GEM MONSTER?
NOT NECESSARILY... I HAVE A THEORY...
WHAT IF THESE MONSTERS ARE REALLY JUST DOPPLEGANGERS... LIKE THE ONES LAPIS MAKES OUT OF WATER? MAYBE THE REAL GEM MONSTER IS IMMOBILE, SENDING OUT DOPPLEGANGERS TO CARRY OUT TASKS FOR IT. IT MUST BE DRAWING THIS "AVOCADO" FLUID YOU SPEAK OF FROM A CENTRAL SOURCE...

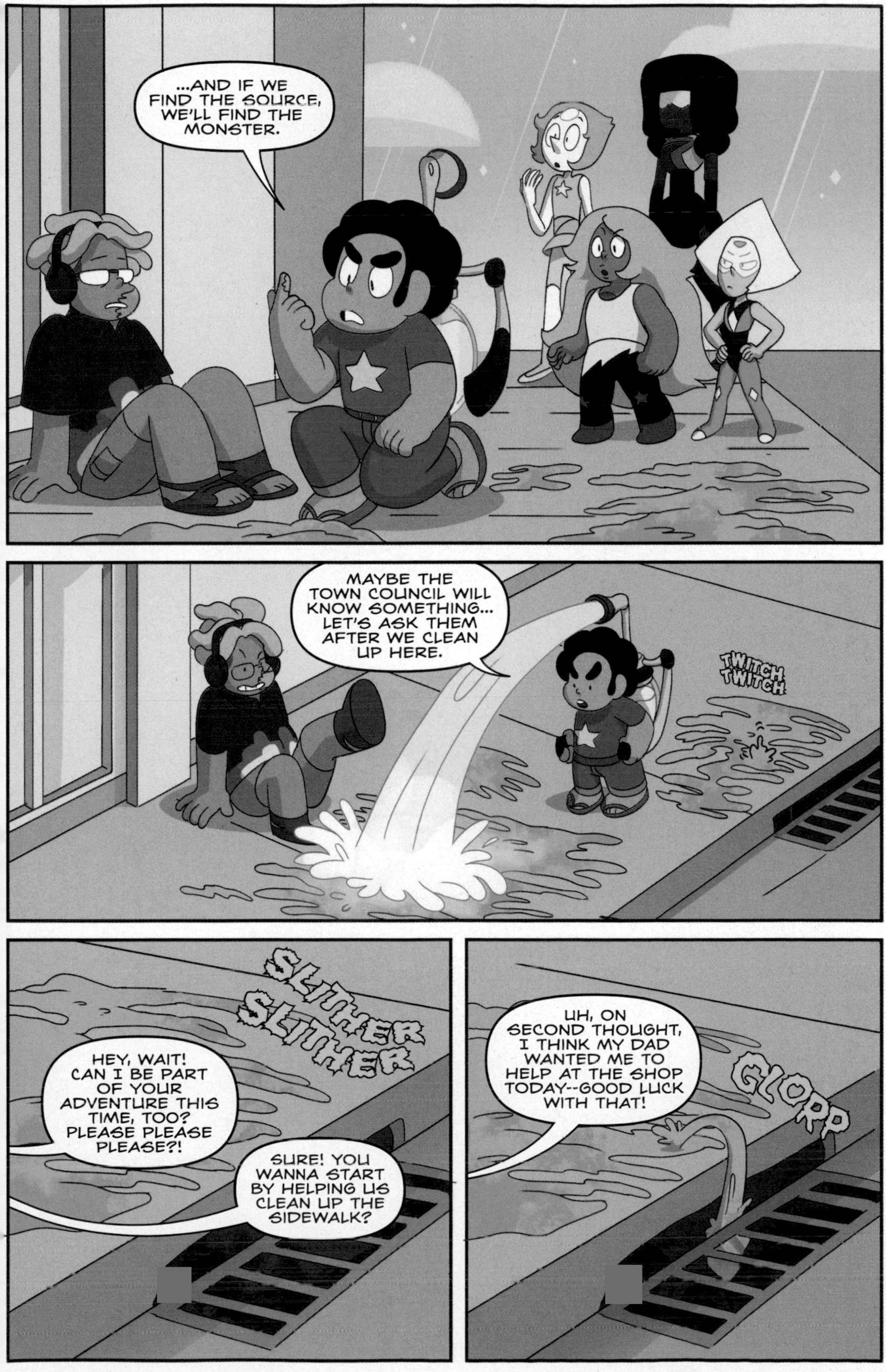
...AND IF WE FIND THE SOURCE, WE'LL FIND THE MONSTER.
MAYBE THE TOWN COUNCIL WILL KNOW SOMETHING... LET'S ASK THEM AFTER WE CLEAN UP HERE.
TWITCH TWITCH
SLITHER SLITHER
HEY, WAIT! CAN I BE PART OF YOUR ADVENTURE THIS TIME, TOO? PLEASE PLEASE PLEASE?!
SURE! YOU WANNA START BY HELPING US CLEAN UP THE SIDEWALK?
UH, ON SECOND THOUGHT, I THINK MY DAD WANTED ME TO HELP AT THE SHOP TODAY--GOOD LUCK WITH THAT!
GLORP

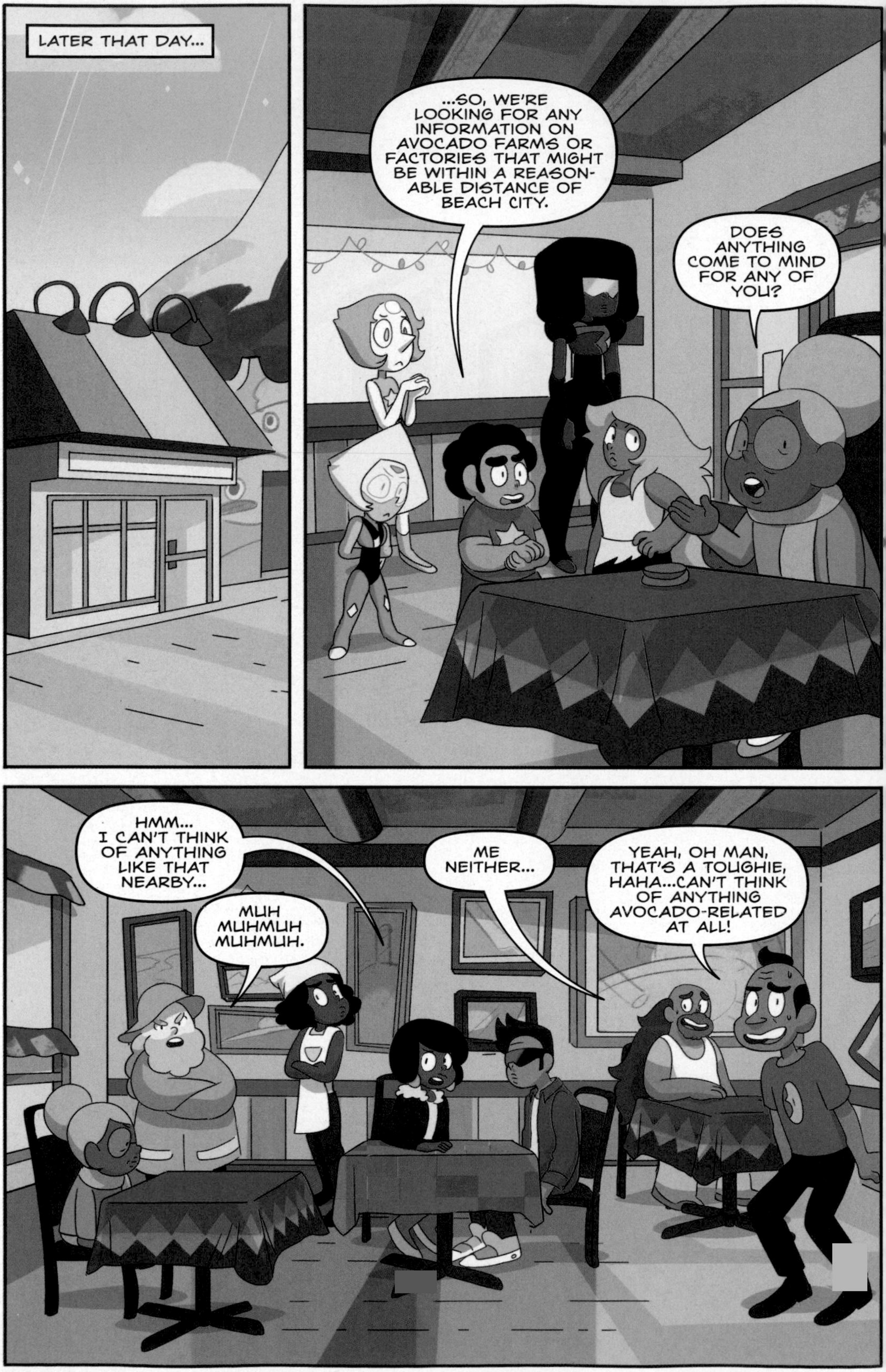
LATER THAT DAY...
...SO, WE'RE LOOKING FOR ANY INFORMATION ON AVOCADO FARMS OR FACTORIES THAT MIGHT BE WITHIN A REASON-ABLE DISTANCE OF BEACH CITY.
DOES ANYTHING COME TO MIND FOR ANY OF YOU?
HMM... I CAN'T THINK OF ANYTHING LIKE THAT NEARBY...
MUH MUHMUH MUHMUH.
ME NEITHER...
YEAH, OH MAN, THAT'S A TOUGHIE, HAHA...CAN'T THINK OF ANYTHING AVOCADO-RELATED AT ALL!

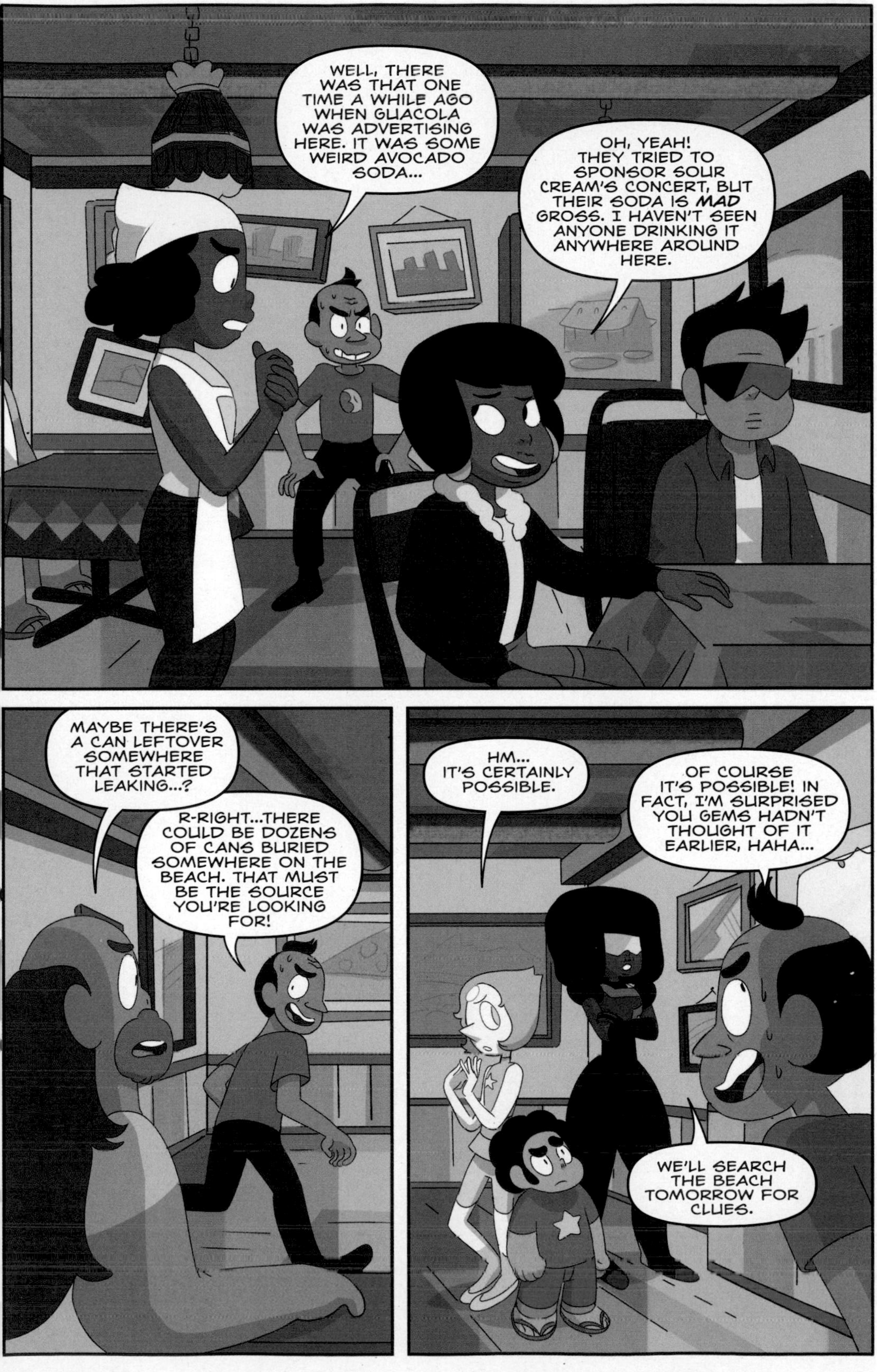
WELL, THERE WAS THAT ONE TIME A WHILE AGO WHEN GUACOLA WAS ADVERTISING HERE. IT WAS SOME WEIRD AVOCADO SODA...
OH, YEAH! THEY TRIED TO SPONSOR SOUR CREAM'S CONCERT, BUT THEIR SODA IS *MAD* GROSS. I HAVEN'T SEEN ANYONE DRINKING IT ANYWHERE AROUND HERE.
MAYBE THERE'S A CAN LEFTOVER SOMEWHERE THAT STARTED LEAKING...?
R-RIGHT...THERE COULD BE DOZENS OF CANS BURIED SOMEWHERE ON THE BEACH. THAT MUST BE THE SOURCE YOU'RE LOOKING FOR!
HM... IT'S CERTAINLY POSSIBLE.
OF COURSE IT'S POSSIBLE! IN FACT, I'M SURPRISED YOU GEMS HADN'T THOUGHT OF IT EARLIER, HAHA...
WE'LL SEARCH THE BEACH TOMORROW FOR CLUES.

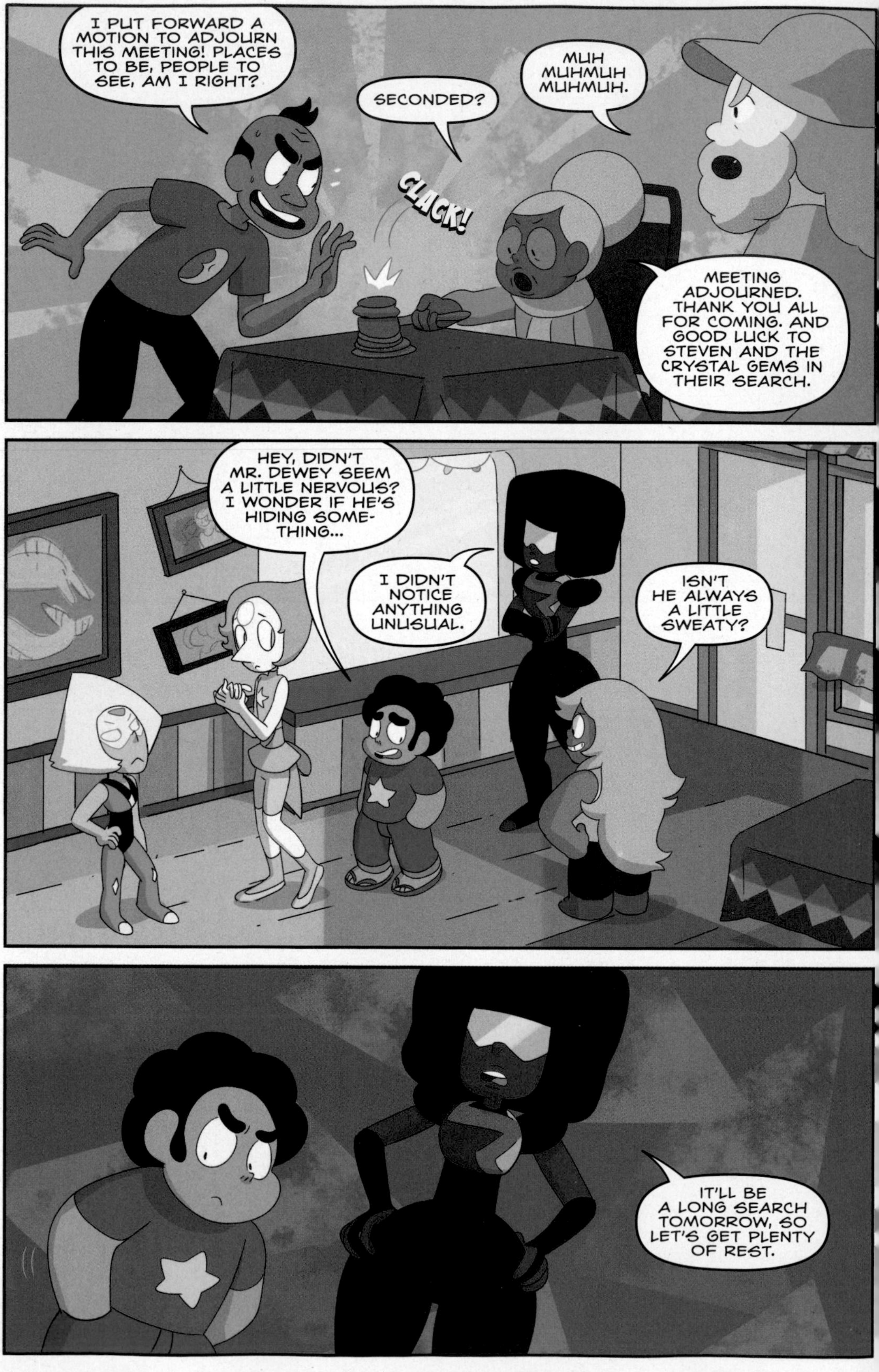
I PUT FORWARD A MOTION TO ADJOURN THIS MEETING! PLACES TO BE, PEOPLE TO SEE, AM I RIGHT?
SECONDED?
MUH MUHMUH MUHMUH.
CLACK!
MEETING ADJOURNED. THANK YOU ALL FOR COMING. AND GOOD LUCK TO STEVEN AND THE CRYSTAL GEMS IN THEIR SEARCH.
HEY, DIDN'T MR. DEWEY SEEM A LITTLE NERVOUS? I WONDER IF HE'S HIDING SOME-THING...
I DIDN'T NOTICE ANYTHING UNUSUAL.
ISN'T HE ALWAYS A LITTLE SWEATY?
IT'LL BE A LONG SEARCH TOMORROW, SO LET'S GET PLENTY OF REST.

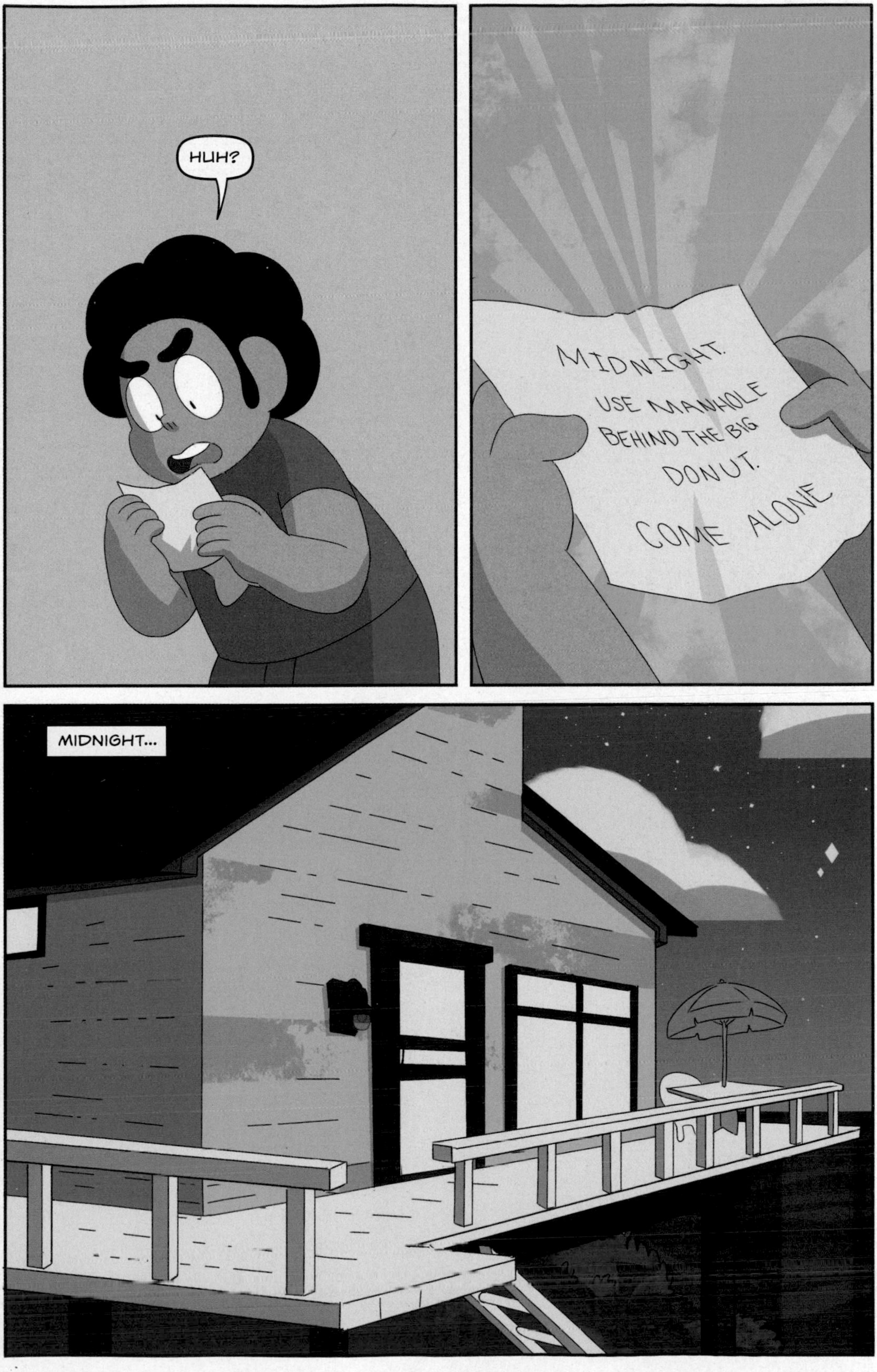
HUH?
MIDNIGHT.
USE MANHOLE
BEHIND THE BIG
DONUT.
COME ALONE
MIDNIGHT...

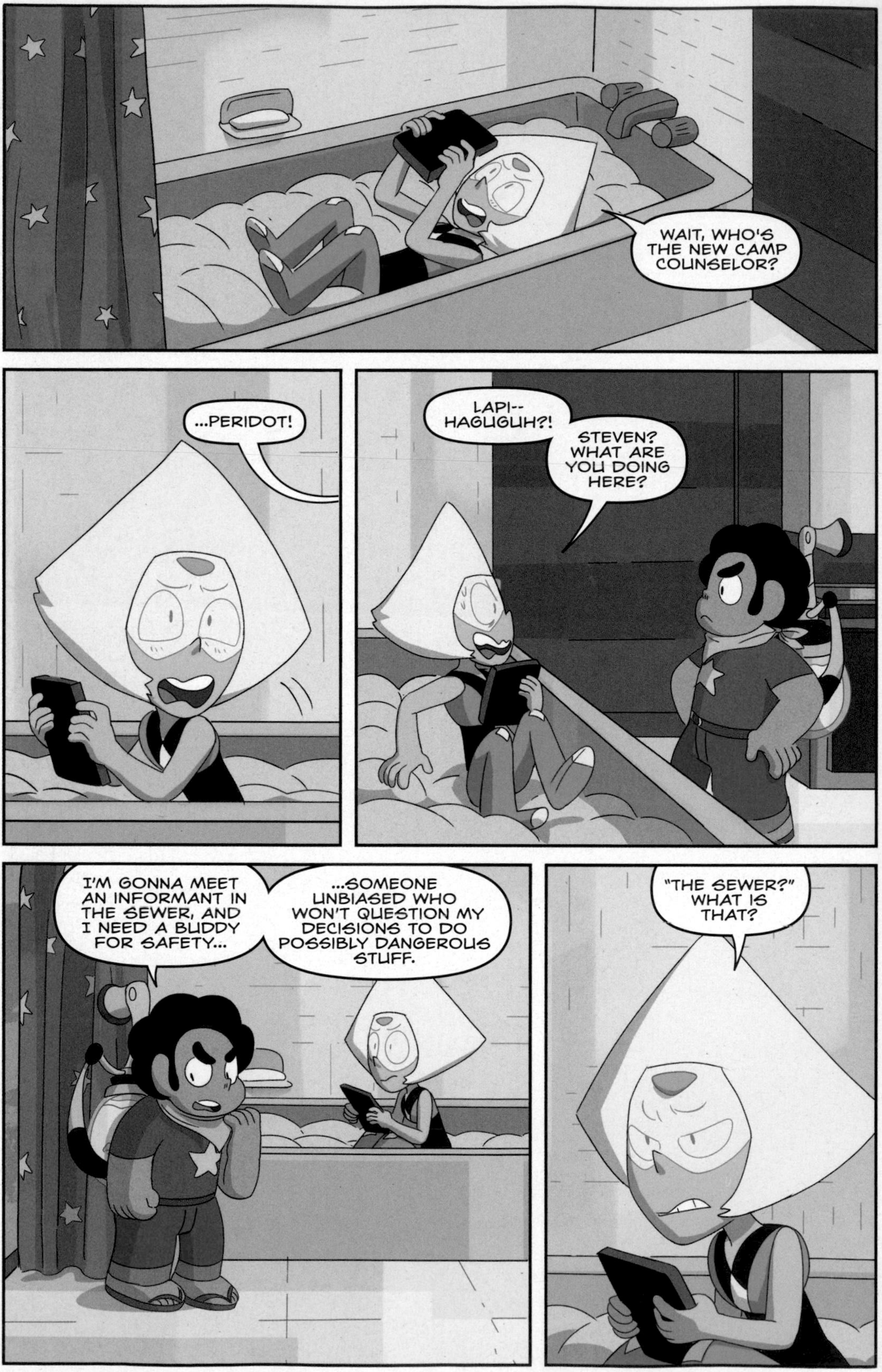
WAIT, WHO'S THE NEW CAMP COUNSELOR?
...PERIDOT!
LAPI-- HAGUGUH?!
STEVEN? WHAT ARE YOU DOING HERE?
I'M GONNA MEET AN INFORMANT IN THE SEWER, AND I NEED A BUDDY FOR SAFETY...
...SOMEONE UNBIASED WHO WON'T QUESTION MY DECISIONS TO DO POSSIBLY DANGEROUS STUFF.
"THE SEWER?" WHAT IS THAT?

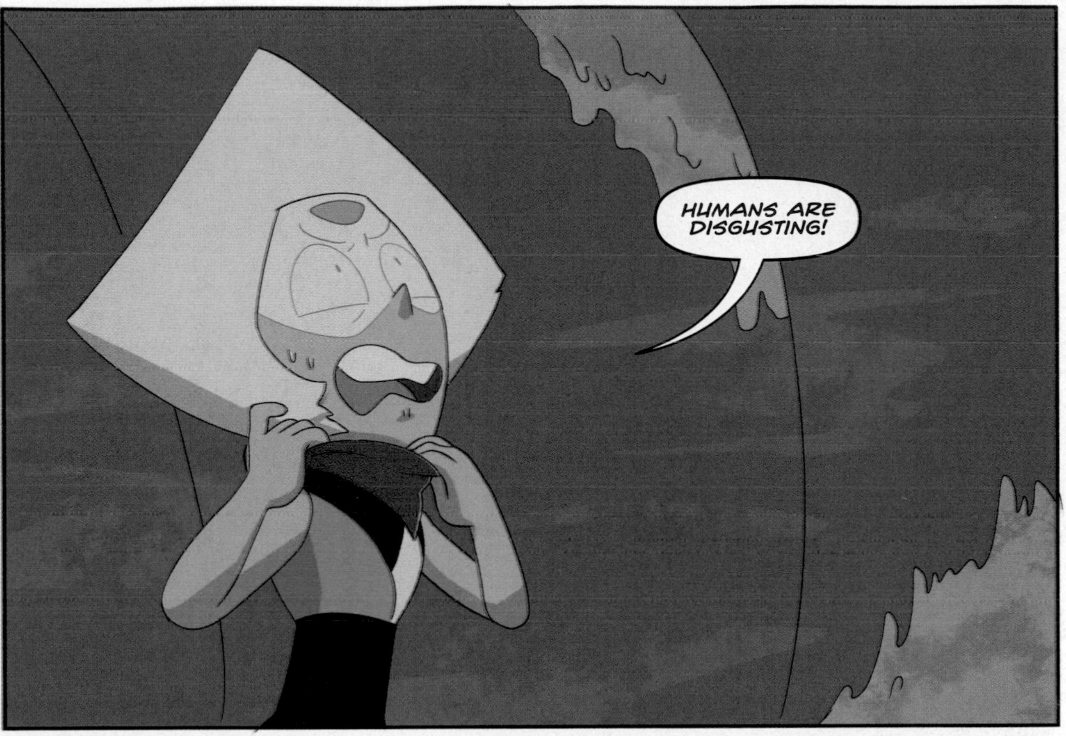
HUMANS ARE DISGUSTING!

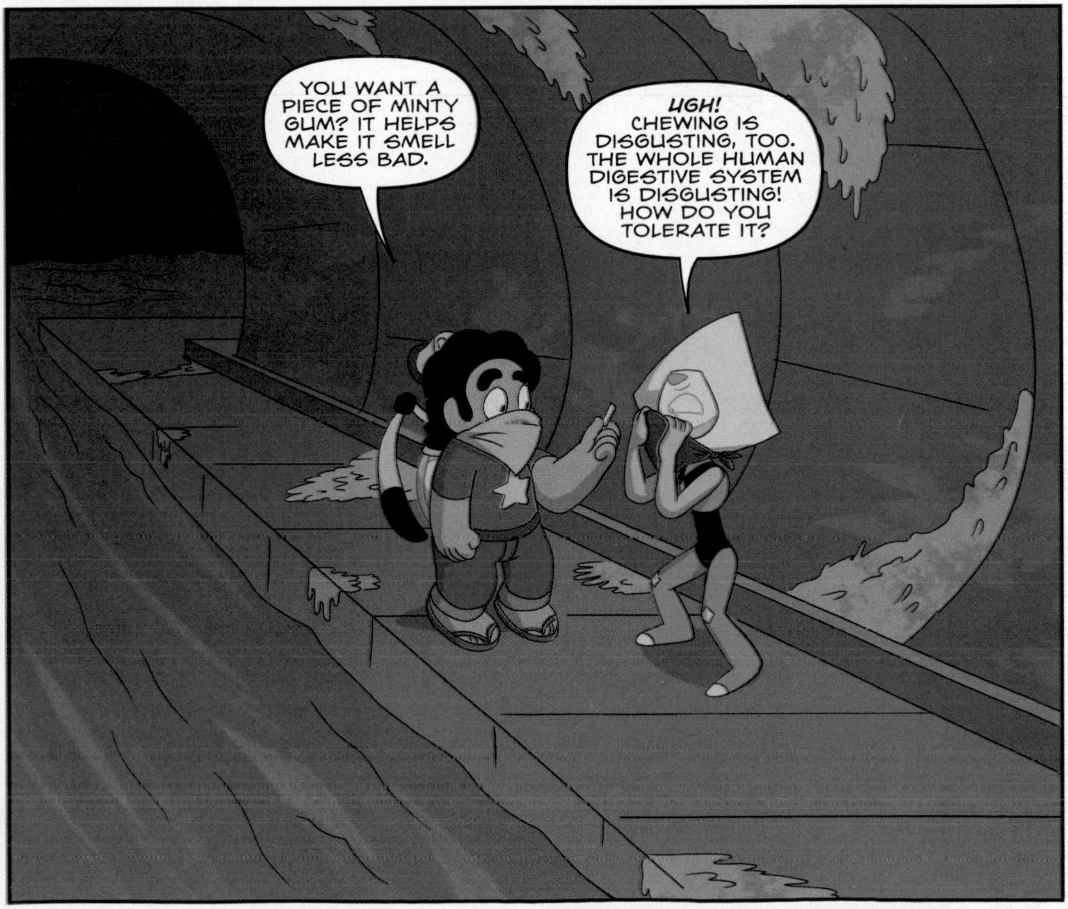
YOU WANT A PIECE OF MINTY GUM? IT HELPS MAKE IT SMELL LESS BAD.
UGH! CHEWING IS DISGUSTING, TOO. THE WHOLE HUMAN DIGESTIVE SYSTEM IS DISGUSTING! HOW DO YOU TOLERATE IT?

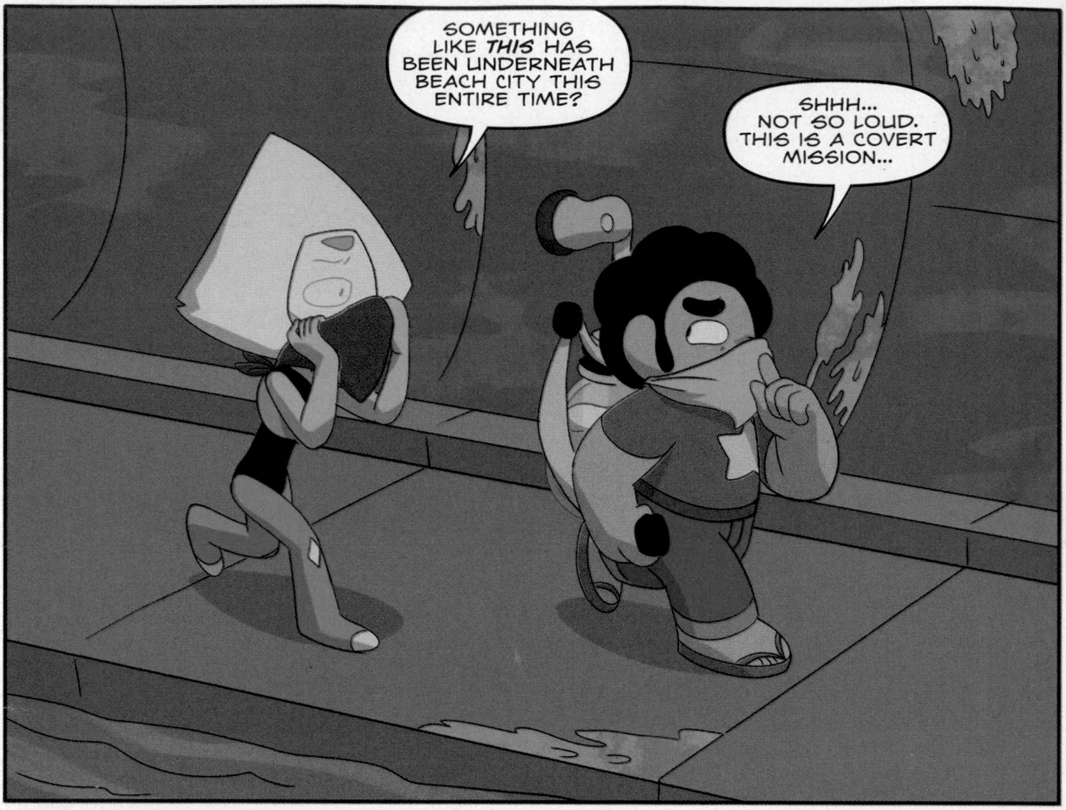
SOMETHING LIKE *THIS* HAS BEEN UNDERNEATH BEACH CITY THIS ENTIRE TIME?
SHHH... NOT SO LOUD. THIS IS A COVERT MISSION...

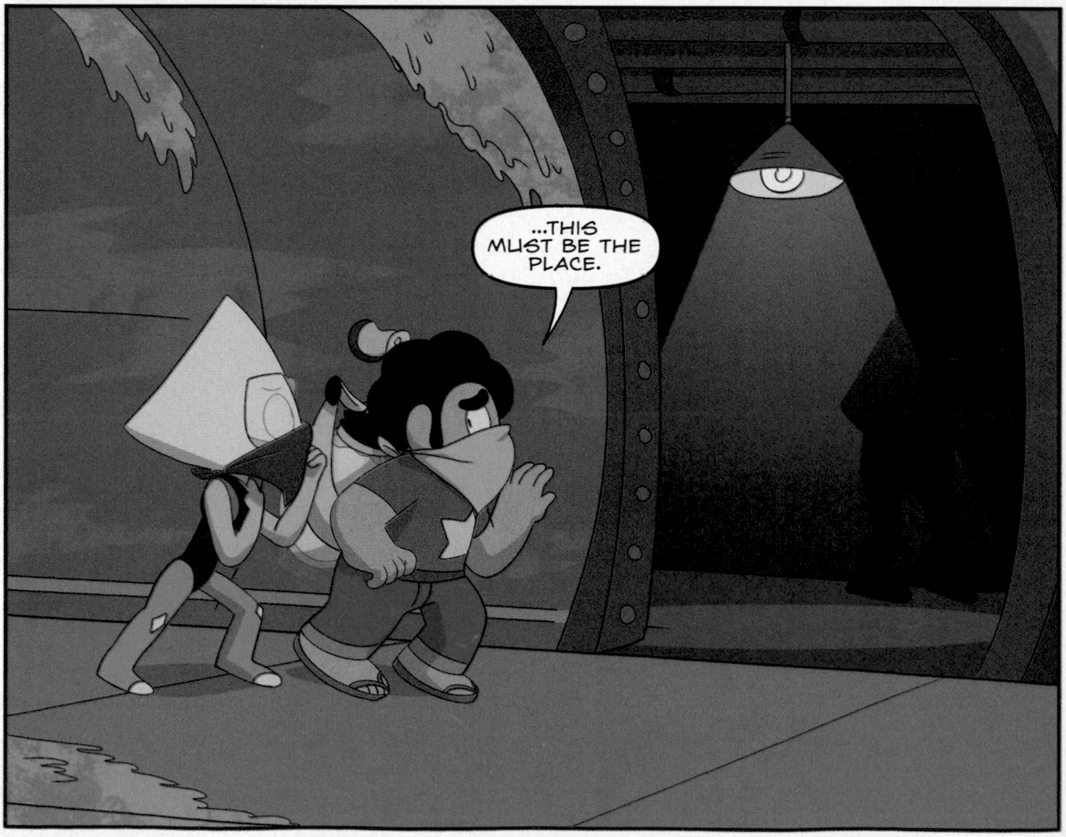
...THIS MUST BE THE PLACE.

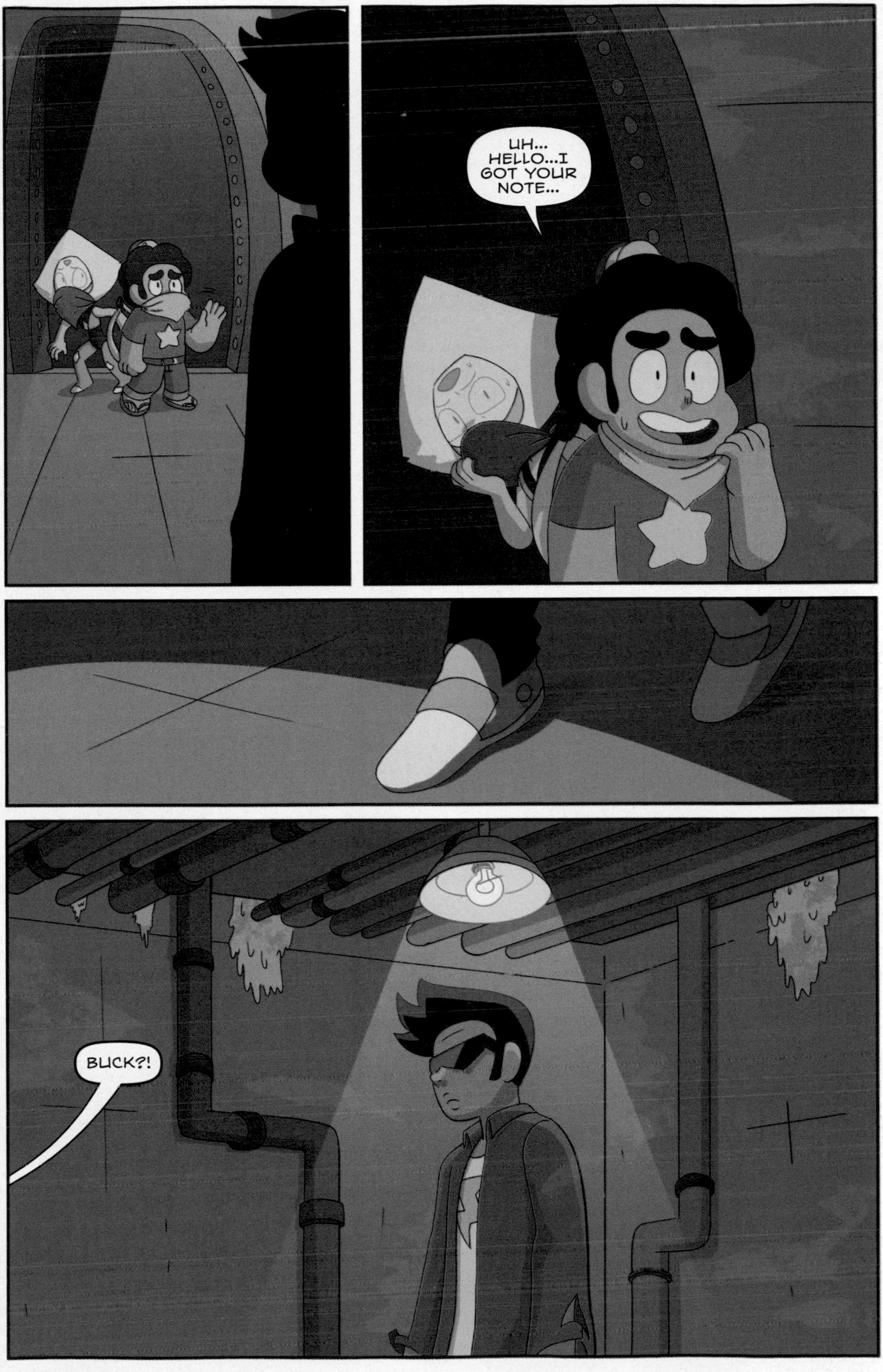
UH... HELLO...I GOT YOUR NOTE...
BUCK?!

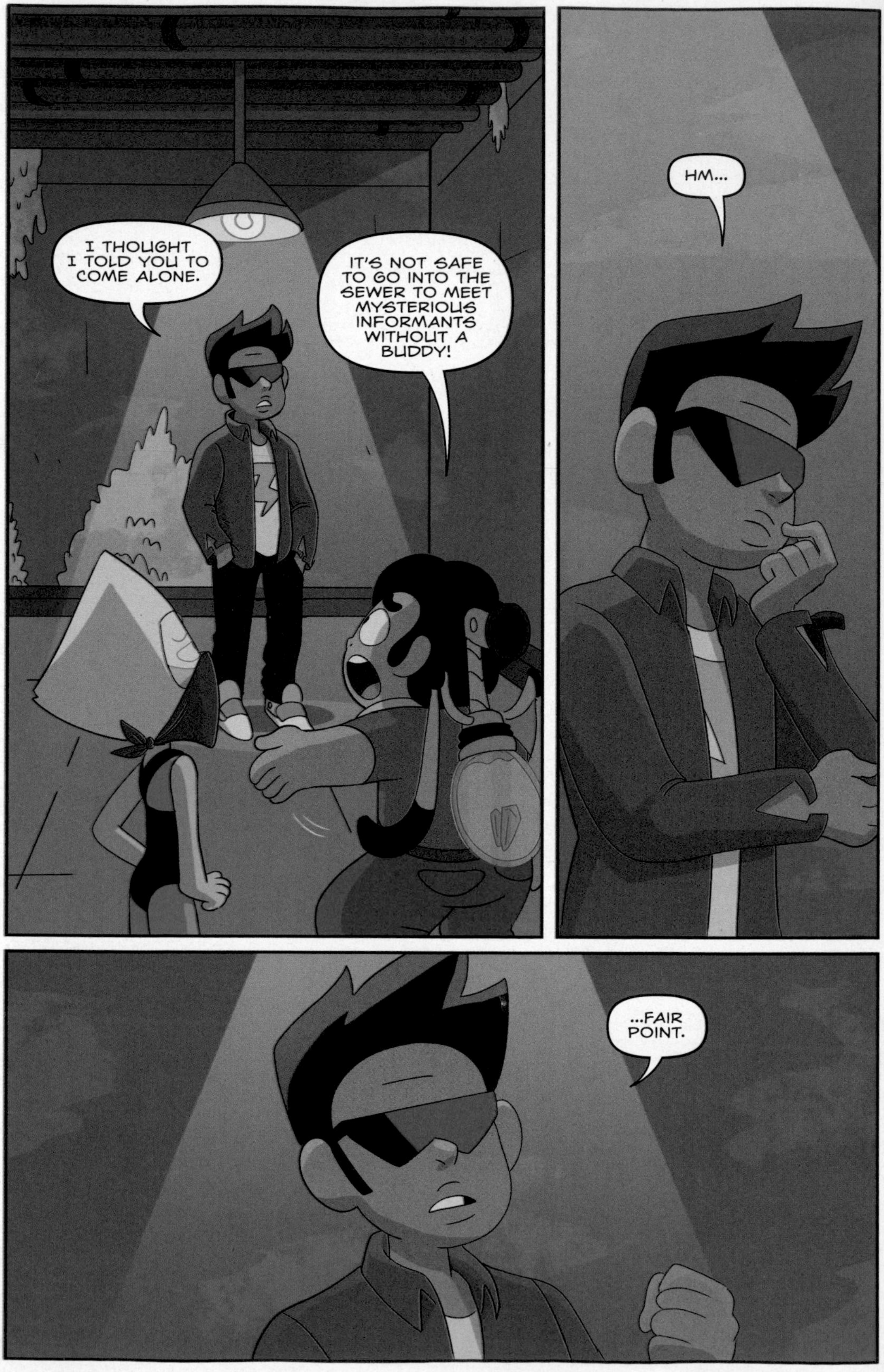
I THOUGHT I TOLD YOU TO COME ALONE.
IT'S NOT SAFE TO GO INTO THE SEWER TO MEET MYSTERIOUS INFORMANTS WITHOUT A BUDDY!
HM...
...FAIR POINT.

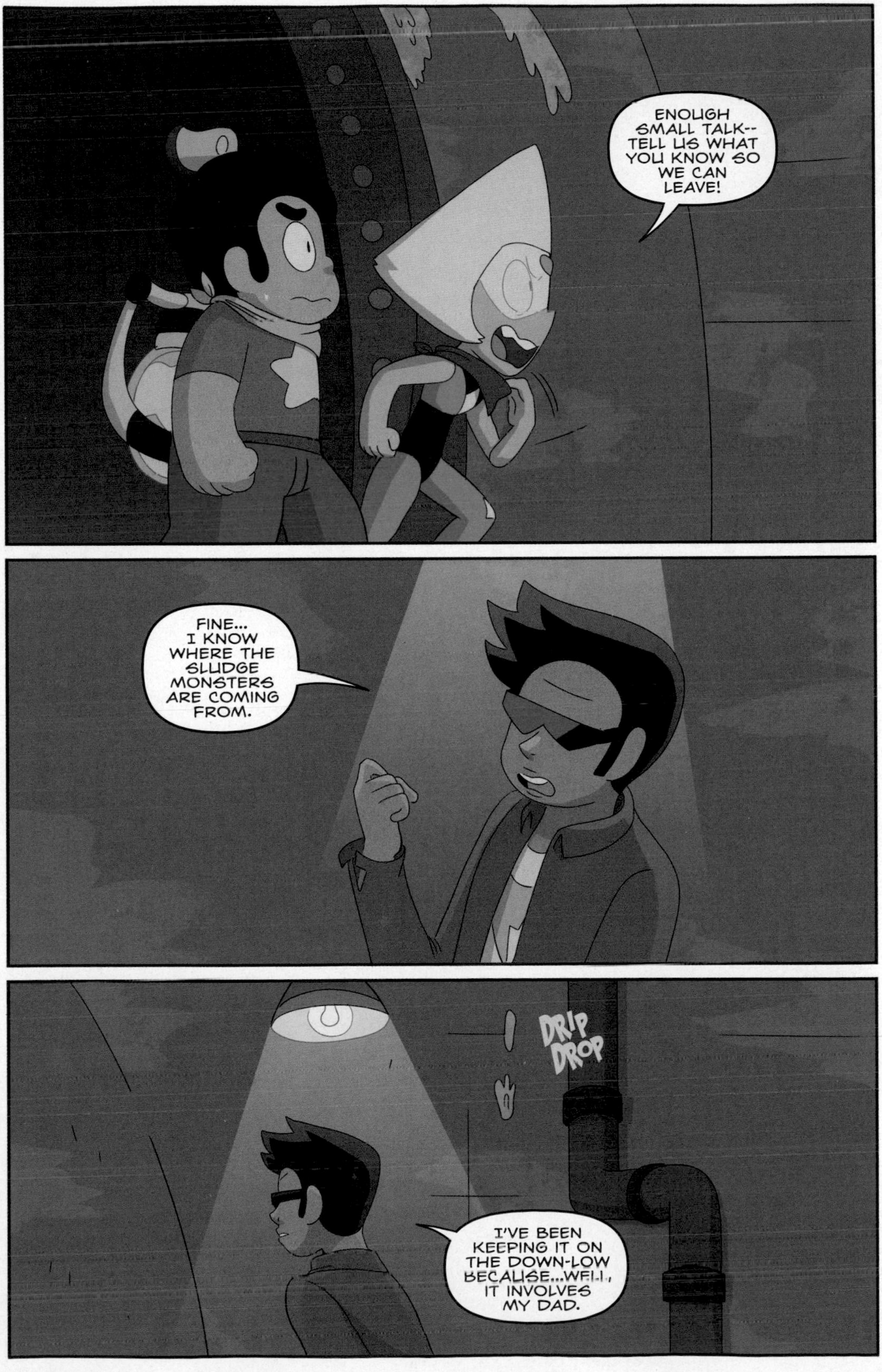
ENOUGH SMALL TALK--TELL US WHAT YOU KNOW SO WE CAN LEAVE!
FINE... I KNOW WHERE THE SLUDGE MONSTERS ARE COMING FROM.
DRIP DROP
I'VE BEEN KEEPING IT ON THE DOWN-LOW BECAUSE...WELL, IT INVOLVES MY DAD.

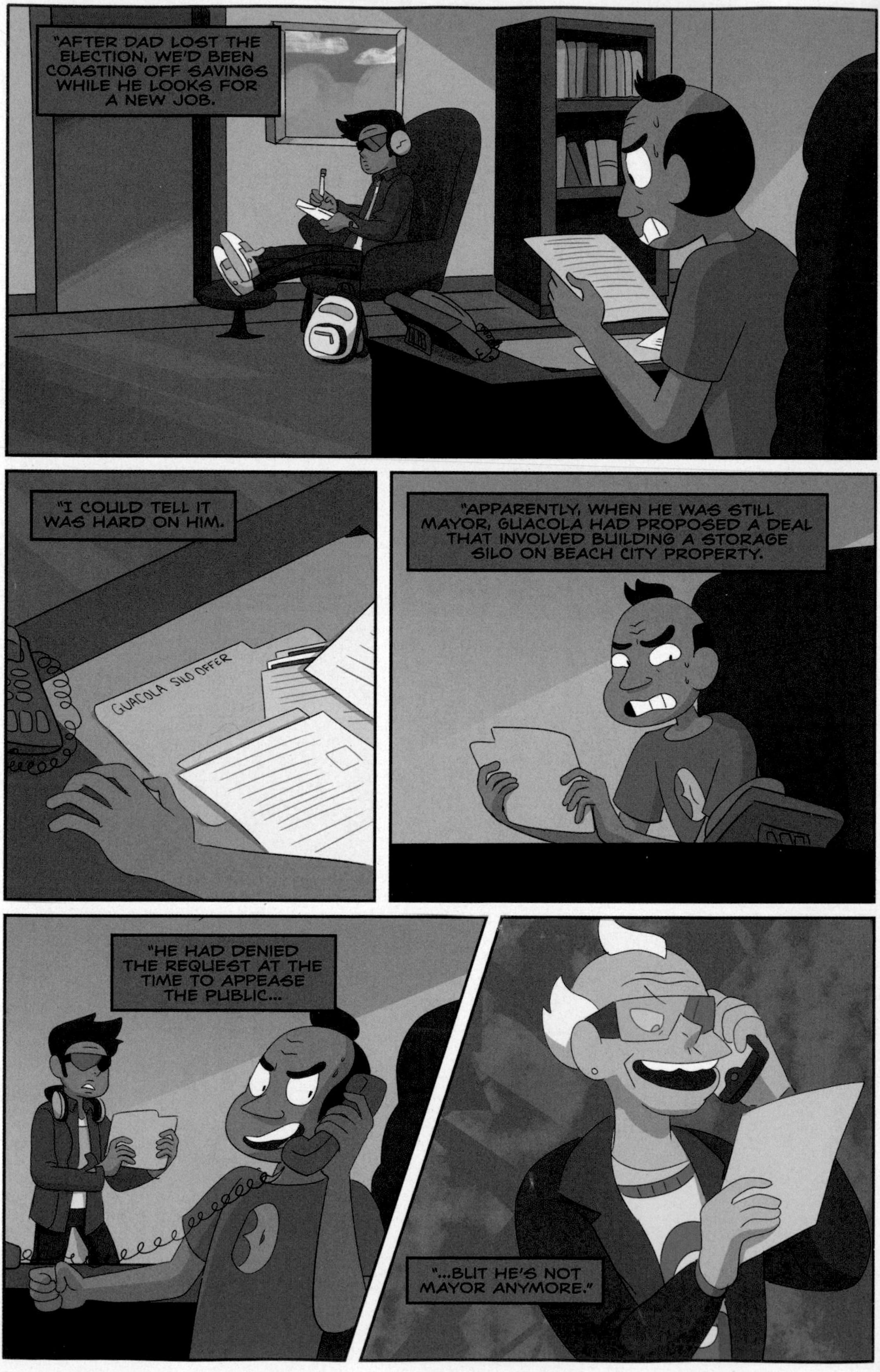
"AFTER DAD LOST THE ELECTION, WE'D BEEN COASTING OFF SAVINGS WHILE HE LOOKS FOR A NEW JOB.
"I COULD TELL IT WAS HARD ON HIM.
GUACOLA SILO OFFER
"APPARENTLY, WHEN HE WAS STILL MAYOR, GUACOLA HAD PROPOSED A DEAL THAT INVOLVED BUILDING A STORAGE SILO ON BEACH CITY PROPERTY.
"HE HAD DENIED THE REQUEST AT THE TIME TO APPEASE THE PUBLIC...
"...BUT HE'S NOT MAYOR ANYMORE."

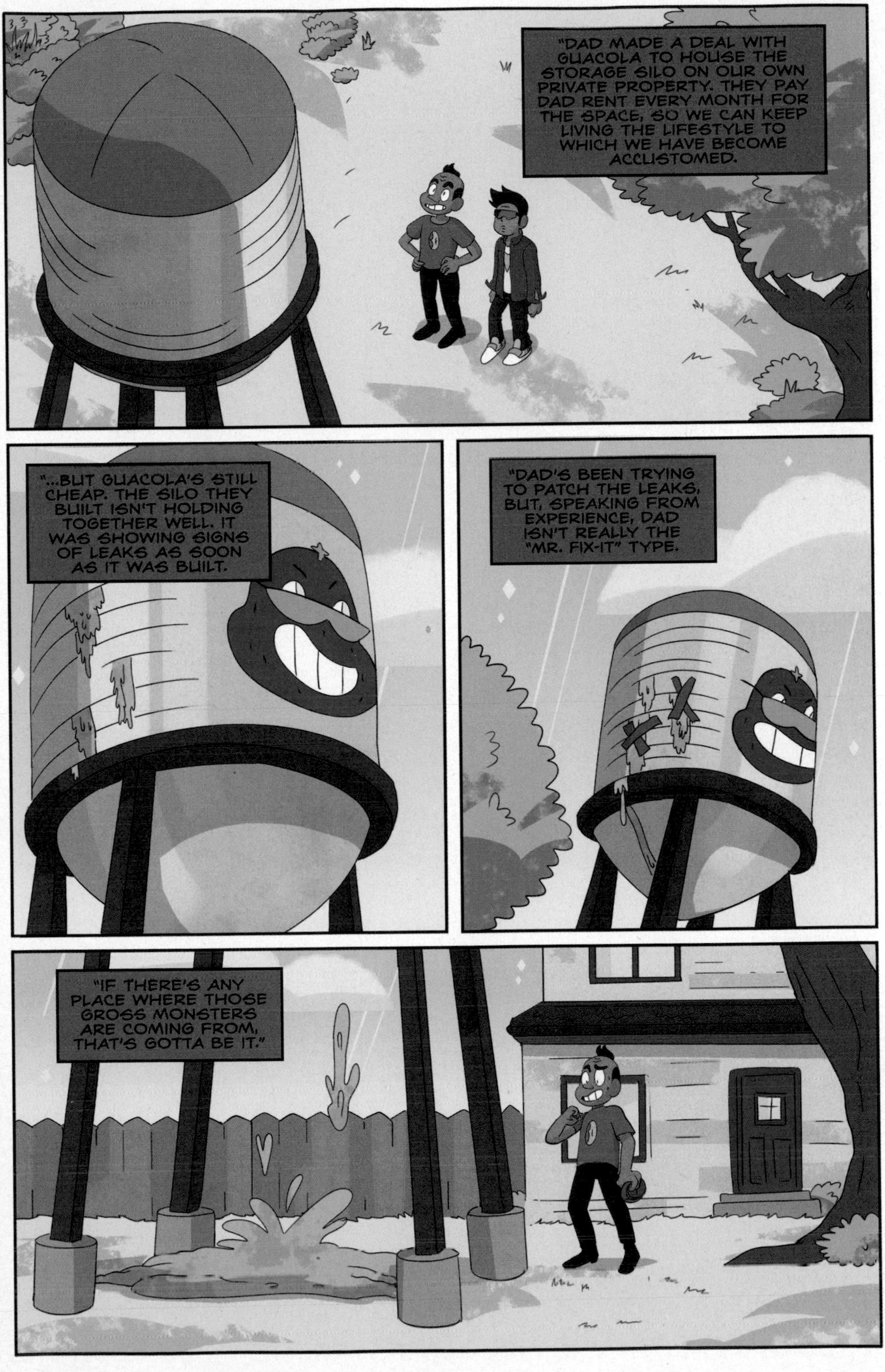
"DAD MADE A DEAL WITH GUACOLA TO HOUSE THE STORAGE SILO ON OUR OWN PRIVATE PROPERTY. THEY PAY DAD RENT EVERY MONTH FOR THE SPACE, SO WE CAN KEEP LIVING THE LIFESTYLE TO WHICH WE HAVE BECOME ACCUSTOMED.
"...BUT GUACOLA'S STILL CHEAP. THE SILO THEY BUILT ISN'T HOLDING TOGETHER WELL. IT WAS SHOWING SIGNS OF LEAKS AS SOON AS IT WAS BUILT.
"DAD'S BEEN TRYING TO PATCH THE LEAKS, BUT, SPEAKING FROM EXPERIENCE, DAD ISN'T REALLY THE "MR. FIX-IT" TYPE.
"IF THERE'S ANY PLACE WHERE THOSE GROSS MONSTERS ARE COMING FROM, THAT'S GOTTA BE IT."

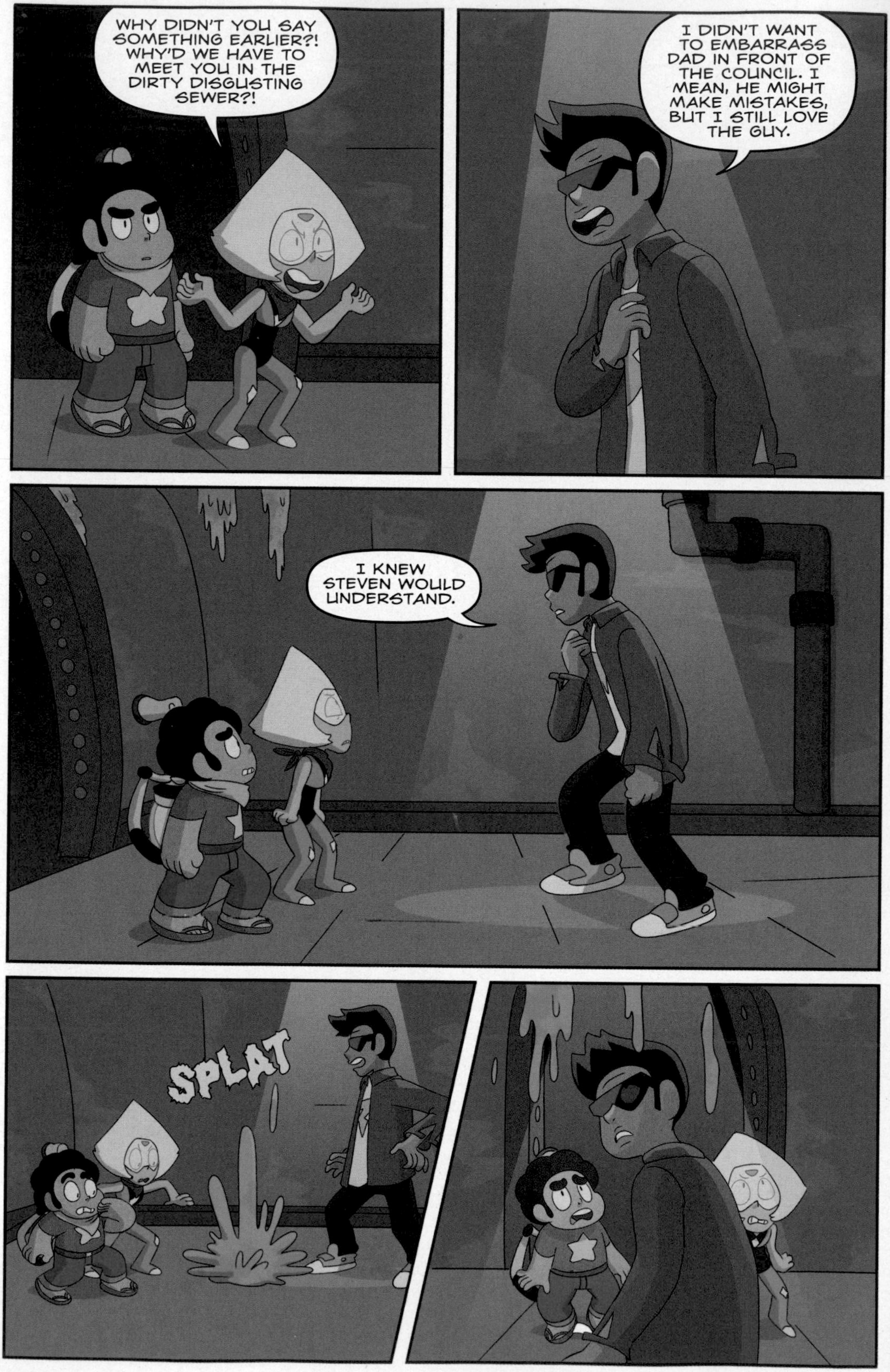
WHY DIDN'T YOU SAY SOMETHING EARLIER?! WHY'D WE HAVE TO MEET YOU IN THE DIRTY DISGUSTING SEWER?!
I DIDN'T WANT TO EMBARRASS DAD IN FRONT OF THE COUNCIL. I MEAN, HE MIGHT MAKE MISTAKES, BUT I STILL LOVE THE GUY.
I KNEW STEVEN WOULD UNDERSTAND.
SPLAT

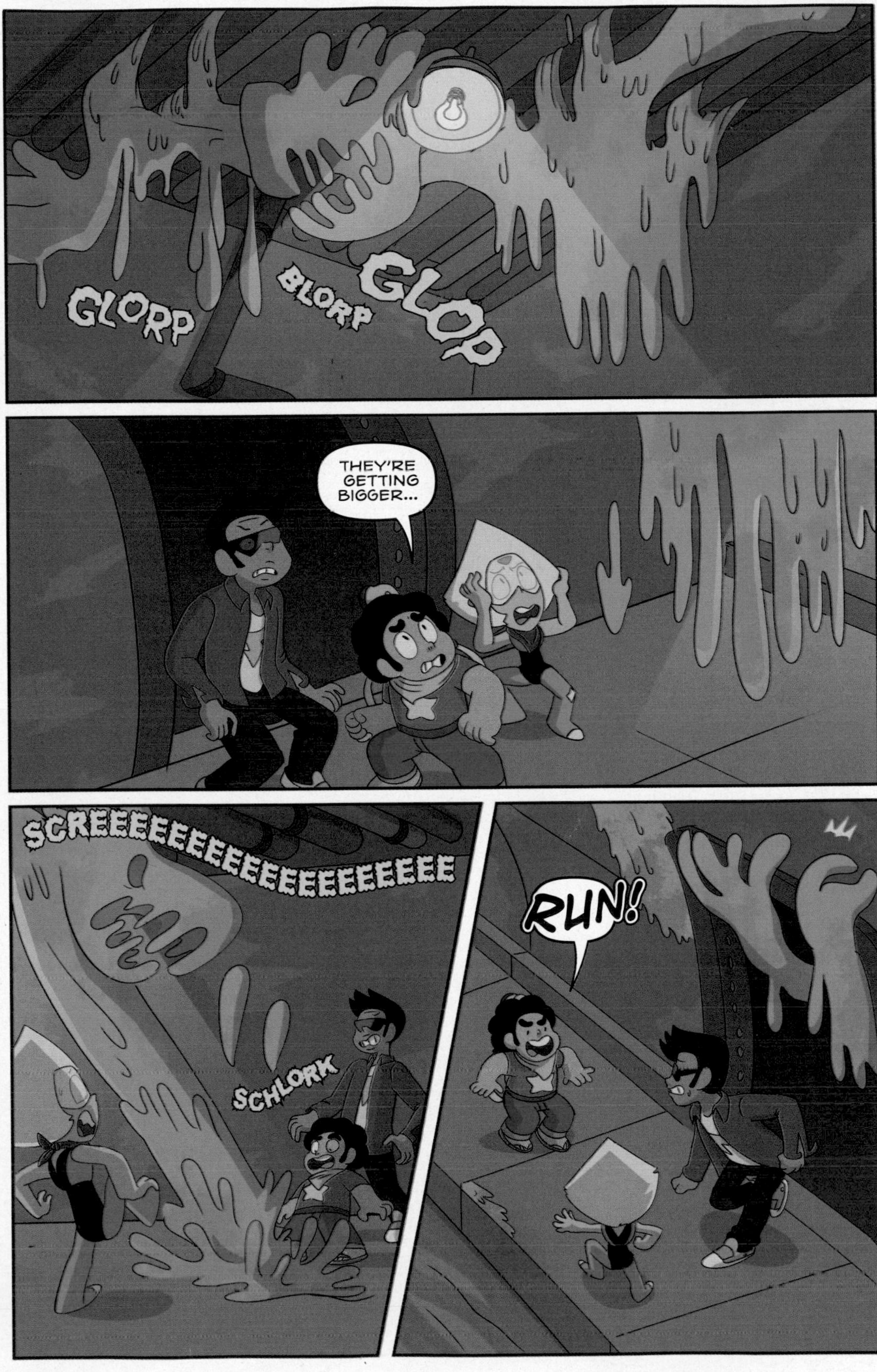
GLORP
BLORP
GLOP
THEY'RE GETTING BIGGER...
SCREEEEEEEEEEEEEEEEEEEE
SCHLORK
RUN!

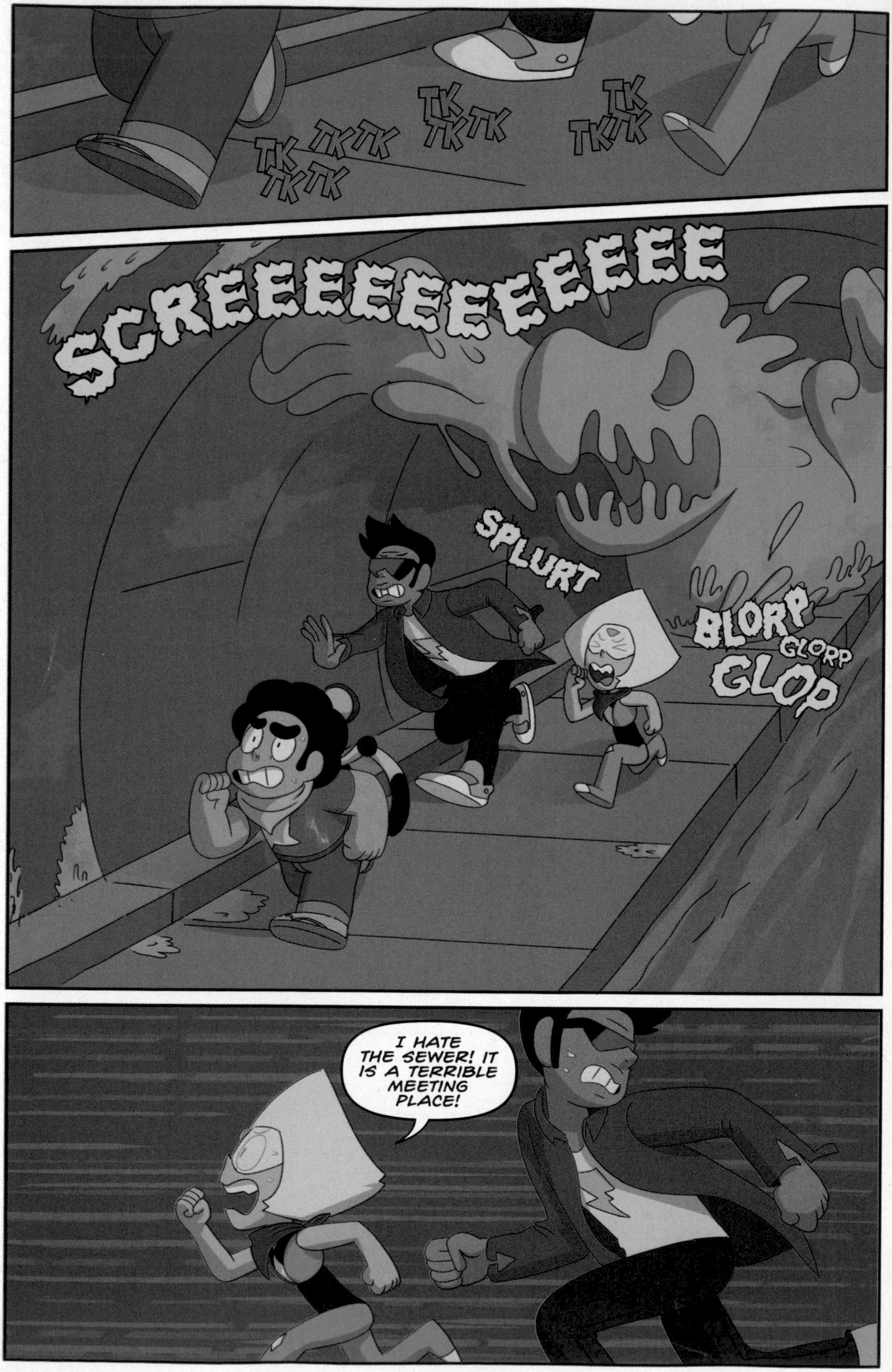
TK TK TK TK TK
TK TK TK
TK TK TK TK
SCREEEEEEEEEEEE
SPLURT
BLORP GLORP GLOP
I HATE THE SEWER! IT IS A TERRIBLE MEETING PLACE!

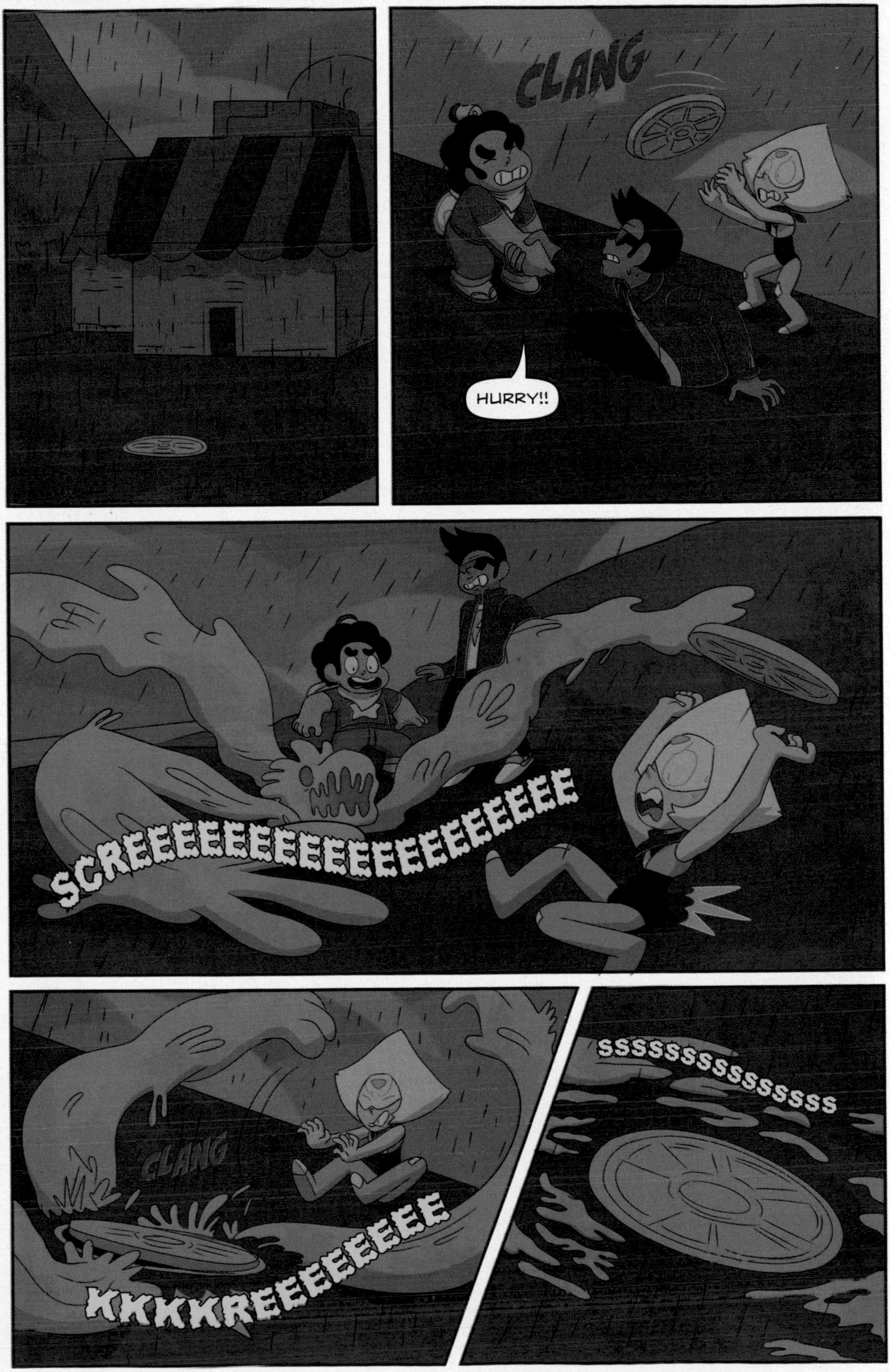
CLANG
HURRY!!
SCREEEEEEEEEEEEEEEEEE
CLANG
KKKKREEEEEEEE
SSSSSSSSSSSSSSS

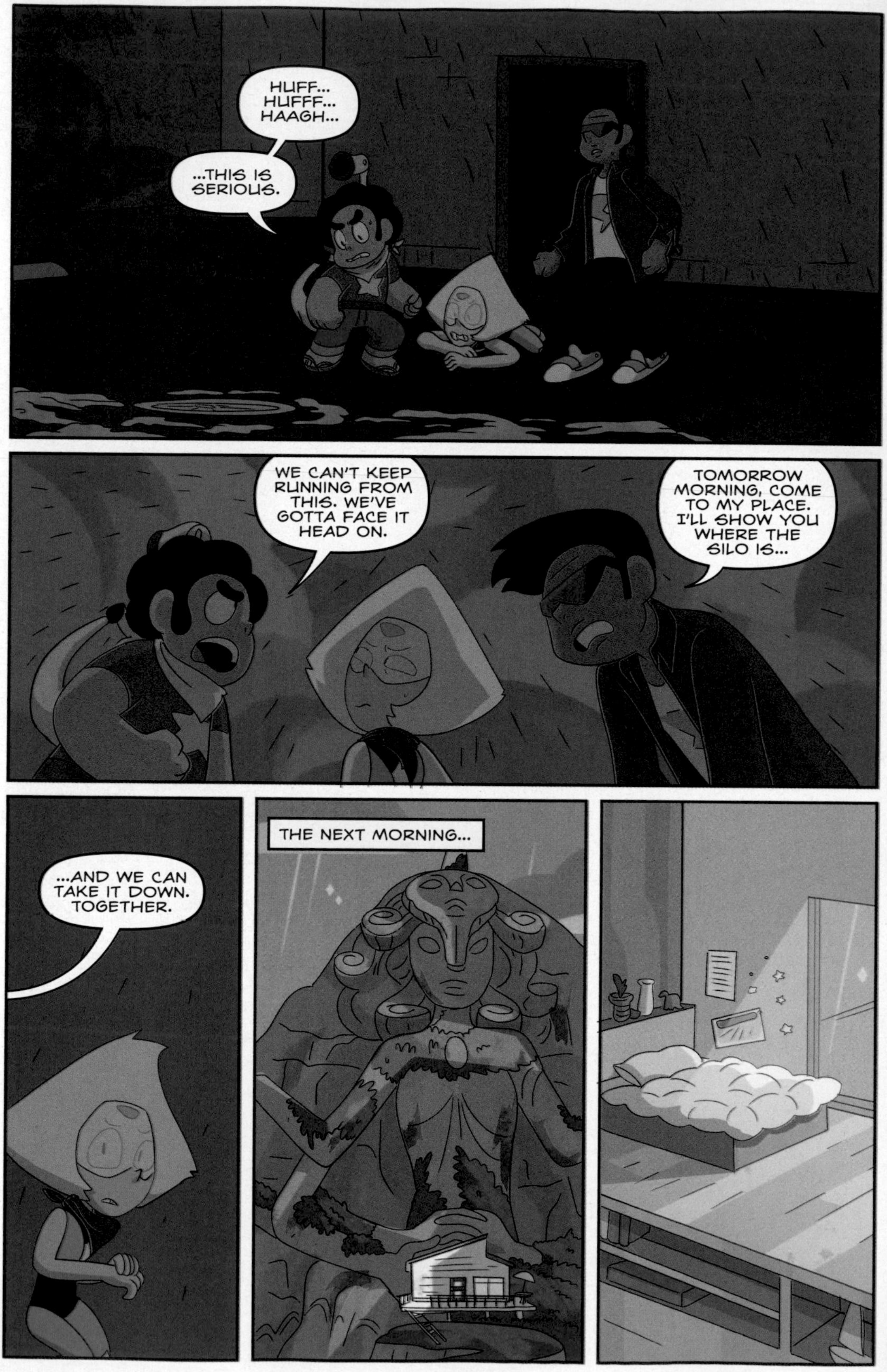
HUFF... HUFFF... HAAGH...
...THIS IS SERIOUS.
WE CAN'T KEEP RUNNING FROM THIS. WE'VE GOTTA FACE IT HEAD ON.
TOMORROW MORNING, COME TO MY PLACE. I'LL SHOW YOU WHERE THE SILO IS...
...AND WE CAN TAKE IT DOWN. TOGETHER.
THE NEXT MORNING...

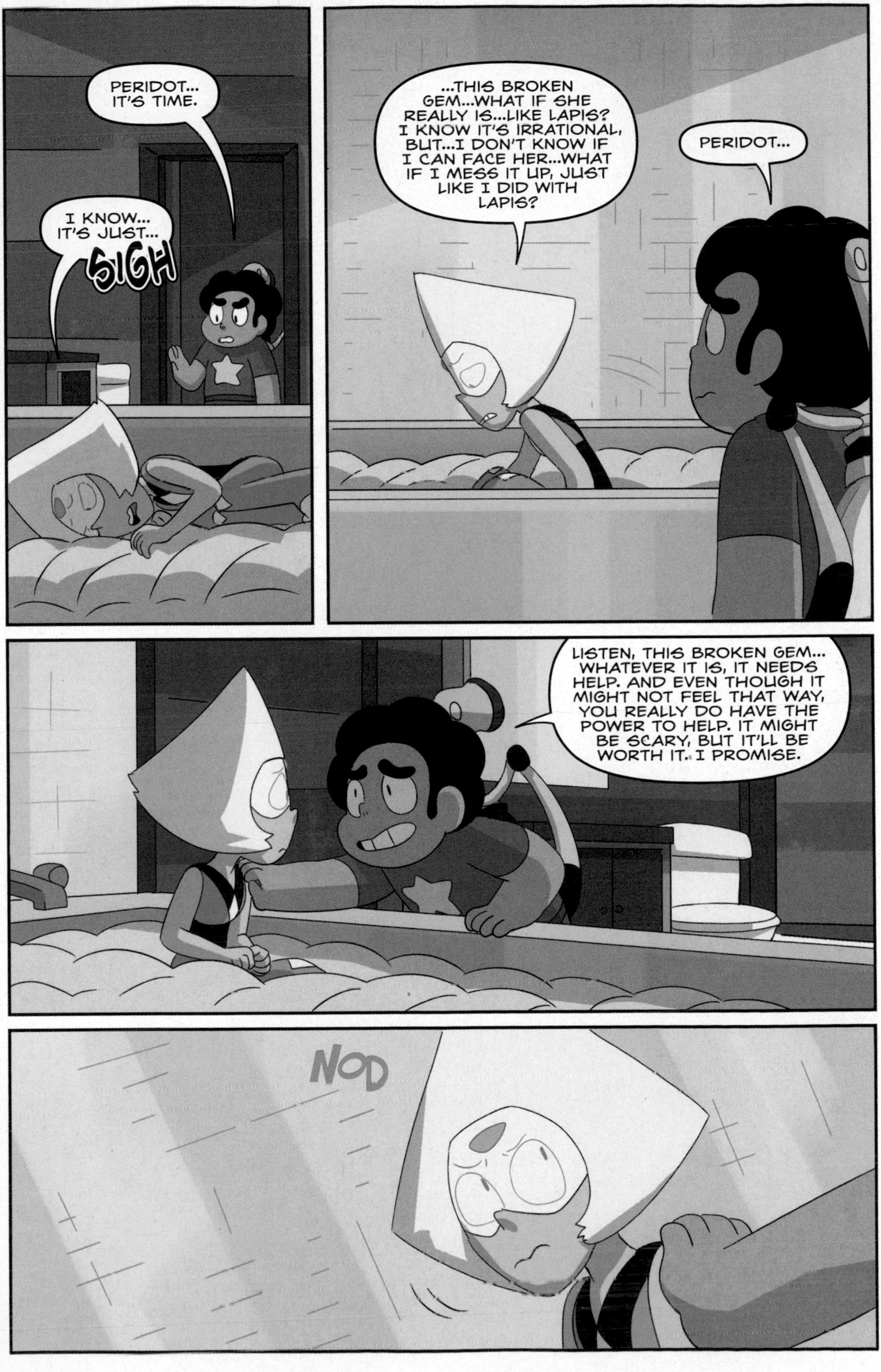
PERIDOT... IT'S TIME.
I KNOW... IT'S JUST...
SIGH
...THIS BROKEN GEM...WHAT IF SHE REALLY IS...LIKE LAPIS? I KNOW IT'S IRRATIONAL, BUT...I DON'T KNOW IF I CAN FACE HER...WHAT IF I MESS IT UP, JUST LIKE I DID WITH LAPIS?
PERIDOT...
LISTEN, THIS BROKEN GEM... WHATEVER IT IS, IT NEEDS HELP. AND EVEN THOUGH IT MIGHT NOT FEEL THAT WAY, YOU REALLY DO HAVE THE POWER TO HELP. IT MIGHT BE SCARY, BUT IT'LL BE WORTH IT. I PROMISE.
NOD

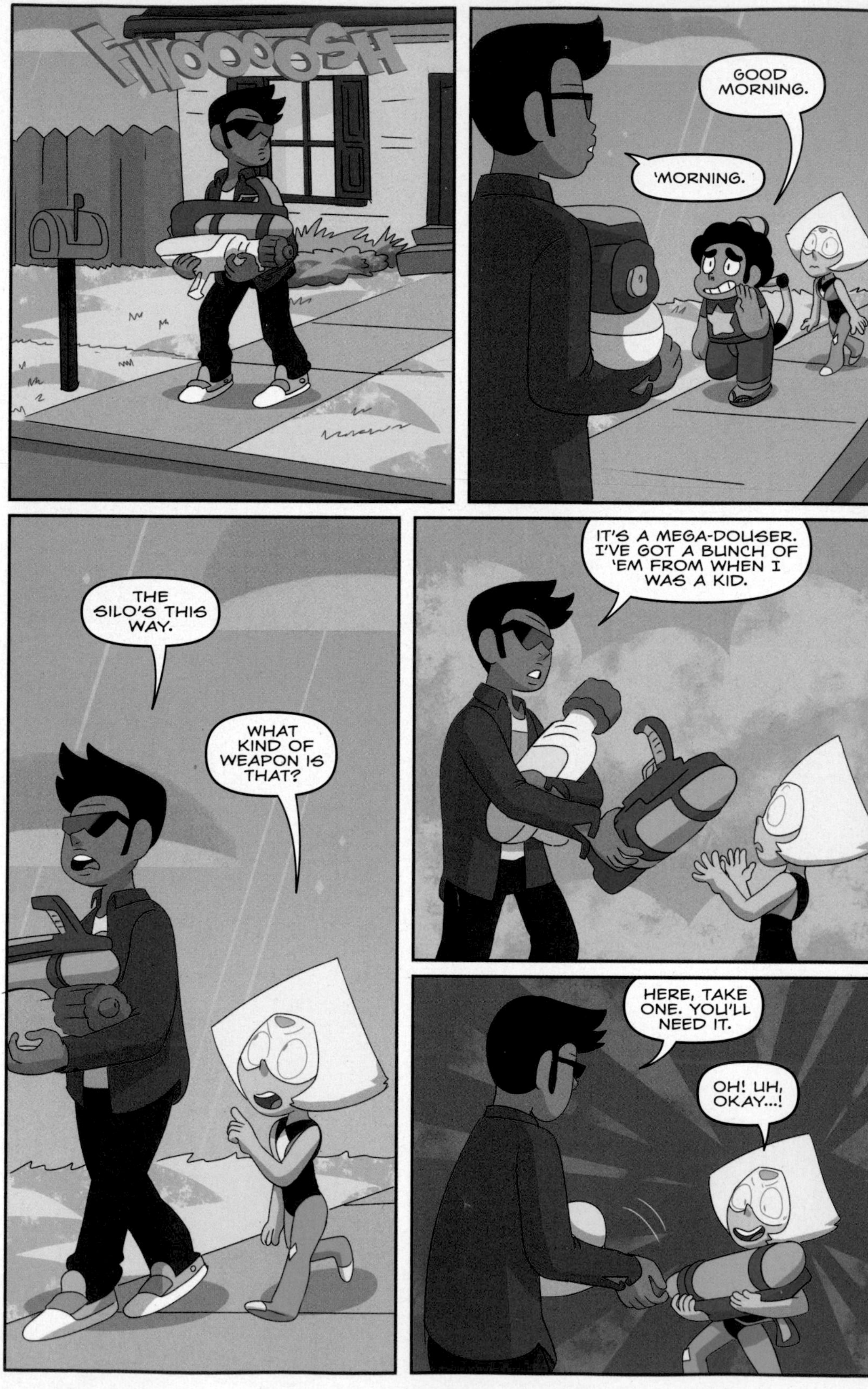
FWOOOOSH
GOOD MORNING.
'MORNING.
THE SILO'S THIS WAY.
WHAT KIND OF WEAPON IS THAT?
IT'S A MEGA-DOUSER. I'VE GOT A BUNCH OF 'EM FROM WHEN I WAS A KID.
HERE, TAKE ONE. YOU'LL NEED IT.
OH! UH, OKAY...!

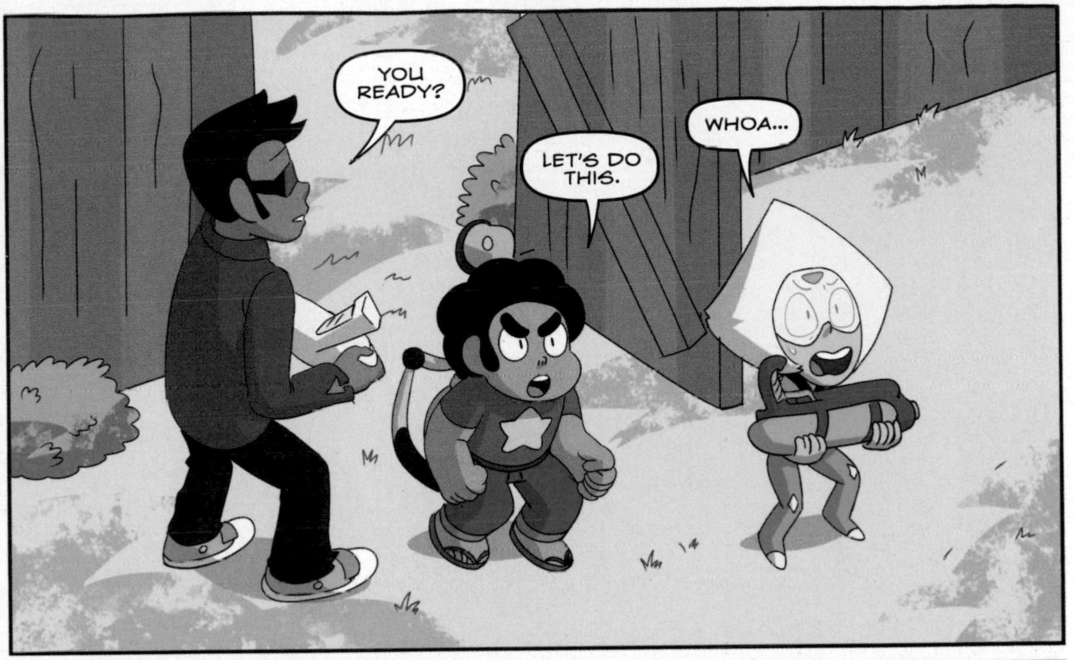
YOU READY?
LET'S DO THIS.
WHOA...

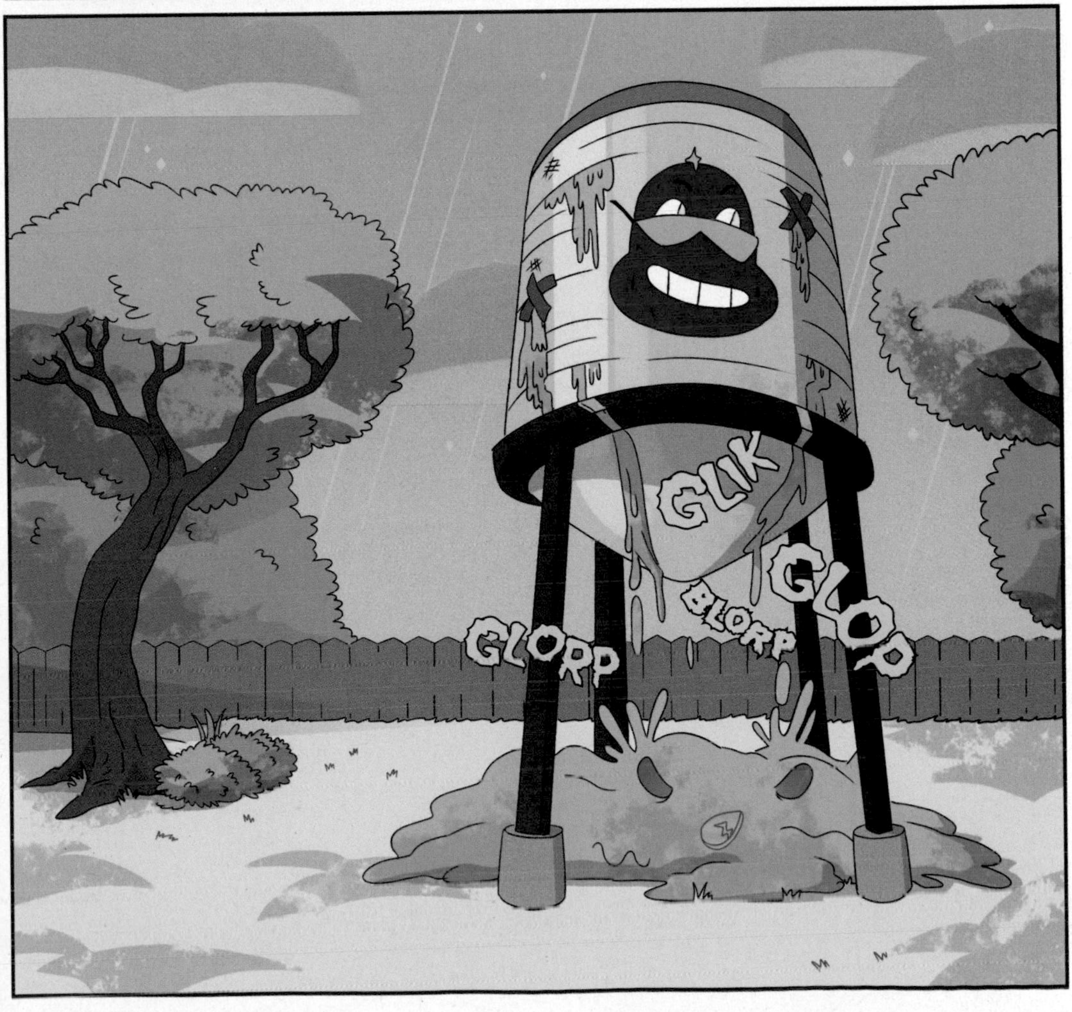
GLIK
GLOP
BLORP
GLORP

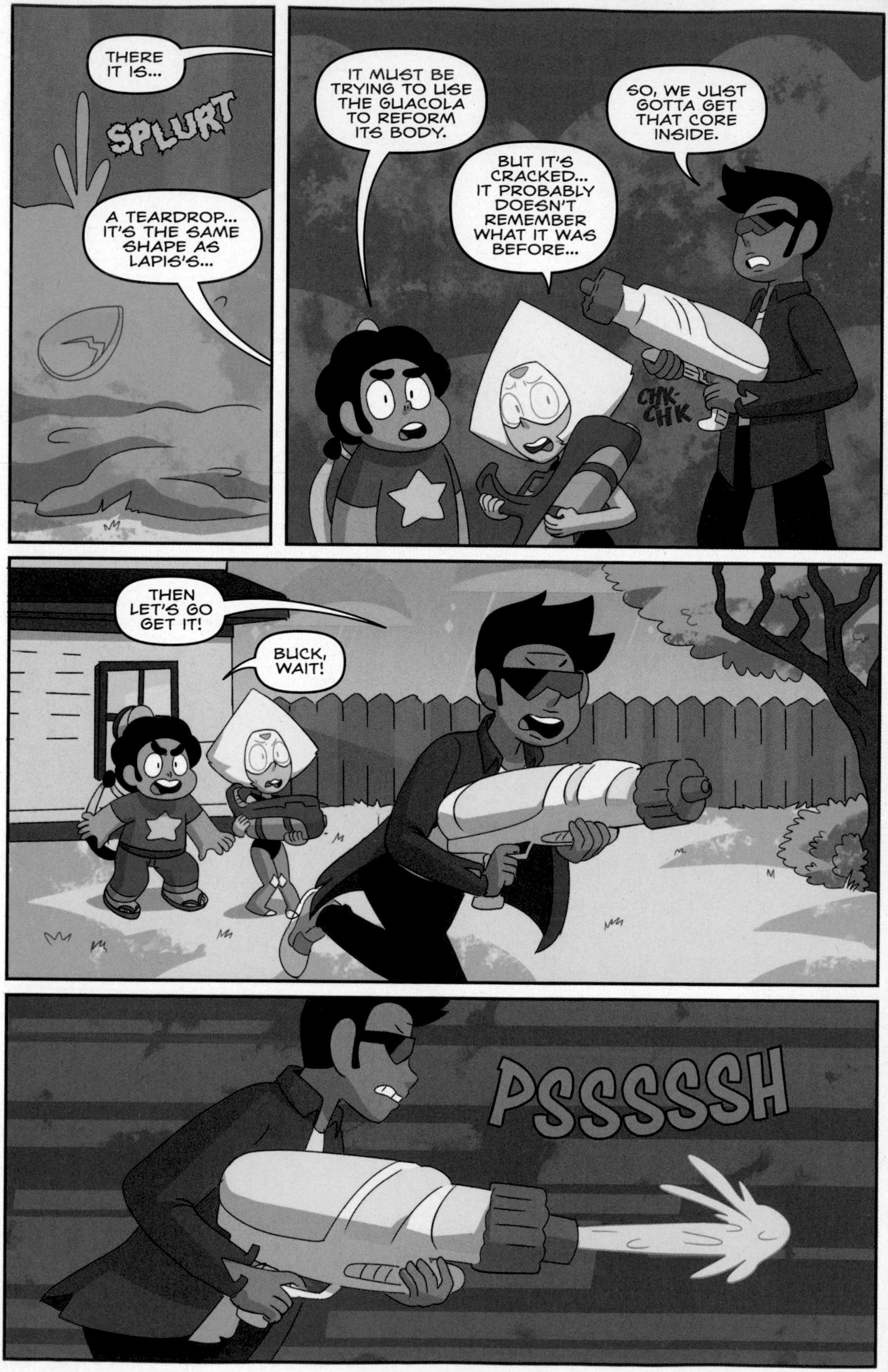
THERE IT IS...
SPLURT
A TEARDROP... IT'S THE SAME SHAPE AS LAPIS'S...
IT MUST BE TRYING TO USE THE GUACOLA TO REFORM ITS BODY.
BUT IT'S CRACKED... IT PROBABLY DOESN'T REMEMBER WHAT IT WAS BEFORE...
SO, WE JUST GOTTA GET THAT CORE INSIDE.
CHK-CHK
THEN LET'S GO GET IT!
BUCK, WAIT!
PSSSSSH

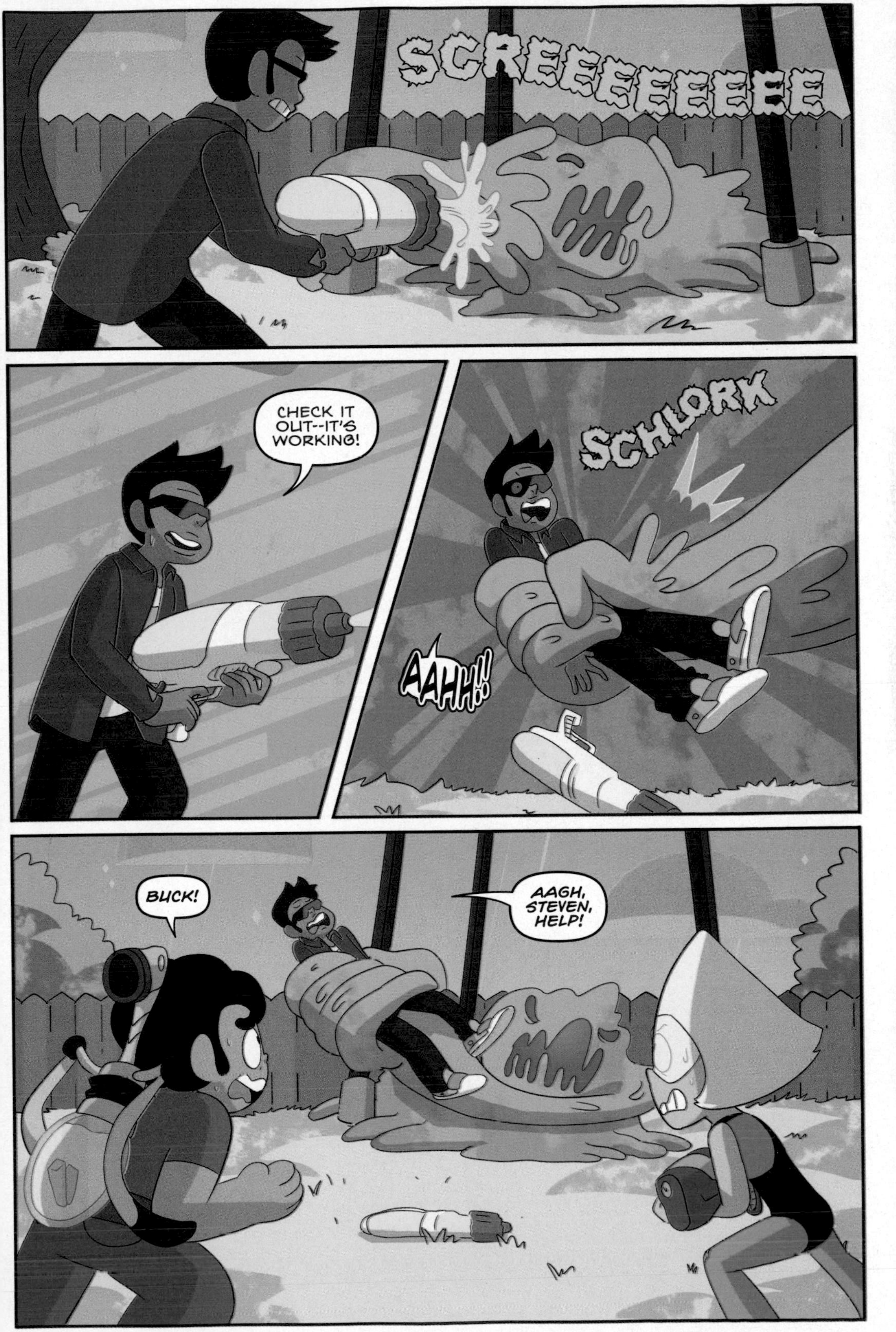
SCREEEEEEEEE
CHECK IT OUT--IT'S WORKING!
SCHLORK
AAHH!!
BUCK!
AAGH, STEVEN, HELP!

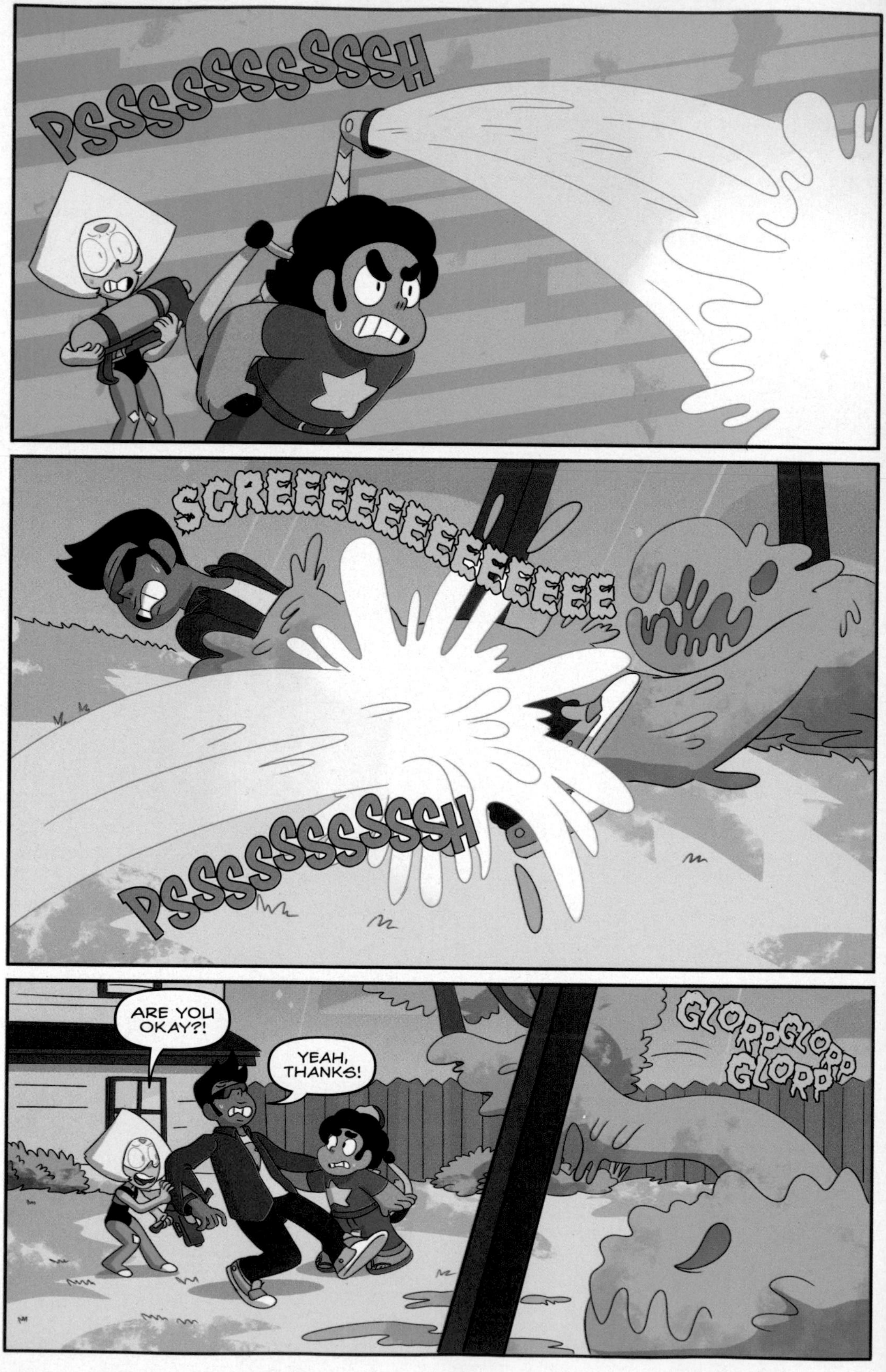
PSSSSSSSSSH
SCREEEEEEEEEEEEEE
PSSSSSSSSSH
ARE YOU OKAY?!
YEAH, THANKS!
GLORPGLORP GLORP

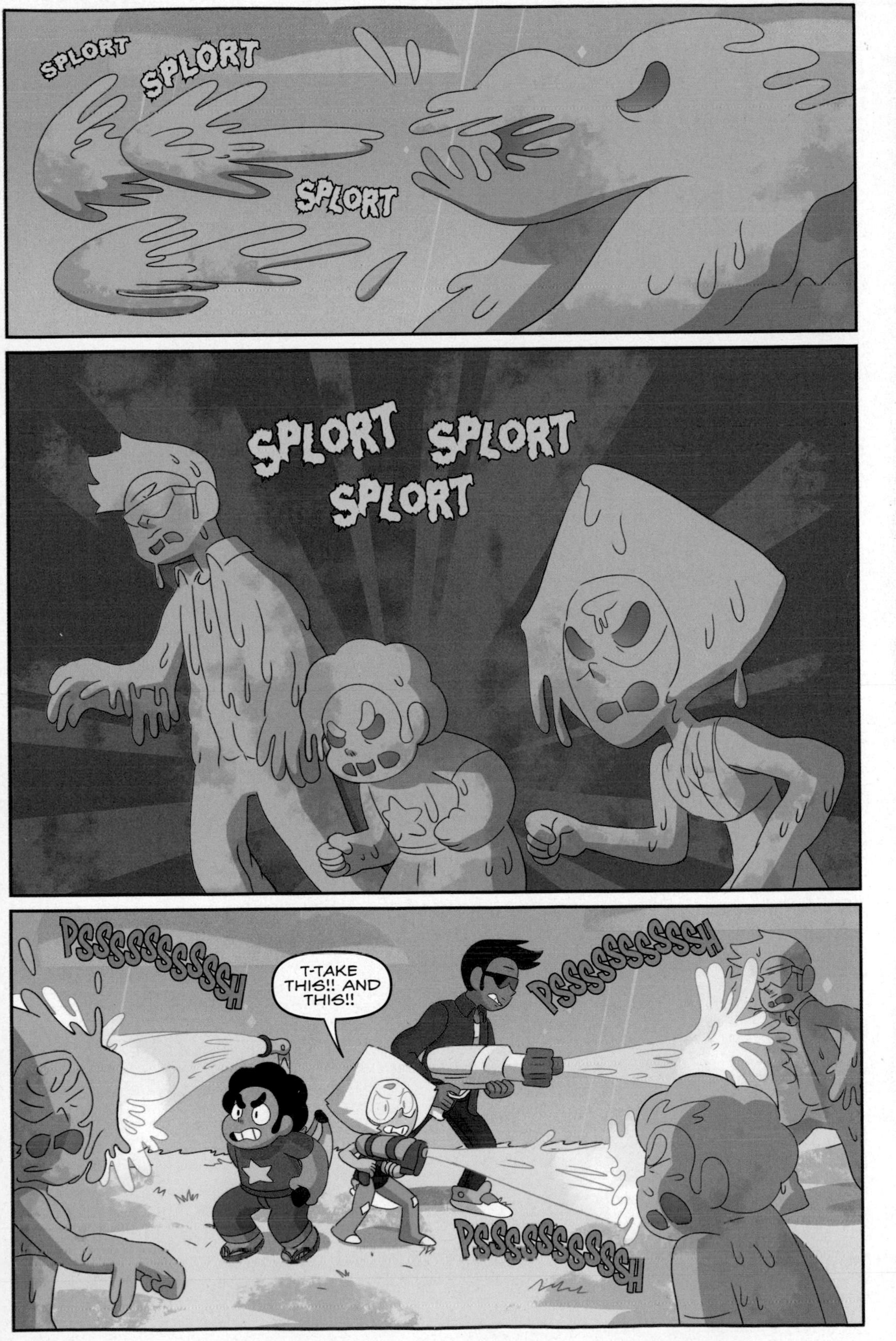
SPLORT
SPLORT
SPLORT
SPLORT SPLORT
SPLORT
PSSSSSSSSSSH
T-TAKE THIS!! AND THIS!!
PSSSSSSSSSSH
PSSSSSSSSSSH

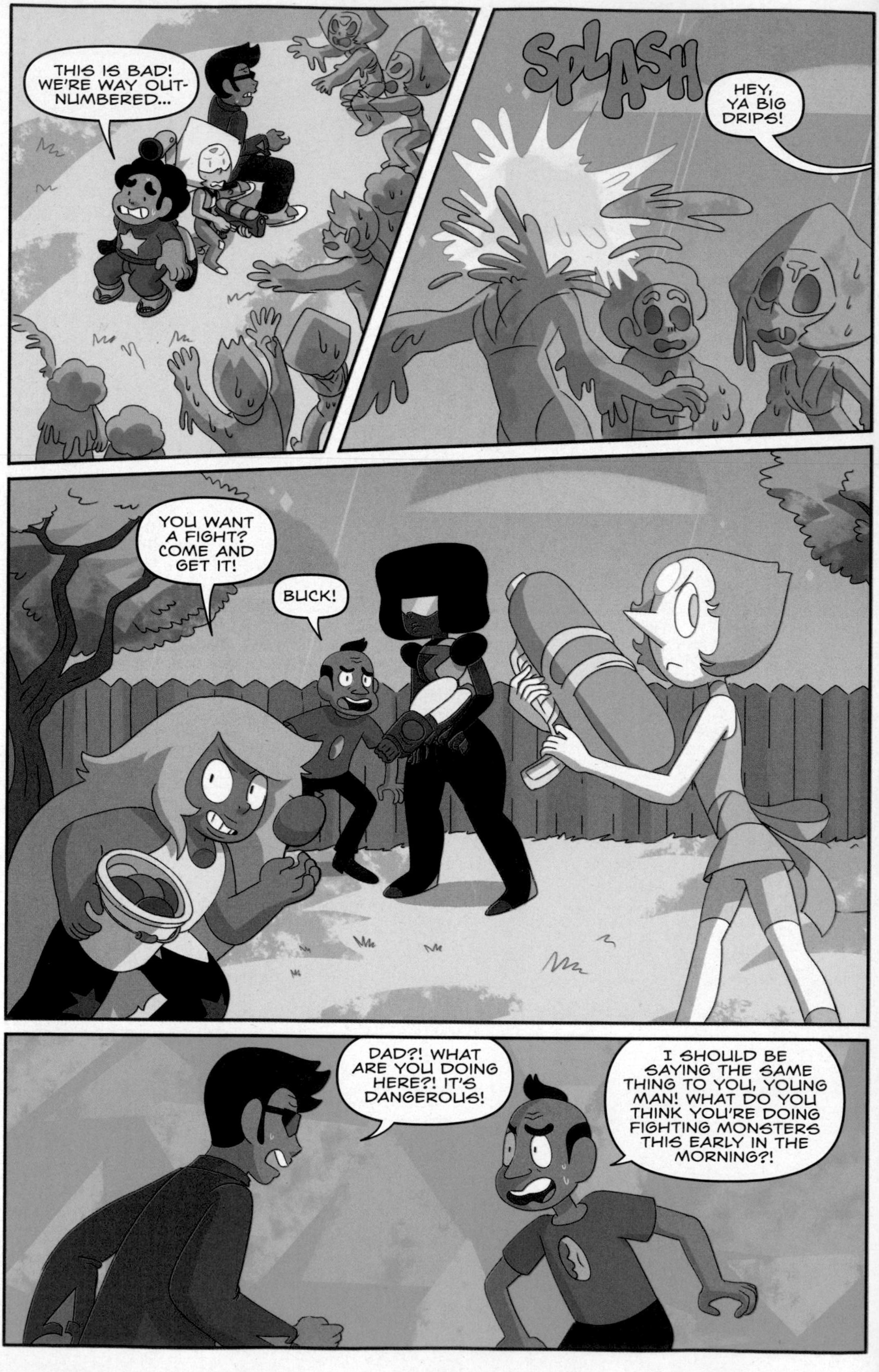
THIS IS BAD! WE'RE WAY OUT-NUMBERED...
SPLASH
HEY, YA BIG DRIPS!
YOU WANT A FIGHT? COME AND GET IT!
BUCK!
DAD?! WHAT ARE YOU DOING HERE?! IT'S DANGEROUS!
I SHOULD BE SAYING THE SAME THING TO YOU, YOUNG MAN! WHAT DO YOU THINK YOU'RE DOING FIGHTING MONSTERS THIS EARLY IN THE MORNING?!

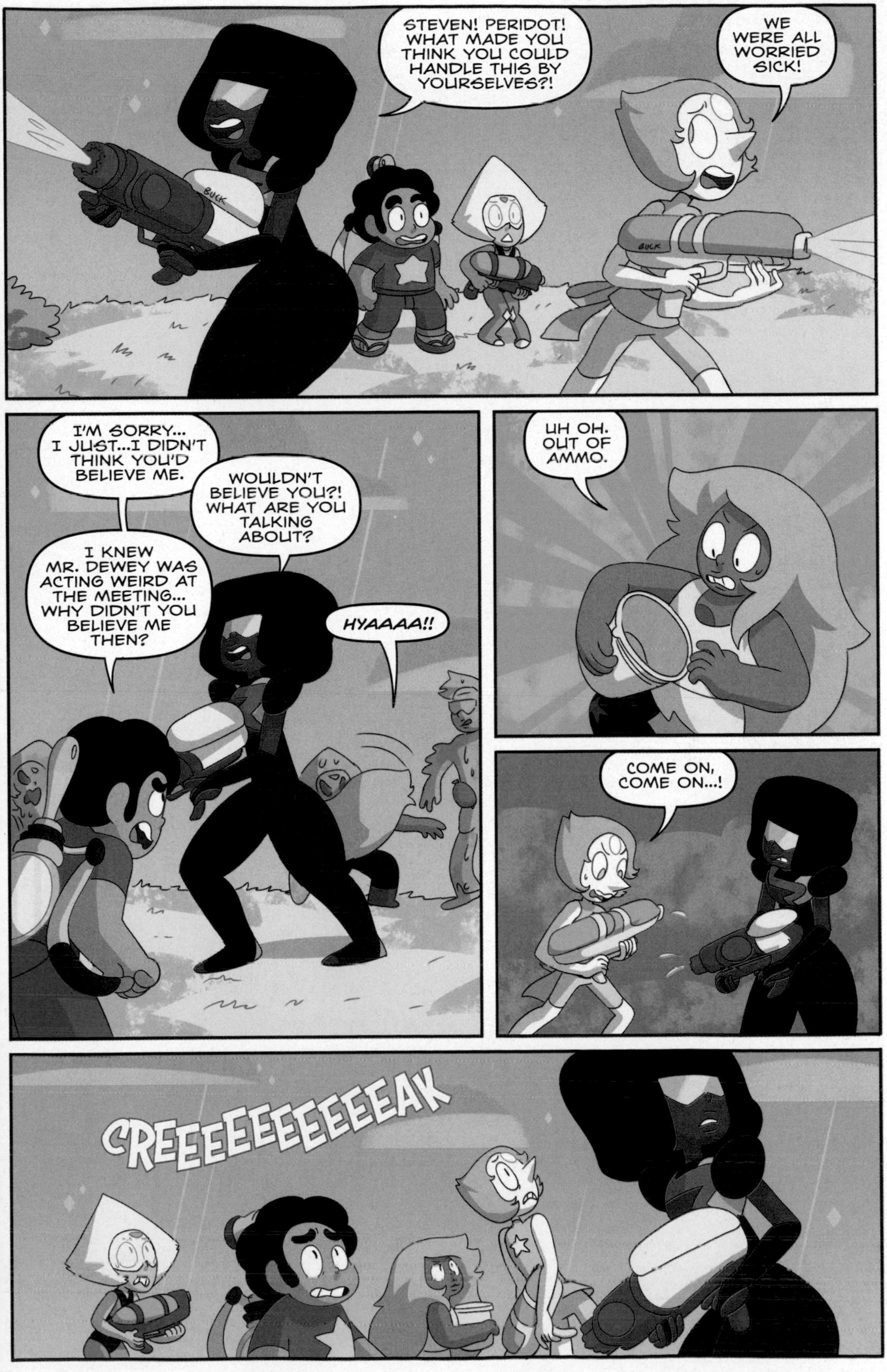
STEVEN! PERIDOT! WHAT MADE YOU THINK YOU COULD HANDLE THIS BY YOURSELVES?!
WE WERE ALL WORRIED SICK!
BUCK
BUCK
I'M SORRY... I JUST...I DIDN'T THINK YOU'D BELIEVE ME.
WOULDN'T BELIEVE YOU?! WHAT ARE YOU TALKING ABOUT?
I KNEW MR. DEWEY WAS ACTING WEIRD AT THE MEETING... WHY DIDN'T YOU BELIEVE ME THEN?
HYAAAA!!
UH OH. OUT OF AMMO.
COME ON, COME ON...!
CREEEEEEEEEEEAK

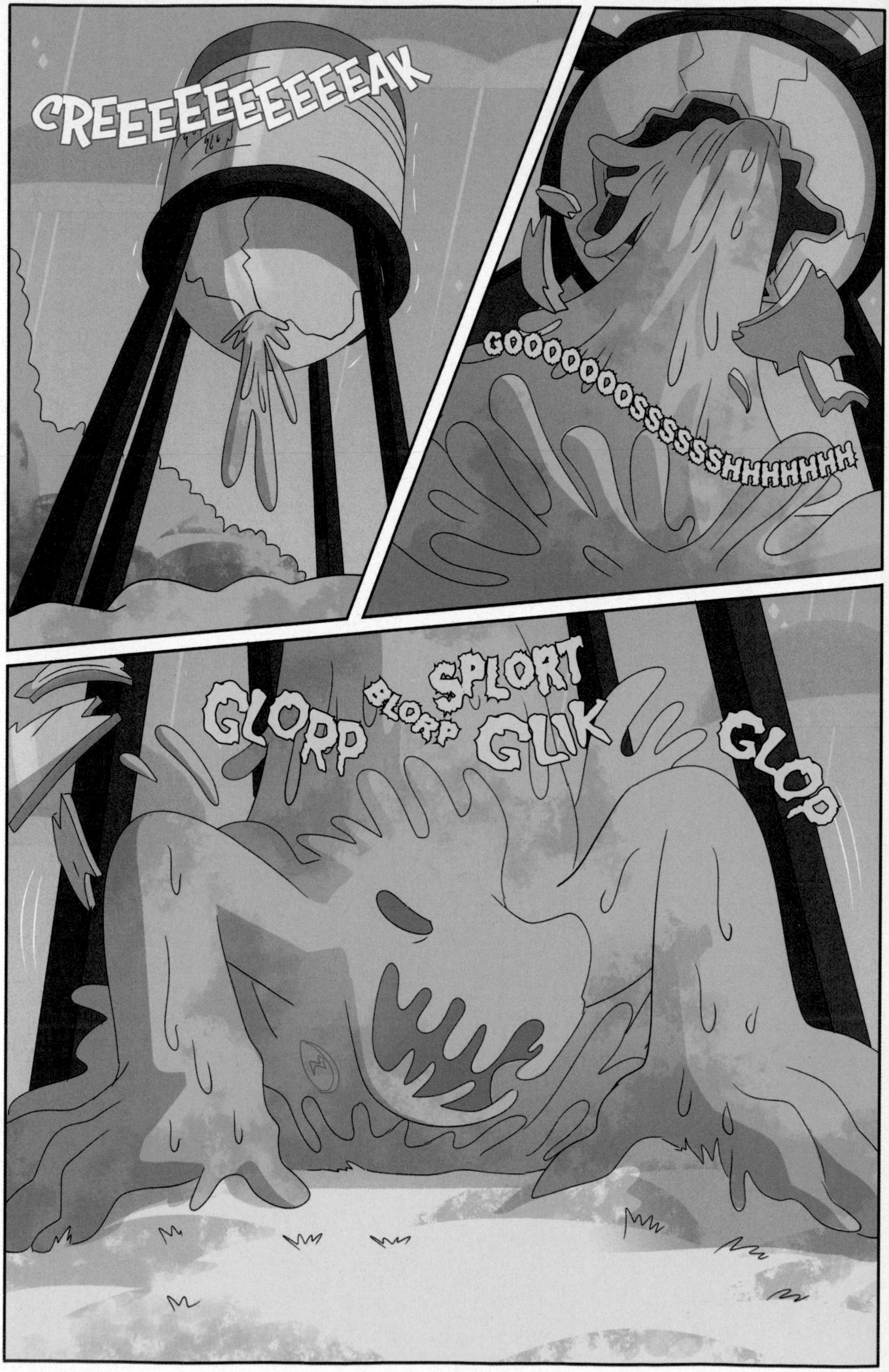
CREEEEEEEEEEEAK
GOOOOOOOOSSSSSSSHHHHHHH
GLORP
BLORP
SPLORT
GLIK
GLOP

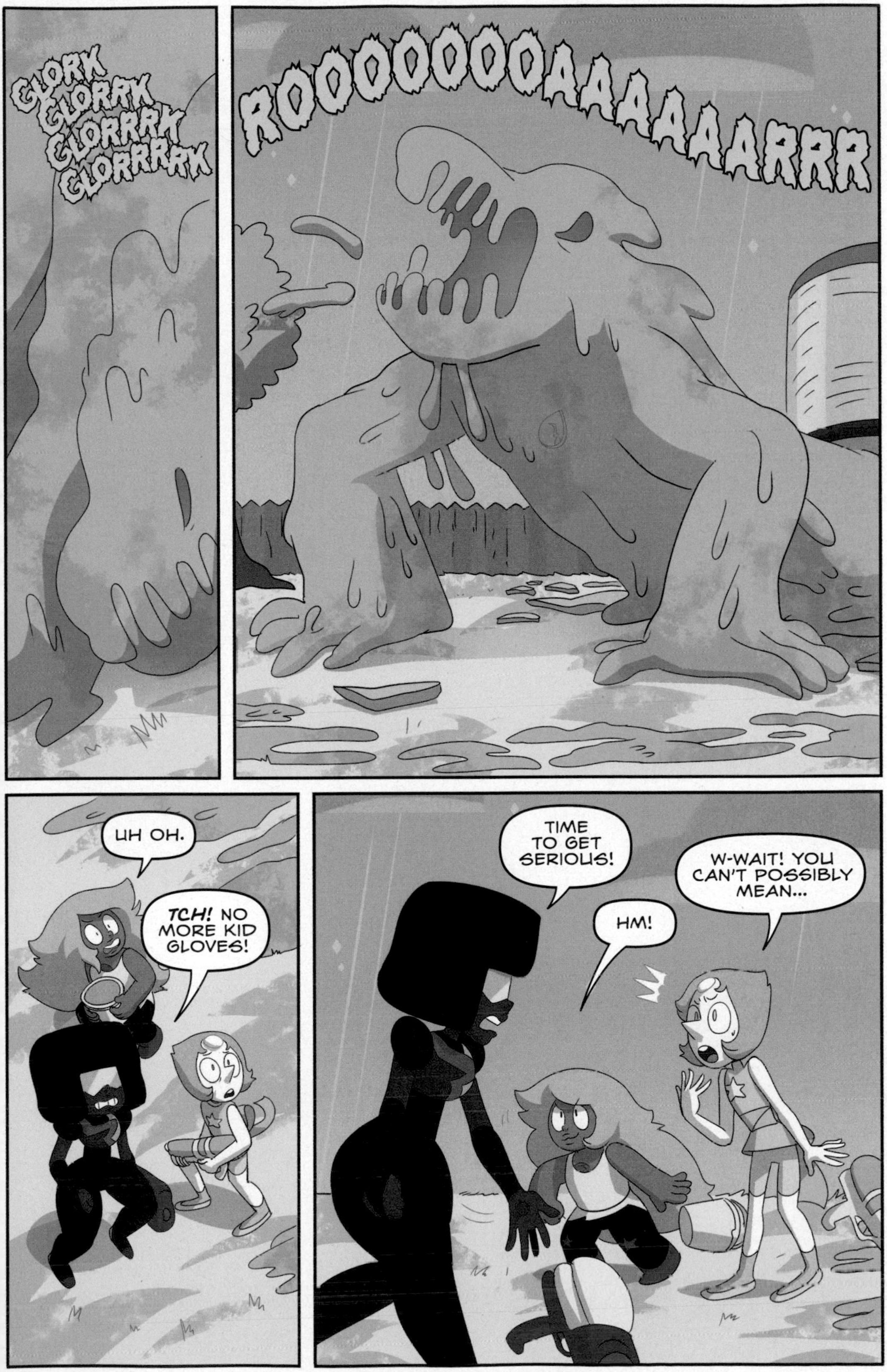
GLORK GLORRK GLORRRK GLORRRRK
ROOOOOOOAAAAAAARRRR
UH OH.
TCH! NO MORE KID GLOVES!
TIME TO GET SERIOUS!
HM!
W-WAIT! YOU CAN'T POSSIBLY MEAN...

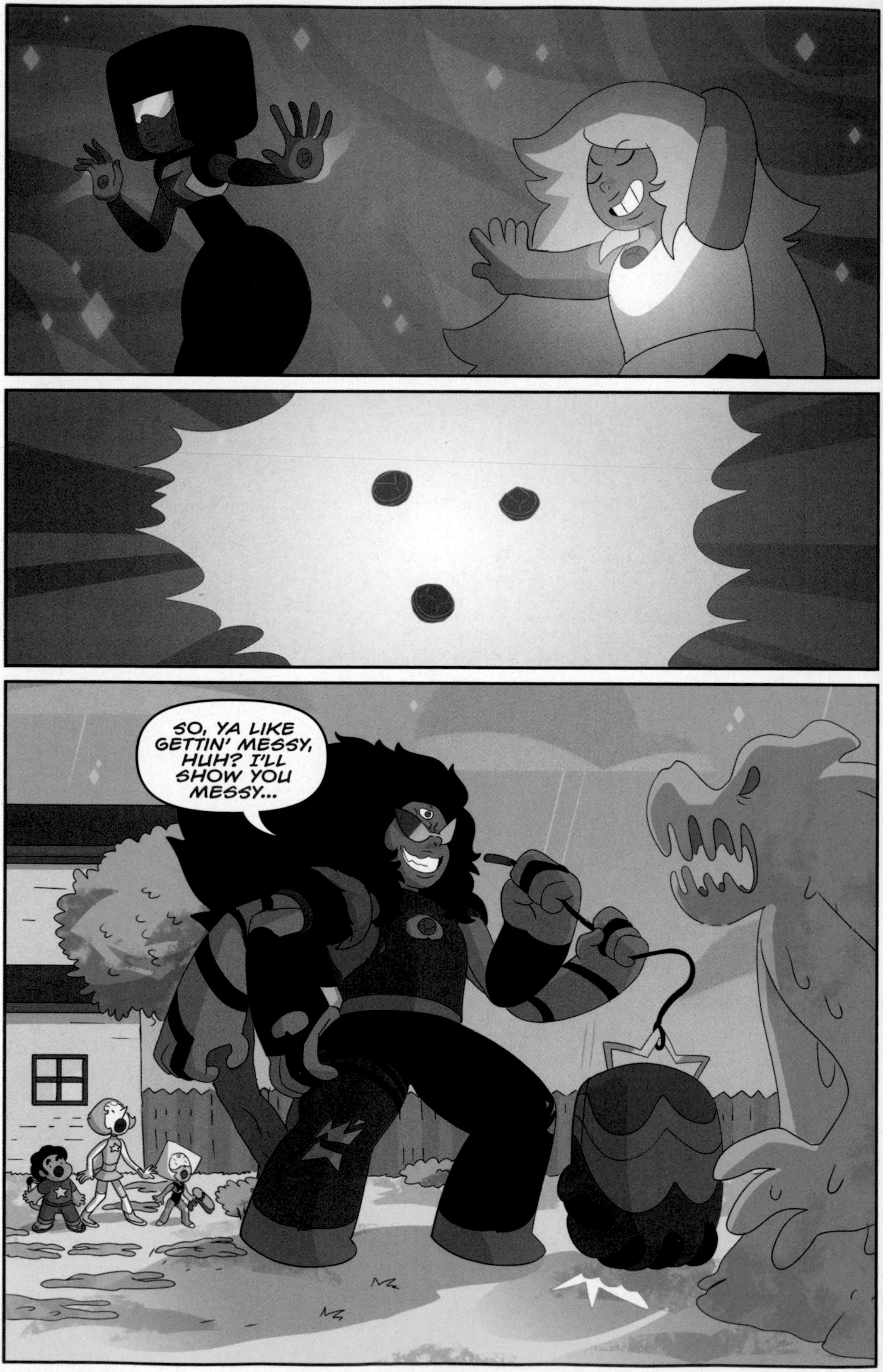
SO, YA LIKE GETTIN' MESSY, HUH? I'LL SHOW YOU MESSY...

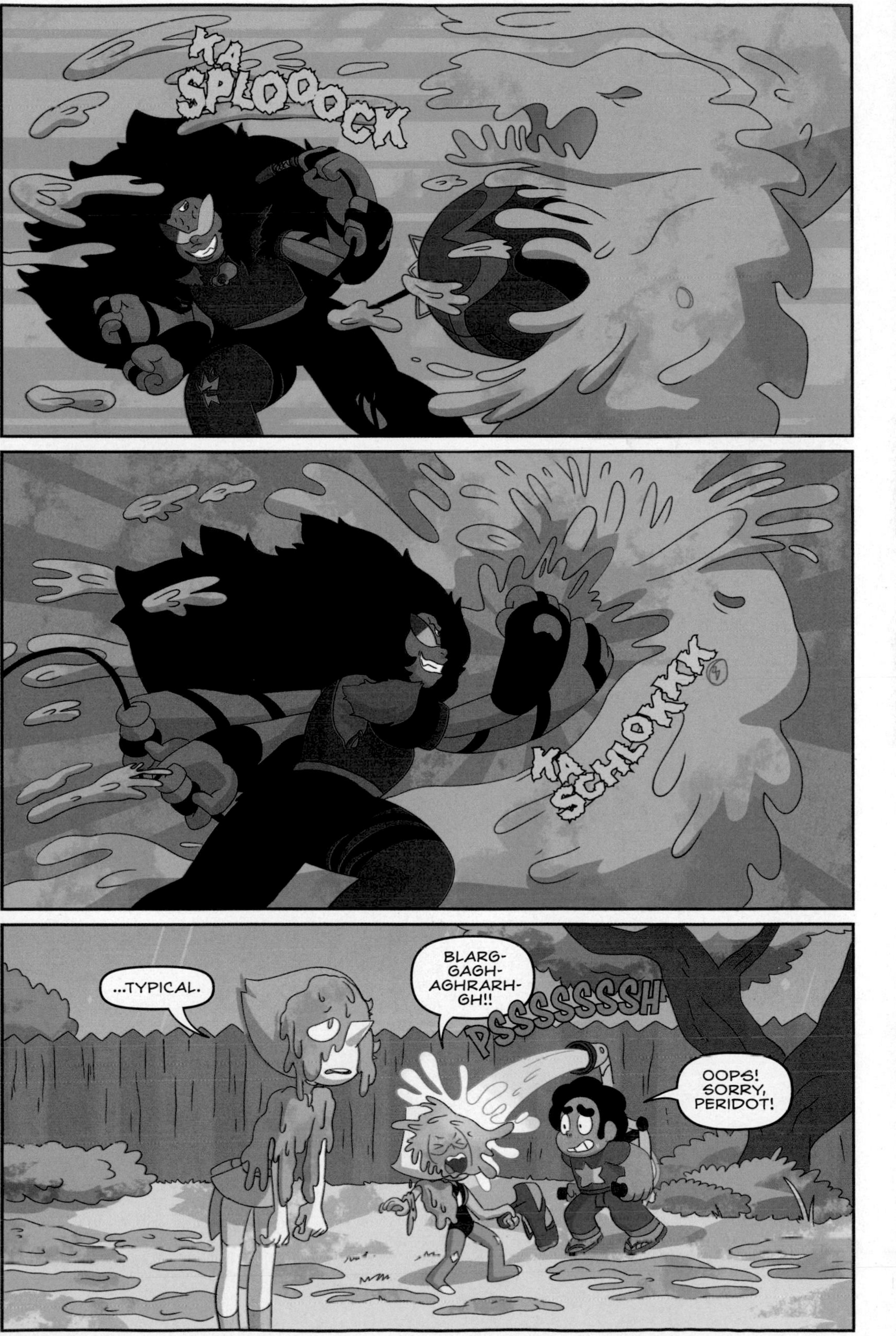
KA
SPLOOOCK
KA
SCHLOKKK
...TYPICAL.
BLARG-
GAGH-
AGHRARH-
GH!!
PSSSSSSSH
OOPS!
SORRY,
PERIDOT!

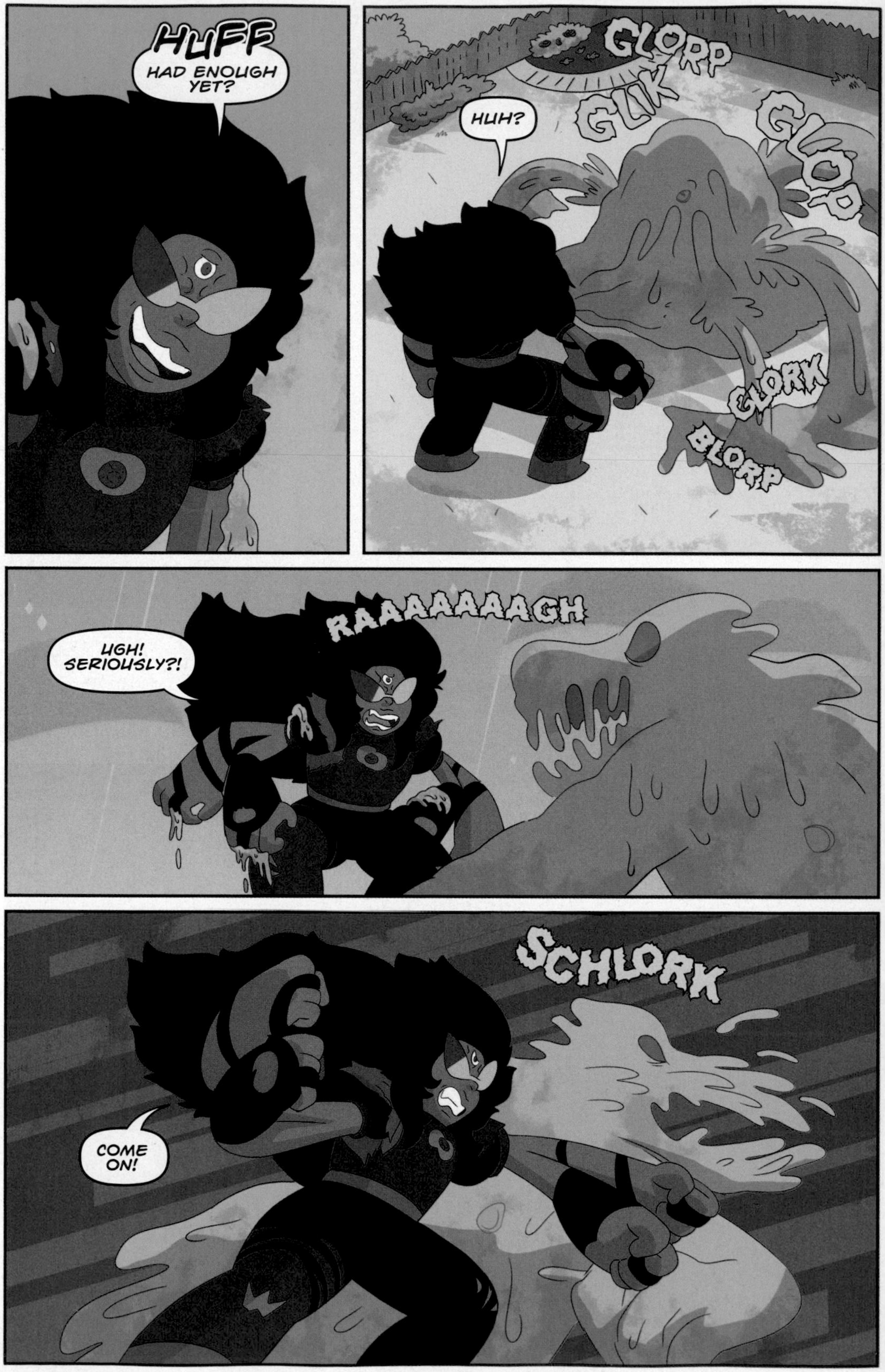
HUFF
HAD ENOUGH YET?
GLORP
GLIK
HUH?
GLOP
GLORK
BLORP
RAAAAAAAAGH
UGH! SERIOUSLY?!
SCHLORK
COME ON!

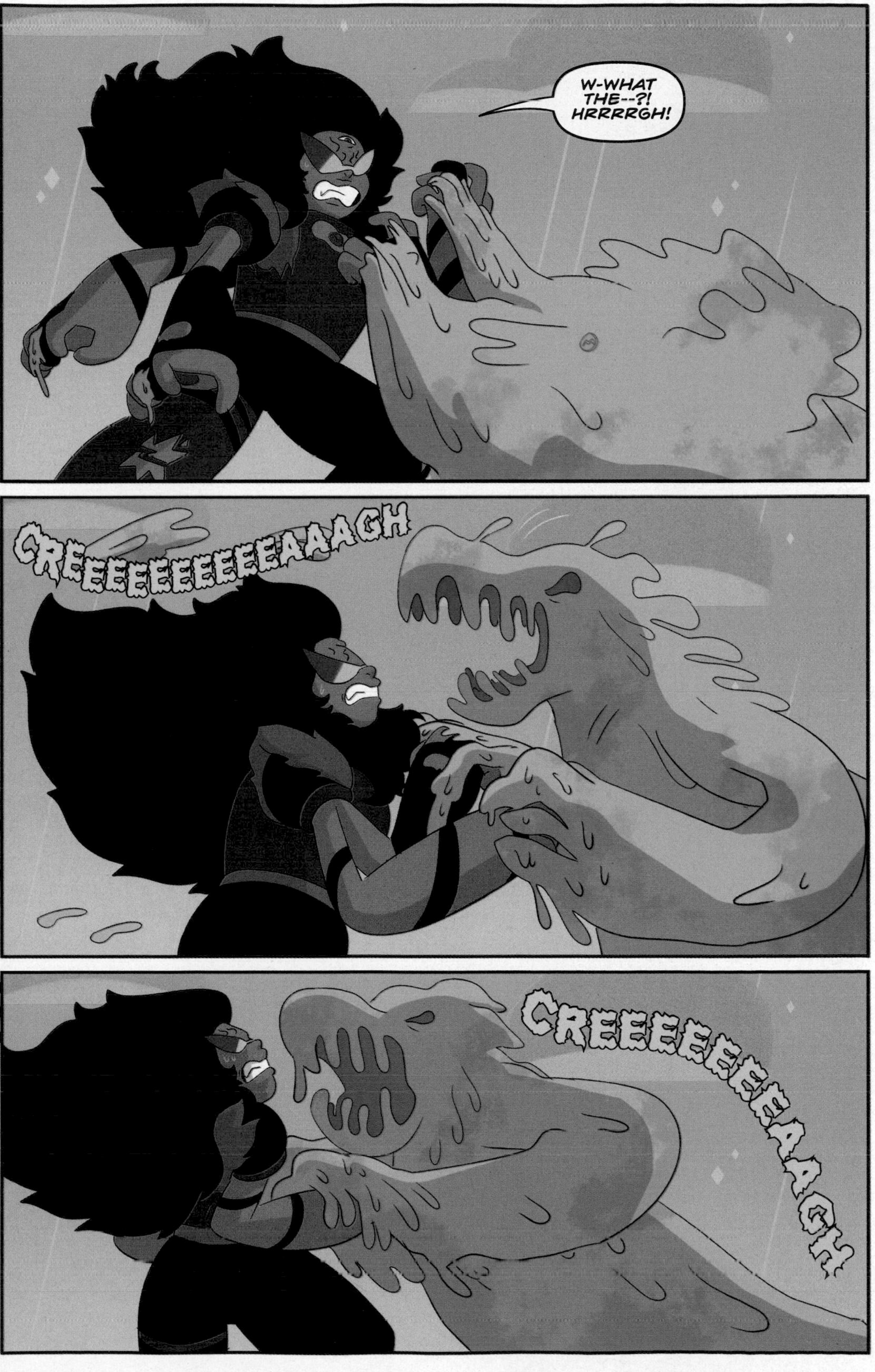
W-WHAT THE--?! HRRRRGH!
CREEEEEEEEEEAAAGH
CREEEEEEEEEAAGH

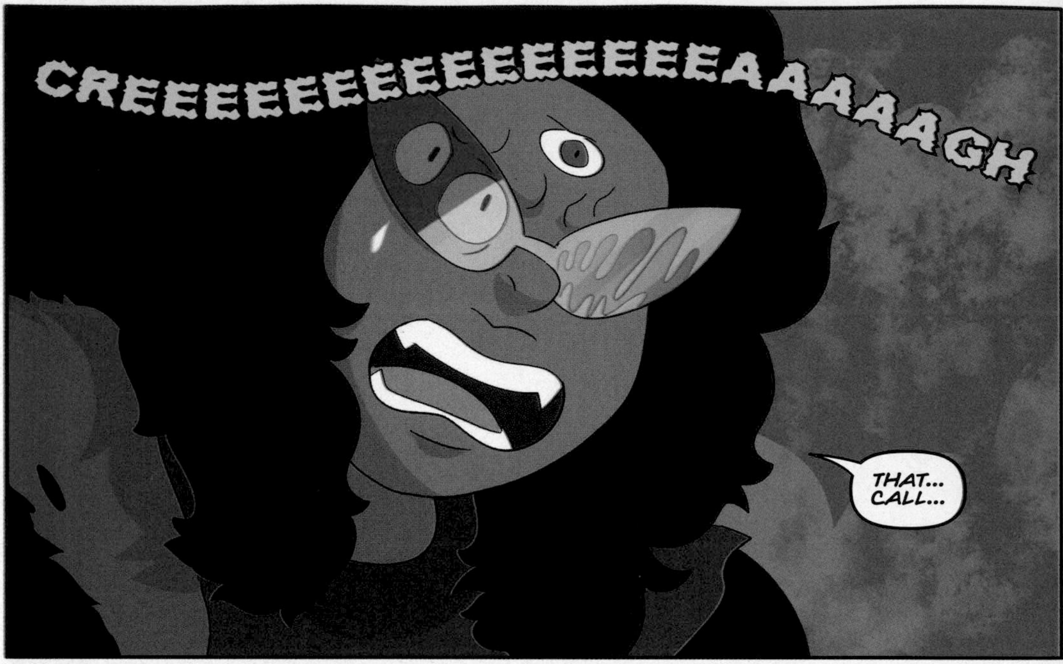
CREEEEEEEEEEEEEEAAAAAGH
THAT... CALL...

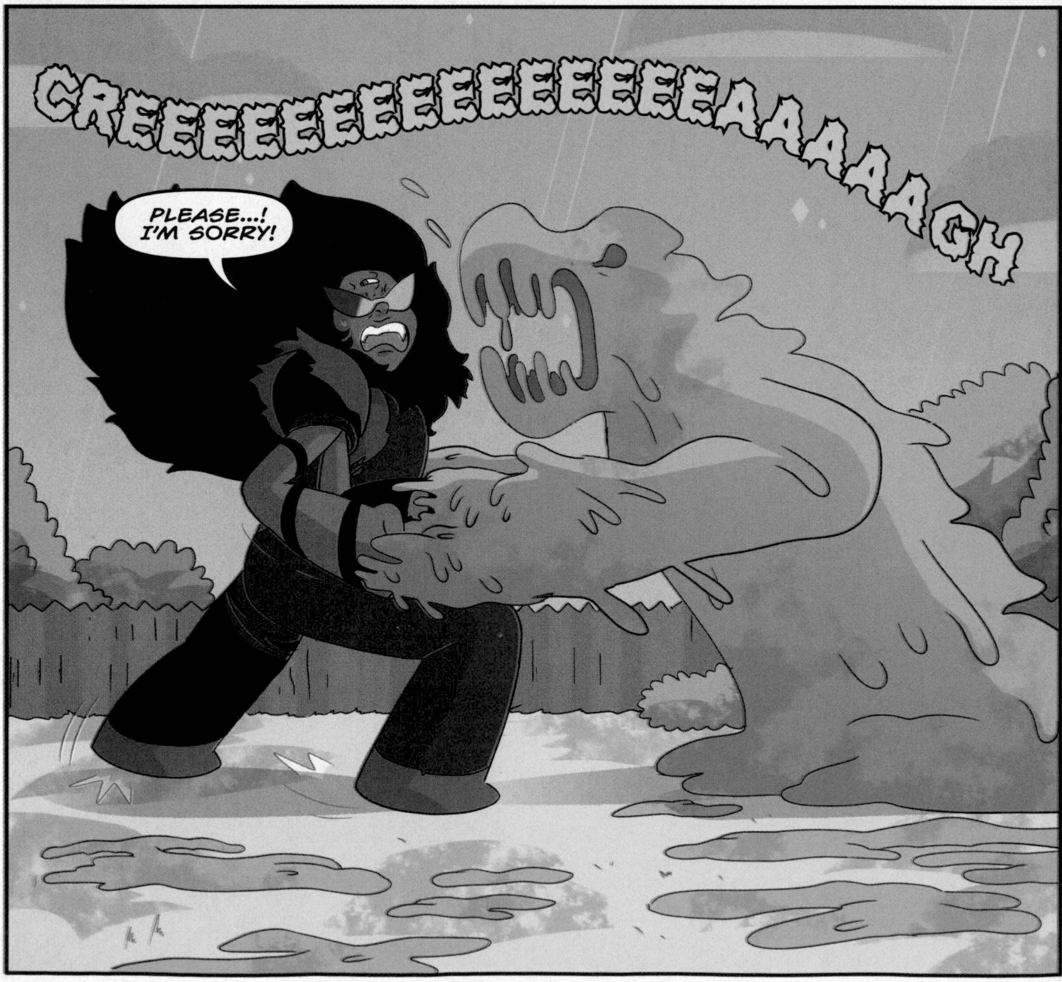
CREEEEEEEEEEEEEEEAAAAAAGH
PLEASE...! I'M SORRY!

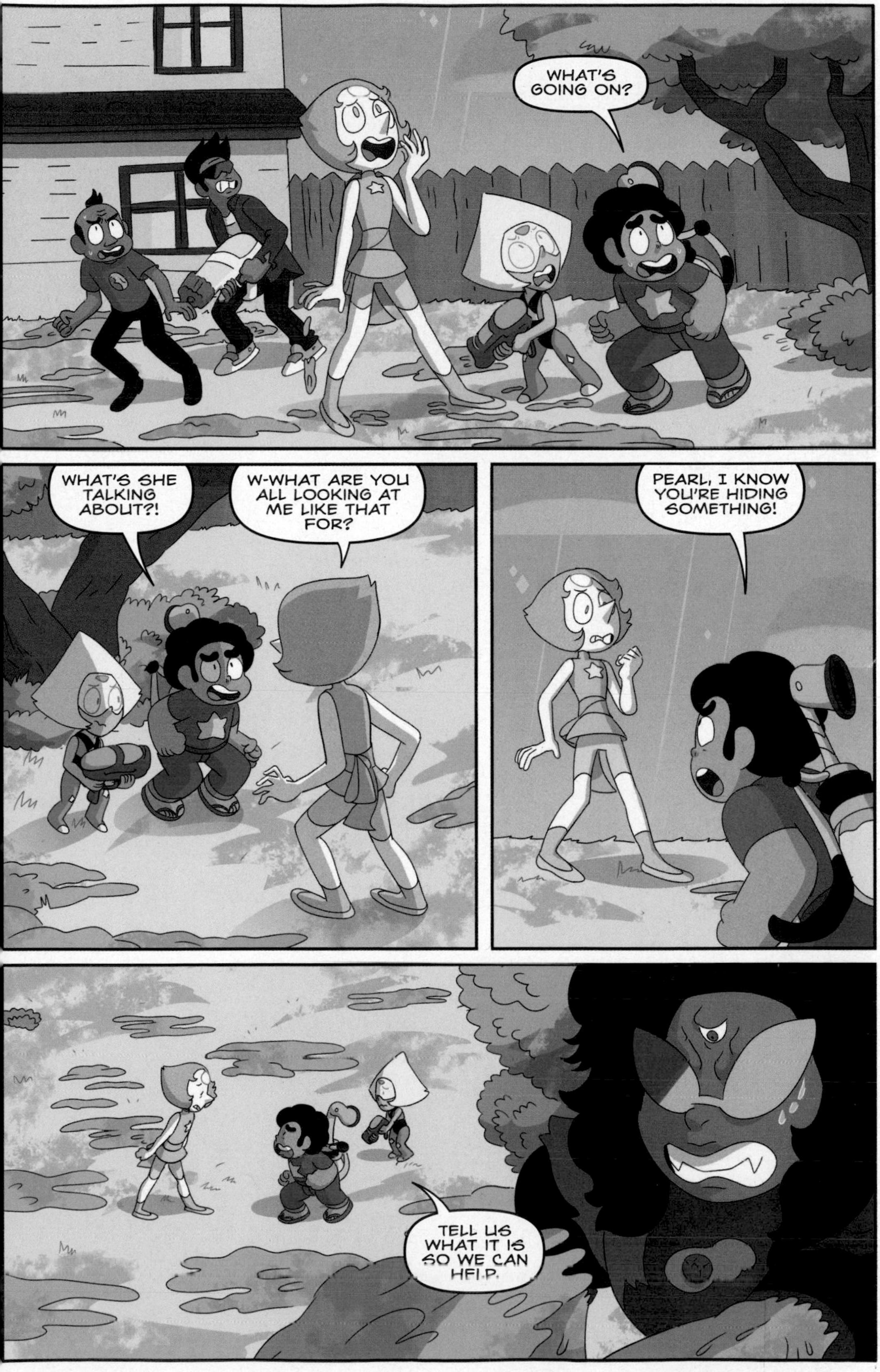
WHAT'S GOING ON?
WHAT'S SHE TALKING ABOUT?!
W-WHAT ARE YOU ALL LOOKING AT ME LIKE THAT FOR?
PEARL, I KNOW YOU'RE HIDING SOMETHING!
TELL US WHAT IT IS SO WE CAN HELP.

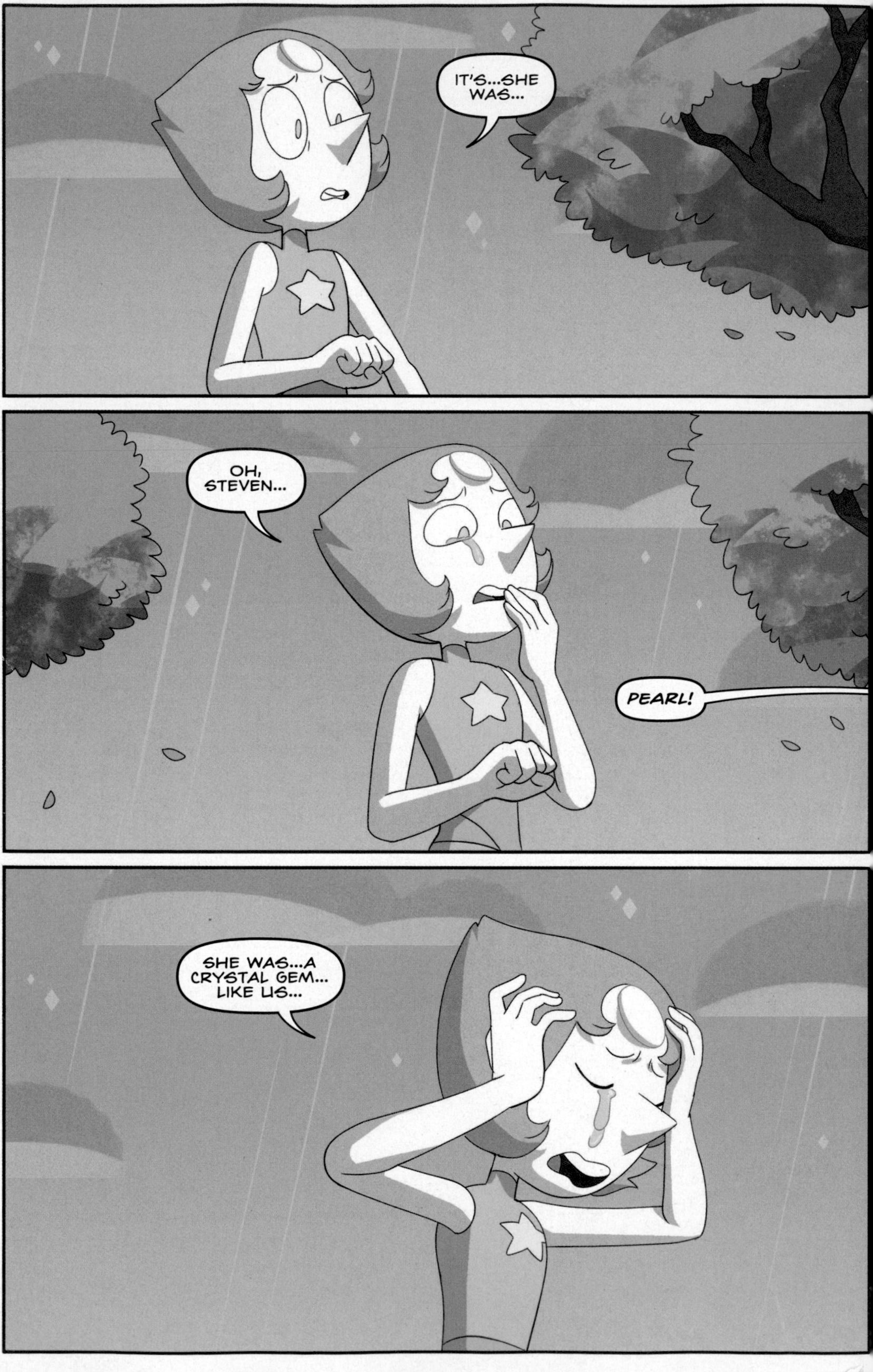
IT'S...SHE WAS...
OH, STEVEN...
PEARL!
SHE WAS...A CRYSTAL GEM... LIKE US...

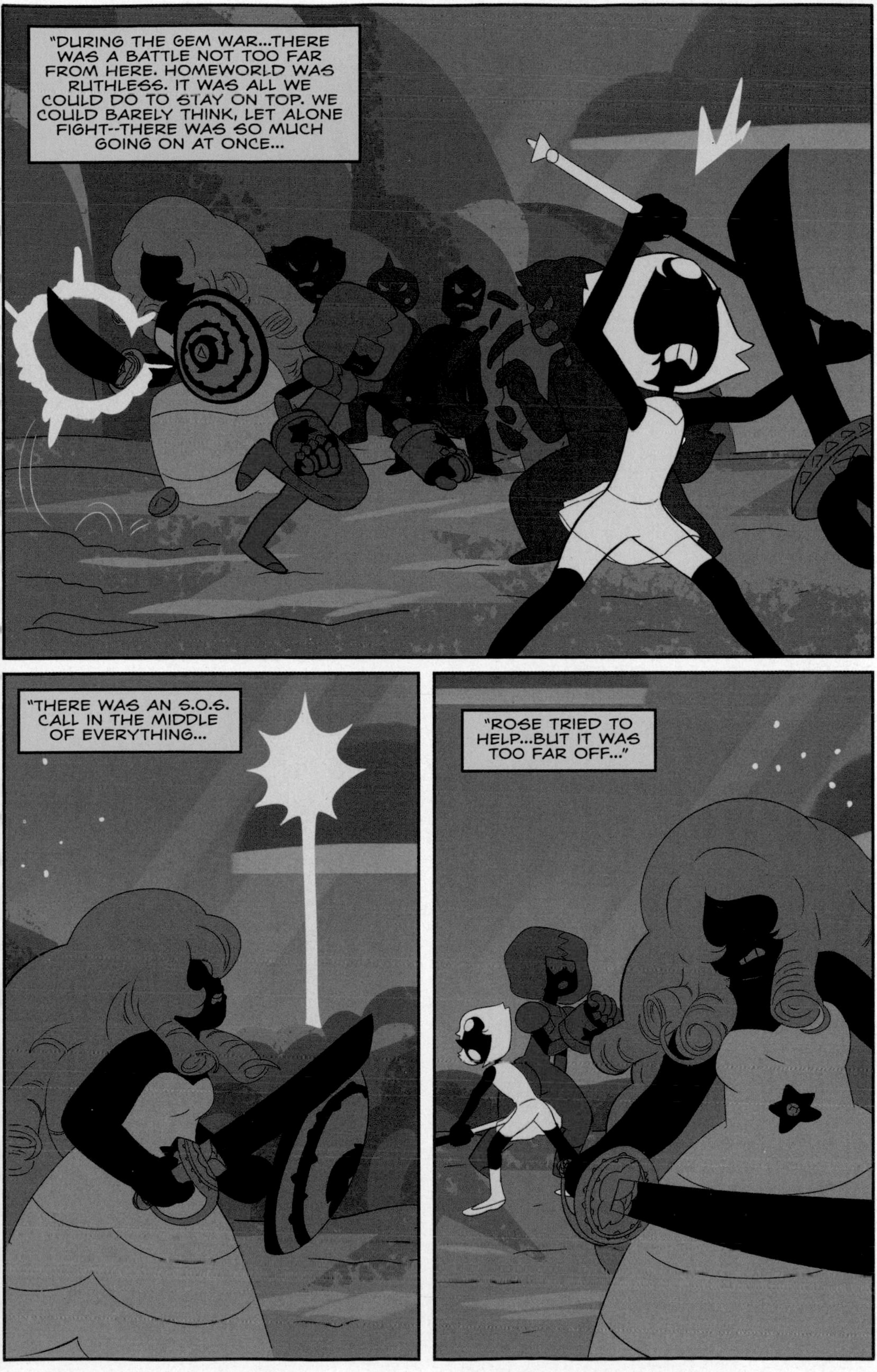
"DURING THE GEM WAR...THERE WAS A BATTLE NOT TOO FAR FROM HERE. HOMEWORLD WAS RUTHLESS. IT WAS ALL WE COULD DO TO STAY ON TOP. WE COULD BARELY THINK, LET ALONE FIGHT--THERE WAS SO MUCH GOING ON AT ONCE...
"THERE WAS AN S.O.S. CALL IN THE MIDDLE OF EVERYTHING...
"ROSE TRIED TO HELP...BUT IT WAS TOO FAR OFF..."

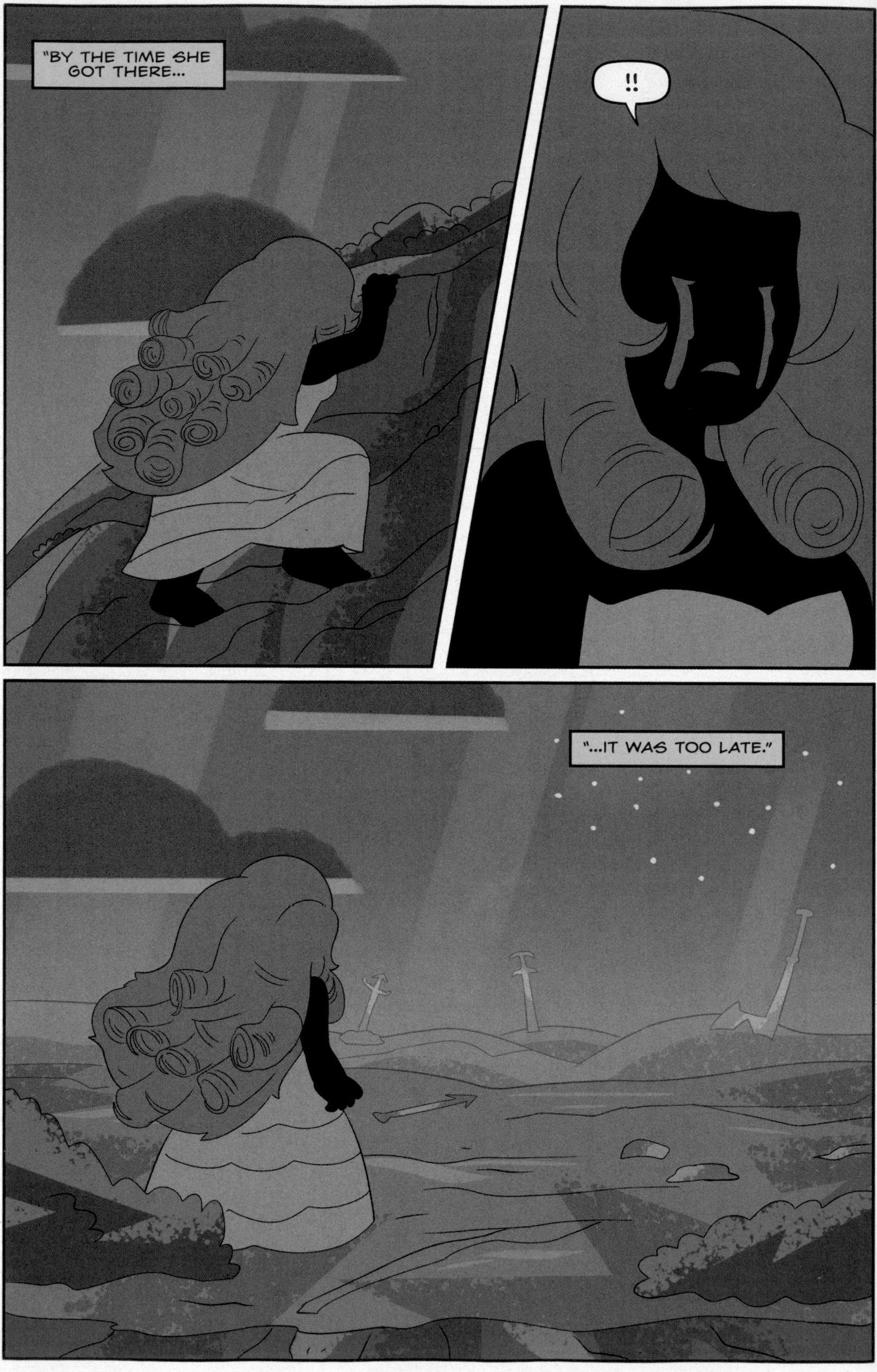
"BY THE TIME SHE GOT THERE...
!!
"...IT WAS TOO LATE."

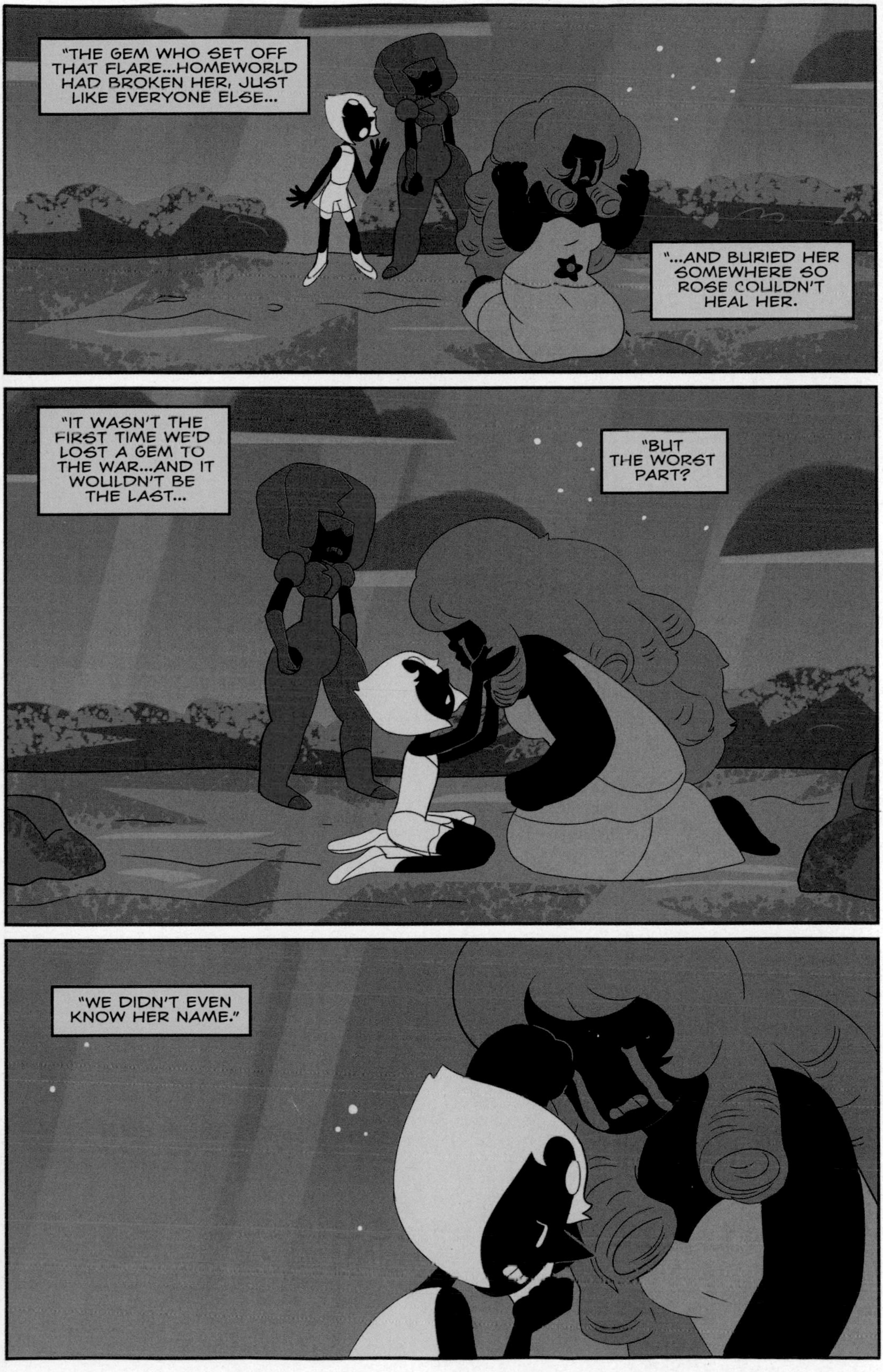
"THE GEM WHO SET OFF THAT FLARE...HOMEWORLD HAD BROKEN HER, JUST LIKE EVERYONE ELSE...
"...AND BURIED HER SOMEWHERE SO ROSE COULDN'T HEAL HER.
"IT WASN'T THE FIRST TIME WE'D LOST A GEM TO THE WAR...AND IT WOULDN'T BE THE LAST...
"BUT THE WORST PART?
"WE DIDN'T EVEN KNOW HER NAME."

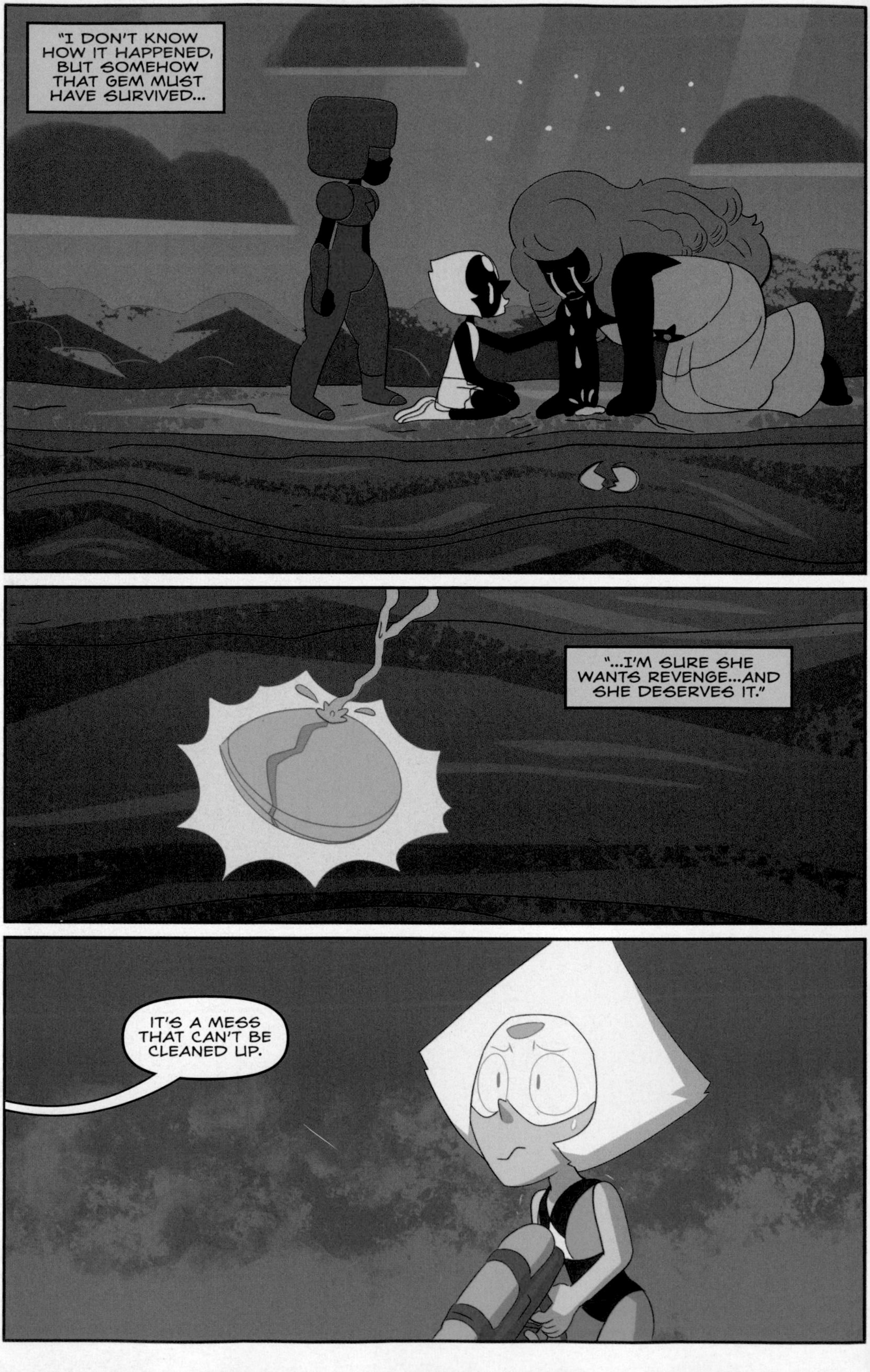
"I DON'T KNOW HOW IT HAPPENED, BUT SOMEHOW THAT GEM MUST HAVE SURVIVED...
"...I'M SURE SHE WANTS REVENGE...AND SHE DESERVES IT."
IT'S A MESS THAT CAN'T BE CLEANED UP.

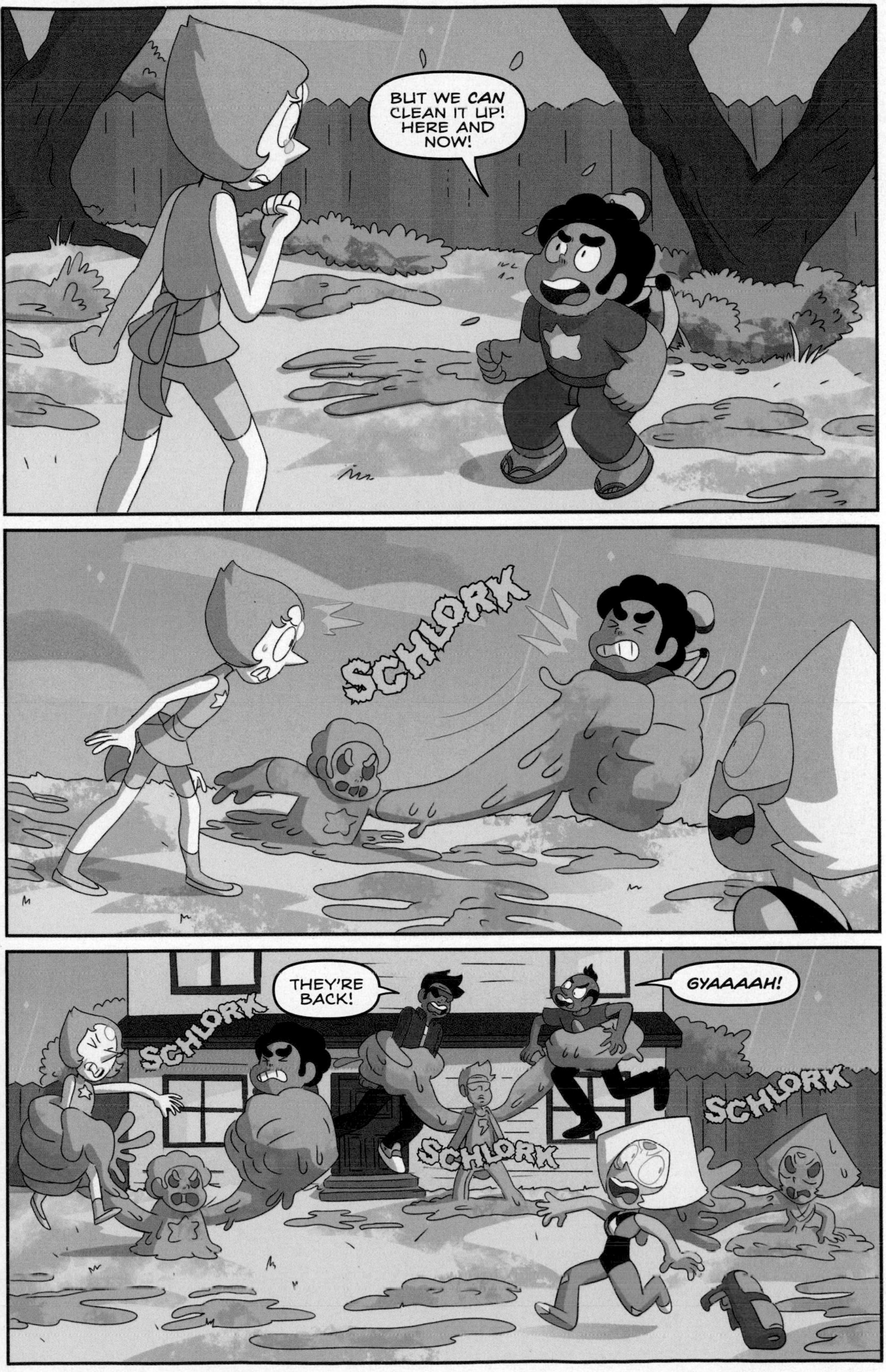
BUT WE CAN CLEAN IT UP! HERE AND NOW!
SCHLORK
THEY'RE BACK!
GYAAAAH!
SCHLORK
SCHLORK
SCHLORK

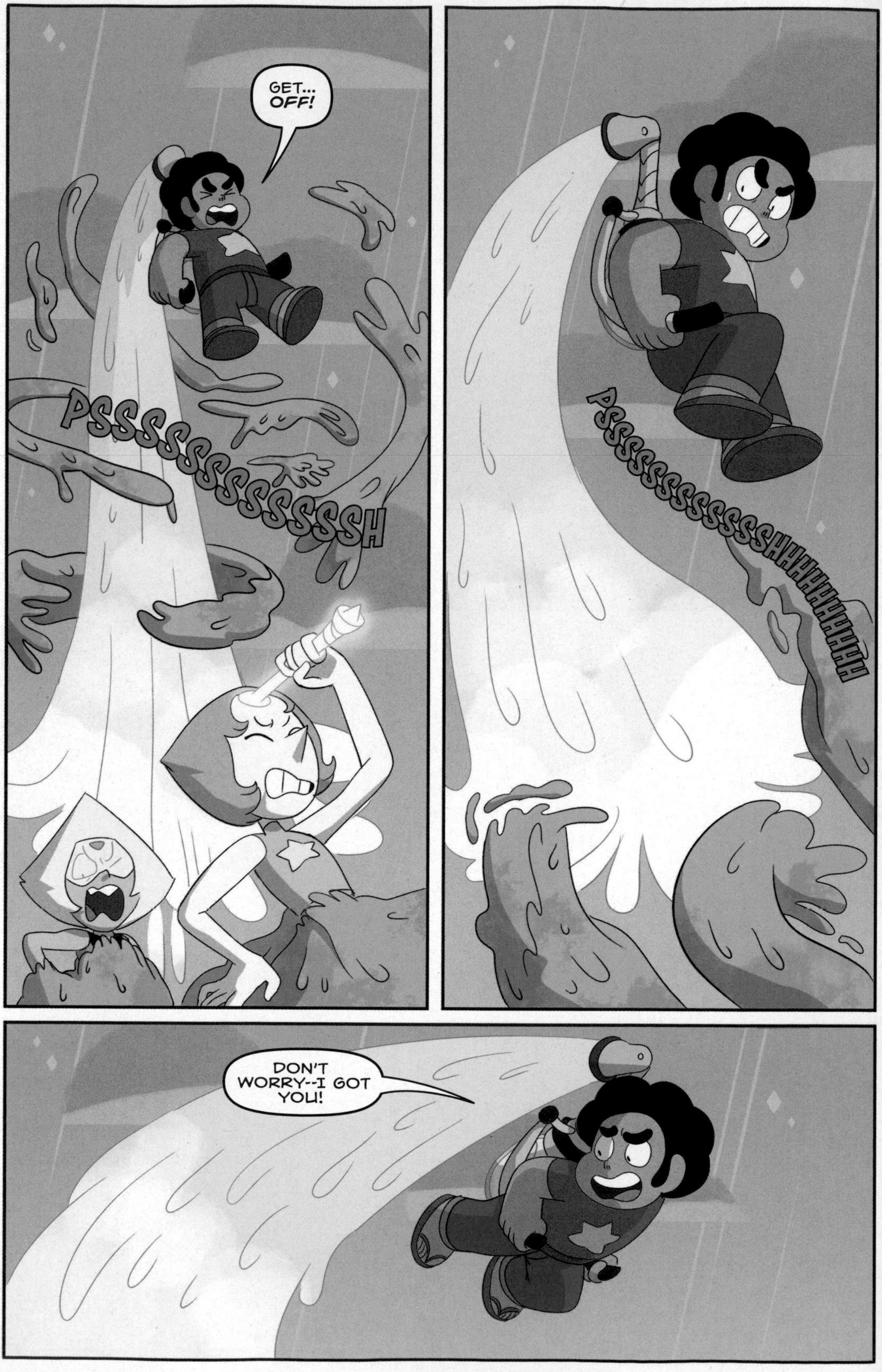
GET... OFF!
PSSSSSSSSSSSSSH
PSSSSSSSSSSSSSHHHHHHHHHH
DON'T WORRY--I GOT YOU!

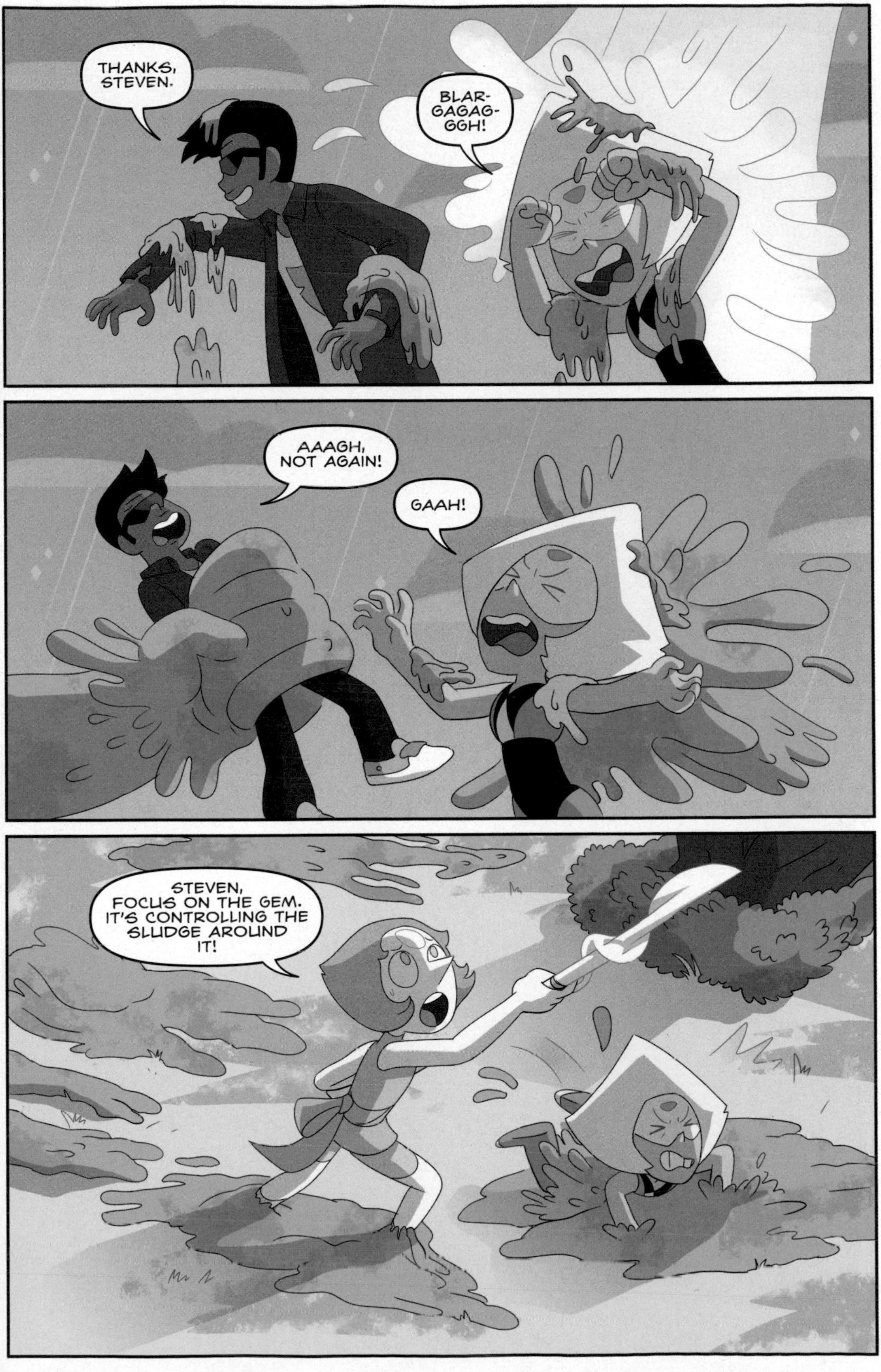
THANKS, STEVEN.
BLAR-GAGAGG-GGH!
AAAGH, NOT AGAIN!
GAAH!
STEVEN, FOCUS ON THE GEM. IT'S CONTROLLING THE SLUDGE AROUND IT!

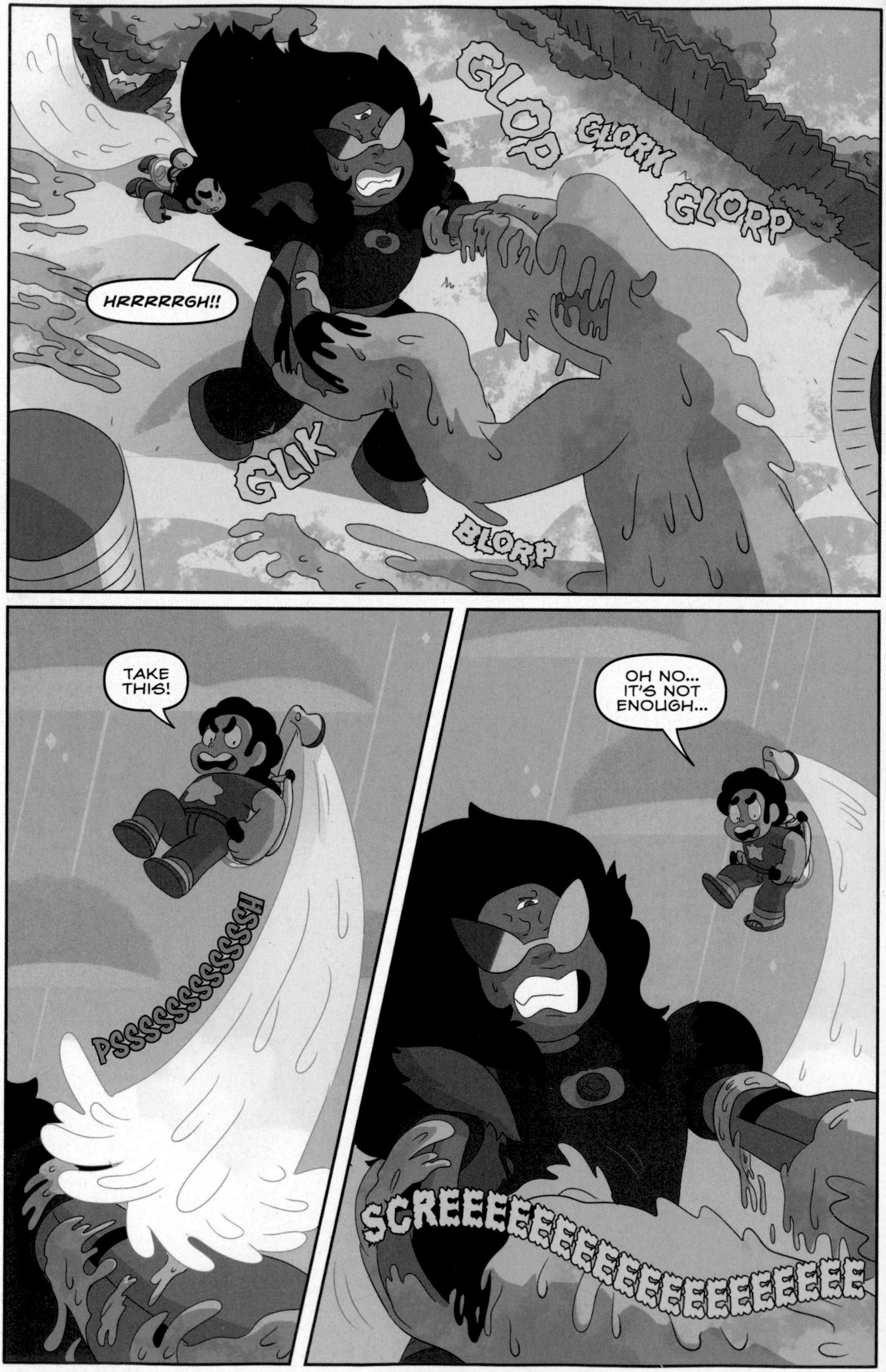

GLOP
GLORK
GLORP
HRRRRRGH!!
GLIK
BLORP
TAKE THIS!
PSSSSSSSSSSSSH
OH NO... IT'S NOT ENOUGH...
SCREEEEEEEEEEEEEEEEEEEEEEE

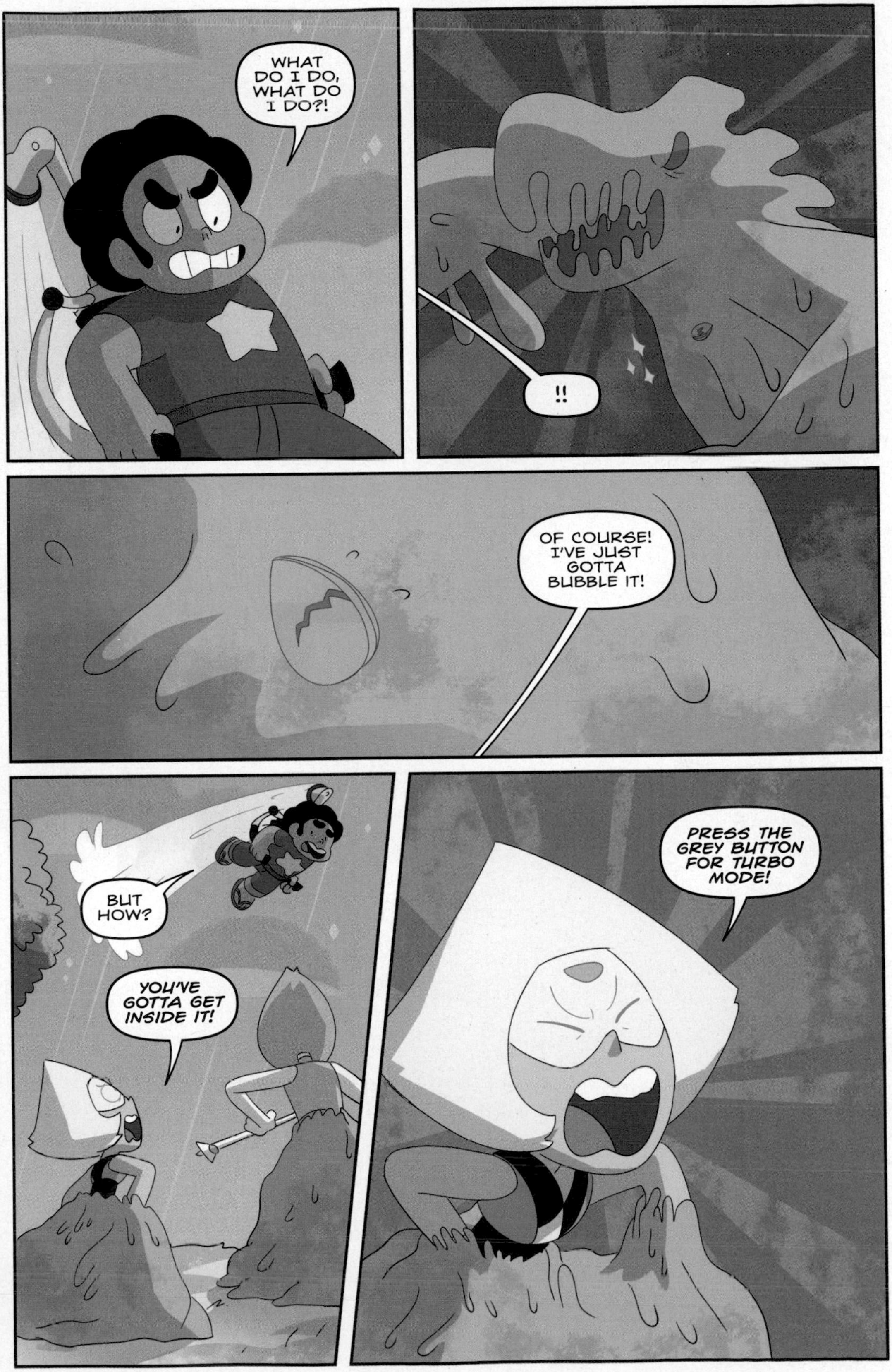
WHAT DO I DO, WHAT DO I DO?!
!!
OF COURSE! I'VE JUST GOTTA BUBBLE IT!
BUT HOW?
YOU'VE GOTTA GET INSIDE IT!
PRESS THE GREY BUTTON FOR TURBO MODE!

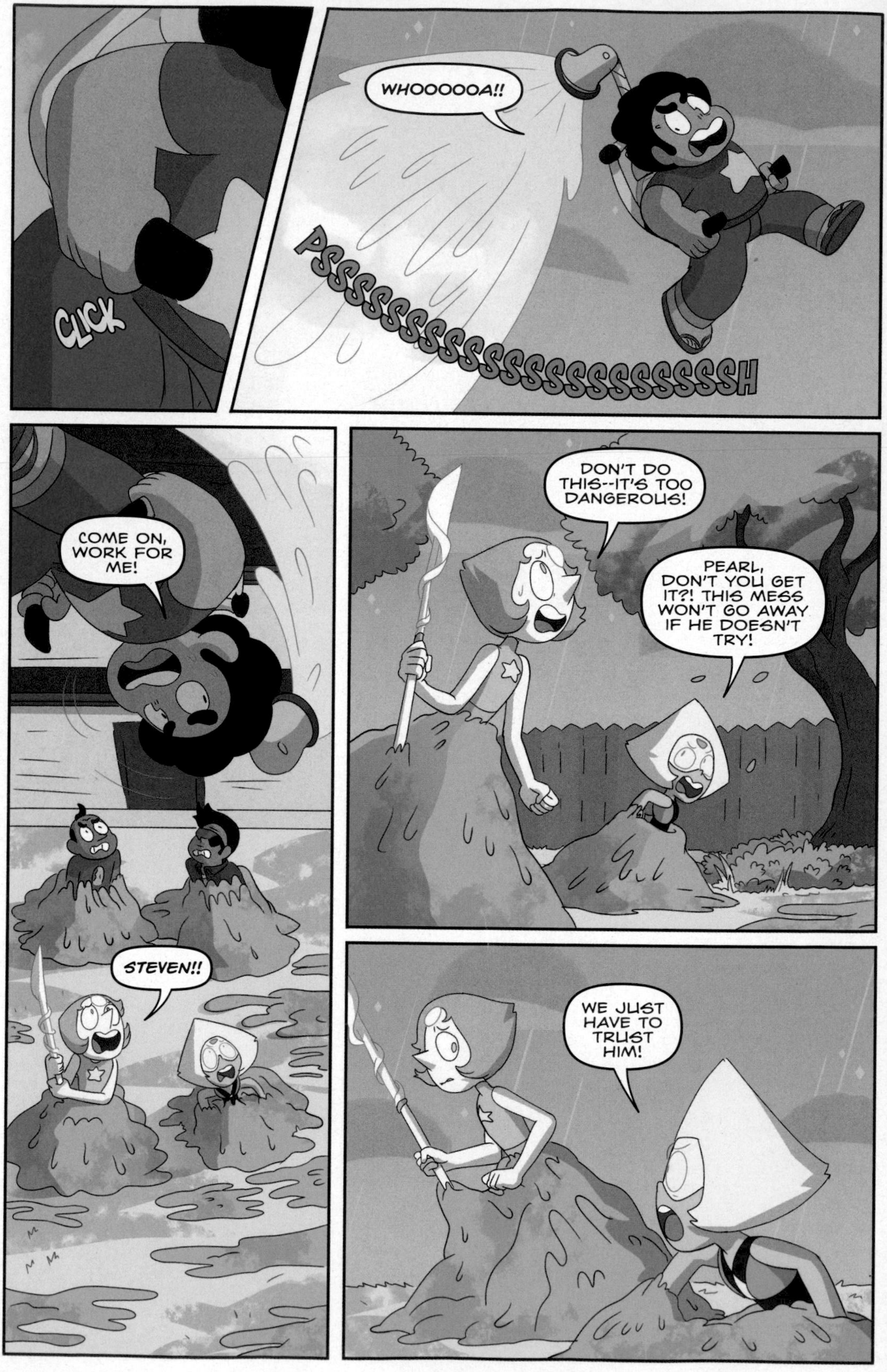
CLICK
WHOOOOOA!!
PSSSSSSSSSSSSSSSSSSSSSSH
COME ON, WORK FOR ME!
STEVEN!!
DON'T DO THIS--IT'S TOO DANGEROUS!
PEARL, DON'T YOU GET IT?! THIS MESS WON'T GO AWAY IF HE DOESN'T TRY!
WE JUST HAVE TO TRUST HIM!

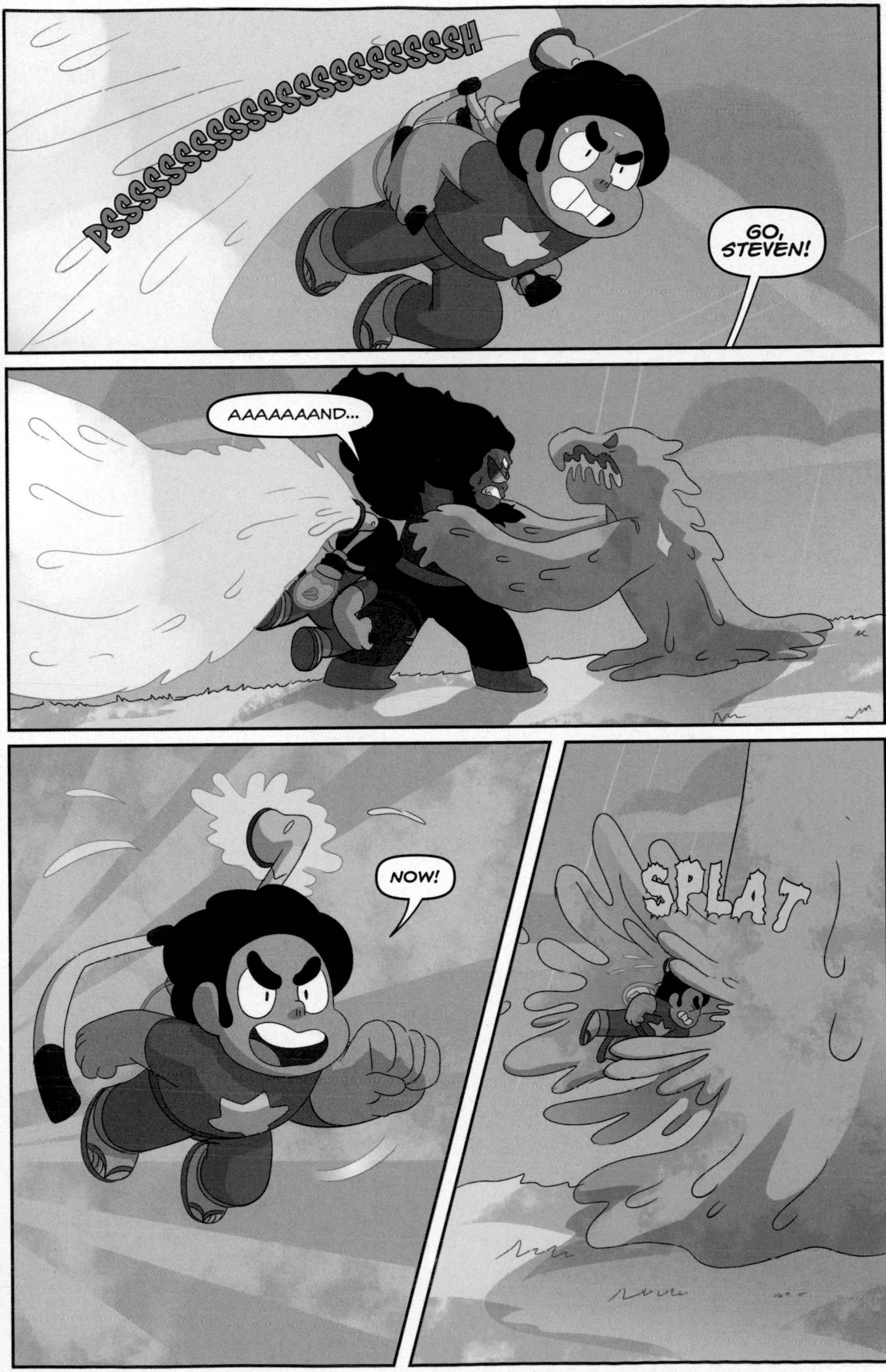
PSSSSSSSSSSSSSSSSSSSSSSSH
GO, STEVEN!
AAAAAAAND...
NOW!
SPLAT

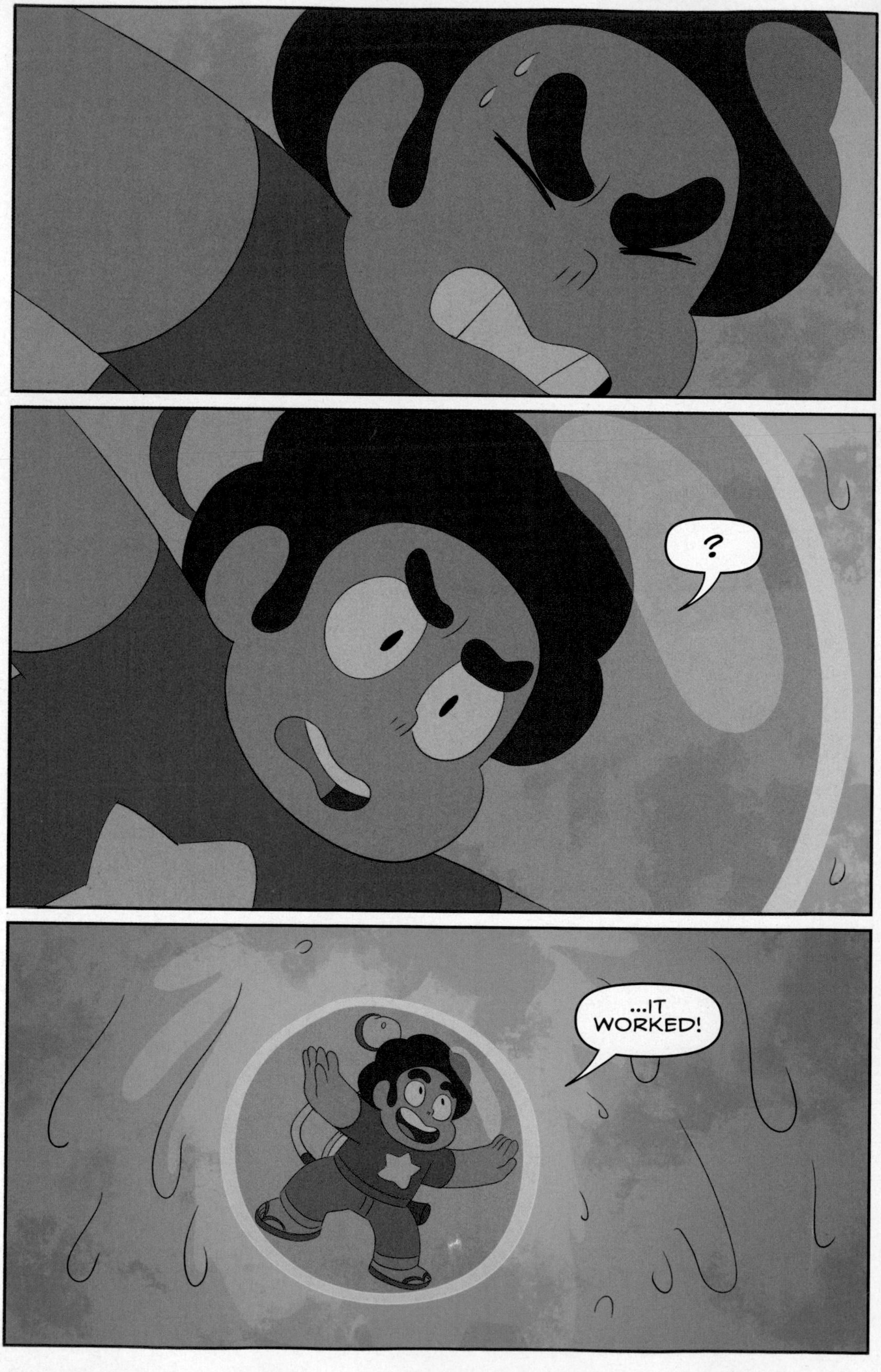
?
...IT WORKED!

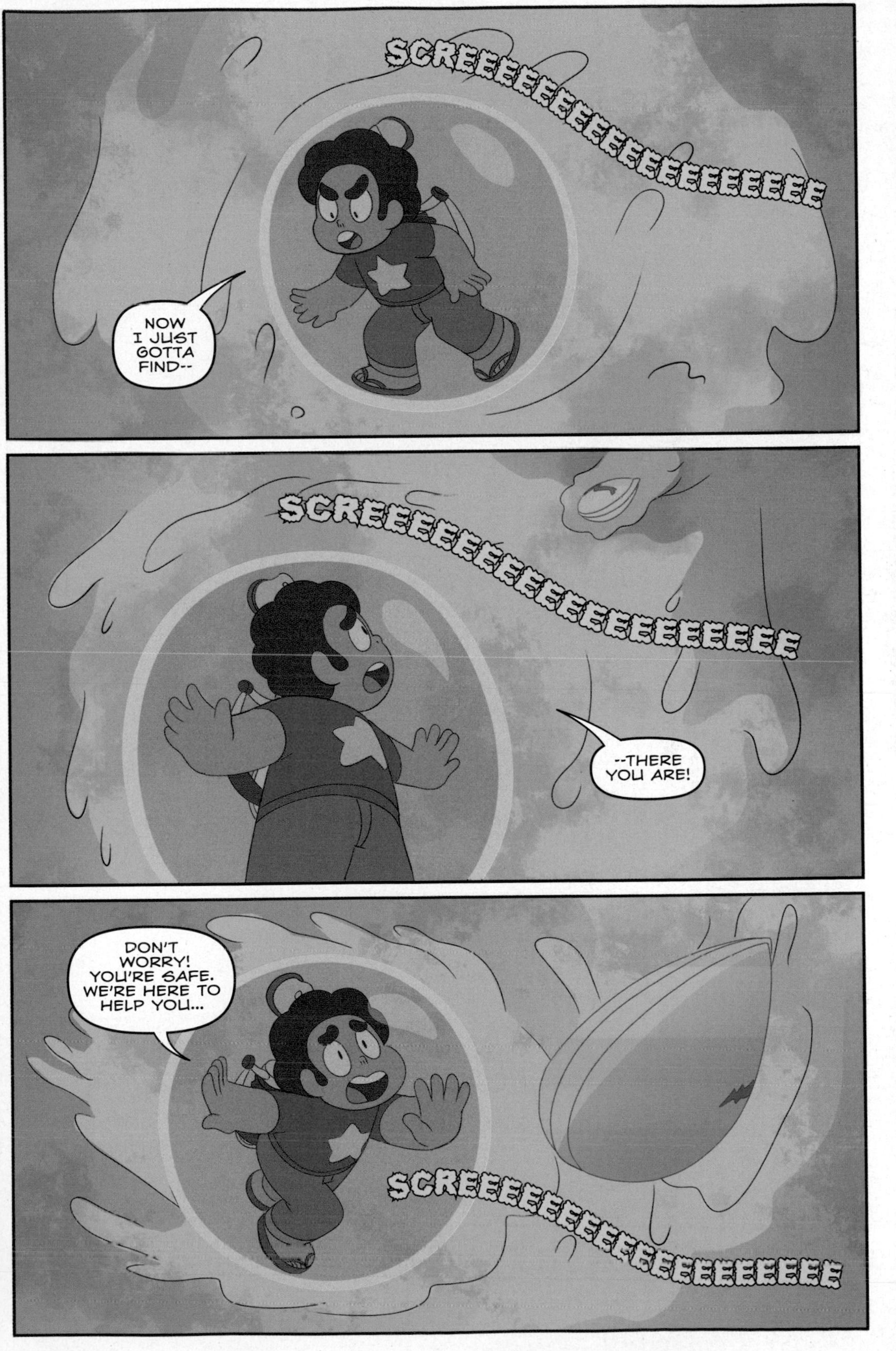
SCREEEEEEEEEEEEEEEEEEE
NOW I JUST GOTTA FIND--
SCREEEEEEEEEEEEEEEEEEE
--THERE YOU ARE!
DON'T WORRY! YOU'RE SAFE. WE'RE HERE TO HELP YOU...
SCREEEEEEEEEEEEEEEEEEE

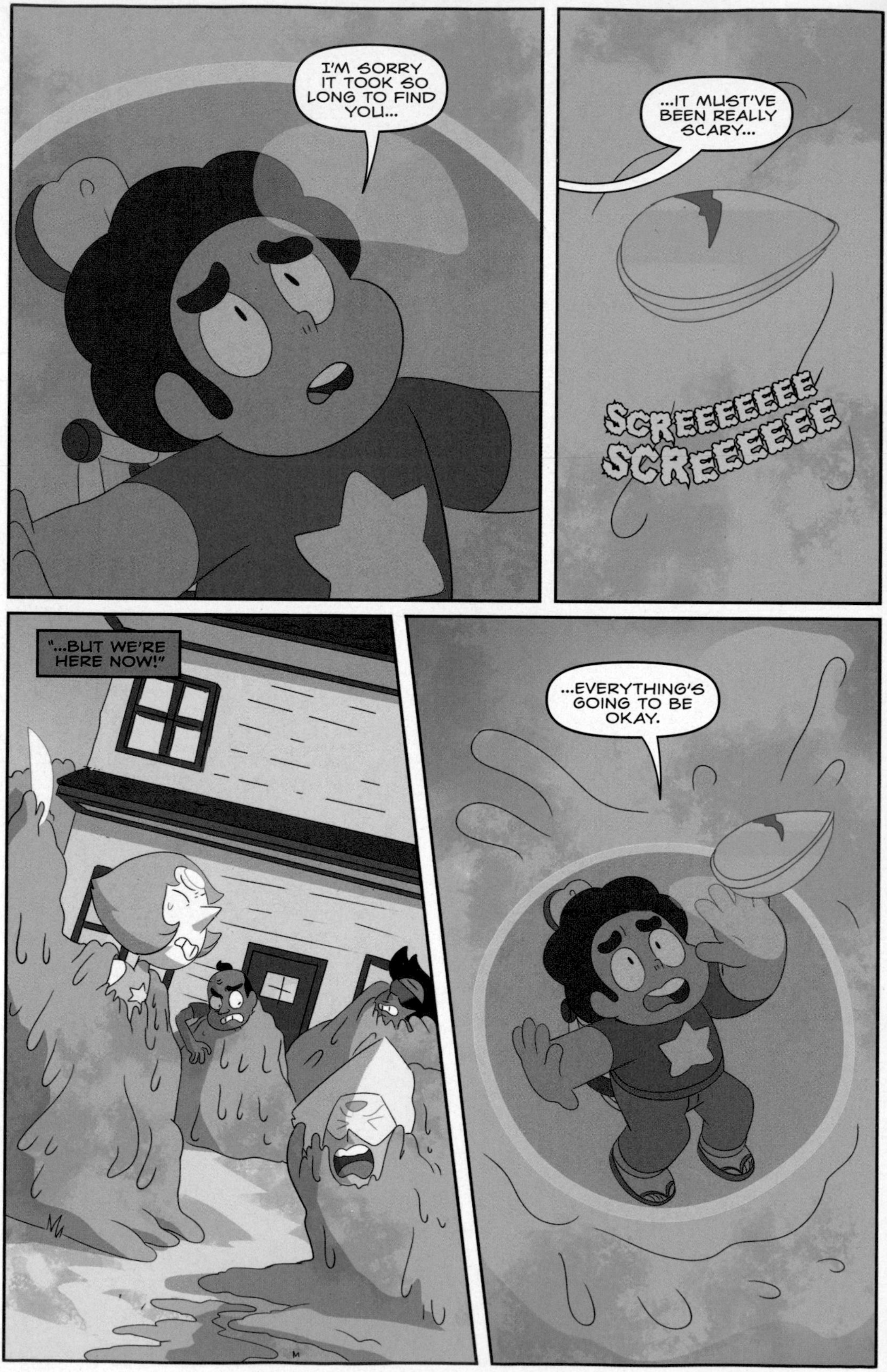

I'M SORRY IT TOOK SO LONG TO FIND YOU...
...IT MUST'VE BEEN REALLY SCARY...
SCREEEEEEEE SCREEEEEEE
"...BUT WE'RE HERE NOW!"
...EVERYTHING'S GOING TO BE OKAY.

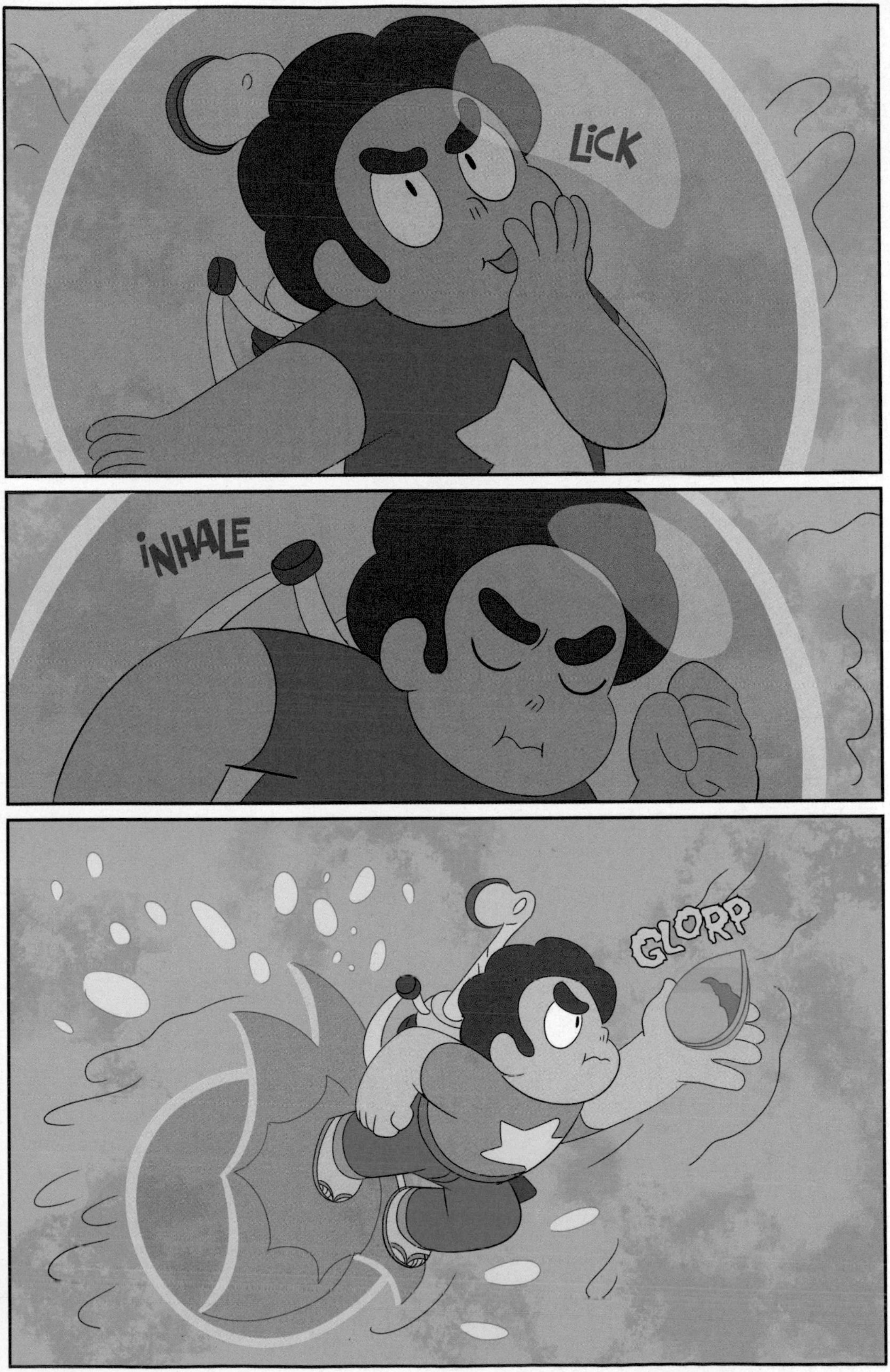
LICK
INHALE
GLORP

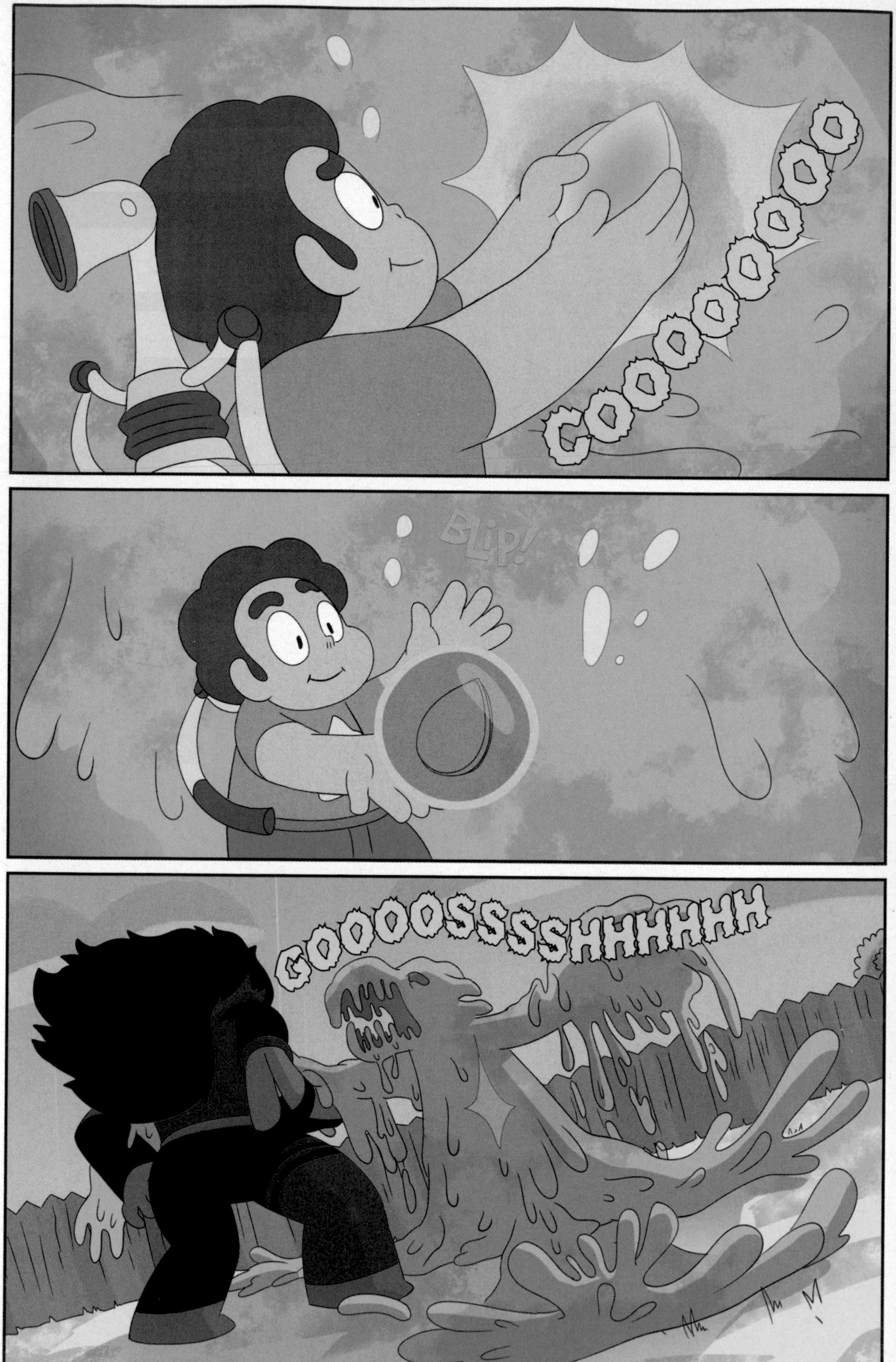
COOOOOOOOO
BLIP!
GOOOOSSSSSHHHHHH

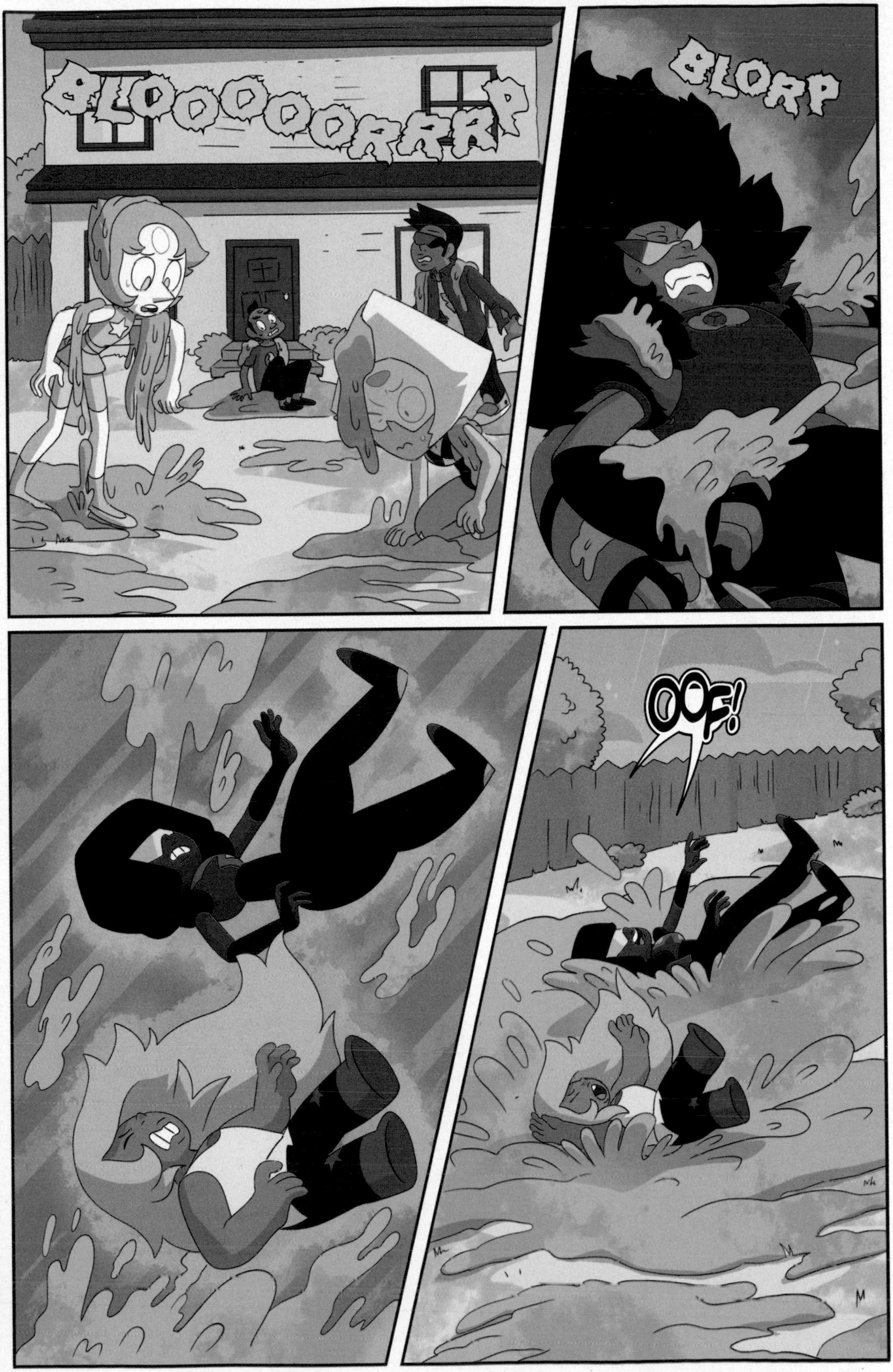
BLOOOOORRRP
BLORP
OOF!

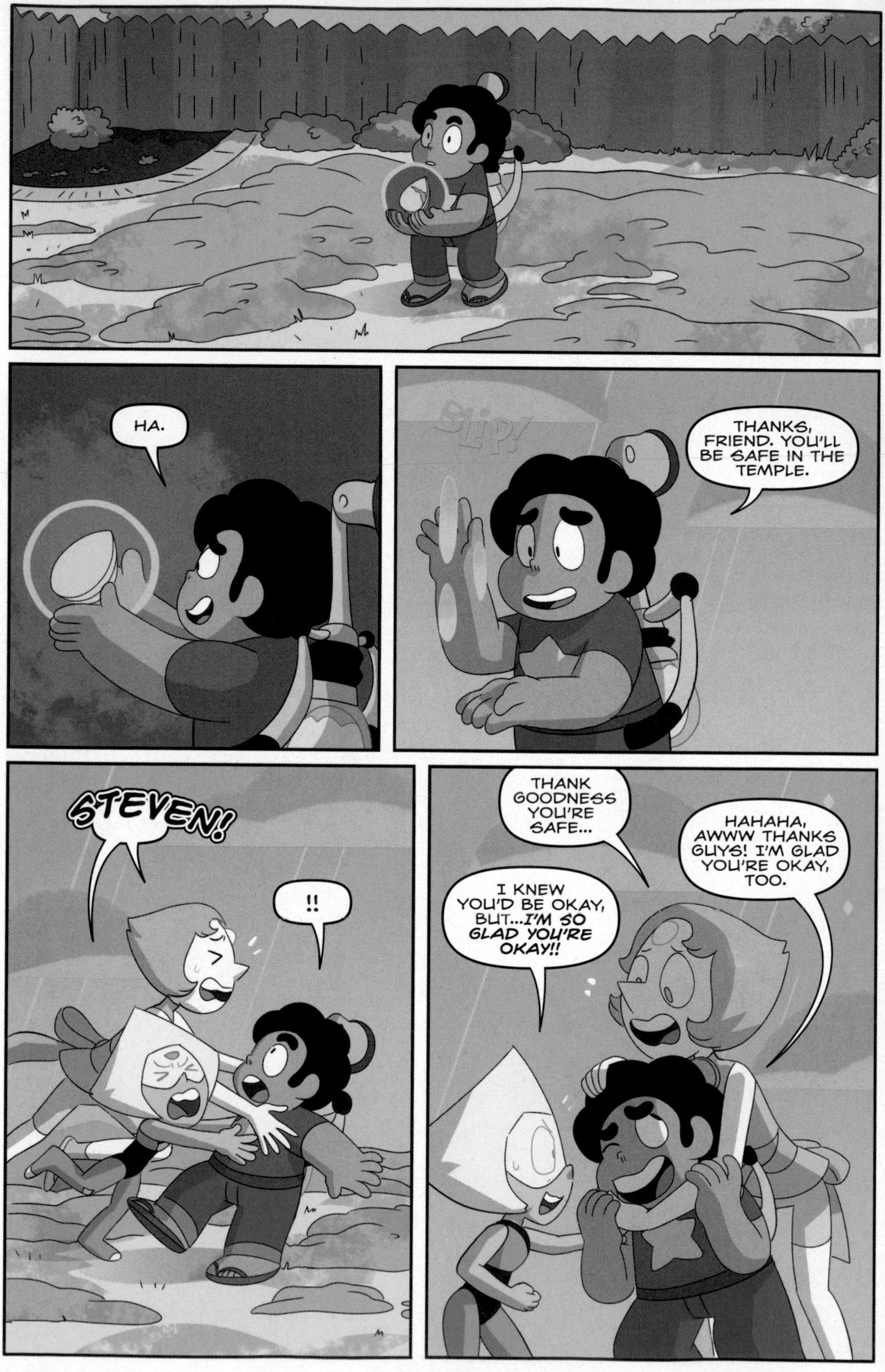
HA.
SLIP!
THANKS, FRIEND. YOU'LL BE SAFE IN THE TEMPLE.
STEVEN!
!!
THANK GOODNESS YOU'RE SAFE...
I KNEW YOU'D BE OKAY, BUT...I'M SO GLAD YOU'RE OKAY!!
HAHAHA, AWWW THANKS GUYS! I'M GLAD YOU'RE OKAY, TOO.

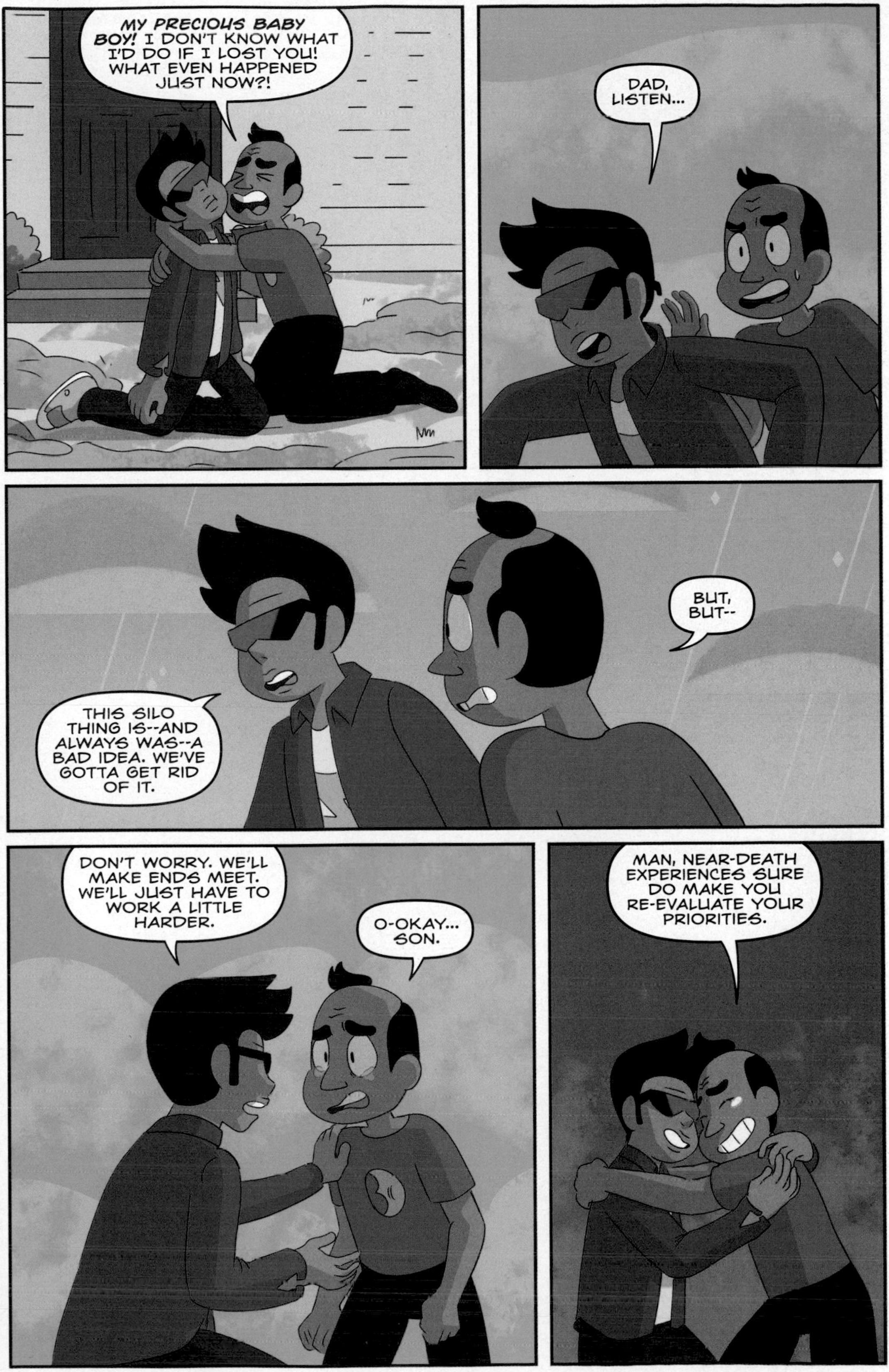

MY PRECIOUS BABY BOY! I DON'T KNOW WHAT I'D DO IF I LOST YOU! WHAT EVEN HAPPENED JUST NOW?!
DAD, LISTEN...
THIS SILO THING IS--AND ALWAYS WAS--A BAD IDEA. WE'VE GOTTA GET RID OF IT.
BUT, BUT--
DON'T WORRY. WE'LL MAKE ENDS MEET. WE'LL JUST HAVE TO WORK A LITTLE HARDER.
O-OKAY... SON.
MAN, NEAR-DEATH EXPERIENCES SURE DO MAKE YOU RE-EVALUATE YOUR PRIORITIES.

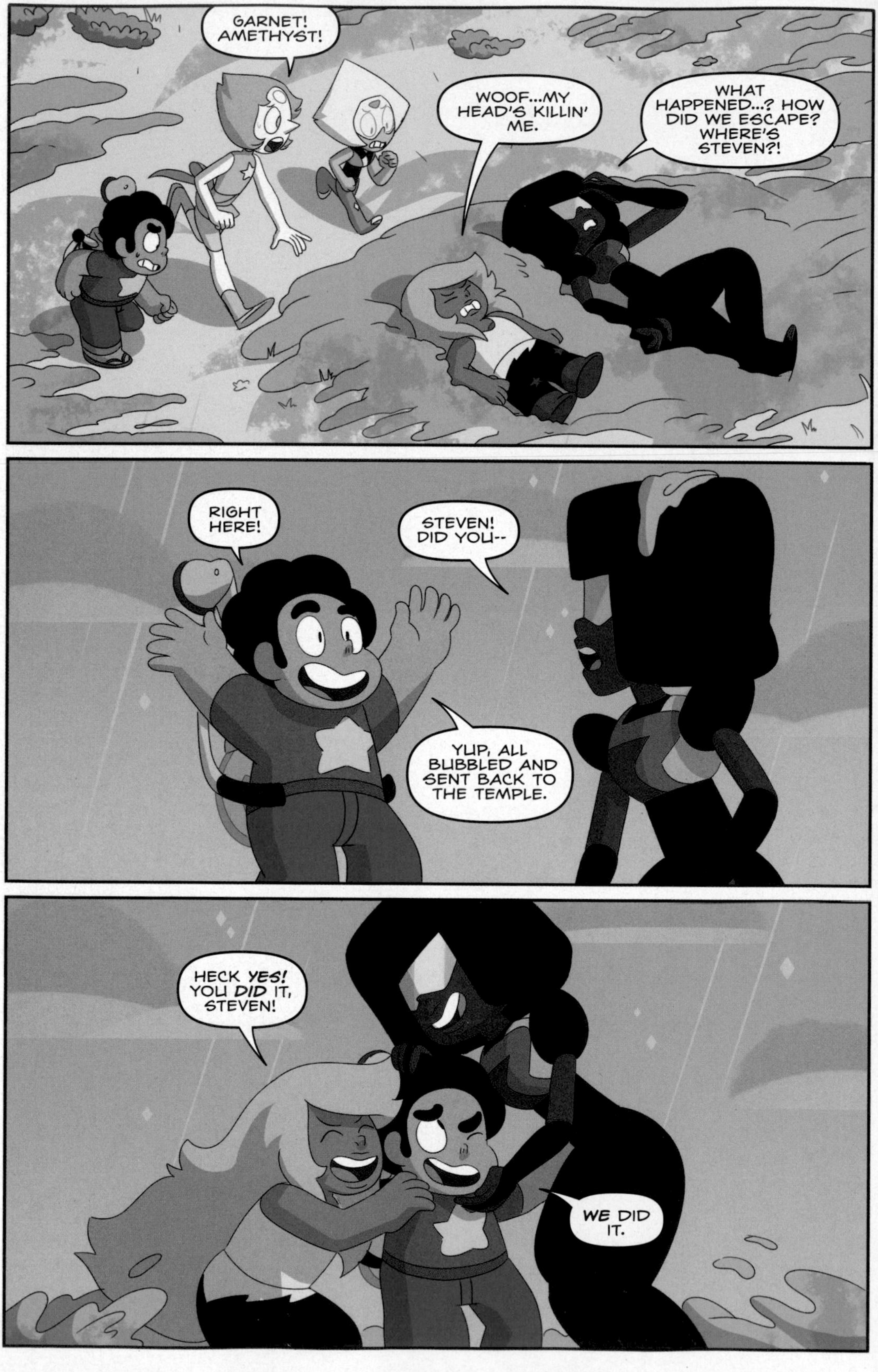
GARNET! AMETHYST!
WOOF...MY HEAD'S KILLIN' ME.
WHAT HAPPENED...? HOW DID WE ESCAPE? WHERE'S STEVEN?!
RIGHT HERE!
STEVEN! DID YOU--
YUP, ALL BUBBLED AND SENT BACK TO THE TEMPLE.
HECK *YES!* YOU *DID* IT, STEVEN!
WE DID IT.

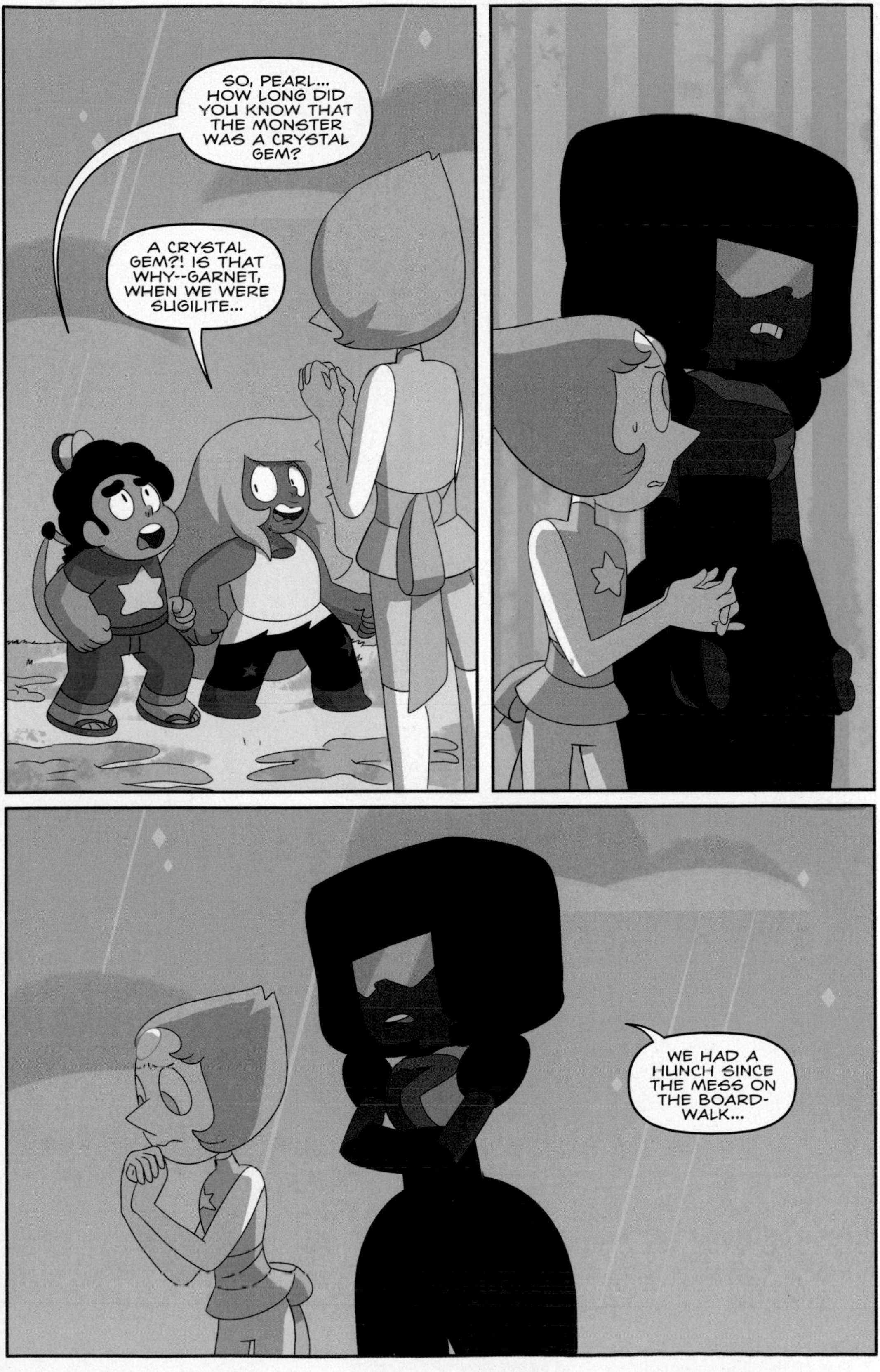
SO, PEARL... HOW LONG DID YOU KNOW THAT THE MONSTER WAS A CRYSTAL GEM?
A CRYSTAL GEM?! IS THAT WHY--GARNET, WHEN WE WERE SUGILITE...
WE HAD A HUNCH SINCE THE MESS ON THE BOARD-WALK...

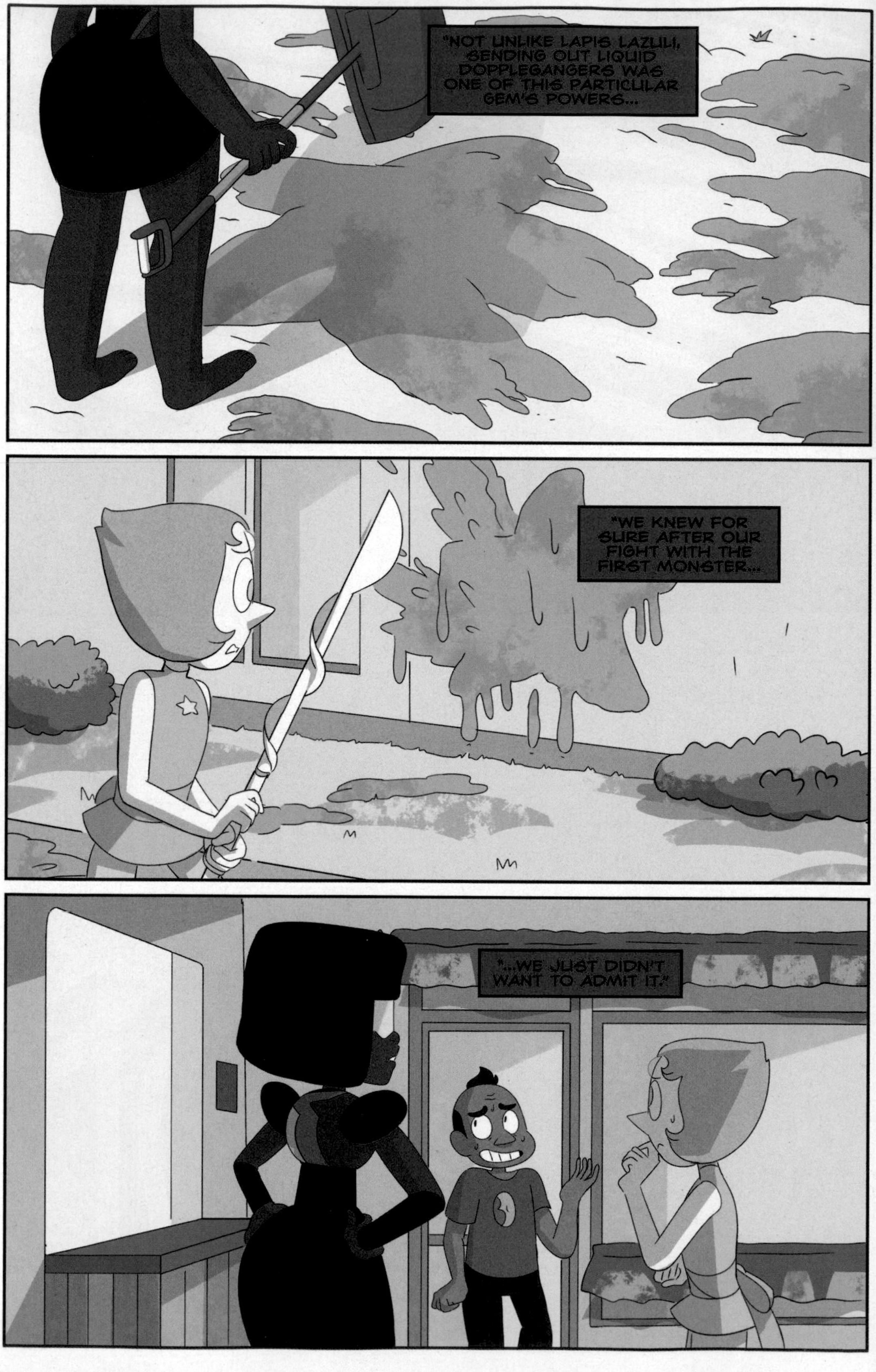
"NOT UNLIKE LAPIS LAZULI, SENDING OUT LIQUID DOPPLEGANGERS WAS ONE OF THIS PARTICULAR GEM'S POWERS...
"WE KNEW FOR SURE AFTER OUR FIGHT WITH THE FIRST MONSTER...
"...WE JUST DIDN'T WANT TO ADMIT IT."

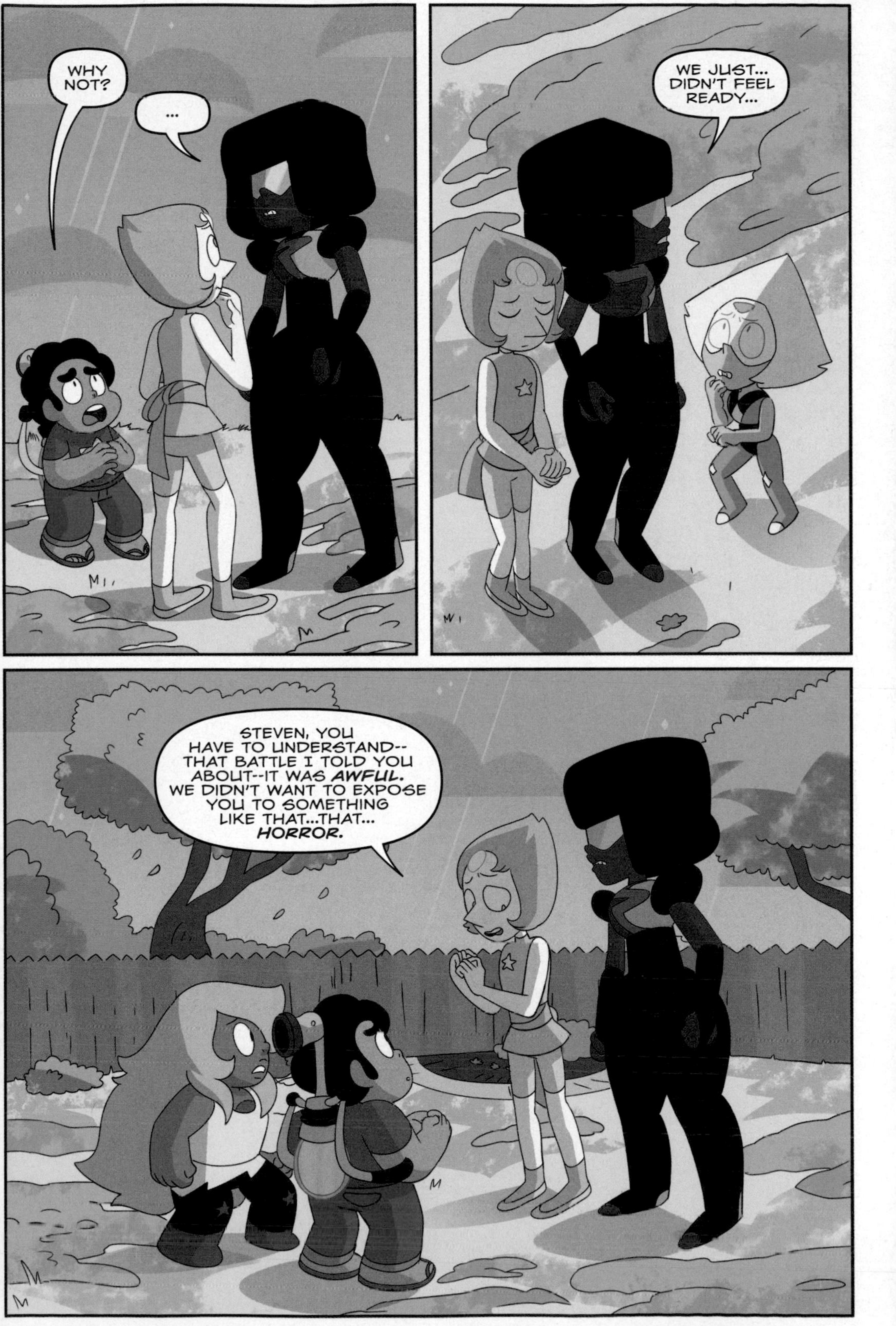
WHY NOT?
...
WE JUST... DIDN'T FEEL READY...
STEVEN, YOU HAVE TO UNDERSTAND-- THAT BATTLE I TOLD YOU ABOUT--IT WAS AWFUL. WE DIDN'T WANT TO EXPOSE YOU TO SOMETHING LIKE THAT...THAT... HORROR.

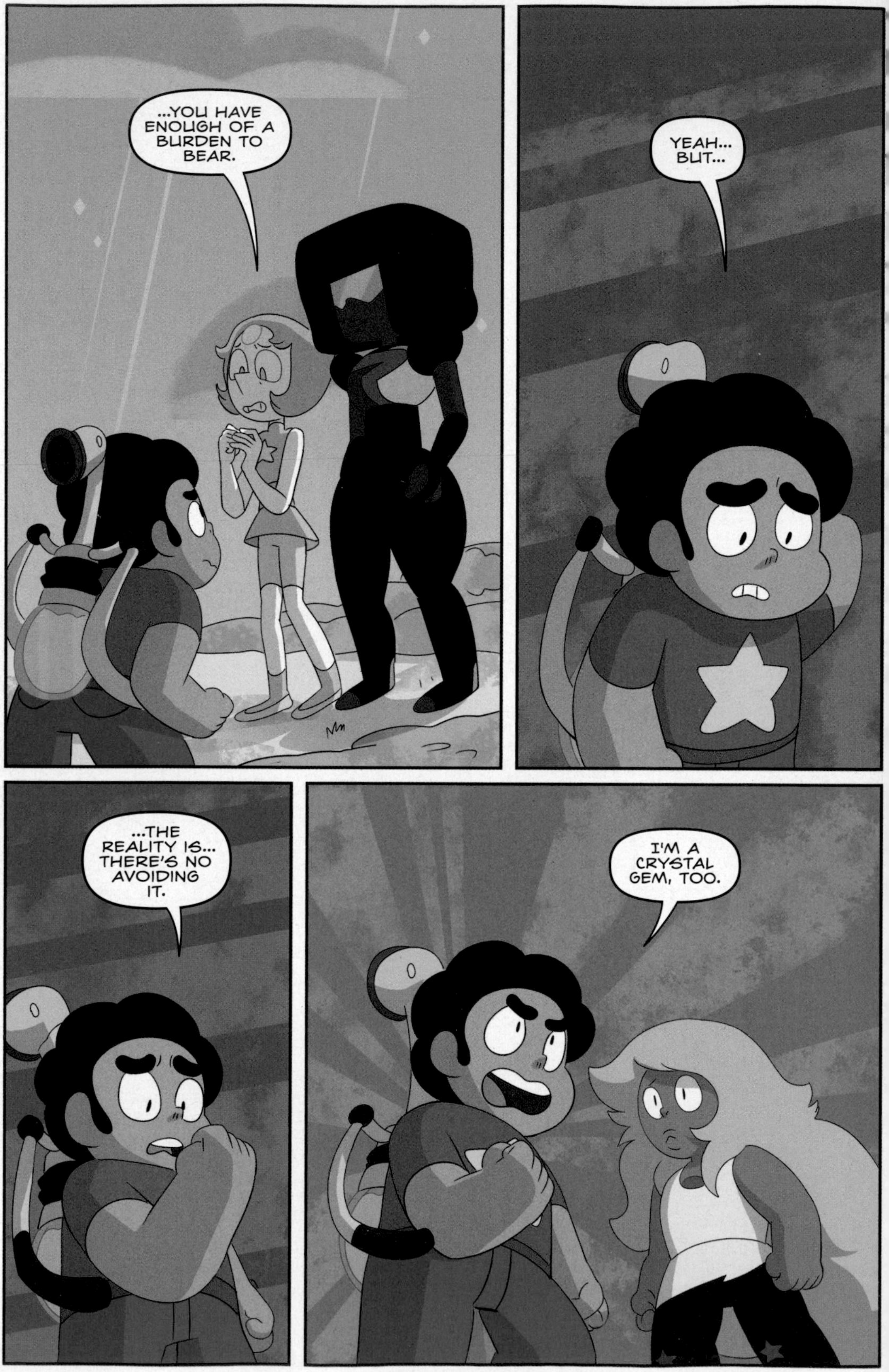
...YOU HAVE ENOUGH OF A BURDEN TO BEAR.
YEAH... BUT...
...THE REALITY IS... THERE'S NO AVOIDING IT.
I'M A CRYSTAL GEM, TOO.

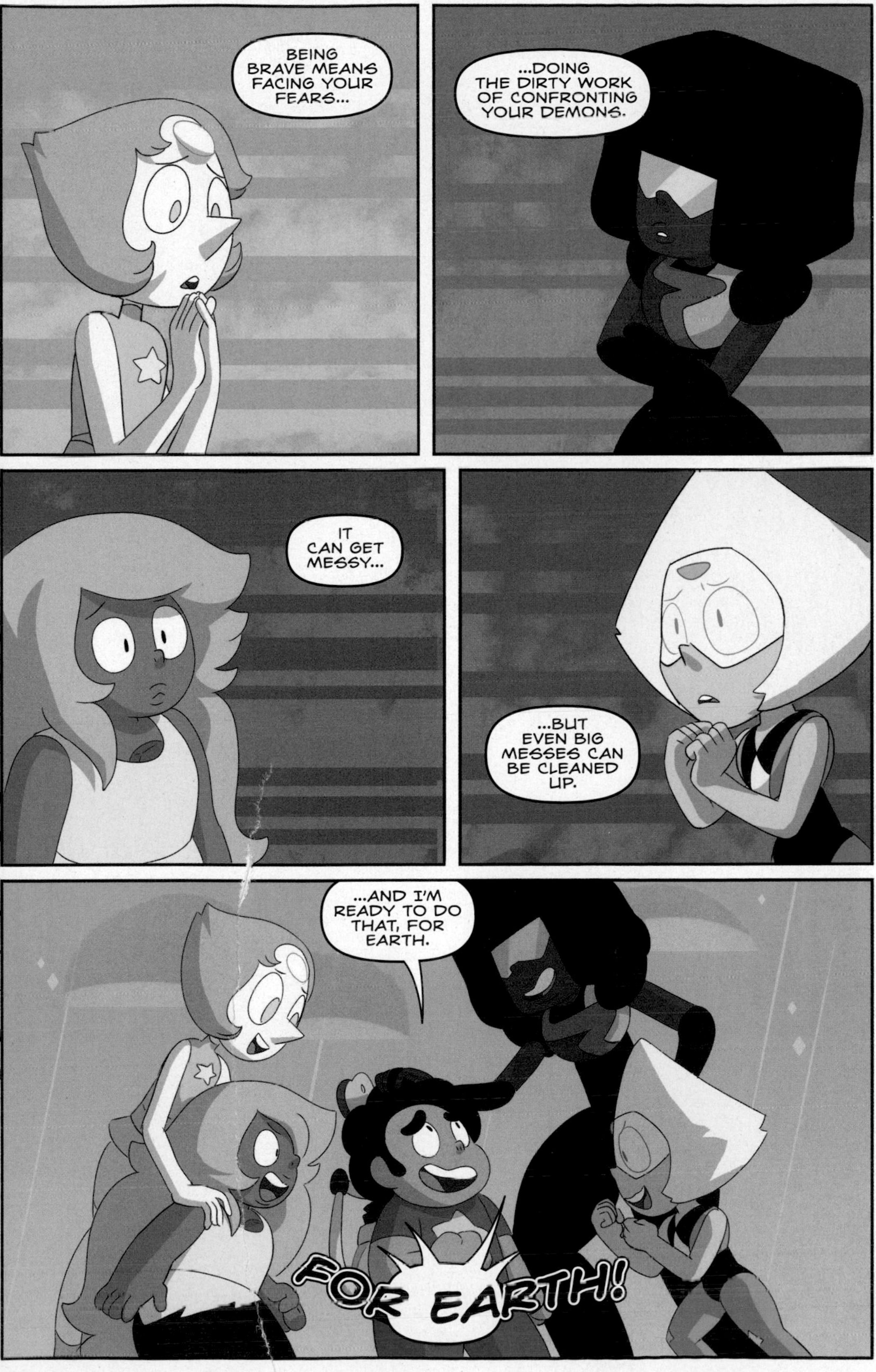
BEING BRAVE MEANS FACING YOUR FEARS...
...DOING THE DIRTY WORK OF CONFRONTING YOUR DEMONS.
IT CAN GET MESSY...
...BUT EVEN BIG MESSES CAN BE CLEANED UP.
...AND I'M READY TO DO THAT, FOR EARTH.
FOR EARTH!

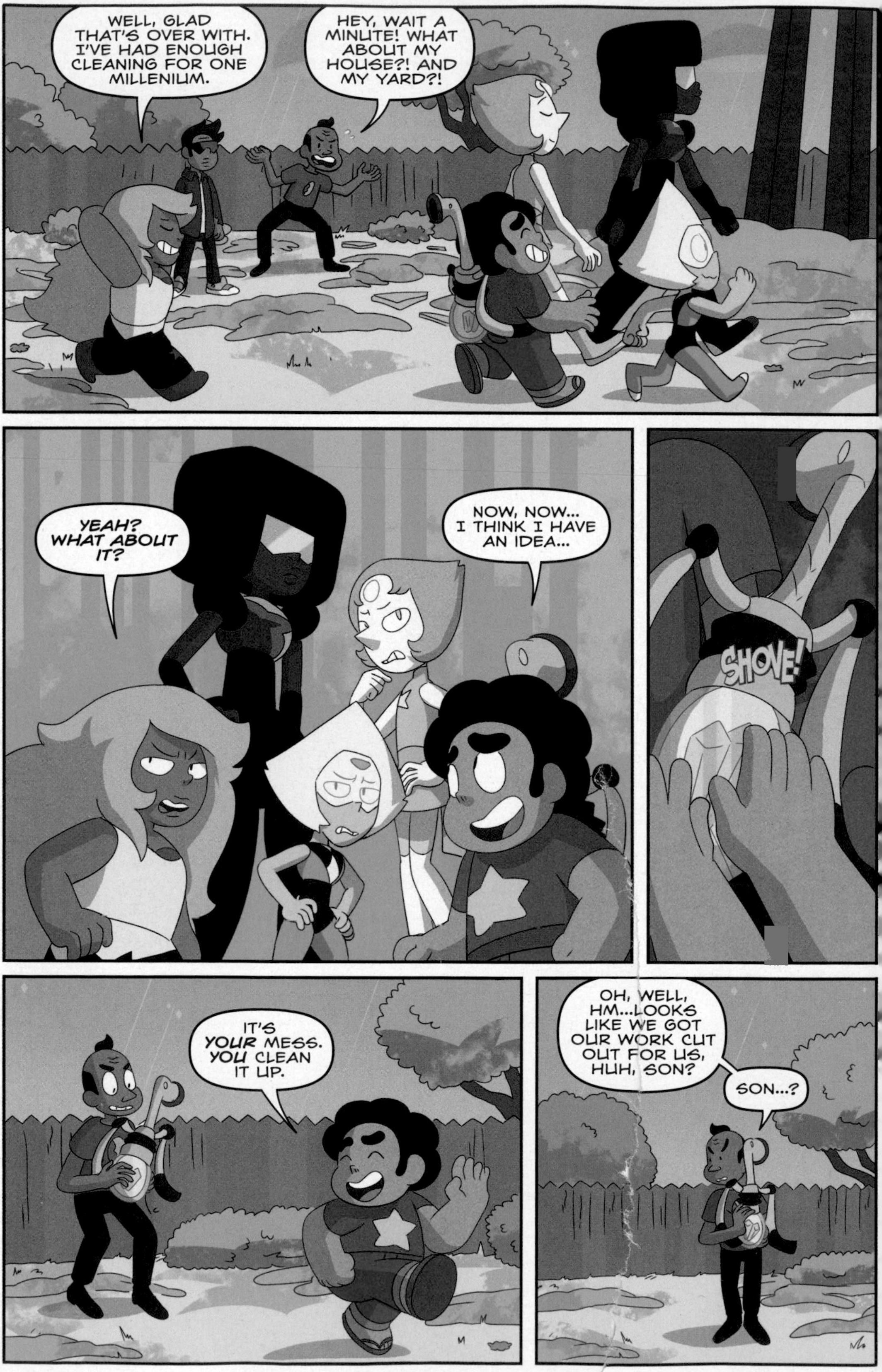
WELL, GLAD THAT'S OVER WITH. I'VE HAD ENOUGH CLEANING FOR ONE MILLENIUM.
HEY, WAIT A MINUTE! WHAT ABOUT MY HOUSE?! AND MY YARD?!
YEAH? WHAT ABOUT IT?
NOW, NOW... I THINK I HAVE AN IDEA...
SHOVE!
IT'S YOUR MESS. YOU CLEAN IT UP.
OH, WELL, HM...LOOKS LIKE WE GOT OUR WORK CUT OUT FOR US, HUH, SON?
SON...?

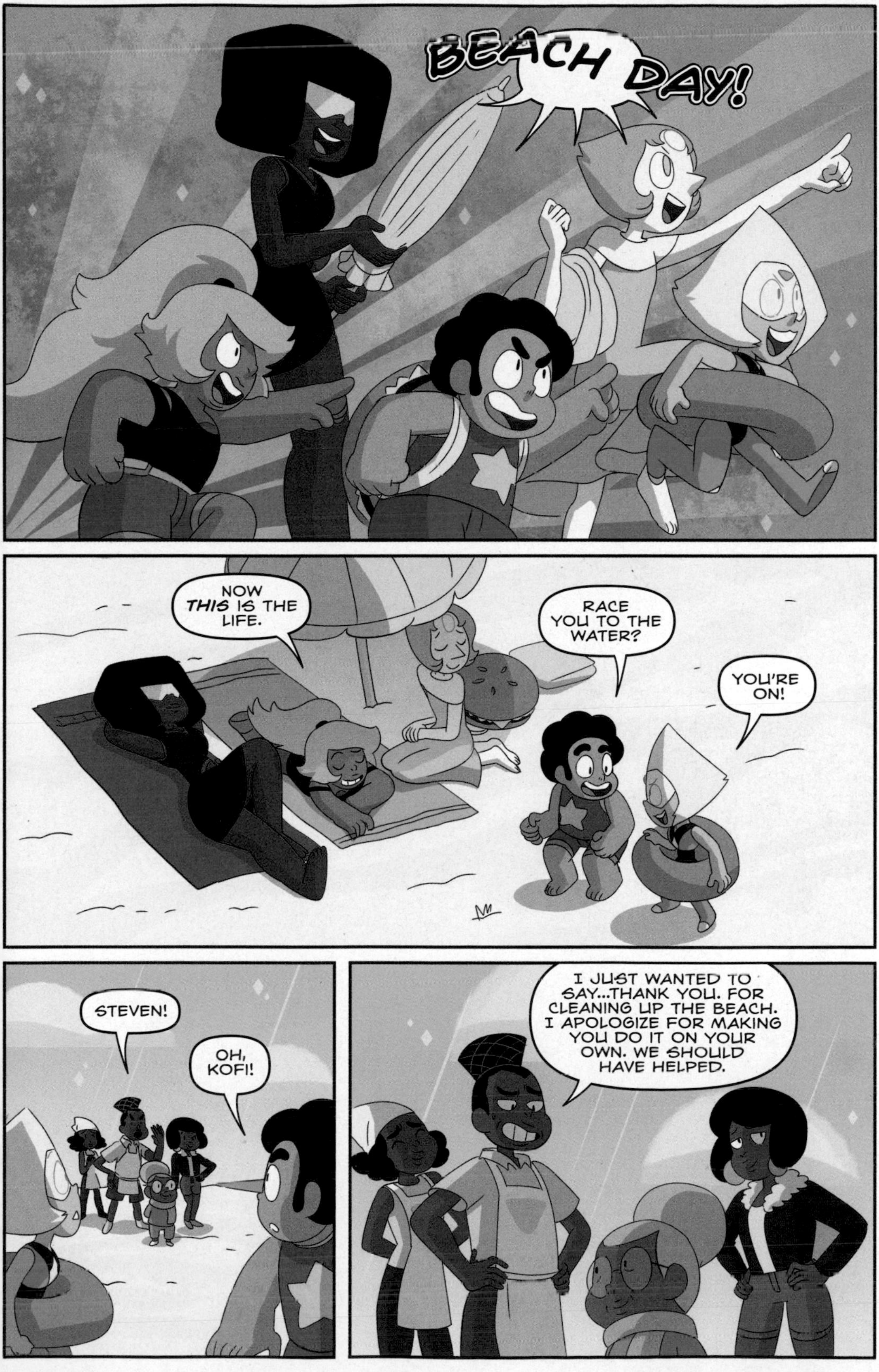
BEACH DAY!
NOW THIS IS THE LIFE.
RACE YOU TO THE WATER?
YOU'RE ON!
STEVEN!
OH, KOFI!
I JUST WANTED TO SAY...THANK YOU. FOR CLEANING UP THE BEACH. I APOLOGIZE FOR MAKING YOU DO IT ON YOUR OWN. WE SHOULD HAVE HELPED.

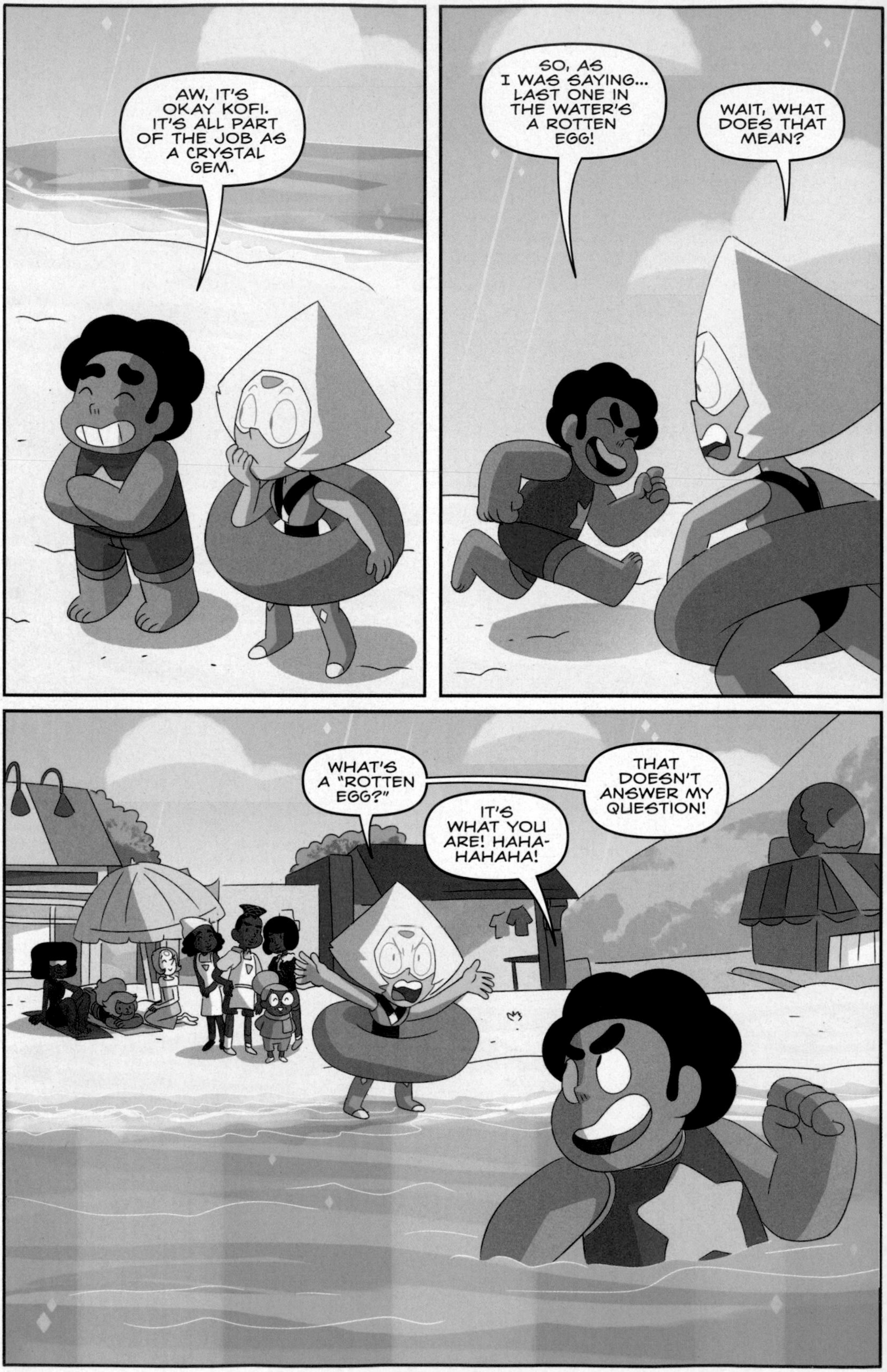
AW, IT'S OKAY KOFI. IT'S ALL PART OF THE JOB AS A CRYSTAL GEM.
SO, AS I WAS SAYING... LAST ONE IN THE WATER'S A ROTTEN EGG!
WAIT, WHAT DOES THAT MEAN?
WHAT'S A "ROTTEN EGG?"
IT'S WHAT YOU ARE! HAHA-HAHAHA!
THAT DOESN'T ANSWER MY QUESTION!

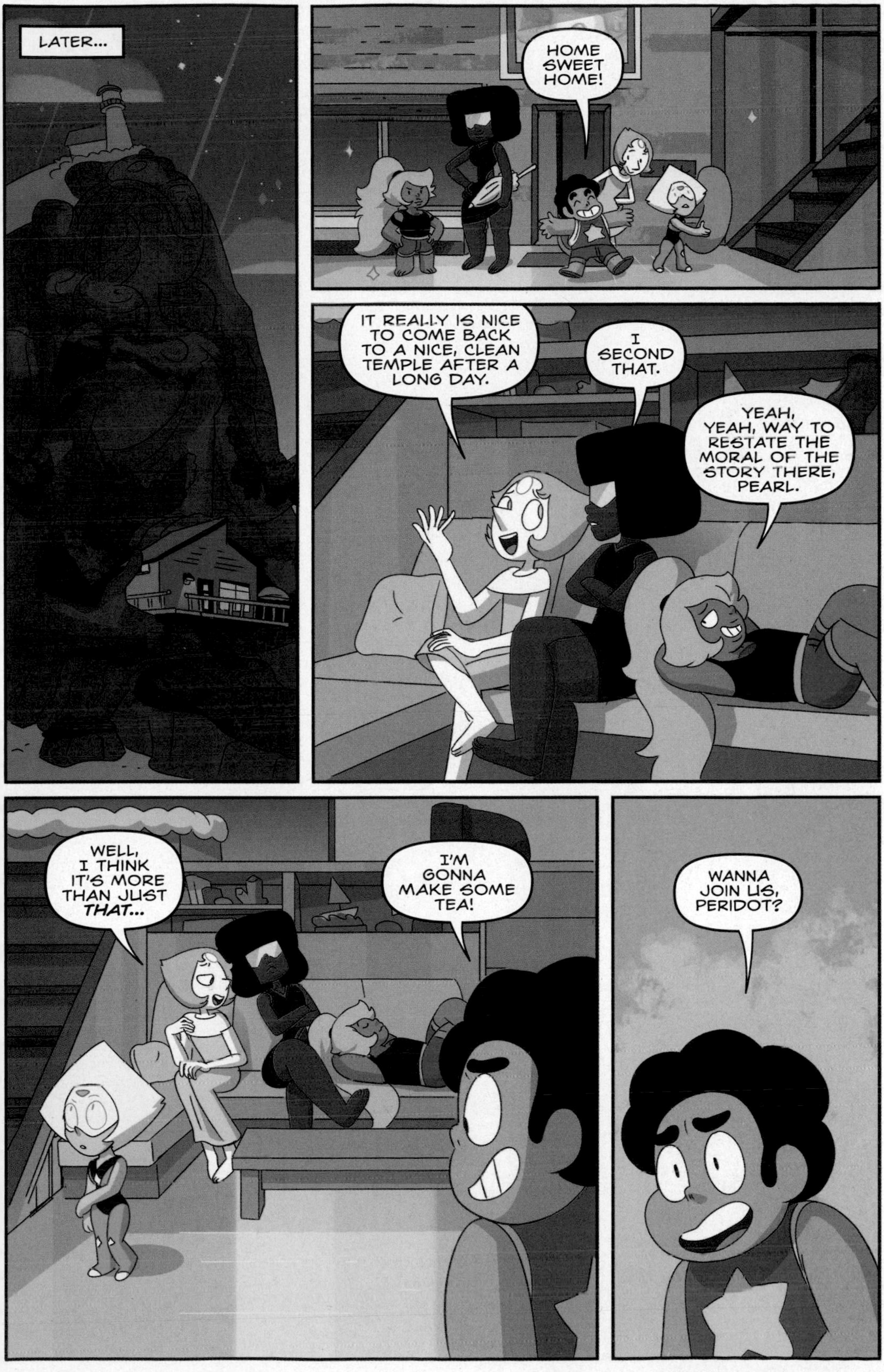
LATER...
HOME SWEET HOME!
IT REALLY IS NICE TO COME BACK TO A NICE, CLEAN TEMPLE AFTER A LONG DAY.
I SECOND THAT.
YEAH, YEAH, WAY TO RESTATE THE MORAL OF THE STORY THERE, PEARL.
WELL, I THINK IT'S MORE THAN JUST *THAT*...
I'M GONNA MAKE SOME TEA!
WANNA JOIN US, PERIDOT?

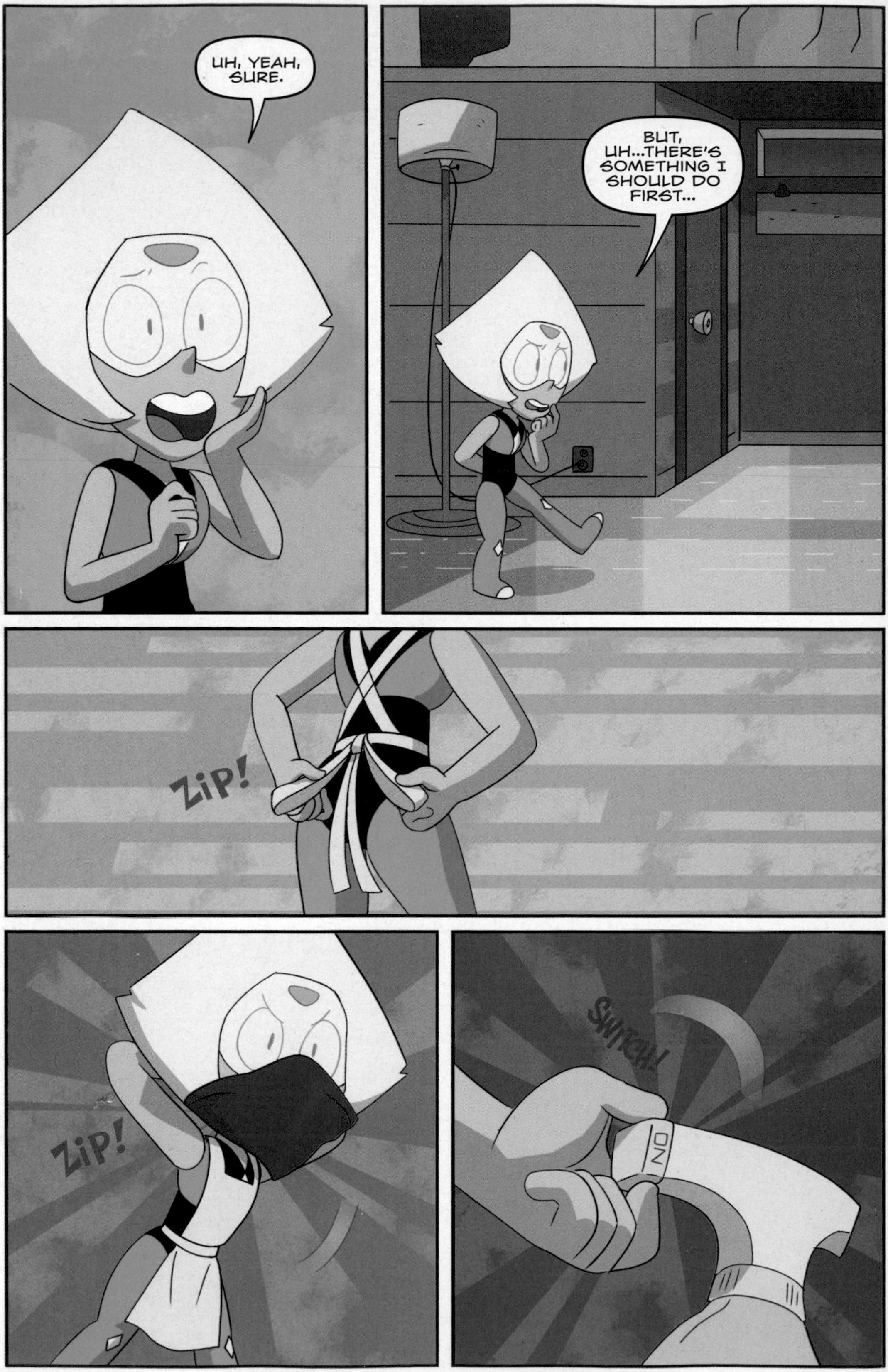
UH, YEAH, SURE.
BUT, UH...THERE'S SOMETHING I SHOULD DO FIRST...
ZIP!
ZIP!
SWITCH!
ON

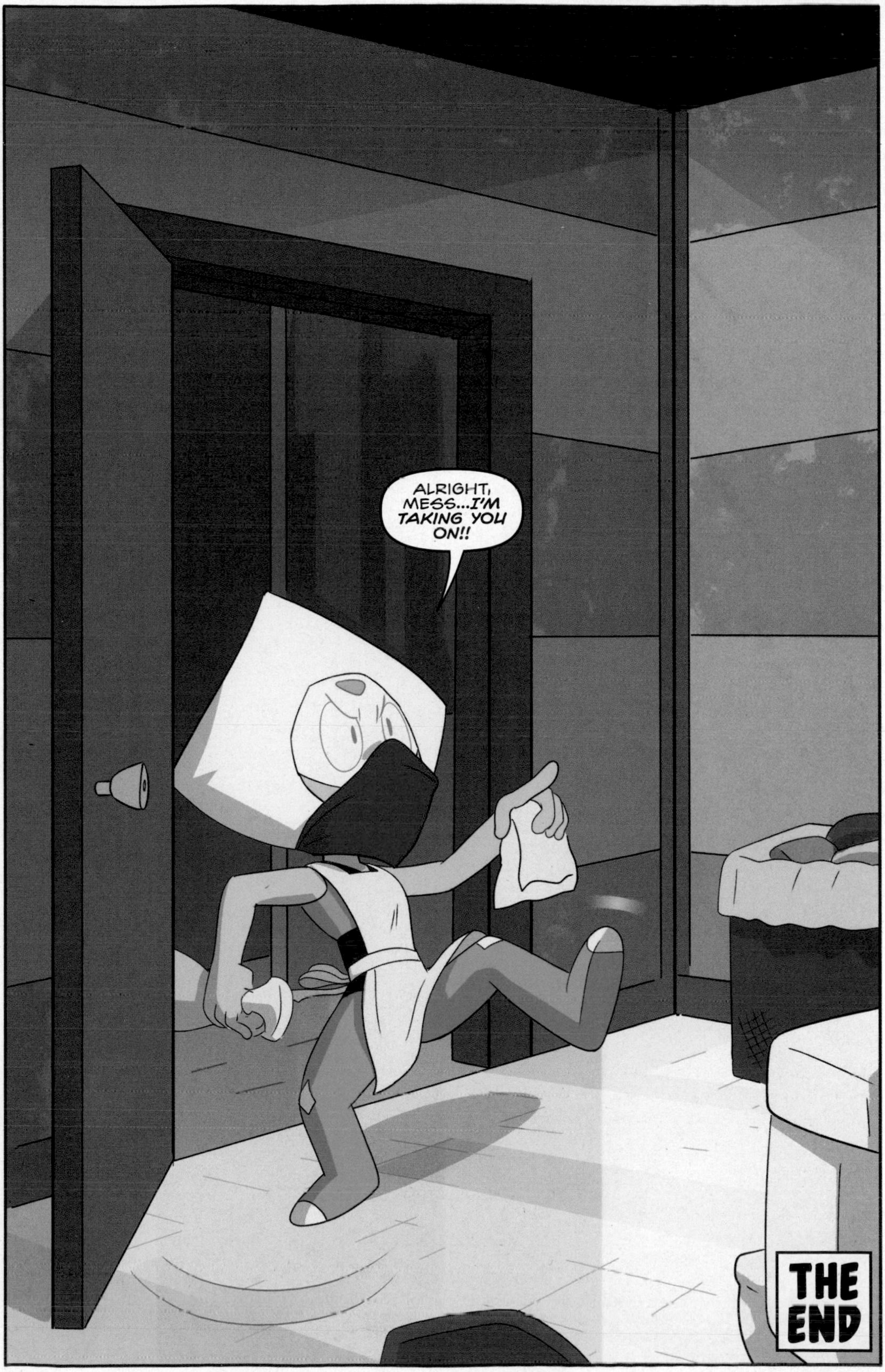
ALRIGHT, MESS...I'M TAKING YOU ON!!
THE END

DISCOVER
EXPLOSIVE NEW WORLDS

Adventure Time
Pendleton Ward and Others
Volume 1
ISBN: 978-1-60886-280-1 | $14.99 US
Volume 2
ISBN: 978-1-60886-323-5 | $14.99 US
Adventure Time: Islands
ISBN: 978-1-60886-972-5 | $9.99 US

The Amazing World of Gumball
Ben Bocquelet and Others
Volume 1
ISBN: 978-1-60886-488-1 | $14.99 US
Volume 2
ISBN: 978-1-60886-793-6 | $14.99 US

Brave Chef Brianna
Sam Sykes, Selina Espiritu
ISBN: 978-1-68415-050-2 | $14.99 US

Mega Princess
Kelly Thompson, Brianne Drouhard
ISBN: 978-1-68415-007-6 | $14.99 US

The Not-So Secret Society
Matthew Daley, Arlene Daley,
Wook Jin Clark
ISBN: 978-1-60886-997-8 | $9.99 US

Over the Garden Wall
Patrick McHale, Jim Campbell
and Others
Volume 1
ISBN: 978-1-60886-940-4 | $14.99 US
Volume 2
ISBN: 978-1-68415-006-9 | $14.99 US

Steven Universe
Rebecca Sugar and Others
Volume 1
ISBN: 978-1-60886-706-6 | $14.99 US
Volume 2
ISBN: 978-1-60886-796-7 | $14.99 US

Steven Universe & The Crystal Gems
ISBN: 978-1-60886-921-3 | $14.99 US

Steven Universe: Too Cool for School
ISBN: 978-1-60886-771-4 | $14.99 US

AVAILABLE AT YOUR LOCAL COMICS SHOP AND BOOKSTORE
To find a comics shop in your area, visit www.comicshoplocator.com
WWW.**BOOM-STUDIOS**.COM